A WORLD OF DESIRE
IN A GENTLE KISS

"I must go, Libby."

"No. Not yet."

He looked down and placed his hand on hers. "There is nothing more to say."

"Case, please . . ." she pleaded softly, raising her hand to caress his cheek. "You're leaving tomorrow, and there might not be another chance. . . ." Stretching up, she pressed her lips to his.

The touch was light and innocent, but it was the sweetest thing Case had ever experienced . . .

Praise for MORNING SKY
by Constance Bennett

Diamond Books by Constance Bennett

MORNING SKY
BLOSSOM

BLOSSOM

CONSTANCE BENNETT

DIAMOND BOOKS, NEW YORK

BLOSSOM

A Diamond Book / published by arrangement with the author

PRINTING HISTORY
Diamond edition / December 1991

ISBN: 1-55773-628-6

Diamond Books are published by The Berkley Publishing Group,
200 Madison Avenue, New York, New York 10016.
The name "DIAMOND" and its logo are trademarks
belonging to Charter Communications, Inc.

PRINTED IN THE UNITED STATES OF AMERICA

10 9 8 7 6 5 4 3 2 1

To my beloved uncle, Miles Hart, who
made the Thunderbird necklace
a reality . . .

and

to Robert Vaughan,
who put up with my endless
cavalry questions and never failed
to have the answers I needed.

PART I

The Legend

ONE

Apacheria, in the white man's year 1847

HIDDEN DEEP in the shadows of branches, He Stalks the Gray Wolf crouched by the river, studying the reflection of the full moon that shimmered on the water at the fork of Cottonwoods Joining. The river was quiet, its voice soft as it spoke to the moon. Gray Wolf strained to hear its words, for the river was wise, and tonight it was wisdom Gray Wolf sought.

On the opposite shore, beyond the trees, he could see the waning campfires of the Many Mountains band, and behind him he knew that identical fires burned inside and out of the Red Canyon wickiups. The two camps reflected each other as the water reflected the moon; so alike, and yet so very far apart.

Would it always be so? Gray Wolf wondered bleakly, remembering all the great and noble speeches he had heard at the peace council that day. Some had advocated peace; others had shouted that there could be no peace. Gray Wolf's people had been at war with the Many Mountains band for longer than any of the elders on either side could remember. If this meeting of the warring bands did not resolve the conflict, the petty, futile feud would continue.

But Gray Wolf did not believe the feud would last for many more generations. In his heart he knew that if all the bands of the White Mountain Apache did not unite as one, there would soon be no Apache left. His people had an enemy

3

lying in wait that was far more powerful than any single tribe, even more fearsome than the hated Mexicans, who had made war on the Apache for a dozen generations. The White Eyes were coming, and they did not understand that this was Apache land, that the Apache were a proud people.

Gray Wolf considered himself a fearless warrior, and there were many in his band who agreed. But it would take more than bravery to hold back the White Eyes. There had to be a way to make his people see that, and so he had come to the river to ask the spirits to tell him how.

Behind him, Gray Wolf heard a rustle of leaves so soft it might only have been a trick of the wind. He tensed, waiting to see who approached, and then relaxed again when a faint tinkle of beads and a rustle of buckskin identified the intruder.

"You should not be here, Mother," he said quietly without turning. "My father has had a difficult day, and he will want you beside him."

The wife of the Red Canyon chief knelt beside her son. "Your father is in council with the elders and will not miss me for some time, I think." She reached out with a mother's hand to stroke Gray Wolf's hair. "You are troubled tonight."

Her show of affection was hardly proper, but Gray Wolf did not pull away. Instead, he smiled and lightly chided her. "If my friends see us, they will taunt me mercilessly and ask if I still suck at my mother's breast."

Round Maiden smiled. "Your friends would not dare taunt you, for they know how swift and sure your vengeance would be. They know that, like your father, you are a great warrior."

"Great warriors' mothers do not stroke their sons' hair and speak to them as though they were children."

Round Maiden withdrew her hand and sighed. "Very well, I shall not treat you as my son."

Gray Wolf turned to her, and his eyes smiled with love and respect. "Now you go too far."

She looked at her strong, handsome son, and pride swelled in her heart. "Tell me what troubles you, my son. Your father said that you spoke most eloquently at the council today. You should be proud.''

His face grew hard and he turned once again toward the rustling river. ''But my words fell on many deaf ears,'' he said, unable to hide his frustration.

''Then tomorrow you will make them hear.''

''And if they do not?'' he asked angrily. ''What will happen then? Will our petty quarrels with the Many Mountains people go on forever?''

''There is much hatred between our two peoples,'' she answered philosophically.

''But for what reason?'' Gray Wolf asked in disgust. ''In the time of my father's grandfather, a Many Mountains brave stole the horse of a Red Canyon brave. He paid for his thievery with his life. The quarrel that began there should have ended there, but instead, many lives were lost. The years passed, but our people and theirs refused to forget, and now we steal each other's cattle to prove our worth as warriors, and we hurl insults at one another.'' Gray Wolf spat into the tall grass at his feet. ''Our foolishness sickens me.''

''That is because you have a wisdom others do not possess, my son.''

''But there is a real enemy awaiting us, Mother, and our people do not see the danger. The Inday of the White Mountain must begin to live as one or we shall perish. Why do they not understand that?''

Round Maiden reached out to touch her son again, but stopped herself. Gray Wolf was right; he was a man now—a fine young brave who no longer needed a mother's comfort. Still, she could not resist trying to soothe him with her words. ''They do not understand, my son, because they have not seen what you have seen.''

Gray Wolf's eyes turned cold at the memory of the Blue Coats, and to ward off the evil of the White Eyes, he instinctively fingered the thunderbird medallion that hung to the center of his chest. Two moons ago he had watched the soldiers march through Canyon Day, their numbers stretching as far as the eye could see. Hidden among the great rocks on the canyon's ridge, he had kept pace with them, studying their fine horses and excellent weapons. They rode foolishly in the open, making no attempt to hide themselves from enemy eyes; but then, with their numbers so great, they had little reason to fear anyone.

When they made camp, Gray Wolf had crept close, as invisible as the wind. He listened to their strange speech and wondered at their even stranger ways. Through the night he had studied them, and when they were asleep, he had moved silently into their camp. When he left, he took with him two of the Blue Coats' rifles so that he could show his people proof of what he had seen.

The experience had made a deep impression on Gray Wolf. He had seen white men before, but never in such numbers. He had heard tales of the Blue Coats who had come to Apacheria to make war with the Mexicans, but until he saw them for himself, he did not realize how formidable an enemy they might be. If the Blue Coats decided to make war on the Apache, the people of the White Mountains would be doomed unless they stood together.

That was why Gray Wolf had urged his father to seek a peace council with the Many Mountains people. The two Apache bands were broken into many local groups, and these were divided into small family clans. To bring the scattered groups together at one time was no small feat, but both bands had made the long journey from their winter homelands to Cottonwoods Joining because their chiefs had demanded it. They had set up their temporary camps and agreed to a truce. Then the talks had begun.

At first Gray Wolf had been encouraged by the peace council, for there were men in both bands who understood the need for unity. There were others, though, who were blind to the danger and preferred to perpetuate a feud whose meaning had been lost long ago. Their stupidity angered Gray Wolf.

"Do not worry, my son," Round Maiden said, wishing she could ease some of the burden he had taken onto himself. "It is a good sign that Blue Bear was able to persuade his people to come here. There will be peace. Wait and see. The elders and the braves will argue, but soon gifts will be exchanged and we will live with the Many Mountains people as brothers again.''

Gray Wolf studied the moon's reflection on the water. ''I hope you are right, Mother.''

Round Maiden stood. ''Pray to the Mountain Spirits for guidance, my son. Perhaps they will give you the words you need to sway the council tomorrow.''

She moved away as silently as she had come, and all was quiet on the river again. Gray Wolf knew that he, too, should return to camp; but whatever had drawn him to the water held him there, as though the answers he sought would be delivered if only he waited with sufficient patience.

A single cloud drifted over the moon, darkening the water and the woods on either shore. Voices from across the river broke the tranquillity of the night, and Gray Wolf peered into the blackness, studying the vague shapes that cautiously emerged from a stand of cottonwoods. The cloud unveiled the moon, and suddenly the shapes were no longer vague; three maidens slipped toward the river's edge carrying their *tus* baskets for water.

Two of them giggled nervously as they scanned the opposite shore for signs of their enemies. Their eyes passed over Gray Wolf several times, but he was deep in the shadows and they could not see him. He watched, wondering if the maidens, despite their nervousness, were secretly hoping to catch a glimpse of a Red Canyon brave. He had seen his sisters behave as these maidens were behaving, pretending shyness and fear while hoping for something unusual to alleviate the dreariness of their daily chores. It would be a wonderful story to tell when they returned to camp—how they had been spied upon by their evil enemy and how they had bravely performed their task despite tremendous fear. But the giggling maidens did not hold Gray Wolf's attention for long. They were foolish, and Gray Wolf had little patience with silly women.

The third maiden was far more interesting. She was taller than her timid companions, but not so tall as to be grotesque, and she moved with a regal grace. She did not giggle or feign shyness, but scanned the opposite shore without fear. With the eyes of a discerning hunter, her gaze moved unerringly to Gray Wolf's hiding place.

He was certain she could not see him, and yet it seemed that she sensed his presence. While the others filled their *tus*, the graceful one stood poised on the riverbank, watching, curiously unafraid of the darkness and the dangers that might lurk within it. The moon made her black hair, bound in a beaded *nah-leen*, shine like ravens' wings, and Gray Wolf wished desperately that he were a little closer, that the moon were a little brighter. He wanted to know if the graceful one was as beautiful as she was brave.

The maidens' voices drifted toward him. Their words were indistinct, but he separated the speakers easily, for the graceful one's voice was musical, like the gently flowing water when it called to the moon. Her tone was soft but stern as she spoke to her companions; Gray Wolf could almost imagine that she was chiding them for behaving so foolishly. She was a stone's throw from the camp of her enemy, but she was not afraid.

Did she trust the truce that had been agreed upon, or did she, like Gray Wolf, believe there were greater things to fear than her Apache cousins?

She knelt by the water to fill her *tus*, every movement poised and elegant, and suddenly Gray Wolf realized why the river had summoned him. The key to his search for peace was revealed to him.

Like a mountain cat he moved to the edge of his shadowed hiding place and stood. The moon touched him, and the graceful one raised her eyes. Upon seeing him, her companions shrieked in surprise and fled into the woods, but the graceful one rose slowly and betrayed no fear.

She Sings by the Willow studied the brave across the river. He meant no harm; of that she was certain, or he would not have revealed himself so boldly. She had known there were eyes upon her, but she had sensed no threat in them, and she sensed none now. The Red Canyon brave stood as though carved in stone, inviting Willow to satisfy her curiosity. Her sister, the moon, bathed him in light, and her father, the river, whispered to her.

Why are you not afraid, Willow?

Because I see nothing to fear, she answered in her mind.

Good. That is as it should be, the river replied. *Go home now, my daughter, and wait.*

For what? she asked, sensing something to fear for the first time.

For your destiny, the river answered as the moon hid behind a cloud. The Red Canyon brave vanished.

Hidden among the shadows once again, Gray Wolf smiled with satisfaction as the graceful one hurried into the sanctuary of the cottonwoods.

He, too, had heard the river speak of destiny, and tomorrow he would test the truth of those words.

"That is good, little sister," Willow said as she inspected the reeds and bear grass her youngest sister, Little Corn Flower, had woven into the shape of a small *me'ts'at*. The cradleboard was a nearly perfect imitation of the baby-carrier their mother had recently made for her newborn son, and Willow was impressed; not many young ones learned to weave so early. "Mother will be proud of you."

"Kayhatin! Kayhatin!"

Startled at hearing her name spoken, Willow stood and looked up to see her cousin hurrying toward her. It was a sign of great disrespect to call another by name, and the offense was forgivable only in times of emergency. From the wild-eyed look on the face of She Carries Water, Willow knew it was not a time to be insulted. "What is it, cousin?" she asked anxiously.

"A brave rides into camp, Kayhatin! A Red Canyon brave. With my own eyes I saw him cross the river!"

"He comes here?" Willow asked, alarmed. "All of our men are gone to council. What could he want?"

"I do not know." She Carries Water looked frantically around Blue Bear's large encampment. "Where is your mother? Someone must greet our enemy."

Willow glanced at her family's wickiup where her mother had disappeared only a short time ago to nurse her son. "She is tending to my brother's needs and cannot be disturbed."

"Then you must welcome him."

Willow pursed her gently bowed lips, for she knew her cousin was right. As the daughter of a chief, she had been taught the ways of making visitors welcome. It was her duty. Other maidens, whose fathers had less influence than hers, were allowed the luxury of shyness. They were permitted—even expected—to hide their faces in the presence of strangers, but the daughter of a chief was required to act with bravery.

Deathly quiet reigned where only moments ago there had been laughter and the sounds of children at play in the many smaller camps that formed the larger one. Only the slow, steady clip-clop of a horse's gait marred the stillness as a single rider wound his way through the sprawling encampment.

"I will greet him," Willow said finally, moving out of the shade of the cottonwood where she and her sister had been weaving. As she hurried toward her mother's wickiup, past the smaller dwellings of her aging grandmother and her married sister, she glanced back and found that her shy cousin had disappeared. Her sister was trotting along behind her as though trying to keep up, but as soon as they reached the wickiup, the little girl rushed inside, leaving Willow to face the Red Canyon brave alone.

She walked forward several paces, and a moment later the brave came into view. He was mounted on a magnificent black horse outfitted with a fine Mexican saddle. Both proved that he was a great warrior who had fought bravely and successfully against the Inday's enemies to the south.

Willow was impressed by the brave's show of wealth, but she was even more impressed by the man himself. Dressed only in a breechclout and supple buckskin moccasins that clung to his calves, he was as fine a young man as Willow had ever seen. His broad chest and powerfully muscled thighs showed him to be a great runner, and the corded sinews of his arms and shoulders testified to his extraordinary strength.

Gleaming black hair, bound only by a red headband, flowed onto his shoulders, framing a lean oval face with high cheekbones and a firm, square jaw. Around his neck was tied a choker with four strands of eagle bone and nuggets of silver and turquoise; from this hung a medallion carved with the symbol of the mighty Thunder Eagle, and from this hung a single eagle feather. It was a necklace that invoked great power, and only a mighty warrior who had earned the right could wear it; otherwise, the god Usen would be displeased and would strike him down.

Willow's maiden heart leaped in her breast at the sight of him, and she realized that this was the brave she had seen at the river. Throughout the long night her thoughts had turned to him and to the words the river had spoken to her. Could the two be intertwined? she had wondered. And now, with the sun, not the moon, high overhead, the brave appeared before her again. The river had told her to wait for her destiny, but Willow dared not believe that this strong, handsome warrior would be part of her future. If all went well at the peace council, his people and hers would be brothers again, but it would be many years before resentment between the bands died away enough for a brave from the Red Canyon band to risk tying his heart to a woman who had once been his enemy.

But knowing that did not stop Willow from feeling as shy as a maiden at her first social dance. For the first time in her life, she wished she were not the daughter of a chief. She had never seen such a wondrously handsome brave before, and she felt compelled to shyly hide her face as other women were allowed to do. But she had to do honor to her father, and so she stepped forward, her face tilted upward, her shoulders drawn back with pride.

"I bid you welcome, my friend. I am Kayhatin, daughter of the great *nant'an* of the Many Mountains people."

Gray Wolf looked down at the girl from his lofty perch. As he had known he would, he had recognized her as the graceful one the moment his eyes fell upon her. And she was the daughter of Chief Blue Bear, as he had suspected last night as he lay awake thinking of the encounter at the river. He had not dared believe, though, that she would be so lovely to look upon.

Her soft, dark eyes were fringed by long lashes, and every

line of her face was perfection. As before, her shimmering black hair was bound in a maiden's bow with ribbons that trailed down her back to her trim waist, and her loose-fitting buckskin dress, trimmed with fringe and bits of iridescent shells, could not conceal her generous woman's curves. It seemed impossible to Gray Wolf that such a maiden had not yet taken a husband, and yet he knew that if she had, her hair would be unbound. Her voice was as rich and gentle as he remembered, and her courage was just as unmistakable.

Gray Wolf threw one leg over his horse's neck and slid smoothly to the ground, landing directly in front of her. Though her eyes widened, she did not step back. *"Enju"*— it is good—he said with an approving smile. "You welcome me as a friend, even though I am an enemy of your people and you know not why I come."

"If I welcome you as a friend, you are bound by honor to act as a friend," Willow replied softly. The visitor was tall, and he towered over her in a most disconcerting fashion. His smile was warm, though, and Willow felt her heartbeat quicken in her breast.

"You are not afraid of me?"

Willow felt many strange and wondrous things, but fear was not among them. Though it was difficult, she gazed steadily at his face. "No."

Gray Wolf nodded. "Just as you were not afraid of me at the river last night."

She lowered her head. The brave's gentle, knowing smile was too wonderful to look at. It made her ache with feelings she had never experienced before. "I was not afraid. Then or now," she replied softly.

"Enju. You do great honor to your father."

"I try in all things to do honor to my father and to my people."

Her head was still bowed, and Gray Wolf paused a moment to study her. Her beauty moved him so profoundly that for a moment he forgot the purpose of his visit. She was the most exquisite woman he had ever seen. "Do you believe that our two peoples should be at peace?" he asked finally.

The question surprised Willow and she glanced up. "It is not my place to decide what is best for my people."

"No," Gray Wolf said gently. "But you, too, have thoughts, and I wish to know them."

Willow frowned. "Is that why you came here? To ask this question of all the women?"

"I came to ask only you," he replied, capturing her gaze and holding it with an intensity that left them both feeling a little breathless.

The sensation was so overwhelming that Willow wanted to look away, but she could not. "I believe the Inday have too many outside enemies," she answered, amazed that she had the power of speech. "We should not fight among ourselves as well."

Gray Wolf smiled again. Her words were the ones he hoped to hear, but he had never expected to be so moved by them—or by this lovely maiden. *"Enju."* It is good. He turned and mounted his magnificent black stallion as gracefully as he had left it; then he paused to look down at Willow. "Your father has a wise and beautiful daughter."

For the first time since the brave had ridden into camp, Willow felt a smile forming on her lips. "I will tell him you have said so," she replied, but the brave shook his head.

"You need not," he responded seriously. "I will tell him myself." Without another word, he turned the stallion and rode away as slowly and purposefully as he had come.

Rooted to the earth, Willow watched until he disappeared behind the wickiup of her uncle, and even after the brave had gone she stood there, pondering the meaning of the handsome warrior's strange visit. Her heart would not stop its errant drumming, and she realized with distinct pleasure that she did not want it to.

TWO

CHILDREN AND ANIMALS scattered with shrieks of surprise as Blue Bear thundered through his own camp, his horse's hooves throwing great clouds of dust into the air. Behind him, the other men were returning from the council fire on the spit of land that divided Cottonwoods Joining into two smaller rivers, but they could not guess what had agitated their chief. Many suspected that a new outbreak of war, rather than peace, was at hand, and they hurried into camp, ready to participate in the war dance if Blue Bear called for it.

But the chief was not thinking of war. His wife, Great Star, saw him coming and waited, as did two of his younger children. The child Blue Bear sought, however, was not among them.

"Where is Kayhatin?" he asked as he slid off his horse and tossed the reins to his son, He Runs Swiftly. Despite his curiosity about his father's agitation, the boy led the horse away to the field where his family's stock was held. Blue Bear threw back the blanketed flap of his wickiup and stepped inside with Great Star following. Except for their infant son, who was strapped safely in his cradleboard, the wickiup was unoccupied.

"What is wrong, my husband?" Great Star asked anxiously.

"I wish to see my daughter," Blue Bear replied, taking a dipper of water from the *tus*. "Where is she?"

"Gathering wood for the fire."

14

Blue Bear sat in his place in the wickiup, which faced the morning sun, as befitted a chief, and looked sharply at his wife. "Find her and bring her to me."

Great Star was usually quick to do as her husband bade her, but she had never seen Blue Bear behave so strangely. "You have heard of the mysterious visit that was paid to our daughter by the Red Canyon brave," she guessed, kneeling at her husband's right hand while he drank deeply from the gourd. "Kayhatin did nothing wrong, my husband. When Little Corn Flower told me that our enemy was riding into camp, I watched from the wickiup. You would have been proud of our daughter. She should not be punished for doing as she was taught."

"Punished?" Blue Bear handed her the water dipper. "Why would you say I wish to punish her, wife? I said only that I wish to see her."

"But you are not yourself, husband," Great Star pointed out. "You seemed angry as you rode into camp, and I thought—"

Blue Bear put out a hand to silence her. "Bring Kayhatin here, and you will learn that I am not angry."

Great Star bowed her head. "It will be as you say." She rose and moved quickly out of the dwelling. Her search for Willow was brief, for the girl was hurriedly returning to camp, her burden basket only half filled with firewood.

"What is wrong, Mother?" she asked, twisting her body so that the basket slipped off her back, around her shoulder, and into her hands in one easy movement. "I saw my brother tending to Father's horse. He said there is great trouble—that we may go to war."

Great Star took the burden basket from her and placed it near the cook fire. "I know not what the trouble is, daughter. Your father rode into camp as though the evil Coyote were on his heels, and he asked to see you."

Willow was surprised. "Me?"

"Yes. And we dare not keep him waiting." She guided Willow toward the wickiup. "Come."

Because it was improper for a man to be alone with a grown unmarried daughter, Great Star accompanied her inside. Both women knelt near the door, and Willow grew alarmed when she saw Blue Bear's stern expression. "I am here, Father."

"A Red Canyon warrior visited you today," he said without preamble.

How had he learned of it so quickly? Willow wondered. He had been in camp only a short while. "Yes, Father."

"What did he say to you?"

"He asked if I believe there should be peace between our tribes."

"And how did you respond?"

With her head bowed, Willow repeated the answer she had given the brave. When she glanced up, she found that Blue Bear's frown had turned to a smile.

"*Enju*. What else did the brave say to you?"

"Very little," she answered, her eyes falling again to hide her guilt. For hours she had thought of nothing but her brief encounter with the brave, and she was still no closer to understanding it. The final words he had spoken were dear to her, and she was reluctant to share them with anyone, even her beloved father.

But Blue Bear understood his daughter's sudden shyness. "Did he speak of your beauty and wisdom?" he asked slyly.

"Yes," Willow said, her face filled with wonder. "How did you know this, Father? There was no one close enough to hear the words we exchanged."

"The brave told me himself. And he said a great deal more as well. He came to me while I was alone in the sweat lodge, purifying myself."

Willow was impressed. It was not forbidden for another man to enter the sweat lodge of a chief, but only those who were willing to risk the *nant'an*'s wrath did so. For a friend the risk was seldom great, but for an enemy . . . The Red Canyon brave was indeed a fearless warrior.

"We offered prayers of peace to the great god Usen," Blue Bear continued. "And then we spoke of my daughter."

"I am honored." -

"You should be, daughter. Do you know the name of the brave who visited you?"

"No. He did not speak it."

"His name is He Stalks the Gray Wolf, a son of Tall One, the *nant'an* of the Red Canyon people," he informed her gravely, and was pleased with her expression of surprise and reverence. "He is a great warrior, and someday he will be a great chief because the spirits have given him wonderful powers. Before his first hunt he went into the high mountains, as all Inday boys must, to fast and to pray. There the Thunder Eagle befriended him and followed him home. Now the shadow of the great bird sits always on his shoulder, keeping him safe in battle and giving him strength against his enemies."

Willow had heard the story before and knew that even among his enemies He Stalks the Gray Wolf was regarded with respect. She swelled with pride to think that so great a young man had sought her out and praised her to her father. Yet the purpose of his visit became even more incomprehensible. "Why did he come to me, Father? What could such a great warrior want of a maiden from his people's enemy?"

"He wishes peace, my daughter. It was Gray Wolf who persuaded his father to ask for a peace council. When I brought our people here, I was not certain that peace between our tribes was possible or even wise. Gray Wolf's words have convinced me I was wrong. Many others now think as I do."

"Will there be peace?" Willow asked hopefully.

"That may depend on you, daughter," he replied cryptically.

"What have I to do with peace? Only women who are old and wise are permitted to speak their minds in the council of elders. No one would listen to me."

"No, but your example may be the light that leads us out of darkness," Blue Bear told her. He gestured for her to come closer, and Willow went to him, kneeling at his left hand. Gently he touched her bowed head. "Gray Wolf has asked to court you, daughter, and if you find him pleasing, his father will present our people with a worthy marriage gift."

Willow could hardly breathe. He Stalks the Gray Wolf wanted her as his wife? It was impossible to imagine. "Will it please you if I marry him, Father?"

"You must follow your heart. I cannot order you to marry him. You are free to choose your own husband." He paused thoughtfully, and Willow waited, knowing he had not finished. "It has been many seasons since you did the Maiden's Dance and became a woman, but though you have been courted by many braves, you have chosen none."

"I know I have disappointed you, but my heart did not ache for any of those braves, and I do not believe that theirs ached for me. They wished only to marry into the family of a great chief so that they could enjoy your wealth and your favor."

"I know this," Blue Bear replied. "That is why I have never spoken of it before. Gray Wolf could choose any maiden from among his own people, but if he marries my daughter he will be required to live with us, separate from his own family. Many of our tribe respect him, but they will still see in him an enemy. He will have to work hard to earn the position of power he enjoys in his father's camp. Yet for peace he is willing to make this great sacrifice."

For peace, not for love, Willow thought sadly, but she dared not speak the words aloud. She had seen love before. It was in her mother's eyes every time she looked at Blue Bear, and in her father's as he looked upon his wife. Willow longed to see love in the eyes of the man who would be her husband. She had sworn never to marry until she did.

He Stalks the Gray Wolf would be as fine a husband as any woman could wish for, but because he was an enemy, life with him would not be easy. Those who did not support the union could never be called upon in time of need or trouble.

The thought of marrying a man whose eyes did not glow with love displeased her, but Willow could find no other fault. The image of Gray Wolf was strong in her mind. He wanted her for reasons that were noble, and the union could lead to great prosperity for both their tribes.

"I will meet with the *nant'an*'s son," she said at last. "There is a trail through the valley below the bend of Cottonwoods Joining. I have had much luck there finding firewood and herbs. My cousin and I will be there when the sun is high tomorrow."

Blue Bear smiled. "Perhaps He Stalks the Gray Wolf will hear of this," he said, confident that the brave would indeed receive the message, for Blue Bear would deliver it himself.

Willow nodded and stood. As she turned, her eyes met her mother's, but Willow found the meaning there unreadable. She hurriedly left the wickiup, leaving her parents alone.

"Speak, wife," Blue Bear commanded. He had lived many years with Great Star, and he knew when she was troubled.

"You ask our daughter to make a great sacrifice. Our people will not accept Gray Wolf as one of us, and his people will not accept Kayhatin. They will both be outcasts. Their life way will be hard. Is that what you wish for her?"

"I wish for peace and prosperity for all my people," Blue Bear snapped, rising. "If the union of Kayhatin and Gray Wolf will achieve that, then yes! That is what I wish." He stormed out, but Great Star remained in the wickiup, deep in thought. Blue Bear seemed certain, but his wife was not. As a chief, he was charged with seeing to the good of all; Great Star had a mother's heart. She was a practical woman, but she also knew what it meant to make a marriage of love.

That was what *she* wanted for her daughter, for she knew that prosperity mattered little to a woman if her heart withered and died.

The valley below Cottonwoods Joining was alive with color. Wildflowers of every hue swayed in the breeze. In the midst of a faint trail that led to a nearby copse, two rows of stones, wide enough for only one person to walk through, formed a narrow path. Willow knew, even before she saw them, that He Stalks the Gray Wolf was nearby. He had collected the stones, laid them along the path for Willow, and now he was watching her from some hidden place.

If she chose to walk between the rows, it would be a sign that she looked favorably upon his suit and would welcome his courtship. If she walked around the stones, Gray Wolf would know that she did not favor him, and he would quietly disappear, his honor intact. Willow would never see him again.

"Look! The courting stones!" She Carries Water stopped

on the trail and stared at the neatly spaced stones. "Who are they for, cousin?"

Willow glanced over her shoulder at her uncle's daughter and experienced a stab of guilt. She had not told her cousin that a suitor might make his presence known today. "They are for me," she replied quietly, slipping her burden basket off her back.

She Carries Water was astonished. "Why did you not tell me you were being courted?" she whispered, realizing that they were most certainly being watched.

"Because I am not being courted . . . yet," Willow said, keeping her voice low as well. "I feared you would not come with me if you knew what was to happen today."

"Why would I not come? You are my cousin, and I have always accompanied you to the first meeting." She leaned close to Willow's ear. "Who is he? Is it Black Rope? He has spoken of offering for you."

Willow shook her head, exasperated by the idea. "It is not Black Rope, and he is foolish if he thinks I would marry him. He boasts too much and treats his sisters badly. If you wish to spare him humiliation, you will tell him I said so."

She Carries Water frowned. "Then who?"

Willow looked around quickly, then whispered, "It is the brave who rode into our camp yesterday. He is the son of the Red Canyon *nant'an*."

"Oh, my cousin, why do we stay here? Come!" She grabbed Willow's hand in alarm and tried to draw her to one side of the courting stones, but Willow pulled away.

"He is an enemy!" She Carries Water whispered.

"Cannot an enemy become a friend?" Willow asked evenly.

"A friend, perhaps, but not a husband!" her cousin replied, no longer concerned with keeping her voice low. She wished instead to let the brave watching them know her heart, for she expressed a sentiment that would be felt by many. "Come away from here, Kayhatin! Now!"

"No." Resolutely, Willow placed her burden basket on the ground and approached the courting stones. Fear and anticipation warred within her, but she refused to let her mixed emotions show. "I have promised my father, and I will do honor to him."

"Then you will honor him alone." She Carries Water turned brusquely away and hurried down the trail in the direction they had come.

Feeling forlorn and abandoned, Willow watched her cousin leave. It was not forbidden for courting couples to spend time alone; cousins came along only to ease any shyness or embarrassment. She Carries Water's words were distressing. They were a sign of what was to come should Willow walk between the courting stones.

"Your cousin is unhappy."

The quiet voice startled Willow, and she whirled to find Gray Wolf standing beside the path he had made for her. He was dressed in buckskins, his fabulous Thunderbird necklace the only adornment. He needed no other. He was so handsome he seemed to be from another world. His dark eyes were so compelling, so mesmerizing, that Willow nearly trembled under his gentle scrutiny. Her legs felt too weak to hold her. "My cousin is frightened of what she does not know," she whispered, amazed that she had any voice with which to speak.

"Yet you stayed," he pointed out with the same gentle, knowing smile Willow could not erase from her mind.

"Yes, I stayed." She bowed her head, embarrassed by the thoughts and feelings he inspired in her.

"Would you like to talk awhile before you make a decision about the courting stones?" he offered. "You must have many questions to ask me."

Willow nodded.

"Then come. We will go to the river." Gray Wolf stepped off the trail, and Willow followed him down the hill, through the carpet of wildflowers. The proud, tall warrior looked out of place among the delicate blossoms, but if he felt foolish he showed no sign of it. There was no arrogance in his stride or in the set of his broad shoulders, but every move he made bespoke confidence and power. He was a man at ease with himself and with the world he lived in. He was a man any woman would have been proud to follow.

The murmur of the water grew louder as they neared the river. Gray Wolf led her to a cluster of boulders, and they sat, keeping a respectable distance between them. With her legs curled beneath her, Willow watched the swiftly flowing water, keenly aware of Gray Wolf's eyes upon her, but unable to return the glance. He studied her intently, and Willow ached to know his thoughts. She dared not to ask, though, and for a long time they were silent.

Gray Wolf, too, was absorbed in thought. As he looked at Willow, he was remembering his mother's urgent counsel to abandon the path he had chosen. Her arguments against choosing a wife from an enemy band had been good ones, but even though a marriage to this young maiden would mean hardship, Gray Wolf still believed it was the only sure path to peace. His mind told him he was doing the right thing, and as his eyes searched Willow's profile, his heart, too, told him he had not made a mistake.

"I am sorry your cousin deserted you," he said when the silence grew long.

Willow swallowed hard and kept her eyes fixed on the river. "If I agree to the courtship, many will turn their backs to me."

"And to me as well."

"Then perhaps you have not chosen wisely," she said, her voice barely audible over the rush of the water.

Gray Wolf frowned, disturbed by her averted face. "Why will you not look at me?" he asked. "You were not so shy yesterday."

She did not move. "Yesterday I was the daughter of a chief greeting a stranger to our camp. Today I am only a maiden."

"We have no time for shyness. Our people need us, even though they do not see their need."

Willow's eyes darted to his, then away. "I have displeased you."

"No, pretty one. You please me well," he replied, softening his voice.

Willow's heart fluttered at his words and the tenderness of his tone. "But you do not know me."

"I think I know your heart. It is strong and true."

Willow searched for a wellspring of courage and found enough to look at him. "Is that why you wish to court me?"

Gray Wolf nodded. "Yes."

"My father says you seek a joining so that our people will be joined, too." She tilted her head in curiosity. "Do you truly believe our marriage could accomplish this?"

"I do."

"How?"

His gentle smile faded. "The peace council does not go well, pretty one. The feud between our people is old, and much pride is involved. Even those who believe we should live as one cannot agree on how to heal the breach between us. You know as well as I that honor will have to be satisfied on all sides before there can be peace."

Willow nodded, mesmerized by his voice. "Yes."

"Beside the council fire, my uncle shouts that if the Many Mountains braves present our people with twenty horses and that number of cattle, honor will be satisfied."

Though Willow did not know Gray Wolf's uncle, she knew enough of the nature of the Inday to imagine the scene he described. The image made her smile. "And when your uncle finishes his demands, my uncle rises and proclaims that the Many Mountains people will give twenty horses and cattle to satisfy honor *if* the Red Canyon people will give twice that number in return, plus twenty blankets and as many hides."

Gray Wolf laughed with delight. "You have been at the council fire, hiding among the rocks and listening to the speeches."

Willow blushed with pleasure at his teasing and lowered her head. "I would not do such a thing, but I do know how our people think."

"Then you know that if there is to be peace, one side must give more and accept less," he said, growing serious again. "Will your people do that?"

Willow looked at him, her face somber. "No."

"Nor will mine."

"Then there can be no peace, and you and I will remain

enemies.'' She could not keep her eyes from betraying her emotions.

Gray Wolf saw what was in her heart, and it touched him deeply—more deeply than he had imagined possible. ''Unless you and I marry,'' he said quietly.

''I do not understand how our marriage could satisfy our people's honor.''

This time it was Gray Wolf who found it necessary to look away. ''We are the son and the daughter of two great chiefs, and no one would risk incurring the anger of his chief. If you and I agree to marry, my father will collect from our people a wondrous marriage gift for you—many fine horses and cattle, blankets, hides, furs . . . beads and cloth and baskets.''

Willow finally saw the logic of his thinking. ''Then my father will distribute these gifts among my people according to custom, and to keep from being shamed by your people's generosity, mine will respond with gifts equally as wondrous. All things will be equal. Honor will be satisfied, and our people will be tied together as one. Your people will be my people, and mine, yours.''

''Just as your enemies will be mine, and mine, yours,'' Gray Wolf replied, remembering the long line of Blue Coats he had seen.

''You are wise,'' Willow told him reverently.

''As are you,'' he returned, amazed at how quick she had been to understand his thinking. Gray Wolf had never met a woman who seemed to embody so many desirable qualities— beauty and grace, intelligence and humor, courage and honor. She was in all ways remarkable. Yet he could see that, despite her understanding, she was troubled. ''Tell me what you are thinking, pretty one.''

''Living with my family will not be the same as living among your own people. You will have no friends.''

Gray Wolf met her eyes and held them with his own. ''I will have you,'' he said softly. ''I think no man could ask for more than that.''

Willow's breath stilled, and tears pooled in her eyes. She had never seen such tenderness in a man's face. It was the look she had dreamed of, the look she had prayed she would someday see in the eyes of a man she loved. Suddenly, Willow knew what the river had meant two nights before when it told her to go home and await her destiny. Her life and everything she would ever be were bound to the man beside her.

"I will be a good husband to you, pretty one." Gray Wolf's voice was sure and strong. "I have led many hunting parties, and my family has known no lack of meat for food or hides for warmth. I would respect your father as my own, and I would honor your mother as she deserves. I would be patient and pray to the Mountain Spirits for guidance in earning the trust of your family, your clan, and all your people."

"And would you love me?" The words were out before Willow could stop them.

The need and hope on her lovely face moved Gray Wolf in a way no woman had ever moved him before. Only honor prevented him from taking her into his arms. "That, I think, would be the simplest task of all."

His eyes were dark and warm. Willow's heart expanded, reaching toward Gray Wolf like a wildflower blossoming in the sun. Without another word, she stood and hurried uphill until she reached the courting stones in their bed of wildflowers. A rustle of grass told her that Gray Wolf was not far behind, that he was watching her every move. She went to the head of the path and did not hesitate before walking between the stones. At the end of the path, she found Gray Wolf waiting for her. Their eyes met and a look of tenderness, longing, and pride passed between them. Their courtship had begun.

"Tonight, in the place of the council fires, our people will gather for a social dance," she told him. "There will be food and music, and all the maidens will dance with the braves their hearts favor. Will you come and see who chooses you for the dance?"

He nodded. "I will come."

Willow smiled. *"Enju."*

THREE

WHEN WILLOW RETURNED to camp, she found all the women deep in preparations for the feast. The night before, Blue Bear had told his people that they would gather for a social dance with the Red Canyon band, but he had not explained that a wedding feast might soon follow. He thought it best to await the outcome of his daughter's tryst with Gray Wolf before making such an announcement.

It was a wise decision, since the announcement of a simple social dance had caused considerable dissension. Some had grumbled because they feared it was too soon for the bands to mingle without some trouble arising. The same rumblings were heard throughout the Red Canyon camp, but Tall One and Blue Bear had reminded their braves that starting trouble at the dance would shame them all—everyone knew that the truce was to be honored at all costs. The men were to be treated as brothers or fathers; the women as sisters, mothers, wives, or sweethearts. The social dance would be the first test of whether the two bands could learn to live in peace.

But Willow's mind was not on peace as she helped her mother prepare the feast. She knew that Gray Wolf's proposal was for the good of their people, but the welfare of her family and friends was of little concern to her at that moment; the workings of her own heart were much closer to home. She could not wipe from her mind the tender look in Gray Wolf's eyes. Her thoughts echoed with the sound of his voice and the sweetness of his words. She smiled often, oblivious of the concern on her mother's face.

Willow had never believed that love would come to her so quickly. She had been courted several times, but none of those braves had made her feel so anxious, as though all the butterflies on the ridge of Sugar Loaf had flown into her stomach and were working their magic there. The feelings Gray Wolf generated were so overwhelming that Willow even wondered if perhaps the brave had cast a love spell on her. To win her husband, Willow's older sister had purchased such a *godistso* from an old woman, Para-ah-dee, who was said to know all manner of spells and potions to bind a man and woman together.

Had Gray Wolf worked a similar magic on her? she wondered. Some forms of *godistso* were bad and might cause madness, but Willow could not believe that Gray Wolf would work evil magic on her. In fact, it did not seem likely that he would ever call upon love magic at all. A man so strong and intelligent, so wonderful to look upon, whose voice was like the river and whose words were sweet enough to coax the birds from the trees, would not need *godistso* to win a maiden—not even a maiden who was supposed to be his enemy.

But if this was magic, it was wondrous magic indeed. Yet despite the glorious feelings Gray Wolf had awakened in her, Willow was a practical maiden. Her arguments against marriage were still as valid as they had been before he told her how simple it would be to love her. She thought of the hardships that awaited her if she married Gray Wolf, and her spirits plummeted. Then she remembered his smile, and her spirits soared. It was a war between her mind and her heart, and Willow did not dare try to guess which would win.

Several times as she worked around the camp Willow caught sight of She Carries Water, but her cousin refused to look at her. It was obvious she had not told anyone about the courting stones, and Willow suspected that her cousin was hoping she would come to her senses before the rest of the camp learned of Gray Wolf's interest. She had always been close to her cousin, and it saddened Willow to think that she might lose that friendship.

As the sun began to set, Blue Bear and Tall One sent messengers into camp to tell their wives it was time for the women to bring food to the council. It took considerable effort to transport the huge quantities of roasted meat, but there was little else to take to the feast. It was the season of Little Eagles, and the mescal was just beginning to ripen; aside from meat, which was available throughout the year, the only food either band had to offer was that which had been dried and stored after last year's harvests. The season of Ghost Face—winter—had been hard, and supplies were running low, but the women did their best with what they had.

On the spit of land in the fork of the river, the men of the council were neatly divided in half-circles around the fire, with each group facing its homeland. The feast was brought across the river on horseback, and each woman served the men of her own family. Knowing there would be little left when they finished, the women had sampled the meal generously as it was being prepared, and they had encouraged their children to do likewise.

The braves and elders ate with relish, and when they were finished, the central fire was built into a roaring blaze. The men moved back, widening the circle around it in order to clear a space for dancing.

When the sun was completely gone, the drums began, and from seemingly nowhere, the Gan dancers appeared. Dressed only in loincloths and intricately decorated hoods and headdresses, the dancers represented the Inday Mountain Spirits. Their bodies were decorated with paint—white dots indicating purity of heart; white triangles representing the sacred mountains; and the sun, moon, and stars to frighten away angry powers.

They danced around the fire until finally they were joined by the Clown. His headdress and hood were more intricately decorated than the others, and his entire body was covered with dots of black and white. Evergreen boughs were tied to his wrists, and he danced among the other Gan, drawing close to the fire, then far away to the outskirts of the circle.

He gathered into the boughs any harmful spirits that were lurking nearby and then cast the evergreens into the fire to burn away the evil.

Then, as quickly as they had come, the Gan disappeared. It was time for the social dance to begin. Without prompting, the maidens and unmarried braves from each band took their places. The braves moved to an area beyond the fire and sat while the maidens moved into a dance ring.

As Willow moved into the circle of the fire, she noticed that the bands were still neatly divided, as though an invisible line cut the circle in half, with the Red Canyon people on one side and her own on the other. No one save the Gan dancers had dared to cross the line. The maidens began moving among the braves, choosing their partners for the dance by tapping the chosen brave on the shoulder, but still no one crossed the line.

When at first Willow made no move to choose a partner, many eyes went to her, but it was only Gray Wolf's gaze that Willow truly sensed. She had been aware of him from the moment she arrived, and the excitement within her had continued to mount. He had watched her covertly, without seeming to watch her at all, but Willow had known his whereabouts at every moment. At times she even seemed to sense his thoughts, for there was something sweet and warm touching her, urging her to have courage. Throughout the meal and the dance of the Mountain Spirits, she had envisioned the moment when she would resolutely cross the invisible line between his people and hers, tap Gray Wolf on the shoulder, and join him in the dance.

Now, though, when it was finally time to call upon that courage and declare her intentions, Willow found herself hesitating. There was no commitment in choosing a brave to dance, and one maiden might have many partners during the course of the night. But Willow knew that when she chose Gray Wolf, she would be risking the censure of both bands. And if she danced with him a second time and a third and a fourth, she would be telling the Many Mountains band and the Red Canyon people that she had chosen the man she wished to court her.

It was a moment of tremendous decision, and despite her awareness of Gray Wolf's intent gaze, Willow hesitated a moment too long. Just as she found the courage to take a step toward Gray Wolf, a Red Canyon maiden touched his shoulder and returned to her place in the dance circle. Though his eyes were still on Willow, he had no choice but to rise and follow the girl who had chosen him.

Disappointment knifed through Willow, but that was not the only keen emotion in her heart. As Gray Wolf took his place facing his partner with only a few paces between them, Willow felt a kind of twisting jealousy she had never known before. The maiden was beautiful, and in the dancing firelight it was clear to see that she was in love with Gray Wolf.

Willow knew she had only herself to blame, and her moment's indecision angered her. Now she had no partner, and there were only a few Many Mountains braves who had not already been chosen. She could not stand in the circle unattended, and to leave would cause much commotion, so she moved toward the remaining braves. The first her eyes fell upon was Black Rope, but, remembering She Carries Water's warning that he had been boasting of his plans to offer for her, Willow quickly looked away from him. She had no intention of encouraging a brave for whom she had no affection. Instead, she looked beyond him, searching for one of her cousins who would not misunderstand her invitation to dance.

She spotted Quick Killer, a distant cousin who liked to joke with her, but to reach him she had to pass Black Rope. The insolent young brave's eyes were fixed steadily on Willow, and he smiled arrogantly as she approached. His smile turned to a scowl of anger when it became clear that she was about to move past him, and before Willow knew what was happening, Black Rope was on his feet. He took a step back, blocking her path, and Willow realized that to those at a distance, it appeared that she had chosen him.

He glared at her, daring her to humiliate him by choosing another, and though Willow disliked the brave, she did not have the heart to shame him. She returned to the dance circle and took a place opposite Black Rope. The drums changed rhythm, and the dance began.

Though Willow normally danced without shyness, her anger with herself and with Black Rope would not allow her to look at her partner. She kept her eyes fixed on the ground as she performed the intricate steps, moving forward as Black Rope moved back, then the reverse; to one side, then forward and back, then to the side again. All the dancers performed the same steps, moving toward the fire, then away from it, like the spokes of a great wheel slowly turning, until finally each couple arrived back at the point from which they had started, and the music stopped.

Except for those courting, whose intentions were already known to all, the braves returned to their places to await being chosen again. Willow kept her head down so that she could see only the upturned toes of Black Rope's moccasins as she waited for him to depart. But he did not move. Her eyes went to his, and again she found the look of defiance.

"Go back to your place," she whispered desperately.

Black Rope's shoulders straightened proudly. "I am where I belong," he replied quietly.

"No." Willow shook her head. "The dance is my choice, and I do not choose you."

A knowing smile hovered around his lips. "You will not shame me."

His insolence was too much for Willow to bear. If she did not move quickly, another Red Canyon maiden—or perhaps even the same lovely one—would select Gray Wolf. And worse, if she danced again with Black Rope, Gray Wolf might take it as a sign that she had dealt falsely with him. She had to rid herself of Black Rope immediately, and he was giving her no choice but to humiliate him in front of his own people and his enemies. A brave could suffer no greater shame, but Willow could not allow herself to be controlled in such a manner.

"You do this to yourself, Black Rope," she hissed, deliberately using his name to show her contempt. She barely saw his look of shock as she turned away and moved to another location on the wheel.

Frozen in disbelief, Black Rope barely heard the murmurs that rippled through the crowd of spectators, but the laughter that began among the Red Canyon braves and quickly spread to his own friends cut him to the bone. Shock turned to humiliation, and humiliation to rage before he finally whirled away. He hurried out of the circle and through the crowd, with the sound of mockery chasing him into the night.

Willow shuddered as the laughter died away. This was not what she had wanted, and even though she did not like Black Rope, she ached for him. It would be a long time before he could hold his head up proudly among his friends, and that was a fate she would wish on no Inday. He would, most likely, leave camp for a few days or even weeks, as many young men did after finding themselves in an embarrassing situation, and when he returned, everyone would pretend to have forgotten.

The slow, steady drumbeat began again, directing each maiden to choose a new partner, and Willow tried to dismiss Black Rope from her mind. She looked for Gray Wolf and found him in the same spot as before. His eyes held sympathy for her, as though he knew how hard it had been for her to shame Black Rope. Willow's heart reached for him again, and without hesitation she moved around the fire.

After her rejection of Black Rope, all eyes were on Willow to see whom she would choose. There were murmurs of speculation and ripples of laughter, but when she boldly crossed the invisible line that divided the bands, the night became as silent as death. Even the steady drumbeat faltered for one beat, then two; but Willow kept moving, keenly aware that all the other maidens had frozen, waiting to see what she would do.

Seeking and finding reassurance in Gray Wolf's dark eyes, Willow went to him. Her hand trembled slightly as she touched his shoulder, but it was not fear that made her quiver; it was the tenderness and the gentle smile of approval on his wondrously handsome face. She withdrew her hand and returned to her place at the wheel without a backward glance.

And then it was Gray Wolf's turn to cross the line that divided the two bands. The stunned spectators watched as he came to his feet in one graceful move and followed Willow. With his back to the fire, he took his place in front of her. She raised her face to his, and they looked at each other without embarrassment, oblivious of everyone and everything.

The drumbeat quickened slightly, as though to remind the other maidens that they had yet to choose partners, and the camp came to life again. The couples moved to their places, the drums made music, and the wheel began to move. In perfect rhythm, Willow and Gray Wolf danced together, forward and back, almost as though they were bound together. The distance between them never varied, but as Willow lost herself in Gray Wolf's eyes, it seemed there was no space separating them at all. The drumbeats were the beats of their hearts, and the warmth that enfolded her was the warmth of Gray Wolf's arms.

Gray Wolf felt the magic, too. Before tonight, the social dance had been nothing more than an obligation, and sometimes even an embarrassment. Many maidens had given him signs that they favored him, and some, like Her Hair Streams Down, who had chosen him for the first dance, were particularly persistent. Gray Wolf had never favored any of them, though. He had seen twenty-four harvests, which made him of an age when most braves were marrying or already married, and yet no maiden had ever touched his heart.

One or two—strong women and good workers—had made him consider the possibility of marriage, but he had resisted, mostly because of his family. Gray Wolf's older brother and younger brother had both married and moved to the homes of their wives, leaving the responsibility of providing for the rest of the large family to Tall One and Gray Wolf. Marrying and moving away would have made life harder for the family, and so Gray Wolf had remained single. Two seasons ago, though, his oldest sister, who was eight harvests younger than Gray Wolf, had finally taken a husband, leaving Gray Wolf free to marry.

Her Hair Streams Down knew of this and had done everything in her power to ensnare the son of the *nant'an*. She had even purchased a *godistso*, but Gray Wolf's spirit guide, the

Thunder Eagle, had warned him so that he could ward off the persistent maiden's magic. Her Hair Streams Down was a maiden of great beauty, but her heart was cold.

There was no coldness in She Sings by the Willow, though. She was as warm as the firelight that danced on her face. Her eyes held no secrets, but instead invited Gray Wolf to enter their depths and see into her heart. It was a pure heart, as gentle as the elegant tree from which she had obtained her name, and as strong as that tree, as well. In his own heart, Gray Wolf knew that he could search a lifetime and never find a woman as perfect as the one who danced the wheel with him, her eyes locked with his, her heart open wide. Before the dance was finished, the desire for peace was no longer the desire that burned strongest in his breast.

Blue Bear watched his daughter and knew from the enraptured look on her face that she was in love with Gray Wolf. When the dance ended, the couple stood in place until the next dance began, and then the next, their eyes never leaving each other.

Blue Bear was well pleased. In a few days his daughter would signal her suitor that she was ready to share the blankets with him. A marriage gift would be presented, and once she had given herself to Gray Wolf and he had taken her as his wife, a second giving of gifts would take place. The two bands would be bound together, honor would be satisfied, and there would be peace—for as long as the Blue Coats would allow it. Blue Bear could not have asked for more.

Great Star was not so happy, though. Unlike Blue Bear, who saw only Willow and Gray Wolf, she was studying the faces of her family and friends around the fire. There was no rapture in their eyes as they watched the Red Canyon brave lay claim to a Many Mountains maiden. There were frowns and murmurs of disapproval on both sides of the fire. Peace would not be as simple as Blue Bear and Tall One wanted to believe, and Great Star's heart wept, for she feared that her gentle, innocent daughter was about to be caught in the middle.

FOUR

FOR THE THIRD DAY in a row Willow rode away from the camp when the sun was high overhead. As on the two previous days, she had decided upon no particular destination, but she did not doubt that Gray Wolf would find her. He always seemed to know where she was. Even more miraculously, he seemed to know what she was thinking and feeling. Today when he met her, he would comment on the heaviness in her heart.

For the first time in her life Willow felt like an outsider among her own people. She had known that being courted by Gray Wolf would make her life difficult, but she had not dreamed it could be this bad. Friends of her childhood avoided her. Cousins and aunts spoke to her only when she addressed them directly. A look of infinite sadness never left her mother's eyes.

Black Rope's father, an influential subchief who was as hot-tempered as his son, was openly trying to create dissension. He spoke out forcefully at the peace council during the day; at night he quietly made his way from camp to camp trying to convince the Many Mountains people that Blue Bear's quest for peace was madness. He reminded them that it was time for the harvesting of mescal. They should be traveling to the places where the plant grew in abundance. They should be cutting and curing the food that was the staple of their diet rather than wasting time talking about peace and waiting for a flighty maiden to make up her mind about marrying an enemy of her people.

His argument was having the desired effect, and Willow feared that any day now the people might rise against her father and choose a new chief.

Blue Bear did not seem concerned, though. He believed his people were wise enough to understand that Black Rope's father was creating trouble only because his son had been shamed into leaving the camp. No one had seen the brave since the night of the dance, and his humiliation was felt by many in his family. At first Willow had been glad that he was gone because she had feared he might force a confrontation with Gray Wolf. But his leaving had caused a different set of problems, and Willow sometimes wondered if things would have been better if he had stayed. With him gone, the people felt pity for him. If he had stayed, his arrogance would have been a constant reminder that he had brought his disgrace upon himself.

With so much dissension around her—*because* of her—confusion had become Willow's constant companion . . . except when she was with Gray Wolf. Only then did her feelings of bewilderment and loneliness vanish, replaced by a sense of belonging more powerful than any she had ever known. She had finally fallen in love, but it was costing her everything she held dear.

Would it always be so, she wondered, or was Gray Wolf right? He seemed certain that someday her people would accept him. He was wise and in all ways wonderful. In her brighter moments—when she was with him—Willow could easily envision her people coming to respect Gray Wolf as much as she did. But when she was alone again, her bright hopes burst and reality crept in. Even if Gray Wolf was tolerated by her people, would he ever truly belong?

And what would her life be like when she visited Gray Wolf's people? She had yet to meet his mother and sisters. Would they welcome her, or did Gray Wolf's mother feel the same despair that Great Star could not hide?

Mired in confusion, plagued by questions she could not answer, Willow rode on, caring little where her pony took her. This valley below the Mogollon Rim was not her home, but she knew the country well. In the seasons of the harvests, her clan often came here to collect piñon nuts and juniper berries. She was surprised, though, to look up and realize that she was approaching Sugar Loaf. That was appropriate, for it was said to be a place of strong love magic. Perhaps she would find wisdom here as well.

The sound of a single horse drew her attention, and she reined in her pony. From the direction of the sunrise, Gray Wolf appeared at the mouth of a small canyon. He rode toward her and, as always, her heart swelled with love.

"You have found me," she said in greeting as he drew his horse alongside hers.

Gray Wolf smiled at her. "Did you intend that I should not?"

Willow laughed lightly. "I think you could find me anywhere, whether I wished it or not."

"That is because there is nothing in my head but you. If I were stalking deer, my family would go hungry."

The compliment pleased Willow, but she could not resist teasing him. "That is not a wise thing to say to a maiden who might someday depend upon you for food."

"Ah, but after we are married, there will no longer be a reason for my wits to be scattered," he replied, leaning toward her with an intimacy that stilled Willow's breathing. "I will be content, and your love will make me twice as strong. My arrows will fly straight and true."

His words and his deep voice created an ache deep in Willow's loins, and she looked away from him. "You grow too bold," she scolded without conviction.

"Only because you make me bold," he answered. When she did not respond, he surveyed the countryside. "Come, let us ride. Were you bound for Sugar Loaf?"

Willow nodded, unwilling to tell him that she had been riding without a destination, oblivious to everything but her confusion about him.

"Have you been to the home of the Butterfly People before?"

As she nudged her pony forward, Willow glanced ahead

to the cone-shaped hill known as Sugar Loaf. ''Never in this season of Little Eagles—only later, when the land is Thick with Fruit.''

Gray Wolf smiled. ''Then you should be prepared to see something wondrous. Come.'' He urged his horse into a gallop, and Willow followed suit. They crossed the dusty yellow floor of the valley until they reached the rocky base of the hill. Gray Wolf slid down from his huge black horse and resisted the urge to grasp Willow by the waist to help her dismount. It would not have been proper to touch a woman who was not his wife in such an intimate fashion, but he burned with thoughts of caressing Willow's womanly curves. Every moment he was with her, it required more strength to keep a respectful distance between them. Gray Wolf knew he was a strong swimmer and a tireless runner, but he was not certain how long he could maintain this kind of strength.

He hobbled his horse and then Willow's after she had dismounted. ''Should I run as fast as I am able to the top?'' he asked with a feigned innocence that Willow found almost laughable.

''Why would you? Do you have need of the magical *bitgo'dzo* plant?''

Gray Wolf hid a smile and shrugged. ''If I perform the ritual, the Butterfly People will look kindly upon me and help me win a wife.''

Willow looked toward the summit of the hill, feigning indifference. ''If you think you cannot win one without magic, go ahead. Run without stopping to the top and see if the plant is there.''

Gray Wolf leaped onto a rugged boulder and held out his hand. ''Run with me, pretty one.''

Though she knew he was teasing, for a moment Willow considered doing as he asked. If they both performed the ritual and were blessed to discover the imaginary *bitgo'dzo* plant, her confusion about marrying Gray Wolf would surely end. The Butterfly People would take control of her heart and give it to Gray Wolf. She would have no choice but to marry him or die of the madness that came from longing; it would not matter to her that she might lose the love and support of her family in the process.

But Willow did not want love that came from magical sources and clouded the mind. She wanted Gray Wolf to love her for herself, not because a love Gan willed it. "I will walk up the hill," she announced at last, ignoring his outstretched hand.

"Then I will walk with you."

Moving slowly up the rugged terrain, they climbed toward the summit. As they neared the top, a shadow passed over Willow, and she frowned. There were no clouds in the sky today. Puzzled and a little alarmed, she stopped and looked up toward the crest of the hill. The cloud that darkened the sun was still there, but it was not high in the sky; it hovered, shifting and shimmering, on the plateau above her. It changed shapes, then disappeared into the rocks.

Fear darted through Willow. "We should not be here, Gray Wolf! Let us go before we anger the Gans." She turned away, but a gentle hand on her arm stopped her.

"There is nothing to fear, pretty one. Trust me." His hand slipped into hers, and the warmth of it spread through Willow, replacing fear with desire. Trusting him completely, she allowed him to guide her up the hill.

They reached the plateau, and Willow gasped with surprise and delight as she discovered what had created the eerie shadow. Around them, on the ground and on every rock and plant, were butterflies—thousands of them—of every size and description. The rocky plateau was a rainbow of color. Mesmerized by their beauty, Willow stepped forward. Gray Wolf let her hand slip from his and watched as she moved among the delicate insects. She walked slowly, careful not to disturb them, but when she finally turned toward Gray Wolf, the butterflies took flight, surrounding her in color.

"They are beautiful!" she cried, laughing with joy as butterflies danced in front of her and even settled on her hair and fringed buckskin dress.

"*You* are beautiful," Gray Wolf replied, awed by the magnificent smile that lit her face. He stepped toward her, and the butterflies enveloped them both. They laughed together as the colorful creatures frolicked, darting this way and that, settling on their clothes, then fluttering away.

And then, as suddenly as they had surrounded the couple, the butterflies rose in a mass that sheltered Willow and Gray Wolf from the sun for a moment before they disappeared over the boulders above.

Disappointed by the loss of so much beauty, Willow scampered up the rocks to another plateau, but there was no sign of the butterflies. "Where have they gone?" she asked as Gray Wolf joined her.

He pointed to a great fissure in the rocks. "Into the cave."

Willow knelt, her eyes fixed on the place he indicated. "Then I will wait for them to come out."

Gray Wolf smiled as he knelt behind her. "You may have a long wait, pretty one. They might not return until tomorrow."

Willow sighed mournfully, but did not dispute him. "You have seen this wondrous sight before?"

"Yes, but never so many. They must have known you were coming," he said gently, giving in to the great temptation to place his arms around Willow's waist.

She stiffened at the intimacy, but only for a moment before leaning back against the hard wall of his chest. She had never felt so safe or so cherished. Her head rested against his cheek, and she could feel the warmth of his breath caressing her hair.

"We have been blessed, pretty one," he said huskily, but he was not thinking of the dancing butterflies . . . nor was she.

"Yes," she whispered.

"I love you," he confessed for the first time, and felt Willow stiffen once again. He frowned but made no move to release her. "Do you doubt me?"

His words were the ones Willow had longed to hear, but she could not lie to him. "Yes."

"Why?"

"Because we have talked often of the reasons you seek peace. It is important to you, and a man will sometimes do many things—even lie—to achieve an important goal."

Gray Wolf's arms tightened around her, pulling her closer as though he wanted to draw her into his own body. "I will never lie to you, pretty one. How can I make you believe that?"

"I do not know."

He released her suddenly and stood, leaving Willow bereft. "I think you look for excuses to deny what is in your heart," he said, unable to mask his frustration.

She twisted her body toward him. Though she found anger on his face, she was not at all afraid. "I seek to do what is right."

"It is right that you should be my wife!"

"So that our people will be at peace?" she challenged.

Gray Wolf grabbed her shoulders and pulled her to her feet. "So that I may touch you as I long to do. So that you are free to touch me. I want to give you children, Kayhatin. I want to grow old sharing the blankets with you." He pulled her to him intimately, her body pressed along his, his face close to hers, his voice lowered to a silken caress. "Say that you do not want what I want, and I will leave you."

Willow had never been so close to a man before, and the heat that coursed through her left her weak and trembling. She wanted Gray Wolf, no matter what the cost, and at long last she realized that the endless agonizing she had done these last days had all been for naught. She was fated to be Gray Wolf's woman. She could allow nothing else to matter to her.

"I want . . . what you want," she whispered.

Gray Wolf's eyes darkened with hunger. "Then come to me tonight so that we may marry."

Willow nodded. "I will."

The need to possess her was almost more than Gray Wolf could bear, but he did no more than cup her face in his hand and urge her to rest her head upon his shoulder. "We will not regret this, pretty one. I promise you."

"I pray you are right, beloved," she replied, her voice made hoarse by the love and need that coursed through her.

When Willow returned to camp, she went quietly about the task of preparing herself to be Gray Wolf's bride. While the

other women in her family were outside preparing the evening meal, Willow took advantage of a few moments alone
in the wickiup. She spread her best dress and overshirt on
the blankets where she normally slept; on these she placed
her best moccasins and her favorite adornments—three strands
of turquoise beads that fit tightly around her neck, bracelets
that matched, and dangling earrings made of turquoise and
eagle down. She rolled the dress carefully, and while the sun
was still hot, she slipped quietly out of the wickiup and disappeared into the thicket behind the camp. If she did not
return by nightfall, her family would know that she had finally made her decision.

Hoping she would not be seen, she made her way to the
cold spring where many fathers took their children to swim
each morning. Exercise was not Willow's intent, however. A
high wedge of rocks surrounded the pool on three sides, and
once she was certain there was no one about, she slipped out
of her dress and into the water until it covered her hips. The
cold made her shiver, but she ignored it. She untied her *nah-
leen* and shook out her waist-length hair as she tossed the
maiden's bow back to shore. Taking a deep breath, she
plunged deep into the center of the pool.

Using soapweed that had been pounded into pulp, Willow
lathered her hair and rinsed it by dunking her head until she
was satisfied that all of the aloe had been removed. She
washed her body in a similarly vigorous fashion, climbed out
of the pool, and slipped into the sleeveless underdress. Using
a bundle of stiff grass tied with a strand of sinew, she worked
the tangles from her hair, then spread the tresses over her
uplifted arm to dry in the sun.

It took a long time, but it was worth the effort. By the time
she used the grass bundle again, her reflection in the pool
told her that her hair was as shiny as the blue-black wings of
the raven. The hip-length shirt that slipped over her head
matched her brightly decorated underdress, its long fringes
of buckskin strung with bits of iridescent abalone shell that
ran across the front and down the sleeves.

For the last time Willow pulled her hair back and twisted
it into a bow-shaped knot. Over this she tied her beaded *nah-*

leen, keenly aware that after tonight she would never wear the bow again. She felt no sadness over the loss of the maidenly custom; her mind was too full of growing speculation about what her wedding night would be like. She had tended her father's animals enough to know a little about mating, and though her older sister had not spoken of her wedding night directly, Willow had seen the secret smiles of happiness the newly married couple had exchanged once they began to share the blankets. Willow experienced a fear of the unknown, but it was tempered with the certainty that no matter what was to come, Gray Wolf would never hurt her.

As the sun began to set, she bundled her old clothes, hid them in a thicket behind her camp, and slipped into the woods to await her wedding night.

FIVE

AFTER SUNSET, with only waning cook fires to guide her steps, Willow went in search of her husband-to-be. Knowing that the wickiups of Tall One's family would be located at the head of the encampment, she worked her way quietly northward until she came upon the four dwellings. The largest belonged to the *nant'an*, and the two that flanked the chief's belonged to Gray Wolf's grandfather and married sister. The fourth wickiup, smaller than the others, sat a short distance away. Behind it was tethered Gray Wolf's beautiful stallion, just as he had told her it would be, so that she could locate him.

From the shelter of some rocks, she watched the camp until she was certain all was as it should be. For a time she feared that the thunderous beating of her heart would awaken those who were already asleep, but no matter how firmly she commanded it, her heart would not be still. The night was cold, but that did not account for the trembling of her limbs. She gathered courage from the memory of Gray Wolf's arms around her, let the remembered warmth still her trembling, and finally left her hiding place to walk boldly into the camp of her enemies.

Without looking right or left, she approached the wickiup. As was polite, she paused a moment outside. Had this been a visit to the abode of a friend, she would have spoken some casual phrase as a warning, but her voice failed her. Instead, she deliberately wrung her hands together, making the bracelets on her wrist tinkle gently to alert Gray Wolf that she had arrived. Then, without waiting for a response, she eased back the rawhide flap of the dome-shaped dwelling and stepped into the opening.

Beyond a small, bright fire that bathed the room in flickering golden light sat Gray Wolf, bare-chested, his legs crossed. His dark eyes were lit from within by a fire more intense than that in the center of the wickiup.

Somehow Willow found her voice. "I have come, as I promised."

"I have been waiting," he answered softly.

Dropping the flap behind her, Willow moved into the dwelling and knelt across the fire from him.

Gray Wolf sensed the wild beating of her heart. He longed to reach for her and pull her close so that she would know her heart was not alone, but he chose to touch her with calming words instead. "I was not certain you would ever come to me like this, pretty one. I know how hard the disapproval of your people has made this for you."

The tenderness in his face made Willow certain she had chosen wisely. "You have known disapproval, too," she reminded him. "Some call you a coward. They say you seek peace only because you are afraid of the White Eyes."

"I am afraid for the fate of our people. If that makes me a coward, so be it."

She smiled at him. "You are no coward. My heart would not reach out to you if you were."

"My heart reaches for you, too, pretty one—more strongly than I had ever dreamed possible," he confessed. "But are you sure that marriage to me is the course you wish to follow?"

He was offering her one last chance to change her mind. Instead of taking it, Willow gathered her courage and moved to him. As she knelt by his side, the long ribbons of her *nahleen* fell over her shoulders. "I am sure."

He turned to her. "But you are also frightened."

Her gaze fell to the fire as she nodded mutely.

"Of coming to me as a woman comes to a man?"

"Yes."

Longing to touch her, Gray Wolf reached for one of the ribbons and wrapped it around his hand. "I do not fear taking you, pretty one. I ache for it. . . . But if you would prefer, we can go to my family's wickiup and pass the night there with my mother, father, and sisters lying between us. The result would be the same—your intention to take me as husband would be declared. The choice is yours to make."

The kindness of his offer touched Willow and convinced her, more than ever, that she had chosen a husband who would always cherish her. But even though she was frightened of the unknown, she knew that sleeping with Gray Wolf's family would not ease her fear, nor would it ease the powerful longings of her body. Only lying in Gray Wolf's arms would do that.

His hand, wrapped in the ribbon, was close to her face, and as Willow raised her eyes to his, she cupped one hand around his larger, stronger one and raised it to her cheek. "I will pass the night here. With you, alone."

Gray Wolf's throat tightened with so much emotion that no words could escape. He opened his hand, and Willow nestled her face in his palm. The heat of that simple, tender contact swept through them both.

"Come," he whispered hoarsely. He stood, bringing Willow with him, and led her to the pile of blankets that would be their marriage bed. When Willow knelt, Gray Wolf moved behind her and dropped to his knees. He touched the hem of her shirt, gathering the material into his hands, and Willow raised her arms. He slipped the shirt, then the underdress, over her head.

Embarrassment coursed through Willow, and she folded her arms across her breasts as Gray Wolf untied the *nah-leen*. Her hair fell into a long rope down her back, and Gray Wolf ran his fingers through the raven mass until it formed a soft, shimmering mantle that covered her back and shoulders.

"So beautiful," he whispered huskily. "I have longed to see this sight since the moment we met." He showed her the beaded *nah-leen*. "Will you give this to me, beloved? When we are old and our children grown, it will remind me of this night."

Tears formed in Willow's eyes. "It is yours."

"Enju." He slipped away from her, but Willow did not turn to follow his movements. Instead, she bowed her head and waited, not knowing what to expect next.

From across the room Gray Wolf studied his bride. She was magnificent, and she was his. He longed to go to her and take her swiftly. He desperately needed to ease the fire in his loins. But as he unfastened his breechclout, freeing his manhood, he knew that he would have to go slowly. There was pleasure to be experienced between a man and a woman—great pleasure for both—but only if he took care to see that his frightened bride was ready for him. Willow's heart was already his, but her body was still her own. Soon, though, she would reach for him with her body and cry for him to take it as well.

Gray Wolf had enjoyed this experience with only one other woman, a widow who had subtly let him know that she found him desirable. He was not proud of the hours he had spent with her, but he had been young then, barely past the age of maturity. His blood had been hot, and the widow had been eager to initiate him into the mysteries of man and woman. He had not known how to refuse her, nor had he truly wanted to. She had taught him much about what pleased a woman and what did not—how to go slowly and where to touch, when to give and when to take.

He had thought his secret relationship with the older, experienced woman was something special, but when he learned that he was not the only young brave the widow had instructed, he never went near her again.

Those memories had faded with the passing of many harvests, but what he had learned was easily recalled. He went to Willow, gently eased her onto the blankets, and told her with his hands, heart, and body how much he loved her.

When morning came, Willow understood the meaning of her sister's secret smiles. She crept away from Gray Wolf's small wickiup to return to her own camp before sunrise, but the wonders of the night went with her. Her heart sang like the birds as she remembered every touch and sigh she had shared with her husband, and she marveled at wonders she had never dreamed existed.

Willow had much to do that day, but she was in no hurry to return to camp. Before nightfall, Gray Wolf's father would bring marriage gifts. If Blue Bear found the gifts satisfactory, as she was sure he would, the union of the two tribes would be sealed. Return gifts would have to be presented over the next few days, but Willow wanted her wickiup built by dusk so that her husband could spend the night in the camp of his new family.

Ordinarily Willow would have counted on her family to help build the wickiup, but this was not an ordinary marriage. As she drew closer to her camp, she began to wonder if they would support her decision or leave her to fend for herself.

The answer came more quickly than she had anticipated, when she found her mother waiting for her on the trail just outside the camp.

The two women came face to face, and Great Star studied her daughter for a long moment before reaching out to stroke her unbound hair. "It is done," she said simply, her eyes filled with sadness. "You are his wife now."

Embarrassment blazed through Willow, but she could not keep a faint smile from forming on her lips. "Yes, Mother, it is done. He will be a good husband to me and a good son to you. Tall One will bring gifts before the day is through."

Great Star nodded noncommittally. "Your father will be pleased."

Her sadness tore at Willow's heart. She wanted everyone—particularly her mother—to be happy for her. "Can you not be pleased, too?"

"You have chosen a difficult path, my daughter. It has always been my hope that your life way would be simple."

"Gray Wolf makes me very happy. We will face our problems together and overcome them, but I wish you would share in my joy. If you cannot accept my husband, how can we ever expect the rest of our people to do so?"

Great Star knew Willow was right—and she also knew that her daughter was in love. No amount of sadness or disap-

proval was going to change that. All she could do was accept
the marriage and try to ease the burden her daughter had
taken upon herself. "I share in your happiness," she said,
opening her arms to Willow.

Willow stepped into the loving circle. "All will be well,
Mother. I promise. You will see."

Some of Willow's serenity passed into her mother, and for
a time Great Star could almost believe that her daughter was
right. "Come, we must build a home for you. Our people
must begin learning to accept your husband today."

Willow's eyes filled with tears. "They will come to love
him as I do, Mother. I know it."

She stroked her daughter's hair. "If he makes you happy,
how can it be otherwise? Now, come, there is much work to
do."

By the time the sun was low in the sky, the wickiup was
complete. Stout poles had been drawn together to form the
dome, and bear grass, brush, and yucca leaves had been woven into a covering. Hides were stretched over this, and a
blanket was attached to form the entrance. A fire pit was dug
beneath the opening in the center of the dome, and Willow
happily moved all of her belongings into her new home. In a
few days, when the two bands broke camp, the wickiup would
be dismantled, but that did not bother Willow. With the help
of her mother, sisters, and aunts, she had built the first structure that she could truly call her own.

The importance of what was taking place in Blue Bear's
camp was not lost on the rest of the Many Mountains people.
There was no peace council that day. No formal declaration
was made regarding what was taking place, but word spread
like wildfire that She Sings by the Willow had married an
enemy of her people. Those who favored the union began
deciding what they would contribute to the marriage gift.
Those who disapproved were suddenly faced with an unpleasant decision: What were they to do when Blue Bear came to
them and asked for gifts? Blue Bear was wealthy and powerful. His skill as a hunter and his generosity after a successful kill had made life easier for all members of his band.

To refuse him might mean hardship in the future. Only the wealthy and the foolish dared risk the wrath of their chief.

Throughout the day, Black Rope's father spoke to anyone who would listen, arguing against contributing to the marriage gift. Black Rope himself returned to camp and immediately joined his voice with his father's in urging the people to elect a new chief. But many who had once supported their cause now turned a deaf ear. Talk of insurrection was one thing; acting against a man as powerful as Blue Bear was another, particularly when that man had just doubled his power by marrying his daughter to the son of another chief as powerful as he. Though many were not happy about the union of the two bands, few were willing to openly oppose the marriage. If Tall One's marriage gift was a generous one, the Many Mountains people would respond with an equally generous gift.

The question of the size of the Red Canyon gift was answered an hour before sunset. A cry went up that Tall One was crossing the river with a dozen braves and twice that many women behind him. Each brave led three fine horses, and no woman's arms were empty. The people gathered in silence to watch them parade through the camp, and no one could doubt the generosity of the gift they brought.

Blue Bear was in his wickiup when he heard the shouted warning of Tall One's approach. He stepped outside and found Willow hurrying toward the wickiup. "Go inside, daughter," he instructed tersely.

Though she was consumed with curiosity, Willow nodded and complied. She had never understood this portion of the marriage ritual. It made little sense. This was her marriage, after all, yet neither she nor Gray Wolf would be allowed to participate or contribute. None of the gifts received would be given to her; they would be distributed among the other members of the band. Gray Wolf would not be in attendance, and neither would she. It was almost as though the reason for the giving—the union of two people in love—was irrelevant to the proceedings.

Yet Willow felt very much involved. The most she could do, though, was to kneel by the door of the wickiup and peer out through a slit in the blanket. She was aware that a crowd was gathering around the perimeter of her father's encampment, but she kept her eyes fixed on the approaching procession.

The number of horses being brought, many with fine saddles, staggered her. Though her line of sight was limited, she counted thirty at least. To her knowledge, no Apache bride had ever brought a higher price, but the horses were only the beginning. She saw blankets, hides, and baskets filled with food. There were precious rifles, taken in battle from the Mexicans, and several freshly killed deer. It was a truly impressive gift. Seeing it, how could anyone doubt the wisdom of her marriage to Gray Wolf? she wondered with pride.

She watched intently as Tall One dismounted and approached Blue Bear. "My friend," he began, speaking loud enough for all those assembled to hear him clearly. "You have a daughter who has found favor in the heart of my son, and so I bring you presents." He raised his hand, and the women came forward to place their baskets around the door of Blue Bear's wickiup. Tall One did not speak again until they were finished; then he pointed in the direction of the setting sun. "Beyond that hill, past the edge of your people's camp, I have sent cattle—as many as you see horses here."

A murmur went through the crowd, but Willow could not tell if it was approval or surprise—or perhaps both. Seemingly oblivious to the noise, Tall One continued, "If you find this gift worthy of a daughter of a great chief, our people will be yours, as yours will be mine. We will stand together and help one another as all families must."

"You honor us with a great gift, my friend," Blue Bear replied. "You have a fine son whom I would be proud to welcome into my family. I will talk with my people on his behalf. If they approve, I will send word to you tonight so that your son may join his bride in their new home." He gestured toward the wickiup Willow and Great Star had built.

"*Enju,*" Tall One pronounced heartily, knowing that Blue Bear's speech was only a formality. Though some in his camp opposed the marriage, Tall One had had little trouble collecting the bride price. He did not believe that Blue Bear would have a problem with the reciprocal gifts.

Tall One turned toward his horse, but a murmur through the crowd stopped him and he looked up to see his son riding toward Blue Bear's wickiup. The stunned crowd parted to make way for him, and by the time Gray Wolf reached his father, not a sound could be heard save the steady tread of his horse.

Willow could hardly believe what she was seeing. Why was her new husband defying custom in this manner? Had he changed his mind? Had she somehow displeased him during the night they had spent together? But if he no longer wished her for his wife, why had he allowed his father to bring the marriage gift?

Hardly daring to breathe, she waited as Gray Wolf dismounted and approached her father.

"I have come to see your daughter," he told Blue Bear without ceremony. "I have a gift I would add to the bride price, but it is for her alone."

Blue Bear studied his future son-in-law, uncertain what to do. He had never known a brave to make such a bold request, but nothing in the custom of his people forbade it. Most maidens were too shy to participate in the negotiations that would determine their future. "If my daughter wishes to see you, that is her choice," he said finally.

Inside the wickiup, Willow was trembling and her hands were moist. Why was Gray Wolf doing this? What gift was he bringing her? Something in exchange for the *nah-leen* she had given him? There was nothing attached to his saddle, and he was dressed as she had seen him the first day he rode into camp, in his breechclout, moccasins, and headband, and wearing, as always, the magnificent Thunderbird necklace. What gift was so important that he felt it must be given to her in the presence of all of her people and a large number of his?

The question went through her mind swiftly, but the possibility of refusing his request never crossed her mind. Her trust in Gray Wolf was so strong that she knew instinctively he was doing this for a reason; whatever his purpose, it was for her good. There was only the slightest pause before she drew back the blanket and stepped out of the wickiup to her father's side.

The look of love in Gray Wolf's eyes and the memories of the previous night gave Willow all the courage she needed to ask, "Why does my husband wish to see me?"

Gray Wolf smiled. She had chosen her words wisely, letting her people know that no matter what they decided, she considered herself married already. "I came to give you this, beloved," he said quietly, not caring whether the others heard him, because his actions meant more than words. Unhurriedly he reached beneath his dark mane of hair to untie the rawhide thongs that held his necklace.

Willow froze in amazement as Gray Wolf moved behind her and fastened the necklace around her throat. She noticed with surprise that two feathers now hung from the medallion.

"Since the day I became a man, the Thunder Eagle has been my guiding spirit. It has protected me from harm and given me strength against my enemies." When the necklace was in place, he turned Willow to face him. "I give it to you so that you will always know the protection of my spirit. One feather has become two, and as long as you wear this, my beloved, we can never be separated . . . even by death."

Tears stung Willow's eyes, and she was not alone. Great Star, too, had tears on her face, and there were others—old women for whom the power of love was only a dim memory, young women who dreamed of a husband to cherish them, married women who had settled for less than their hearts desired. All were touched by Gray Wolf's bold gesture.

Blue Bear was mightily impressed. The look that passed between Willow and the Red Canyon brave was clearly a look of deep love and devotion. He was happy that his daughter had finally found a man worthy of her, who would use every means at his disposal to see that she was protected and provided for. But while he had no doubt that Gray Wolf was sincere, Blue Bear couldn't help wondering if there was a subtler purpose behind his gesture. Was Gray Wolf so keensighted that he had realized the effect his bold presentation would have on Willow's people? He had won the favor of every woman in the camp. From this day forward, maidens would judge their suitors by the romantic standard this brave had just set.

Planned or not, it was a clever ploy. Women did not often oppose their men in public, but in private a wife had considerable influence on her husband's decisions. "You have given my daughter a gift beyond price," Blue Bear told him proudly.

Gray Wolf looked at his father-in-law. "Your daughter herself is a gift beyond price. She is all that a woman should be and all that I will ever desire in this life."

Without waiting for a response, Gray Wolf returned to his horse and mounted. Swollen with pride for his son, Tall One mounted his own horse and motioned for his warriors to lead the horses to the place where the cattle had been taken. No one spoke as the Red Canyon chief led his people out of the Many Mountains camp.

Her eyes never leaving her retreating lover, Willow gingerly touched the eagle feathers that dangled from the Thunderbird medallion. "Father, what will I do if our people refuse to accept the marriage gift?" she whispered forlornly.

Blue Bear looked down at his daughter and started to speak, but when a shadow passed over her face, he directed his eyes to the sky. Others saw the shadow and looked up as well, and an astonished cry went through the crowd. Overhead an eagle soared, circling the camp on barely discernible currents of wind. Though the sun was low, casting only long shadows, the great bird made shadows where none should have fallen. Only the Thunder Eagle—Gray Wolf's guiding spirit—could create such wonderful magic. The bird soared, and its shadow followed it, over the Many Mountains camp, then beyond, toward the Red Canyon camp, where it disappeared. When it had gone, no one doubted that the spirit had given his blessing to the marriage of He Stalks the Gray Wolf and She Sings by the Willow. And no one would dare oppose the will of the powerful Thunder Eagle, for to do so would mean disaster.

Blue Bear looked down at his astonished daughter and gave her a wry smile. "Do not fear, daughter. They will accept the gifts and your husband, I think."

PART II

The Shadow

SIX

Arizona Territory, 1863

"TOP DOLLAR, gentlemen! That's what the New Arizona Mining Company is paying to enterprising men like yourselves who sign on for our White Mountain expedition. You'll receive an honest wage of thirty dollars a month, plus a generous bounty for every Apache scalp you bring back—one hundred dollars for each brave, fifty dollars for a squaw, and twenty-five per child!"

Jedidiah Longstreet heard the announcement, and his blood ran cold. The glass of whiskey in his hand was forgotten as he looked across the room toward the planks and barrels that made up the bar in the Hell's Bent Saloon. The imbecile who'd made the revolting offer was at the head of the bar waving a sign-up ledger, and it was everything Jedidiah could do to keep from flying across the room and pounding the jackass to a bloody pulp.

Bounties on Apache scalps? It wasn't a new idea—the Mexicans has been doing it for years—but it was stupid, inhuman, gut-wrenching barbarity . . . and it was entirely legal. After all, the Apache weren't human, were they?

Jedidiah knew with sickening certainty that every one of the two dozen men in the Hell's Bent Saloon would answer that question with a resounding " 'Course they ain't!" And the dandy who was proposing wholesale slaughter of Apache men, women, and children knew it, too. Jedidiah had never

57

met the man, but he knew the type—an ignorant city-bred buffoon who thought he could waltz into the newly formed Arizona Territory and waltz out with a fortune in his pockets. A spate of gold and silver strikes had brought scavengers like this one in by the hundreds. And what was worse, the strikes had attracted thousands more who wouldn't bat an eye at accepting an offer like the one just made.

"Well, what do you say, gentlemen? Do I have any takers?" the dandy asked, wiggling his ledger.

"Jest what, exactly, is this ex-pedition of yours fer?" asked a grizzled old miner at the end of the bar.

Grover Bannon, chairman of the New Arizona Mining Company, craned his neck to look at the miner. "I thought I made that clear. We're mounting the expedition for the express purpose of killing Apaches. My company has obtained exclusive mining rights to the entire White Mountain area. We are ready to begin our initial survey of the area, and we want to be sure we'll have no trouble from those heathen Indians. Instead of opening a mine and waiting for them to descend, we're going to drive them out now."

Bannon's absolute confidence branded him as a rank greenhorn and elicited laughter from some of the more seasoned Indian fighters in the saloon. They knew from bitter experience that wiping out Apaches wasn't as simple as Bannon obviously believed. "You make it sound easy," one of them shouted scornfully.

Bannon smiled tightly, trying to look like a good sport. He'd nurtured this project for too long—and collected too much money from eastern investors—to be daunted by the skepticism of this motley crowd. "If it was easy, we wouldn't be paying such an exorbitant bounty, gentlemen."

"You ever come face to face with an Apache, mister?" the old miner asked.

"No, I can't say as I have, yet," Bannon admitted reluctantly.

The miner stood on wobbly legs and hobbled through the crowd toward Bannon. "Well, mister, we got a sayin' around here: 'It takes an Injun to kill an Injun.' "

"Nah, Pete, you got it wrong," Duke Haas, the bartender,

said with a laugh. "Killin' an Apache ain't no problem—it's *findin'* 'em. That's what you need another Injun fer."

Everyone had a good laugh at that, and Bannon raised his voice over the din. "Actually, that problem has been solved, gentlemen. As you probably know, the territorial governor has authorized citizens groups to employ friendly Indians in the hunt for Apaches. I have already done just that."

Everyone stopped laughing and began taking Bannon a little more seriously. If he had the foresight to hire Indian guides it was just possible that he wasn't as much of a greenhorn as he'd first appeared. "You got some Papago willing to track for you?" Haas asked, referring to the Indian tribe that had long been one of the Apaches most deadly enemies.

"I have a group of Papagos, yes, but we have also procured an even more formidable ally," he replied. "I have just received word from my partner in Tucson that our search will be joined by a dozen renegade Chiricahuas led by an Apache known as Gato."

The announcement sobered the crowd. Gato had a reputation as black as midnight; even his own people had rejected him. If Bannon could control the renegade, the expedition's chances of success would be greatly increased. Some of the men expressed the opinion that Gato couldn't be trusted, but that didn't stop several men from crowding around the mining president to sign on.

Sickened by the entire proceeding, Jedidiah Longstreet finished his final swig of whiskey, stood, and started toward the door. He'd made it only halfway when the bartender noticed him.

"Hey, Longstreet! This greenhorn's lookin' to get rid of some of those 'Paches out your way! Maybe you'd like to give him a little advice." The laughter rose to new heights, and Haas winked at Bannon, who was clearly mystified about why that was so funny. Jedidiah ignored the bartender and kept moving, but the mining company president's curiosity had been aroused. He glanced at the nondescript man headed toward the door and noticed with satisfaction that a scalp hung from the belt of his buckskin jacket. Thinking he had found an important ally, he hurried to cut him off.

"Pardon me, Mr. Longstreet, but did I understand correctly? Do you live in the White Mountains?"

A pair of piercing blue eyes pinned Bannon with a look of pure hatred. "Get out of my way, you jackass."

Bannon took a step back in surprise. He hadn't sensed anything threatening in the man until now. Longstreet was only average height, but his brawny shoulders bespoke considerable strength. "Sorry, sir. I didn't mean to detain you— I just thought that if you lived under a constant threat from those Apache heathens you'd be as anxious as I to eradicate them."

Jedidiah lost control of the thin thread that was holding his temper, and before Bannon knew what had happened he found himself pinned to the wall by the door, his feet dangling an inch or two off the floor. "Mister, I've lived in Apacheria for more than ten years now, and the only *heathens* I've ever seen are jackals like you. This country belongs to the Apache, and you don't have any right to drive them out." He dropped Bannon and was surprised that the dandy had enough gumption not to run away.

Bannon straightened his coat and tried to regain some of his dignity. "If it's *their* country, what gives you the right to live here?" he asked haughtily.

Jedidiah's gaze never wavered. "I asked their permission," he said with quiet intensity.

"And married one of their squaws!" someone in the back of the room shouted. "Ain't that right, Jed?"

For just a second the anger in Longstreet's eyes turned to anguish, but it disappeared so quickly that Bannon wondered if he'd imagined it. The burly Indian-lover stepped toward the door and left the saloon without another word.

Shaken by the encounter, Bannon returned to the bar. Someone bought him a shot of whiskey and asked for more information about his expedition. Bannon answered the questions by rote, but his mind was still on Longstreet. To the best of his recollection, he'd never met anyone so quick to defend a red man—particularly an Apache.

"Is that man really married to an Apache squaw?" he finally asked the bartender.

Haas nodded. "Was."

"Was?"

"She died 'bout two years ago." The bartender grinned. "A couple of prospectors went to the cabin while Longstreet was out hunting. Killed his wife 'n' kid and took their scalps for souvenirs. It took Jed and his wife's Apache relatives less than a week to track them down."

"He killed two white men?" Bannon asked in astonishment. "Why wasn't he punished?"

"Mostly it was a question of survival. If we'da hanged Longstreet, the 'Paches would have burned this town to the ground."

Bannon supposed it made a strange sort of sense, but when he remembered the scalp he'd seen on Longstreet's belt, he shuddered with distaste. "He carries around his own wife's scalp? That's revolting."

Everyone within earshot of the comment laughed, and Bannon wondered what faux pas he'd committed this time. Duke Haas was only too happy to enlighten him.

"No, mister, you got it backwards. Those scalps on his belt belonged to the prospectors who killed his family." Haas reached across the bar and clapped Bannon on the shoulder. "If you're goin' after White Mountain Apache, you got more to worry about than Injuns. You better watch your back, 'cause you can bet your last dollar that Jedidiah Longstreet will be watchin' it, too."

"These are very good," Gray Wolf said as he studied the cane shaft arrows his son had brought for his inspection. It was excellent workmanship for a boy who had seen only fifteen harvests. "When the other braves learn what fine work you do, they will ask you to make weapons for them."

Seated outside the wickiup, his cross-legged position mirroring his father's, He Brings Peace straightened his shoulders proudly. He was not yet a brave, since he had participated in only three hunting parties, but knowing that his father considered him worthy of the title made him very happy. "My grandfather taught me well. He knows many secrets for making an arrow fly true."

Gray Wolf studied his son with pride—he was truly an amazing young man. At an age when other youths were eagerly boasting of their accomplishments, He Brings Peace was always quick to give credit to others. It was a trait that had earned him the favor of the Thunder Eagle; like his father, He Brings Peace had gone into the mountains before his first hunt and returned with the shadow of the eagle on his shoulder. The boy's thirst for knowledge was extraordinary, and his skill as a hunter had already earned him considerable respect among men twice his age. He was almost as tall as his father, and as soon as he had taken part in one more hunt or war party he would be considered a full-fledged brave. Gray Wolf could not have asked for more from his only son.

"Father, look! I have arrows, too!"

Gray Wolf turned barely in time to catch the tiny body that hurtled toward him in a blur of motion. Miraculously he managed to avoid being impaled by the crooked branch "arrows" his daughter, Morning Star, held in her fist. Behind her, Willow was entering the camp with their other daughter, One Who Sings, walking sedately at her side. Both were carrying burden baskets filled with juniper berries. With a laugh, Gray Wolf settled Morning Star onto his lap.

"See, good arrows." She held them out proudly for inspection.

"Very good indeed," Gray Wolf said, trying to appear solemn. He looked at He Brings Peace. "Do you not agree, my son?"

Morning Star held the "arrows" out to her brother, waiting expectantly, and the young man leaned forward, his expression serious as he studied the motley collection of tangled branches. Quail feathers, most of them hanging precariously, had been bound to the ends of the limbs with strands of yucca, and the little girl had made a valiant attempt at sharpening the other ends of the sticks into points. For the most part, though, the effort had yielded only frayed bark. They were, without question, the most pitiful arrows He Brings Peace had ever seen, but not for all of Usen's power would he have crushed his sister by saying so.

"Indeed, Father, they are excellent. Perhaps I should take lessons from this young one."

Morning Star beamed at the praise, and Gray Wolf stroked her dark hair. "Is this what you have been doing this fine morning while your mother and sister gathered berries?"

"Yes, Father."

Gray Wolf looked at Willow, who had placed her basket next to the door of the wickiup. "Your daughter will make a fine warrior someday," he told her with a teasing smile.

Willow moved to him and knelt. "She is too much like her father and brother," she said wryly. "I tried to coax her into picking berries, but she was determined to play, not work."

"She is only five," he reminded her.

Willow looked at her husband and their younger daughter. Like her mother, the child was never happier than when she was in Gray Wolf's arms, for it was a place of great security and love. "She has been indulged too much," she said without any conviction or remorse. One Who Sings had come to stand beside her, and Willow reached up to touch her daughter's face. "But at least I have one child who is eager to learn what it means to be a woman."

One Who Sings bowed her head shyly. "Should I begin preparing the berries, Mother?"

Willow shook her head. "Divide them first, and take half to your grandmother. She is not well, so you may stay and help her prepare them," she replied. She plucked Morning Star off Gray Wolf's lap. "And take this little warrior and her arrows with you. Perhaps together you and my mother can teach her the proper use of a woman's weapon—the *metaté*."

One Who Sings took charge of her sister and hurried off to do as she was told while Willow turned her attention to He Brings Peace. "Are these yours?" she asked, gesturing toward the quiver of arrows.

"Yes, Mother." He picked up the quiver and held it out to her. "Would you like to see? Father says they are good"— he grinned—"but he said that of my sister's arrows, too."

Laughing, Willow started to reach for the arrows, then

abruptly withdrew her hands. "If your father says they are good, then I will trust his word."

Gray Wolf looked at his wife, puzzled by her behavior. Clearly she had wanted to inspect her son's craftsmanship, but had changed her mind. A woman was forbidden to touch a man's implements of war only when she was carrying a child, for it was believed that a pregnant woman made arrows too heavy to fly straight.

Was it possible? he wondered, hardly daring to hope. He Brings Peace had been born amid much rejoicing the first spring after their marriage. Gray Wolf had added another feather to the Thunderbird necklace, and four harvests later—exactly as custom and practicality dictated—a feather had been added to protect One Who Sings. But four harvests after that, Willow had given birth to a stillborn son, and for two long years she had tried desperately to conceive again. Just when she had given up hope, Morning Star had come to them, but the birth had been a difficult one, and Willow had resigned herself to the sad possibility that she would bear Gray Wolf no more children.

Had their dream of having another child finally come to pass? After so many barren harvests, would they finally add a sixth feather to the necklace? Gray Wolf had seen no change in his wife's body, and Willow had given him no indication that she might be pregnant again. But if his suspicion was unfounded, why had she refused to touch her son's arrows?

He Brings Peace, too, was puzzled by his mother's reluctance, but he did not try to force the arrows on her. Instead, he withdrew one from the quiver and showed her the lightning symbol he had carved into the shaft.

"Would you like to see how well they fly?" he asked.

"I would," Willow replied.

The young man stood. "Then I will demonstrate by bringing rabbits for our supper." He slipped into the wickiup and returned a moment later with the bow Gray Wolf had helped him craft out of a mulberry limb. He trotted off toward the hills behind the encampment.

Willow smiled at her husband. "How many do you think he will bring?"

"He is such a fine hunter, I would not be surprised if he returned with enough to feed the whole camp."

"Your pride is showing," she warned him lightly.

"My pride is deserved. We have raised a fine son."

"And fine daughters," she replied as she stood and moved into the wickiup. Gray Wolf collected the buckskin and rawhide he had been using to repair his favorite moccasins and followed his wife inside. He put his belongings away while Willow collected the *metaté*—a smooth, hollowed-out food-grinding stone—and the other utensils she needed for preparing the juniper berries.

"Why did you refuse to touch our son's arrows?" he asked finally, when the question would no longer remain inside him.

Willow paused, but refused to look at her husband. "It did not seem right."

"Because you are carrying our child?" he asked quietly.

Willow could hear the hope in his voice, and it hurt her to have to answer, "I do not know for sure. Our son was so proud of his arrows that I thought it best not to take the chance, lest he have to destroy his creations later."

Gray Wolf moved across the room and knelt by his wife. "But there is a chance?"

A smile that started deep inside her crept its way to Willow's lips. "Yes. A very good chance."

With a joyous laugh, Gray Wolf gathered Willow into his arms. She leaned against him and rested her head on his shoulder. "This makes you happy?" she asked.

"Why would it not?" He stroked her back and pressed his cheek to her hair. "We have said many prayers for this."

"But it is not a good time, beloved." Her voice was laced with sadness she did not want to feel. "Ghost Face season will soon be upon us. You and our son will not be able to hunt with the other men. Without meat, winter will be hard."

Gray Wolf could not contradict her, for she was right. A wife's pregnancy made her husband and unmarried sons too heavy to travel quickly and caused their arrows and rifles to shoot poorly. Over the years, Gray Wolf had led many hunting parties with great success, but there would be no hunting parties this winter if Willow was pregnant.

Gray Wolf did not fear starvation, though. The fruit harvests had been good, and there were great quantities stored in secret places throughout the mountains. But, more important, he had been generous to all members of Willow's band in the years since he had become one of them. After hunting parties, his gifts of fresh venison and bear meat had kept families alive when starvation would otherwise have claimed them. With parties of Red Canyon and Many Mountains braves, he had led many successful raids against their enemies, and he had always made certain that everyone in both bands benefited. He was already a respected subchief of Willow's clan, and no one doubted that he would someday follow in his father-in-law's footsteps as chief of the entire Many Mountains band.

He had given much to his wife's people and asked for nothing in return. As a consequence, he had no doubt that the people would return his generosity and see his family through the difficult season of Ghost Face. It was the Apache way.

And Willow knew that; Gray Wolf was certain of it. So why was she concerned? "I think you do not speak all of the truth, beloved," he said gently, and was not surprised when Willow slipped out of his arms. When she looked up at him, her smile was no longer there.

"You have had dreams," she reminded him reluctantly, tracing the strong line of his brow and cheek with gentle fingertips. "You do not talk of them, but I know they are not good."

Gray Wolf found it difficult to look into her eyes. "The dreams have not yet been explained to me. I do not know what they mean."

"Now it is you who speak falsely," she said quietly.

He shook his head. "No, beloved, I do not. The dreams are but shadows. I do not know what they mean."

"Do they foretell danger?"

"They are dark dreams. That is all I can say."

Willow studied him closely. "They are dreams of the White Eyes, yes?" she asked, knowing that he had received such dreams before. In the years since the White Eyes made peace with the Mexicans, the White Mountain Apache had been fortunate, for they had had less contact with the White Eyes than many other tribes. Stories passed from tribe to tribe and camp to camp about the brutal murder of women and children, of how trusting Apache leaders had been lured into "peace" talks under a flag of truce, only to be slaughtered mercilessly. The White Eyes had forced entire tribes off their hunting grounds, robbing them of the ability to feed their women and children.

Like a disease, they spread their destruction in every direction, and when the Apache retaliated with a life for a life, as was only just, the White Eyes called the Apache savages and declared that not one deserved to live. Yet it was the White Eyes who had taught the Apache, by hideous example, the fine art of scalping. Who could not believe that such butchers deserved to be butchered themselves?

Several times Blue Bear had sent braves to aid other Apache tribes in their fight against the White Eyes, and several times the Many Mountains band had sought revenge against white men who had murdered members of their clan, but most of the time, there had been peace in the White Mountains.

Willow believed that if that peace was about to come to an end, her husband would know it, for since their marriage, Gray Wolf had been visited by many dreams that foretold the future. Willow's people considered it the blessing of the Thunder Eagle, and that blessing was responsible for their immediate acceptance of Gray Wolf.

But the dreams had never disturbed Gray Wolf in the way they seemed to now, for he was reluctant to answer her question. "They are dreams I cannot explain," he said finally, "and it troubles me that the eagle has not come to tell me what they mean. I have sung songs and said prayers to him, but he remains silent."

Willow touched the Thunderbird medallion that hung between her breasts. "The eagle will return. I know it. He has blessed us with his power many times."

"But what if the White Eyes have driven him away?" Gray Wolf asked, allowing Willow a glimpse of his deepest fear.

"You must not say that! The spirit of the eagle is stronger

than the White Eyes' medicine. The eagle has shielded us from our enemies in the past, and he will continue to do so!''

Gray Wolf knew that he had upset his wife greatly, and he regretted it. It was his responsibility to protect Willow, not frighten her with the darkness that troubled his heart. ''You are right, of course,'' he said soothingly, drawing her back into his arms. ''Tonight I will hold a ceremony to ask the spirit again to explain my dreams, and he will answer.''

Willow nodded and let Gray Wolf's strength surround her, but when he finally left her so that he could make plans for the ceremony, she found that she could not forget the fear she had seen in her brave husband's eyes. That alone was enough to terrify her.

SEVEN

‖‖‖‖

SOMEONE WAS watching him. Jedidiah had lived in Apache country too long not to know it. His instinct for such things was as finely honed as the blade of his bowie knife. There were only two questions in Jedidiah's mind: Was there one Apache or a dozen? And were they friend or foe? At one time he had traveled among nearly all the Apache tribes with impunity, studying their customs and learning their strange, fascinating ways. Those days were gone, though. Too many white men had flooded New Mexico and Arizona, bringing with them a good reason for the Apache to strike first and ask questions later—or not at all. Jedidiah still had good friends throughout the territories, but he no longer felt as safe as he had in the old days.

Back then he'd supported himself by trading cloth, grain, and glass beads for furs, buckskins, and an occasional gold nugget or two. It hadn't been a particularly lucrative pastime, but it had suited a young loner who had itchy feet and a longing to see more of the world than could be found in the stuffy drawing rooms of Philadelphia.

Though his education had prepared him for a career as a civil engineer, he had signed on for a mining survey of the unexplored territory that had been ceded to the United States after the war with Mexico. His parents, Casewell and Georgina Longstreet, had thoroughly disapproved of his adventure, but he departed for the vast unknown despite their objections. He never regretted his decision.

The land he'd discovered was one of harsh extremes, and he had quickly learned to respect the fierce, proud people who lived as one with the magnificent mountains and deserts. When the survey team left Apacheria to return east to report their findings of rich gold, silver, and copper deposits, Jedidiah Longstreet had stayed.

Miners had started arriving, and towns had sprung up here and there. When the Apache objected to having their land usurped, troops had arrived to "subdue" the savages. Over the years they had developed a broad and uncompromising extermination policy. Soldiers and citizens were authorized to kill Apache men, women, and children on sight. As a result, virtually every tribe in New Mexico and Arizona was on the warpath—a state of affairs that had made Jedidiah's quiet life more than a little difficult.

He was now only about twenty miles east of his ranch on the White River, and normally he'd have felt confident that the Apache observing him from the hills on his right was friendly—this was White Mountain country, after all. But so many tribes had been driven from their usual hunting grounds that Jedidiah knew better than to be confident about anything. The Tontos to the west were having a rough time of it with the army, thanks to a gold strike near Prescott, and it was entirely possible that one or two bands had slipped over this way for a little peace and quiet.

To a casual observer, Jedidiah, with his pack mule in tow behind his horse, appeared to be an easy target. Fortunately, Apaches weren't casual observers. Whoever was watching him would immediately have taken note of the six-shooters strapped to his waist and the rifle resting across his lap. His erect posture suggested a combination of confidence and wariness. An Apache never attacked unless he was certain of victory, so Jedidiah did his best to look like the formidable foe he really was. As long as he didn't let down his guard for even a moment, he had a pretty good chance of surviving the day.

He continued steadily toward the mountains. The terrain grew rougher and the hills started closing in. It was great ambush country, but Jedidiah didn't consider turning back.

The conversation he'd heard in the Hell's Bent Saloon nearly a week ago was weighing heavily on him. His friends had to be warned that trouble was headed their way. It wouldn't take Bannon long to collect the men he needed, and once they started pushing into the White Mountains, blood was going to flow more freely than water. Jed was determined to do whatever he could to stop it.

At midafternoon he came to a creek bed that had enough water to service his animals, and he dismounted to let them drink their fill. Cradling his rifle in his arms, he took his canteen and some jerked beef from his saddlebags and warily sauntered to a spot shaded by a towering outcropping of rock. There was plenty of cover nearby, should he need it, and with the rock at his back he felt relatively safe.

He studied the rough terrain, wondering which crevice his Apache shadow was hiding in. By that time he was convinced there was only one Indian dogging him, but it was impossible to guess where he was, so Jedidiah kept a sharp lookout in every direction. In the end, all his analysis was for naught. He had thought the Apache was in the hills to the east. He was wrong.

"You guess ver' bad, Pindah Dak'é."

The quiet voice, which seemed only inches from Jedidiah's ear, made him jump, but when he recognized the halting English and excellent guttural Apache he relaxed. He glanced up and saw nothing above him, but the Apache was there, all right, and close.

Jedidiah chuckled. "And your English is atrocious, my young friend."

The rocks above Jed came to life, and a sturdily built boy of fifteen dropped to the ground beside him. "What mean"— the boy struggled to form the word—" 'trocious?"

"Bad."

The boy considered the pronouncement and shrugged. "Long time you no come teach."

"Well, I'm here now. Perhaps I'll give you another lesson tonight if you will take me to your father."

He Brings Peace understood what his friend Longstreet meant, even though he knew only about half of the words.

The man his people called Pindah Dak'é—His Eyes Blue—
had long been a friend to the Inday of the White Mountains.
His marriage to one of Gray Wolf's cousins in the Red Canyon band had made him family, and He Brings Peace always
looked forward to his visits.

"*Enju*. I take."

"Where are you camped?" Jedidiah asked as he collected
his horse and mule.

He Brings Peace thought about how to answer the question,
but he did not know how to say "slender peak standing up"
in the white man's language. "*Nàdohots'os*. Not far. Come."

He set out at a steady trot, and Jedidiah threw himself up
on his horse to follow. To an Apache, even one on foot, "not
far" could mean a distance of twenty miles, but Jedidiah
knew that *nàdohots'os* was considerably closer than that. At
the brisk pace He Brings Peace was setting, it would take
them less than an hour to reach his camp.

Time was of the essence to Jedidiah, but even so, he regretted that traveling with his young friend in this fashion did
not allow him the opportunity to converse with the boy. He
Brings Peace was truly a remarkable young man. He was
exceptionally intelligent and had an insatiable curiosity about
everything. The Apache considered most boys his age too
young to handle the power of many of their rituals, yet He
Brings Peace was already accomplished in the use of lightning power and was learning the ritual for "enemies against"
power.

His thirst for knowledge did not end with his own people,
though. Once he realized that Jedidiah came from a society
with beliefs alien to his own, he had begun pestering Pindah
Dak'é to teach him about the world of the White Eyes.

At first Jedidiah had confined his lessons to descriptions of
the white man's cities and colorful stories from the works of
Shakespeare, Hawthorne, and Dumas. Jedidiah spoke Apache
reasonably well, but even so, putting the stories on a level
He Brings Peace could comprehend had been a delightful
challenge. The story of Romeo and Juliet had held a particular fascination for the boy because it paralleled the legend
that his people told about Willow and Gray Wolf.

Of course, one story had a happy ending while the other did not, but the similarities had made He Brings Peace wonder if perhaps the White Eyes and the Inday had more in common than either group believed.

Such a conclusion was an extraordinary one for an Apache—or a white man, for that matter—and once the boy expressed it, Jedidiah had fully expected Gray Wolf to forbid his son to listen to any more stories from the white man's world. But he had not. Nor had he objected when He Brings Peace declared his desire to learn English.

When Jedidiah questioned Gray Wolf about his willingness to allow his son to learn, the wise Apache subchief had sadly cast his eyes toward a place Jedidiah could not see and replied, "Like the sand driven by the wind, the White Eyes come in a great dark wall that cannot be stopped. The spirit of the eagle has shown me that someday they will rule the Inday. The knowledge you give my son will help our people to survive a time of great sadness and want."

As much as he wanted to tell Gray Wolf he was wrong, Jedidiah had not been able to lie to his friend. The arrogant white man was fulfilling what he considered his manifest destiny, and even the fierce, proud Apache wouldn't be able to stop them from taking a country that wasn't really theirs. Thousands would die, but ultimately the white man would win by the sheer force of greater numbers.

Jedidiah had offered to teach English to Gray Wolf, but he had declined, his eyes sad as he said, "I will not need the White Eyes' words."

So Jedidiah had continued to teach He Brings Peace, telling him stories of the white man's capacity for good, but never neglecting to illustrate the evil as well. English was hard for the boy because the Apache used their voices in such a strange, guttural way. He was quick to comprehend the meaning of words, but speaking them caused him considerable difficulty.

At first the boy had feared that Jedidiah would laugh at his attempts, as he had often laughed at his teacher's inability to master certain Apache sounds. But Jed had never once laughed at him, and a bond of trust had grown between them to such a degree that He Brings Peace even felt comfortable joking with the older man. Tonight many in camp would laugh at how the boy had surprised his vigilant friend on the trail today.

No one showed any surprise when Jedidiah finally reached the small temporary encampment that housed Blue Bear and his extended family. He Brings Peace had sprinted ahead to alert his father to their visitor, but Jedidiah considered it unlikely that their approach had gone unnoticed. His impending arrival had no doubt been announced in camp not long after He Brings Peace joined him.

Women barely looked up from their cook fires as he wound his way toward Gray Wolf's wickiup, but the children were more demonstrative. They gathered around his horse, clamoring for the treat he always brought them. He dug into his saddlebags for the sack of horehound candy he'd purchased in Bledsoe for this very occasion, and just as he started scattering the drops, an exuberant little voice touched his ears—and his heart.

With the determination of a child twice her size, Morning Star fought her way through the crowd, yelling, "For me! For me!" But a share of the candy was not her goal. She held her arms up to him, and Jedidiah laughed as he bent low and scooped the child into his arms. She hugged him with innocent joy, and the rugged frontiersman felt the salty sting of tears behind his eyelids.

He Brings Peace was special to Jedidiah, but Morning Star held a place in his heart that was hers and hers alone. Her childish laugh and huge dark eyes reminded him so much of his own daughter that it was sometimes difficult for him to look at the little girl. Yet, strangely, he welcomed the pain, for it kept the image of his beloved wife and child alive in his heart. It had been two years since their brutal murder, but to Jedidiah, it might have been only yesterday. And he never intended to forget.

"Hello, little princess."

Morning Star drew back and looked at him with an impish grin. "Princess pret-ty?" she asked. Her English vocabulary was limited to only a few words, and those were her favorites.

"My princess *very* pretty." Jedidiah dug into his pocket for the little package of butterscotch candy he had brought just for her. "For you," he said, reverting to her language.

Being very careful, Morning Star unfolded the brown paper. The small disks looked almost the same as the horehound candy he had given the other children, but when Jedidiah popped a piece of it into her mouth, her eyes widened in surprise. This was a new treat—not bittersweet at all, but wonderfully delicious.

"Enju?" he asked, though her enthralled expression gave him all the answer he needed.

Morning Star nodded vigorously, and Jedidiah laughed. He looked away from the child and discovered that Gray Wolf had done him the honor of stepping out of his wickiup to greet him. He was waiting patiently beyond the circle of children, and reluctantly Jedidiah slipped out of his saddle and returned Morning Star to the ground. A word from Gray Wolf sent the children scattering to the four winds, leaving the two old friends to face each other alone.

"My eyes are glad to see you, cousin," Jedidiah said in Apache.

"You have stayed away too long," Gray Wolf replied with a smile.

Since the Apache weren't given to polite chitchat, Jedidiah came right to the purpose of his visit. "I have words to speak to the *nant'an*, and I wish you to hear them as well."

Gray Wolf knew from his expression that what he had come to say was serious. With a nod, he turned and led Jedidiah to his father-in-law's wickiup, which was some distance from his own. When he was close enough for anyone inside to hear him speak, he turned his back on the dwelling and announced, "A friend comes, my father. He has words for both of us."

Jedidiah tried not to smile. This was one Apache custom he had never really understood. Obviously Gray Wolf knew that the *nant'an*'s wife was in the wickiup, and turning his back so that she could leave before he entered was a form of respect. If Gray Wolf was a good son-in-law, it was highly unlikely that he had ever looked Great Star in the face or exchanged words with her.

Sure enough, only seconds after Gray Wolf announced himself, Great Star came out of the wickiup with her face averted so that she would not see her daughter's husband. She hurried off, and as soon as she was out of sight, Jedidiah told Gray Wolf it was safe to go in.

They slipped into the wickiup, and Gray Wolf moved across the room without invitation to sit near Blue Bear. Jedidiah remained by the entrance until the aging chief invited him to sit across from him. There was no fire in the pit, but charred embers from the previous night's fire still remained.

"My eyes are glad to see you," Blue Bear said when Jedidiah was seated.

"My eyes are glad to see you, too, old friend, but my heart is heavy. The reason I come is not good." The expression on Blue Bear's face did not change, but Jedidiah knew he had the chief's undivided attention. "A white man named Bannon is bringing many men to your mountains to seek the yellow iron. I heard him say so myself."

"We have none of the yellow iron," Blue Bear said. "There is white iron to be found in only a few places, but no yellow."

"I know that what you say is true," Jedidiah replied.

"Did you tell the white man this?"

"He would not have listened, for he knows I am your friend."

Blue Bear nodded and gestured toward Gray Wolf. "For many years my son has said this day would come. I did not doubt that he was right, but I am sad the day is here. We will gather our people together and prepare for battle."

Jedidiah shook his head and leaned forward intently. "You must not do that, old friend. When the white men come, they will bring with them Indians who are your enemies. The whites are ready to pay a high price for Apache scalps."

The news didn't seem to shock either man. "The Papago come to fight us?" Gray Wolf asked.

"Yes. And also a band of Chiricahua renegades led by Gato."

Blue Bear spat at the dormant fire pit. "Gato is no good. He is only a young man, but he uses evil magic. Even his own people have cast him out."

"I know."

Blue Bear spat again. "What you say makes no difference. We will drive them all out of our mountains—even Gato."

"No. Hear me well," Jedidiah said. "When the men come, they will find no yellow iron—and you must let them find no Inday, either. Take your people into the mountains where not even Gato can find them. They will look for the yellow iron, and when they see that there is none to be found, they will leave."

Blue Bear's face turned into a mask of stone. "You ask me to hide like a woman? No!"

"Yes," Jedidiah insisted. "If you stay and fight them, many will die—both Inday and white. I know your warriors are strong—strong enough to defeat Gato, even—but Bannon and men like him cannot be stopped. If you drive Bannon away, he will come back again with an army of Blue Coats greater in number than all the White Mountain tribes. They will build a fort and there will be fighting for many years to come."

"He speaks wisely, Father," Gray Wolf said. Despite the disturbing news, Gray Wolf was almost relieved. Last night he had held the eagle dance, as he had promised Willow he would, and though the spirit itself had not appeared, the eagle had answered some of his questions by sending Jedidiah Longstreet. "Dreams have visited me at night, but I did not understand their meaning until now. I have seen our people looking down on White Eyes from a high place. We must do as our friend says."

Blue Bear trusted Gray Wolf implicitly, and he knew that Pindah Dak'é had only good intentions, but the idea of running from a fight did not set well with the old warrior. He had seen more than sixty harvests, but he was still a vigorous man. His people respected him, and he had no desire to have them think him a coward. "I must pray on this."

"You are a great chief who wants only what is good for his people," Jedidiah said.

"If we do as you ask, it will mean spending the season of Ghost Face in the mountains. That is not good," he replied.

"Women and children murdered in their sleep is not good, either." Blue Bear grunted but said nothing, and Jedidiah realized he'd said all there was to say. "Tomorrow," Jedidiah continued, "I will go over the mountain to find my cousin, Tall One. I will tell him all that I have said to you. If you choose the way of peace, I will do all I can to help you through the winter. When the snows come, I will bring cattle and sheep."

"You are a good friend," Gray Wolf told him.

Jedidiah regarded the warrior fondly. "My skin is white, but my heart is Inday. You, better than anyone, know this."

Gray Wolf nodded. His friend was thinking of the wife and child he had lost. He had great respect for the way Longstreet bore his sadness, for Gray Wolf could imagine nothing worse than losing his own beloved wife. When word of the massacre had come, he had lost no time in mounting a war party. Longstreet was already on the prospectors' trail, but Gray Wolf and half a dozen braves had joined him in his quest for vengeance. Their success had permanently sealed an already strong friendship.

"Come." Gray Wolf stood. "You will eat with my family and sleep in our wickiup tonight."

Jedidiah nodded to Blue Bear and followed Gray Wolf out. "Will he do as I say?" he asked as they started across the camp.

"I do not know," Gray Wolf replied hesitantly, though in truth he did know. The news Jedidiah brought had made a number of things clear to him—none of them good. He stopped and looked to the sky, but it was only a vast blue emptiness.

It had been too long since he had seen the Thunder Eagle. Death was in the air.

The firelight flickered over young faces and old as Gian-nah-tah wove his spell on the rapt audience. He was a masterful storyteller, and as his name, Always Ready, implied, he was never without a tale to tell. Gian-nah-tah was a powerful shaman, and it was from him that the children in Blue Bear's clan had learned the stories of Coyote the Trickster and Born of Water. Some of the most important Apache legends could be told only in the dead of winter, though, so Gian-nah-tah was confining his storytelling to a lesser tale—a relatively new one that had been born on the day He Stalks the Gray Wolf married She Sings by the Willow.

Those who sat by the fire had heard the story before, but they listened attentively anyway—all of them except He Brings Peace. His sisters were seated beside the shaman, devouring every word of the cherished romantic story of how his mother had married his father despite the opposition of her people, and how the Thunder Eagle had blessed their union. But tonight the first child born of that union was more concerned with the story he was hoping Pindah Dak'é would tell him. The frontiersman had been occupied in conversation with Gray Wolf all evening, though, and He Brings Peace was beginning to fear that his friend had forgotten his promise.

He needn't have worried. After what seemed like an eternity, Jedidiah finally stood and stretched, then went off toward the remuda to check on his animals. He Brings Peace waited a moment, then quietly slipped into the darkness. As he left the circle, he glanced back once and smiled at the look of delight on Morning Star's face. She was too young to fully understand the story, but like the others, she was spellbound by Gian-nah-tah's oratory. No one by the fire would miss him, least of all his youngest sister.

Using the shadows of night to cloak his movements, He Brings Peace crept toward the remuda, intent on surprising his teacher as he had on the trail, but this time Jedidiah was ready for him. The frontiersman was already seated on a rock, as though waiting. The young brave moved up behind him, not making a sound, but his stealth was for naught.

''You are wasting time, my young friend,'' Jedidiah said quietly when the boy was a dozen yards away.

He Brings Peace abandoned his silent approach. ''How did

you know I was here? I made no sound," he said as he dropped to the ground at Jedidiah's feet.

"You betrayed your intent at the campfire," he replied, smiling fondly at the young man. "You watched me so closely that I knew you would come."

The boy nodded philosophically. "Then I have learned an important lesson."

"Life is full of lessons, my young friend. I have never known you to let one go to waste." Jedidiah slapped his thighs. "Now, what would you like to learn tonight? More English or a story of my people?"

"Both."

Jedidiah laughed. "Very well. I will tell you the story of a man who died seeking revenge on a fish."

The boy's smooth brow furrowed suspiciously. "A fish?"

He nodded. "A great fish named Moby-Dick."

He Brings Peace did a passable job of imitating the unfamiliar name, and the lesson began.

The next morning Blue Bear sent runners to all the nearby camps with word that he wanted to speak to the men. Within a few hours forty braves were gathered in a clearing near the *nant'an*'s wickiup. Gravely he told them about the Bannon party, and the response was dramatic. Braves young and old cried for a war party, but Blue Bear silenced them with a wave of his hand.

"No! We will not make war on them—not now, and perhaps not at all. We will send our women, children, and old ones to the high mountains while our braves scatter in small groups to watch and study the men who seek to destroy us. We will be like the wind, unseen but always there. They will look for us, and we will laugh at them while they find nothing."

Blue Bear's plan did not please many of the braves. His oldest son-in-law, Angry Coyote, was particularly vehement, but Blue Bear talked until he had quieted all the protests.

At the outer edge of the circle Jedidiah listened to the chief's plan and the arguments against it. The plan was an excellent compromise between action and inaction, but Jedidiah didn't like the idea of sending the women and children off alone for an unknown amount of time. Certainly they could all fend for themselves in fine fashion, but they would be virtually defenseless should some of Bannon's party slip past the scouts. Blue Bear seemed confident this could not happen, though, and Jedidiah was content that the old man would hold to his decision not to wage open warfare unless there was no alternative.

The *nant'an* chose his strongest runners to spread the word to other Many Mountains clans camped greater distances away. He offered to send someone to accompany Jedidiah on his long trek across the mountains to the Red Canyon camp, but Jed declined the offer. He knew where his wife's people would be camped at this time of year, and he felt no need of a guide.

When the council members finally began to disperse, Jedidiah found himself flanked by Gray Wolf and his son as Blue Bear approached them. "You have done a good thing," the *nant'an* told him, his eyes still dancing with the fervor he had used to persuade his men.

"As have you," Jedidiah replied. He saw no need to express his doubts. "Will you lead the scouting party yourself?"

Blue Bear nodded. "I will lead one, and my son-in-law will lead the other." He gestured toward Gray Wolf, but his eyes were on He Brings Peace. "And you will join us, my grandson. This will be a good time for you to earn your new name."

The young man's eyes lit up at the prospect of finally becoming a full-fledged brave, but before he could answer, Gray Wolf intervened. "I am sorry, Father, but my son and I cannot go with you."

Blue Bear frowned. He had never believed it possible that Gray Wolf would oppose him, and his son-in-law's disloyalty cut the old chief deeply. "If you doubt the wisdom of my plan, why did you not speak up in council as the others did?"

"I do not doubt your wisdom," he answered with a hint of a smile. "My son and I cannot go with you because my wife believes she is carrying a child."

There was nothing restrained about Blue Bear's smile—or Jedidiah's. "Congratulations, my friend," he said, slapping Gray Wolf on the back.

"Yes, it is good," the chief said happily. "It is time my daughter gave you another child. And perhaps it is good that the time is now. If you go with the women into the high mountains, I know they will be well cared for."

"We will all do as we must until the danger passes," Gray Wolf replied. He looked at He Brings Peace, who was standing beside him with his shoulders erect and his head held high. "You are disappointed, my son."

The boy could not deny it. His mother's pregnancy meant that it would be many moons before he became a brave and earned a name that befitted an Apache warrior. But in his heart he knew that he was ready, and time would not change that. "My time will come," he replied, earning a look of pride from his father that eased his disappointment.

Reluctantly Jedidiah took his leave of Gray Wolf and his family. He left behind a sack of cornmeal as payment for Willow's generous hospitality and hugged little Morning Star tightly. He promised He Brings Peace that he would visit them in the high mountains once he had delivered the news of Bannon's party to the Red Canyon people; in return, the boy promised to practice the new words he had learned the night before.

As he rode away from the camp, Jedidiah turned to look back—something no true Apache would have done. The desire to take one last look at his friends was too overpowering to ignore. Gray Wolf and Willow stood side by side near the wickiup, their hands touching discreetly as they watched him depart.

With great reluctance the frontiersman turned and rode on. Had he known it was the last time he would see his friends alive, he might have taken a longer look.

EIGHT

"I DON'T UNDERSTAND IT," Grover Bannon growled, hurling the dregs of his coffee into the fire. The liquid sizzled and popped, but did nothing to alleviate the mining entrepreneur's agitation. He and his men had been roaming the foothills of the White Mountains for nearly a month, and so far the only things they'd found to shoot at were a few wild turkeys. "Those blasted Indians swore we'd find Apaches in this part of the country picking nuts and berries! So where the hell are they?" he demanded, rounding on Alberto Montega, the Mexican who'd hired on as the party's interpreter. Montega spoke no Apache, but Gato and some of the Papagos understood Spanish quite well. In fact, it was from the Mexicans that Gato had received his name, the Cat; Montega had no idea what his Apache name was.

Bannon's anger didn't faze the Mexican. "The Papago claim we have no luck because we brought Gato with us. They say it is bad medicine. In case you have not noticed, the Papago hate the Chiricahua Apache as much as they hate the White Mountain tribes."

"That's hogwash," Bannon retorted. "They're just making excuses for their ineptitude. What does Gato have to say?"

"I don't know. I have not seen him and his braves for several days. Could be they got tired of smelling Papago and headed south."

Bannon threw his hands into the air. "Wonderful! This is

83

without a doubt the most exasperating situation I have ever encountered.''

''Did you really think it would be easy?'' Montega asked.

Bannon gave him an irritated look. ''I knew that driving them out was going to be hard, but with all these Indian trackers along I never dreamed that finding the damned savages would be nigh unto impossible.''

''I expect they were warned.''

''You mean that mountain man, Longstreet? He warned them?''

''Probably. It is surprising, though.''

''What is?''

Montega shrugged. ''If the Apache knew we were coming, it is surprising that they have not attacked. Gato says he has seen signs that they are watching us, but they do nothing.''

Bannon thought that over. ''Well, if they're going to give us a free rein, I might as well call some of my mining engineers in to conduct surveys. We've certainly got enough men here to guard them.''

Montega shook his head and glanced at the thirty men who had signed on for Bannon's ''expedition.'' Some of them were already asleep; others were talking quietly, drinking, or playing cards by the firelight. In the month they'd been on the trail, they'd heard enough of Bannon's temper tantrums not to be interested in anything the eastern dandy had to say.

Keeping his voice low, Montega replied, ''These men, they did not come with you to be guards for your miners. You promised them many pesos for Apache scalps. If you do not deliver soon, they will desert you.''

Bannon sighed heavily. Montega was right. ''Then we'll just have to find the Apache camps, won't we?''

''I do not think that will happen, Bannon,'' the Mexican replied with a shake of his head. ''We are chasing a wild goose.''

''Damn it, I'm not giving up!''

''You may have no choice. Your plan to kill Apache was good only when surprise was on your side. But they are ready for you. If we fight now, you will lose many men.''

''That's *your* opinion,'' Bannon snapped. ''I say we've still got a chance to—" A noise in the brush behind him had Bannon whirling as he fumbled for his Colt. "Who's there?"

Everyone in camp became instantly alert, but Montega grabbed Bannon's gun hand and forced the revolver down. "The way you stand in front of the fire and wave your arms, if it was Apache, you would already be dead," he said with disgust as he peered into the darkness. "Whoever is there wants us to know where he is." Because he was fairly certain he knew who had made the noise, Montega raised his voice and gave the all clear. *"Ya está bien, amigo mío, puedos entrar."*

"Enju." A moment later a lanky Chiricahua and two of his braves were made visible by the flickering firelight. They came into camp and seated themselves around Montega, their rifles resting across their knees.

Bannon looked at Gato and repressed a shudder. The renegade's flat, lifeless eyes always bore a look of cold contempt that turned Bannon's blood to ice water. He was grateful that the Chiricahua was on his side, but he knew better than to trust the Indian too much. "Ask him where he's been," he demanded. "Did he find any Apaches?"

Montega engaged in a brief dialogue with Gato, then turned to Bannon. "He has been searching for White Mountain camps in the eastern foothills, but he found nothing. The women and children are all in the high mountains, as we suspected."

"Then we'll just have to go up there."

Montega shook his head. "Your men will not like that. The snows will come soon."

"Well, damn it, we've got to do something. If we don't engage the Apaches soon, we're going to have to return to Bledsoe for supplies."

Montega translated the conversation for Gato, and Bannon waited impatiently while the Indian replied. "Well, what?" he demanded as soon as it appeared that Gato had finished.

Montega was frowning, as though he didn't care much for what Gato had to say, but he translated anyway. "He said you would be foolish to take these men into the mountains. There are Apache braves all around us, and they will follow.

If we come too close to the camps of their families, they will attack.''

"Hell's bells, man, that's what we want! Sounds like a damned good way of flushing them out.''

"No. If we fight in the mountains, we will not come out alive. If you cannot be persuaded to give up, it is better that we fight down here.''

Bannon ran both hands through his hair in frustration. "But the Apaches won't fight us! The braves are just watching!''

Reluctantly Montega said, "Then we must give them a reason to fight, but on our terms.''

"And how do you suggest we do that?''

"Gato has a plan,'' he replied with a heavy sigh. "While we fortify our position down here and prepare for an attack, he will take his men into the mountains. He believes they can slip past those who watch us and make their way to the camps. They will kill all the women and old ones and make prisoners of the children. When the braves learn what has happened, they will come for us.''

"Excellent!''

Montega frowned. "It is a dangerous plan, señor. The Apache will not attack blindly. They will choose their time carefully. Their braves are scattered now as they watch us, but they will come together in a great number before they attack. If necessary, they may even enlist the aid of the Tonto and Cibecue. They will outnumber us, and we will be slaughtered.''

"I don't believe that for an instant,'' Bannon scoffed. "If we kill their women and carry off their children, they'll attack out of blind rage, and we'll be ready for them. We've got over sixty men here, including Gato's band. We're obviously more than a match for them, or they would have attacked us before now.''

Montega shook his head. "You think like a white man, not an Apache.''

Bannon jabbed a finger in Gato's direction. "He's an Apache and it's his plan. By God, I think it's a good one. Tell him I said so.''

The interpreter did as he was told, and Gato relayed Bannon's words to the braves who flanked him. As far as Bannon could tell, Gato's expression did not change throughout his conversations with his braves and with Montega.

"If you will give him more ammunition for his rifles, he will leave tonight while the White Mountain braves sleep," the Mexican said. "His braves will separate and travel alone for two days until they are sure no one follows them; then they will come together and attack as many camps as they can."

"That sounds reasonable." Bannon moved to the supply wagon and unloaded a small crate filled with rifle shells. "How will we know when they've attacked?" he asked, placing the crate in front of Gato.

Montega spoke with Gato again, then turned to his employer. "He will send a runner to us so that we may be ready, but it will take a little time for the Apache to learn what has happened to their families. Gato believes that he will have more than enough time to join us with their captives before they attack."

Bannon looked at Gato with a forced, snappy smile plastered on his face. *"Enju, amigo,"* he said, employing the only two foreign words he knew.

Gato glanced at his braves, and the three Indians burst into laughter. *"Tagoon-ya-dah,"* the leader said to Bannon as he and his men rose.

Bannon kept his smile in place as he looked at Montega. "What did he say?"

"I think it was a term of respect," he guessed, unwilling to admit that he wasn't sure what the word meant. He was fairly certain, though, that it wasn't something Bannon would have appreciated. Neither man would have been pleased to know that Gato had called Bannon a fool.

The earth was hard in the high mountains, but a few soft spots showed good sign in places where the sun poked through the trees for long periods. With his face furrowed in concentration, He Brings Peace studied the tracks he had found in one of those places. A group of boys his age and younger were gathered around him, their hunting expedition forgotten for the moment.

"When were they made?" one of the young ones asked.

"A day ago, near sunset," He Brings Peace answered. "See how the ground has frozen and then thawed again? And look here"—he moved to another of the intermittent tracks—"this moccasin was sewn strangely. No White Mountain Inday makes his moccasins in this manner."

"If it was not one of us, then who has been here?" asked He Crawls Away, the son of Angry Coyote. Though he was nearly a year older than He Brings Peace, He Crawls Away had long ago accepted his cousin as the undisputed leader of their band of would-be braves.

He Brings Peace stood, his face serious. "Our grandfather says that the Chiricahua sew moccasins like this."

The boys looked at one another, making a valiant effort not to show their fear. They had been in the mountains from one full moon to the next, and they all knew that Gato and his band of Chiricahua renegades were the reason why. "How many are there?" He Crawls Away asked.

"Five passed this way, I think, but if it is Gato, there are many more." He Brings Peace turned and hurried toward the shelter of a stand of pines. "Come, we must return to camp and warn my father. Move silent and swift like the wind," he cautioned, and seconds later the six young Apache vanished into the woods.

"Lightning alongside dances, they say," Willow chanted.

Gray Wolf looked across the fire at his wife and smiled. Gathered around her in the wickiup were all the materials needed for the making of a baby-carrier, and as she completed each section she said the ritual prayer to bless that piece. The one just completed was for the loops along the side of the frame that would be used to strap the baby into the carrier. Willow's concentration was so fierce that she appeared to be completely oblivious to her husband, but she was not.

"You are wishing that this baby-carrier was for our own child, yes?" she asked without looking up.

Gray Wolf laughed. "You know me too well."

"Wishing will do you no good, beloved," she said wistfully as she began attaching the rawhide laces to the loops. "It will be a long time before our child has need of its first cradleboard. Nah-tanh has paid me well to make this carrier for her and to say the prayers over it. Her baby will come tonight, I think."

"I know. As her time grows near, her husband becomes useless," Gray Wolf said without censure.

"It is their first child," Willow replied as though that explained everything.

Gray Wolf moved across the wickiup and sat beside her. "With me, one child or five will not make a difference, beloved," he said tenderly. "When your time comes, I will be useless, too."

Willow looked at her husband and saw that he was thinking of the child they had lost and of Morning Star's difficult birth. She reached out to touch his face lovingly. "I will give you a strong, healthy son, beloved. There is no reason for worry."

"Are you so sure it will be a son?"

Willow placed one hand on her stomach. She hardly showed any sign of her pregnancy, and yet already she felt as one with the child inside her. "Yes. I am sure. Does that please you?"

"Any child born of our love will please me very well. Here. It is my gift for Nah-tanh's baby." He handed her a rawhide thong onto which he had laced a bear claw.

Willow smiled at her husband's generosity. "There is much power in this bear charm. Nah-tanh will be honored. When the cradleboard is finished, I will attach it to the hood to keep away sickness." She placed the charm with the other materials and went back to work on the baby-carrier.

The voice of One Who Sings outside the wickiup alerted them to the return of both their daughters, and Gray Wolf moved back to his place on the other side of the fire.

"I hear our children," Willow said loudly so that One Who Sings would know that it was all right to enter. Little Morning Star appeared a moment later and ran to her father without stopping, but their older daughter entered more sedately. "How is your grandmother?" Willow asked as One Who Sings took her place by the fire. Great Star had not been well for some time, and the harsh, cold climate of the mountains made Willow fear for her mother's life.

"She is better today, I think," the girl answered. "Her breath does not come so hard, but she has asked for the medicine man to perform the curing ceremony."

Willow looked at her husband, deeply concerned. Giannah-tah was with Blue Bear's scouting party in the foothills. A runner had been sent to find him four days ago, but neither had returned. "What can we do, husband?"

Gray Wolf shared Willow's anxiety, but he did not want to believe yet that some tragedy had befallen the runner. "If Nah-kah-yen does not return with the medicine man by tomorrow's sunset, I will go down the mountain to find him myself," he replied after a moment. "There is no other choice."

The thought of Gray Wolf placing himself in danger alarmed Willow, but she said nothing. Her mother needed the curing ceremony, and she knew that her husband was more than capable of keeping himself from harm. To ward off her fear, she touched the Thunderbird medallion on her necklace and said a prayer as she stroked the eagle feathers.

Gray Wolf saw the gesture and understood its meaning. Since the day he had given Willow the necklace she had never taken it off except to sleep or bathe. With the birth of each of their children, he added a feather so that now there were five. The necklace was as much a part of Willow as Gray Wolf himself. It was growing old, for Gray Wolf had made it many years before he gave it to his wife; yet it still looked as new as it had the day he carved the Thunderbird into the medallion and laced the turquoise nuggets on the rawhide thongs. Even the delicate eagle feathers, which should have needed replacement many times, showed no sign of wear.

Truly, the necklace was blessed. Willow touched it often, as she did now, for she believed in its power to shield her family from harm. She had performed the ritual many times, and it held no less meaning for her now than it had the first time she said the prayer that brought safety to her family.

But this time as she gently touched the feathers, one, then another and another fell into her hand like green leaves falling from a tree that had died before its time.

"Gray Wolf!" Tears of panic and fear formed as she frantically sought her husband's eyes. "What does it mean?"

Gray Wolf rose and went to her, fighting back a panic as intense as his wife's. "They are old and should be replaced; that is all," he said firmly.

"They are like new," she insisted as tears cut slender lines down her cheeks. Almost afraid to believe what she was seeing, she touched the largest feather. "This was the first," she whispered. "And this one you added to protect me." Her voice broke as she touched the third feather. "And this you added on the morning our first daughter was born."

Fiercely she clutched the two remaining feathers on the necklace—those that protected Morning Star and He Brings Peace. Her head fell back and a keening "Ay-eee," like the sound made by a dying animal, pierced the wickiup.

"It means nothing," Gray Wolf said vehemently, as though the force of his words would make it true. He pulled Willow into his arms and held her more tightly than he had ever dared before. Frightened by her mother's tears, Morning Star sought refuge in her sister's arms, and the girls clung to each other, trying to shut out their mother's wails of mourning.

Outside, others heard the keening and came out of their wickiups to search for the source.

They were the first to die.

NINE

When He Brings Peace heard the first shots, he and the other boys froze, their hearts tripping in alarm as they looked at one another.

"Gato has found our camp!" He Crawls Away shouted as he started running again.

"No! We must go carefully!" He Brings Peace called after him, but it was too late. The other boys joined his cousin in a headlong flight toward the camp.

Another volley of gunfire split the cold air, and He Brings Peace fought the foolish temptation to join the others. His father had taught him better. A brave did not run headlong into battle; he approached stealthily until he could assess the situation. Only in this way could he be truly effective in the fight. For all they knew, the other boys might be running directly into the gun sights of the attackers.

Though he was frightened, both for himself and for the fate of his family, He Brings Peace forced himself to be calm and to remember his father's teachings. Making no sound, he slipped through the trees. The frantic screams of his people reached his ears, as did the report of answering gunfire. The sounds echoed through the hills, making it difficult to judge from which direction the shots had originated, but as he ran, he finally identified the location of the attackers. Without pausing, he changed direction and climbed a hill west of the camp.

His own wickiup sat at the base of that rugged hill, and

when He Brings Peace finally reached the crest, he looked down on a scene that tore his heart from his breast. The bodies of his cousin and friends were lying at the edge of the camp where they had been cut down the moment they entered the clearing. Around them, all was chaos.

There were only ten wickiups in the small encampment; five were already on fire. Smoke billowed into the air. Women shrieked as they dragged their frightened children from the burning huts, but their screams were cut short by a hail of bullets and arrows that came from the cover of brush and scrub pines to the east and south.

Some of the old men had found fortified placements and were returning fire, as were some of the women. Though his eyes watered from the smoke, He Brings Peace searched for his parents and finally saw them a short distance away from their wickiup. From behind a pitifully small boulder, Gray Wolf was attempting to hold off the attackers with his bow and arrows while Willow fired at them with her husband's rifle.

Knowing he was too far away for his own arrows to be effective, He Brings Peace realized that his only hope of helping his family was to circle the camp and surprise the attackers from behind. Opposite him was a steep cliff riddled with many small caves, some of which were connected by a series of shelves and ridges. He had played in the caves as a youth, and more recently he had helped his mother store food there.

Running as fast as he could, heedless of any lookout Gato might have posted, the young brave circled the camp. He blocked out the shots and screams and tried not to imagine what was happening to his family. Like a mountain cat, he climbed a steep slope that would take him to the top of the cliff, then began working his way around to the face and down.

Below him, he saw a Chiricahua brave leave his cover in an attempt to flank Gray Wolf. Without pausing to think, He Brings Peace readied his bow and fired. The brave fell, and He Brings Peace dropped to his hands and knees to crawl along the sloping shelf. Another brave showed himself, unaware of a need to guard his back, and he fell, too, with the boy's arrow piercing his leg. The Chiricahua scrambled for cover and searched the cliffs behind him, but He Brings Peace had ducked out of sight.

"In the cliffs! A warrior!" the brave shouted to Gato.

"Be silent, fool," Gato snarled. "Do you want to give them hope? They are almost done for in the camp—only the man and woman oppose us." He turned and gestured to his other warriors. "Flank them and finish them. I will take care of the one on the cliff."

Exercising more caution, the renegades hastened to fulfill his orders. Another arrow streaked harmlessly into the brush near Gato. He studied the angle, then directed his gaze to the midsection of the cliff. He readied a poison-tipped arrow and waited.

Crouched low with his back against the rocks, He Brings Peace nocked another arrow against his bowstring. He rose quickly, fired into the brush below, then dropped and crawled along the shelf until the rocky path ended and there was nowhere to go but straight down.

The sounds of battle were growing less intense. The stand of pines Gato was using for cover made it difficult for He Brings Peace to see what was happening in camp, but he knew it could not be good; there were too many Chiricahua, and his people had been unprepared. His father was a great warrior, but not even he could prevail over so many enemies under these conditions. The smell of death was as strong as the smoke that hung in the air.

If his family was to die, He Brings Peace wanted to die as well, but he would die like a warrior, not like a child. Abandoning caution, he moved to the edge of the shelf to search for a target. None presented itself. He looked below, seeking a way down the cliff so that he could meet the Chiricahua face to face. Not even the smallest handhold was visible to him.

Desperate, he turned to retrace his trail and glanced down to the brush again. This time he saw the renegade who had been lying in wait for him, but it was too late. Before he completely understood what had happened, Gato's arrow pierced his shoulder. With a cry of shock and pain, he crumpled onto the rocky shelf with his face turned to the sky.

The world went dark, but only for a moment. Then it was light again . . . and deathly silent. He Brings Peace opened his eyes. Above him an eagle soared. It swooped toward him, and when it rose it took the boy's soul with it.

From a high place where the smoke and the trees did not seem to exist, He Brings Peace looked down on his own crumpled body. His eyes were now the eagle's eyes as the great bird glided over the camp. He Brings Peace did not wish to see the destruction, but the eagle's eyes were open and the boy had no other choice.

The Chiricahua had overrun the camp. He Brings Peace could not hear their whoops of victory, but he felt them. They pierced his heart with rage. A child was dragged screaming from a wickiup and was carried away. An old woman and man, their eyes devoid of life, were scalped and left to rot.

As the eagle soared, that scene was played out for He Brings Peace again and again as the people he knew best were brutally mutilated. But the people he loved the most . . . where were they? The need to know finally overcame his horror, and he asked the great bird to show him. An instant later the eagle was hovering over the bodies of his parents.

Gray Wolf had been the first to die. He Brings Peace could hear his mother's cry as she had gathered her husband into her arms. But her time to grieve had been short. Three arrows pierced her back. Her body was crumpled onto the man she had spent her life loving.

For He Brings Peace, the pain of seeing his slain parents was more than he could bear, but it was nothing compared to the horror of watching a cold-eyed Chiricahua strip them of their last shred of dignity. With a cry of victory, the renegade cut the Thunderbird necklace from Willow's throat, and with his scraping knife, took her scalp.

The eagle screamed.

The shrill cry startled the renegade. His eyes sought the sky, but when he saw nothing, he returned to his work. He shoved Willow's body aside like a corn-silk doll and scalped her husband.

The eagle screamed again.

When his work was done, the renegade picked up Gray Wolf's rifle and pointed to the wickiup. "Search and fire it!" he shouted to one of his braves. Two men scurried inside and a moment later came out dragging One Who Sings and Morning Star. Both girls screamed and fought their captors, but Morning Star was too small to be a burden to the brave who held her.

With the Thunderbird necklace still dangling from his hand, Gato pointed at Gray Wolf's older daughter. "She will make trouble. Kill her." He gestured to Morning Star. "She will come with us." He turned his back as his order was carried out.

The eagle screamed again.

Gato looked up, searching for the bird that had made the cry, but still he saw nothing. There was magic at work, of that he was certain, but he could not say whether it was for good or ill. Even a practitioner of the dark arts of witchcraft, like Gato, sometimes found it difficult to understand the signs that were presented to him. But as the little girl was carried off, the eagle screamed once more, and Gato looked down at the necklace in his hand. The blood of his victims ran in dark streaks across the Thunderbird medallion. That blood would make him stronger.

With a chilling smile, he fastened the necklace around his throat.

The eagle's scream echoed through the mountains.

"The cry, where does it come from?" one of his braves asked as Gato stalked across the camp.

The renegade touched the medallion. "From a spirit I now control," he answered. He raised his voice to the other braves. "Get the horses from the remuda! We must go quickly from this place of death."

"Gato!" Another brave approached him. "What of the one in the cliffs? If he escapes to warn the other camps, they will come after us."

"He was only a boy, and the arrow that struck him bore my strongest poison. There is no reason to waste time searching for a dead man. Come. We must return south quickly."

The brave smiled. "What of Bannon?"

Gato laughed. "He is a great fool."

"We will not warn him of the camps we have taken?"

"No. We will let him suffer the vengeance of the White Mountain Inday while we take our horses and slaves to Mexico. The scalps will bring a good price there, too. Come." Laughing, the renegade broke into a trot. Seconds later the camp was deserted.

Overhead, the eagle soared toward the cliffs. The shattered world of He Brings Peace grew dark again, and when next he opened his eyes, he was on the cliff. The cold of the rocks seeped through his bones, and he tried to rise. Pain seared his shoulder and he pulled at the arrow, only to discover that the point had passed all the way through. He broke off the feathered shaft, stanched the blood, and tried to rise again. All he could do was crawl.

Like an animal guided by instinct he worked his way toward the camp. A part of his mind—the strongest part—no longer wished for death. Only life mattered now, for with life came his only chance for revenge.

"Gato," he whispered again and again as he crawled on, his strength fading as his resolve grew, until darkness claimed him once more.

The dreams would not let him rest. Images of strange people he did not know visited him and took him on journeys too frightening for his mind to comprehend. A fire burned in his blood, fueled by hatred, as he walked in the netherworld between life and death.

With the shadow of the eagle guiding him, he soared over a great camp where many Blue Coats lived and worked. He flew through mountains and canyons, watching battles beneath him.

For a time a soft hand like that of a gentle, loving woman touched him and eased his torment. Her face swam before him; her gentle eyes beckoned him. She called to him in the darkness, leading him toward the light; but always the fire returned and the journey began again. He saw his people, broken and starving, and then he saw himself guiding them to food and shelter. He heard voices in many languages and heard himself speaking them, too. His sister, Morning Star, called to him from a great distance, but he could not reach her.

Hardship and sorrow mingled with fleeting glimpses of happiness, but always at the edge of every image was the face of Gato as he tore the Thunder Eagle necklace from Willow's lifeless body.

Day after day the eagle took him on new journeys, until finally he awoke with the certain knowledge that the course of his life had been set.

Jedidiah tossed the old compress into the basin and allowed his tired shoulders to slump with relief. After nearly a week the boy's fever had finally broken. His brow was cool and his fitful tossing and turning had become a restful slumber. He Brings Peace was going to live. Jedidiah considered it something of a miracle. The poison that had infected the wound in his shoulder should have killed him within a few hours, or a day at the most. Yet He Brings Peace had survived the difficult journey to Jedidiah's cabin and had hung on to life ferociously. Jedidiah had been caring for him day and night, but he knew that his survival had less to do with his own ministrations than with the boy's incredible resolve to live.

A hazy veil of smoke had still hung over Gray Wolf's encampment on the afternoon Jedidiah arrived on the scene of the massacre. His journey across the mountains to warn the Red Canyon band about Bannon's expedition had been a success, and he had spent several weeks with his wife's family. Luck, or perhaps even fate, had prompted him to leave them earlier than he had planned. On his trip back across the mountain, he had passed through many small Apache encampments, and from these clans he had learned the location of Gray Wolf's winter camp.

But he had arrived too late to do more than mourn for his dear friends. The sight of their mutilated bodies had brought back the hideous memories of his wife's death. It was all he could do to force himself to search for survivors, even though he had no hope of finding any.

And then he had seen his young pupil crumpled near the bodies of his parents. From the signs around the boy it was clear that he had crawled from the cliffs. Jedidiah had removed the arrow protruding from his back and cleaned the wound, which was already beginning to fester.

Sick at heart, he had searched for some sign of his precious little Morning Star, but when he found no young children among the bodies he realized that the attackers had taken them captive. He studied the tracks they had left, and finally concluded that this was not the first camp they had struck; too many riderless horses had been led out of the area. The imprints of Chiricahua moccasins told him the identity of the attackers.

His first impulse had been to follow them and find a way to free Morning Star, but to do so would have condemned He Brings Peace to certain death. The boy's only hope for survival was for Jedidiah to get him back to his cabin where he had salves and a disinfectant that might keep the infection from spreading. If he traveled day and night, he could make the trip in three days. Jedidiah doubted that the boy could survive, but he had to try. Once He Brings Peace was out of danger, or dead, Jedidiah would begin his search for Gato.

With his desperately ill young friend strapped to a travois, the frontiersman had made his way out of the mountains. For a time, he had followed Gato's trail south and had surmised that the renegades were headed for Mexico where their slaves and scalps would bring the best price. Eventually, though, he was forced to abandon Gato's trail and head west to his cabin.

Sleeping only a few hours every night, and stopping only to tend to He Brings Peace, he finally reached his home. The boy's fever was raging out of control, and for the next few days, Jedidiah kept a bedside vigil, expecting every labored breath he drew to be his last. But He Brings Peace clung to life, tossing fitfully, crying out for his parents—and for the man who had slaughtered them.

But finally the fever had broken. Exhausted, Jedidiah kept one eye on his sleeping patient while he prepared another kettle of the beef broth he'd been force-feeding He Brings Peace. Then he napped in the chair beside the bed, and some time later he awoke to find the boy watching him. The dark eyes that stared at him contained a coldness Jedidiah had never seen in them before, but considering the tragedy the boy had witnessed, what else should he have expected?

"Gato?"

Jedidiah moved to the bed and raised the boy's head so that he could drink. "His trail led south," he replied in Apache. "I believe he has gone to Mexico. When you are stronger, I will go after the renegades. Their trail is already cold, but I will find him and return your sister to you."

He Brings Peace took several sips of water and fell back into the bedding. "I will go with you."

Jedidiah frowned. "It will be a long time before you are strong enough to travel. Their trail will already be difficult to follow."

"It does not matter," he said weakly, but with a conviction that startled Jedidiah. "We must go . . . together."

The frontiersman saw no point in arguing. "I have seen smoke signals that call for all Inday warriors to come together. Your grandfather is preparing a war party."

He Brings Peace nodded as though this was an expected piece of information. "He will . . . attack Bannon."

"I believe so," Jedidiah replied. "But he may have sent a war party in search of Gato as well."

"No." He barely had the strength to shake his head. "Gato is mine." His eyelids fluttered and closed.

Jedidiah allowed him to sleep for a while, then brought a bowl of broth to the bedside and roused him long enough to force a few spoonfuls down him. That became their routine over the next two days. He Brings Peace made no further attempts at conversation, and Jedidiah finally realized that he was directing all his strength toward his recuperation.

He began trying to sit and then stand much sooner than Jedidiah thought wise, but He Brings Peace could not be deterred. Before long he was taking feeble steps and seemed to be growing stronger with each foray. Only once more in the week that followed the fever did Jedidiah mention leaving so that he could go in search of Gato, but the boy's response was firm and dramatic: Pindah Dak'é was not meant to chase the renegade alone; the spirits had decreed it.

As the boy's health returned, Jedidiah began to see changes in him that went beyond the effects of shock and grief. His stoicism was pronounced and disturbing, but he displayed an inner strength that was nothing less than amazing. Gone was any trace of the mischievous youth Jedidiah had known. His place had been usurped by a young man who was already old beyond his years.

Toward the end of that week he began spending long hours sitting out-of-doors and staring toward the mountains. The smoke signals had long since stopped. There was nothing to see but sky and yellow earth; yet Jedidiah was often struck by the eerie feeling that He Brings Peace knew exactly what was taking place beyond the horizon. His eyes held a haunting coldness that was seldom tinged with even a hint of sadness.

The Apache did not believe in discussing the dead, so Jedidiah made no attempt to force the young man to speak about his parents. In fact, they did not talk at all except when there was no alternative. The wounded shoulder began to mend, but Jedidiah feared that the scars inside the young man might never fade.

Late in the evening of the eighth day of his recovery He Brings Peace finally broke the long silence of the previous week. Jedidiah was on the porch of his adobe cabin, nursing a cup of whiskey-laced coffee, when the young man rose from the spot where he kept his mountain vigil. With a purposeful stride, he approached the man who had saved his life.

"It is time. Tomorrow we go."

Jedidiah sighed resignedly. "To Mexico after Gato?"

He Brings Peace looked to the mountains. "No. We go to my grandfather first. There are things I must say to him." He pinned Jedidiah with a look that brooked no disagreement. "Things you must hear as well."

The frontiersman could have argued that there was no reason for him to see Blue Bear. He could have explained his concern about Morning Star. But Gato's trail was already so old that it would be useless to follow him in that manner, and a few days more wouldn't make much of a difference. If He Brings Peace needed the support of a friend when he confronted his grandfather, Jedidiah could do no less than provide it.

"I will go with you and listen," he replied after a moment.

The young man nodded and slipped inside the cabin.

They left early the next morning, setting a slow but steady pace toward the mountains. Near midday they spotted the vultures. A few minutes later they came upon the scattered bodies of the Bannon party. From the looks of things, it had not been a long fight.

Knowing that Apache were extremely superstitious about being in the presence of the dead, Jedidiah expected He Brings Peace to skirt the battlefield, but he did not. He rode among the corpses until he had seen them all. The bodies had been stripped of their rifles and revolvers; the supply wagons had been looted and burned. The fires still smoldered, and smoke hung thick in the air, reminding He Brings Peace too much of the destruction of his own camp. Shoving back the images of the people he loved, he studied the tracks at the edges of the death camp and finally returned to his companion.

"Not a one escaped," he informed him.

"But Gato is not here, is he?" Jedidiah asked.

The cold-eyed young brave shook his head. "No."

He wheeled his horse and left the battlefield to resume his trek to the mountains. For nearly an hour they followed the clear trail left by the Apache, who had taken the party's horses with them. As the terrain grew more rugged, the signs were more difficult to spot, for the Inday had separated into smaller groups that had splintered off one by one from the main war party.

Jedidiah wondered which group Blue Bear had ridden with, but He Brings Peace seemed to suffer no such confusion. When the trails diverged, he chose one without hesitation and continued his methodical pursuit. The boy should have been exhausted, but he showed no sign of it. The only clue that he had been wounded at all was that he kept his left arm close to his body. If the shoulder still hurt—as Jedidiah knew it must—he kept his pain a closely guarded secret.

They traveled steadily all day, stopping only when necessary. At dusk it became impossible to read the signs, but He Brings Peace continued as confidently as before. When the sky was completely black, his vigilance was finally rewarded. The golden glow of a fire in the distance told them they had found the war party. The victory dance was already under way.

As they approached, Jedidiah heard the chanting of the braves as they circled the fire acting out the deeds they had performed in battle. Their silhouettes were a dramatic contrast to the blazing bonfire. Bows were drawn back and rifles were raised. Each warrior had painted a band of white across his chest and over his right shoulder. A white band spotted with red crossed the left shoulder. War whoops split the night air, and the dancing became a frenzy of movement.

A huge group of spectators sat just outside the war circle, and beyond them Jedidiah caught faint glimpses of a vast number of wickiups. The entire Red Canyon band as well as clans of Tonto and Cibecue Apache had joined forces with Blue Bear's people. It was no wonder the battle that morning had been brief; the Bannon party had been outnumbered by more than five to one.

He Brings Peace rode steadily forward until he reached the outer rim of spectators. He dismounted, and Jedidiah followed suit, staying at his young friend's side as the boy passed through the crowd. When the glow of the fire illuminated him, the drums stopped, the chanting died away, and the warriors turned to see what had disrupted their dance.

From the other side of the fire, Blue Bear saw the face of his grandson, and his heart leaped with joy. He rose and waited as He Brings Peace came to him, but when the boy drew close, the old chief gathered him into his arms.

"You live. My grandson lives," he whispered, unashamed of the tears that slashed his weathered cheeks. He drew back and looked at him. "When the medicine man returned from the mountains to tell me what had happened, he said that your body was not with the others. I buried my family and grieved for you as well, for I feared that Gato had taken you away to be tortured.''

"Gato believed I was dead, Grandfather.'' He Brings Peace touched his wounded shoulder and glanced at Jedidiah. "Had it not been for my good friend, he would have been right. He took me to his home and brought me back to life.''

Blue Bear looked at the white man. "I owe you my grandson's life. All that I have is yours.''

"Your friendship and his''—Jedidiah gestured to He Brings Peace—"are all the payment I need.''

The old chief nodded, his eyes brimming with tears and gratitude. "Come. You must eat and rest.'' He gestured for the victory dance to continue, then led his grandson and Jedidiah away from the bonfire. Gian-nah-tah and several of the elders accompanied them as they moved toward the *nant'an*'s wickiup. All of the women in Blue Bear's clan had been killed in the massacre, but the camp of the medicine man's family had not been attacked, and those women were now seeing to Blue Bear's needs. The men settled around the cook fire outside the wickiup, and food was brought almost immediately.

He Brings Peace asked about his other grandfather, Tall One, and was told that his war party had not yet returned to camp. "Your father's mother has not taken the news of her son's death well,'' Blue Bear told him reluctantly. "I am told she does not leave her wickiup.''

He Brings Peace stared into the fire, his expression unchanged, but his thoughts raged against Gato for the lives he had destroyed. "I will go to her soon,'' he replied. "But first there are words I must say to you, Grandfather. I rode among our enemies today.''

Blue Bear straightened his shoulders proudly. "It was a glorious battle. The White Eyes had made a camp and were ready for us, but it did not matter. They paid the price for the Inday blood they spilled.''

He Brings Peace frowned. "But it was Gato who attacked our people.''

"I know this,'' the chief responded. "But we could not find Gato. Rain and wind had destroyed his trail. The White

Eyes brought Gato here to destroy us. It was just that they pay the price. Honor is satisfied.''

"No!" He Brings Peace snarled, showing the first signs of anger that Jedidiah had seen from him. "Gato killed my parents and sister. He took Morning Star as a slave. I watched as he cut the Thunderbird necklace from my mother's body and placed it around his own throat." He leaned toward his grandfather, his eyes burning with hatred. "When I have cut that throat and reclaimed the necklace, when I have found my sister and returned her to her people, *then* honor will be satisfied! No blood but his will do."

Blue Bear understood his grandson's hatred, but the boy's desire for revenge against Gato and Gato alone was not the Apache way. "This is your grief speaking, my grandson. We have taken a life for a life. That is all that matters. If Gato and his braves were still *true* Chiricahuas, we would have taken our war party south and spilled Chiricahua blood as payment for White Mountain blood. But Gato is *tsét'a go*— a renegade. His people have disowned him, and we cannot hold them responsible for his acts. But Bannon paid him to come here. Bannon told him to kill us, so Bannon's death satisfies honor. We cannot spend the rest of our lives chasing one man.''

"I can and must!" He Brings Peace said hotly, unswayed by his grandfather's logic.

"It is not the Apache way!"

"It is *my* way!"

"Then your heart is not Apache!"

He Brings Peace drew back as though he had been slapped. A shocked silence pervaded the area around the campfire, and it was a long moment before the boy could finally reply, "I have no heart, Grandfather. Gato has taken it, and I cannot be whole until I force him to return it to me."

Blue Bear regretted his angry outburst, but his grandson was not the only one who had suffered because of Gato. The old chief had lost his daughters, his grandchildren, and his beloved wife, Great Star. His own pain was no less than his grandson's, but he was old and had long ago learned the wisdom of the customs that had been handed down through generations. He could not allow He Brings Peace to spend his life needlessly consumed by grief and hatred. "I feel your pain, for it is as my own," he said quietly. "But I am your chief, and you must do as I bid you. Be satisfied with the revenge we have wrought today."

"I cannot, Grandfather," the young brave replied sadly. "A power greater than yours has shown me the course of my life. As I lay dying, the spirit of the eagle visited me."

A murmur of surprise went around the fire, but He Brings Peace continued. "I was taken on journeys to see things I do not yet understand. I saw wonders too great for my mind to comprehend. But some things I do know: It is my destiny to kill Gato. When he took the Thunderbird necklace, he took a part of our people with him. The necklace must be returned to me. But that will not happen soon. In order to meet my destiny I must learn the ways of the White Eyes. I must speak their language and live as they do."

"No! I forbid it!" Blue Bear roared, but the words were barely out of his mouth before Gian-nah-tah intervened.

"Hear him, my friend," the medicine man said. "If the eagle has truly favored him with the gift of sight, we must listen to what he says."

"No. I have lost too much because of the White Eyes' greed," Blue Bear replied stubbornly. "I will not give them this grandson as well."

"You may have no choice," Gian-nah-tah replied. He looked at He Brings Peace. "Can you not see that your grandson is no longer a child? He is a man now, old beyond his years. The Thunder Eagle has changed him for a reason, and it is not for you or for me to challenge the wisdom of the Gans."

"What he says is true, Grandfather," the young brave interjected. "You must allow me to follow the path the eagle has chosen for me."

Blue Bear shook his head, but his protests were growing weaker. "You cannot live among the White Eyes. They despise all Apaches. They would kill you."

"All White Eyes are not alike, Grandfather." He looked

at Jedidiah and waited until the frontiersman's eyes met and held his own. "This man is different, and someday I will meet others who possess his understanding and his heart. I will live with Pindah Dak'é, and he will teach me all I must know of the White Eyes." His gaze returned to Blue Bear's. "And from you I will continue to learn the ways of my people. I will stand with one foot in each world until I meet my destiny."

Blue Bear saw the resolve in his grandson's eyes and knew it was futile to argue further. Gian-nah-tah was right. The future of He Brings Peace had been ordained by a power Blue Bear could not oppose. With great reluctance, he nodded. "Very well." He looked at Jedidiah, who was clearly startled by the young brave's announcement. "You have been chosen to bear a great responsibility, my friend. Do you accept it? Will you teach my grandson how to survive in your world?"

Jedidiah looked from the old man to He Brings Peace. His thoughts were of the wife and daughter he had lost and of the son his wife had been denied the opportunity to give him. "I can think of no greater honor," he replied.

"Enju." Blue Bear looked at the medicine man. "My grandson needs a new name, worthy of the warrior he has become."

The old shaman nodded and stared into the fire for a long moment. Only the sound of drums and war cries from the victory dance in the distance marred the quiet of the night. "His name must reflect the life he will live and the power he has been given," he said finally, capturing the young brave's eyes. "From this time on, our people will know him as He Chases the Thunder."

The newly christened brave nodded and looked at Jedidiah. "I have a good Apache name now, but I must have a name the White Eyes will know as well. You must choose it."

Honored by the request, Jedidiah thought for a moment, but this was not an easy task. He stared into the fire as the medicine man had, but for the life of him, only one name came to mind. It had always been his intention to name his first son after his own father; somehow it seemed fitting to use it now. "My people will know you by a name I respect," he said finally. "They will call you Case Longstreet."

The young brave with two new names reached out, taking his grandfather's hand on one side and his mentor's on the other, forging his bond with both worlds.

"It is done."

PART III

The Quest

TEN

Fort Apache, April 1874

"WELL DONE, Sergeant Brogan," Libby Ashford said, turning in a full circle to survey the newly whitewashed parlor. "This place is finally beginning to look livable."

Teak Brogan joined her in the center of the room, scratching his head as he looked around. "So it does, miss. 'Course you realize these walls won't stay white for too long, don't you?" He gestured toward the open windows. Crude shutters could keep out some of the elements, but they would never hold back the constant infiltration of dust that contaminated this and every other square foot of the military encampment. Glass-paned windows were an unknown luxury in the Arizona Territory, at least as far as the U.S. Army was concerned.

Libby swiped at a lock of damp hair on her forehead, creating another smudge of grime. "Then we shall paint it again when the need arises," she replied, refusing to be daunted by his prediction. When she'd arrived at Fort Apache with her brother, Meade, three days ago, their apartment adjacent to the post hospital had been so filthy that she'd nearly burst into tears. After weeks of traveling in an army ambulance over almost nonexistent roads, eating meager camp fare, sleeping in tents, and being terrorized by tales of rattlesnakes, scorpions, tarantulas, and—most frightening of all—

hostile Apaches, arriving to find uninhabitable living quarters had been the last straw.

Of the five rooms they would call their home, the kitchen had been the worst by far, but the parlor, dining room, and two sleeping rooms were almost as bad. Layer upon layer of dirt had covered rotted food and discarded bottles of spirits. The few pieces of furniture that the previous tenant had left behind were so ramshackle they were virtually unusable, and the walls of the log cabin structure had been black with soot and dust.

She had struggled to keep Meade from seeing the depth of her despair, but her brother, as always, was sensitive to Libby's every thought and feeling. They had been taking care of each other for so long that words were often unnecessary. Meade had immediately set out to find a striker who could help Libby while he attended to the pressing problem of whipping the hospital into shape; the new post surgeon had been appalled to find that the infirmary was even more of a pigsty than the living quarters.

When Teak Brogan, a middle-aged veteran of army life on the frontier, had learned that the captain was in need of a striker, he'd quickly applied for the position. The part-time job was an excellent way to supplement his pay, and though the doctor's sister had kept him busy every waking off-duty minute of the last two days, the sergeant didn't regret taking the job. Unlike some ladies he'd worked for, Miss Ashford had toiled every bit as hard as he had, and the striker had quickly come to admire her pluck. Later, when she had the quarters cleaned and arranged to her liking, his duties would be less demanding; cooking, doing household repairs, and running an occasional errand would be the sum of his responsibilities.

In the meantime, Teak was determined to do whatever it took to make the young lady comfortable. She was a sweet, charming girl who looked too fragile to survive the rigors of life in the Southwest. Some might have criticized the doctor for bringing such a delicate flower to a godforsaken place like Fort Apache, but Brogan was of the opinion that the West needed a woman's touch. And this young lady was much tougher than she looked, he had decided. She reminded him a great deal of his own sister, and working for the Ashfords was almost like having a family again. For Teak, that was worth far more than the ten dollars a month Captain Ashford was paying him.

"What next, miss?" he asked, collecting his bucket and brushes.

Libby smiled at his eagerness. "Sergeant, you are a jewel beyond price, and I can't imagine how I would manage without you. Frankly, though, I am utterly exhausted. Why don't we put down the rug, replace the furniture, and call it a day?"

Teak couldn't help but return her smile. She was just so darned pretty, even with smudges of dirt and whitewash on her heart-shaped face. "That suits me fine, miss. And after that, I'll start supper while you wash off some of that war paint."

"War paint?" Libby touched her face and only succeeded in spreading a glob of whitewash across her cheek. "Oh, my," she muttered, heading for her bedroom. She returned a moment later with an oval mirror in one hand and a damp cloth in the other. "Sergeant, why didn't you tell me I look a perfect mess?" she asked as she swabbed at the dirt.

"Because the sergeant knows better than to insult my sister," Meade Ashford said pleasantly as he sauntered into the room. Brogan snapped to attention and then quietly departed after Meade muttered, "At ease, Sergeant," as he approached his sister. "My, but you do look lovely today, Libby dear," he teased. "Have I arrived in time for high tea?"

He dropped a kiss on her damp, smudged forehead, and Libby glared up at the tall, dark-haired man whose greatest joy in life was teasing his sister. Over the years Libby had learned to give back as good as she got from him. "Don't make sport of me, you cad," she said, trying to appear stern and failing miserably. "Sergeant Brogan and I have been slaving away like Hercules cleaning the Augean stables. Our quarters are now spotless, no thanks to you."

"My darling Libby, if you think our rooms were bad, you should have seen the condition of the hospital. My predecessor must have received his medical training in the Dark Ages. Believe me, I've had my hands full next door.''

She looked at him suspiciously, noting that not a single blemish marred his appearance. He looked as fresh as when he'd left their quarters this morning in his crisp blue uniform. "If you've been cleaning as diligently as I, how is it that I'm covered in filth while you look as though you've just come from a debutante cotillion?''

Meade ducked his head guiltily. ''Well, I didn't say that I did all the cleaning myself.''

''From the looks of you, you didn't do *any* of the cleaning yourself.''

''Not true,'' he claimed. ''I had to spruce up and pay an official call at headquarters when Major Forsythe returned a few hours ago. And speaking of which—you'd better do a little sprucing yourself. As soon as the major brushes the dust off his uniform he'll be dropping by to pay his respects.''

Libby's heart tripped in alarm. ''You're not serious? I look a fright.'' She glanced down at her soiled gingham frock. ''I can't receive an officer like this.''

''Then I suggest you change. He could be here at any moment.''

''Oh, my word,'' she muttered. ''Just look at this parlor. There's not even a place to sit. Sergeant Bro—''

Meade grasped his sister's shoulders and pointed her in the direction of her room. ''I'll bring in some furniture. You go make yourself presentable.''

''But the carpet! The curtains!''

''Don't worry about it. Believe me, the major isn't coming to inspect the barracks.''

Sighing with exasperation, Libby gave up her protests and disappeared into her room. Meade began carting chairs in from the dining room, but he had no trouble hearing her through the thin walls. ''I swear, Meade, our lives were ever so much simpler before you joined the army. The protocol of these endless courtesy calls alone is enough to make my head swim. Yesterday it was Colonel and Mrs. Dunlevy, Captains Edgemont and Robertson, and Robertson's pretty little wife,

Susannah. And then there was that odious Major . . . oh, what's his name? The one with the bushy muttonchops?"

"Armbruster," Meade supplied.

"That's right." Libby dashed water onto her face and succeeded in erasing the last of the whitewash, then slipped out of her dress. She continued with the list of callers she'd entertained in the last three days, bemoaning the necessity of returning all their calls in order of rank.

Meade chuckled. "After a few weeks out here, I suspect you'll be grateful for any diversion, Libby dear. But if it makes you feel any better, I don't believe Major Forsythe's visit has anything to do with courtesy. The moment he stepped back on post this afternoon he heard that a lovely unmarried lady had arrived in camp. He all but ordered me to make myself ready to accept his call. Personally I think he's anxious to throw his hat into the matrimonial ring."

Libby stopped what she was doing and stuck her head out the door to look at her brother. "Be serious."

Meade placed an oak rocking chair in front of the hearth with a thud. "I am. I can't tell you the number of inquiries I've had about the state of my sister's marriageability."

"You're teasing me again," she accused, not sure whether she should be flattered or appalled.

"I'm not," he swore, raising his right hand to supplement the oath.

A wisp of a smile played around Libby's mouth as she ducked back into her room. "Did you tell them I'm a twenty-two-year-old spinster who's determined to devote her life to caring for her bachelor brother?"

Though she spoke in jest, her words struck Meade as being too close to the truth, and he knew he had no one to blame but himself. Libby didn't see the guilt that crept onto his face, nor did she hear it in his voice, because he made a concerted effort to keep his tone light. "No, I told them you're a fiendish coquette who'd broken the heart of every eligible bachelor in the East and that you'd moved out here to escape the shame of a scandalous affair with a European count."

The absurdity of the notion made Libby laugh out loud. She had never even met a European count, and she'd certainly never engaged in an affair—illicit or otherwise—with any man. "Well, that ought to do wonders for my reputation. Once all the wives learn of my wicked past I'll be about as popular with them as an outbreak of typhoid fever."

"Oh, they'll adore you," he assured her. "You'll give them something new to gossip about."

"That's what I love most about you, Meade . . ." She flounced out of her room, handed her brother a buttonhook, and turned her back so that he could fasten the back of the pastel blue day frock she'd changed into. "I can always count on you to defend my honor and keep the proud name of Ashford unbesmirched."

"I do my utmost," he intoned seriously.

She looked around the room, clucking her tongue as he finished with her dress. "Really, Meade, Grandma Latham's rocker should sit by the window, not on the hearth."

"May we discuss the decor later, Lib?" he asked quietly, handing her the buttonhook. "I believe I hear the major on the porch." A knock at that exact moment confirmed his assumption.

"But my hair isn't combed," she hissed, pushing a mass of errant chestnut locks back over her shoulders.

"You look fine," he whispered, heading for the door. "Now, behave yourself."

Libby gasped, but had no time to retort as Meade admitted their guest. Her first impression was that he was quite handsome. He appeared to be in his mid-thirties and had the deeply tanned face of an outdoorsman. Meade was a good two inches taller than his superior, but no would ever have described him as short.

While the major and the captain went through their ritual mumbo jumbo at the door, Libby tried to figure out what to do with the buttonhook. There was no convenient place to lay it, and her frock had no pockets. In the end, she surreptitiously passed it from her right hand to her left and hoped the folds of her skirt would keep it hidden.

"Major Andrew Forsythe, may I present my sister, Miss Liberty Ashford, known affectionately to her family and friends as Libby," Meade said as soon as the saluting was out of the way.

"It's a great pleasure, Miss Ashford." The major's pale blue eyes traveled discreetly up and down Libby's trim figure, but she refused to allow herself to wonder if he liked what he saw.

"The pleasure is mine, Major," she said sweetly as she moved forward, her hand extended. Forsythe accepted her hand, brushed it lightly with his lips, and released it. "Won't you be seated?"

"Thank you."

She ushered him to the misplaced rocking chair—the sturdiest piece of furniture in the room—and chose a straight-backed chair for herself. Since there was no other place to sit, Meade chose to stand at his sister's side.

"I do hope you'll forgive me for calling on such short notice, Miss Ashford, but I was eager to add my welcome to those already tendered to you and your brother. In fact, I pulled rank on him to arrange this visit."

"Then you deserve what you get, sir," Libby said with an easy smile that Forsythe found utterly charming. "The lady of the house is a perfect mess—and we won't even discuss the condition of the house itself." A wave of her hand encompassed the lifeless, nearly vacant room. "But I could certainly manage to prepare a cup of tea for us—or coffee, if you'd prefer."

"Don't trouble yourself on my account, please, Miss Ashford. I just wanted to pay my respects. It isn't every day that Fort Apache is granted the pleasure of welcoming such a lovely lady to its ranks."

Libby had led such a sheltered life that she wasn't accustomed to blatant flattery, and she tended to discount it as a chivalrous but somewhat hollow courtesy. Still, she knew better than to challenge one of Meade's superiors. "Thank you, Major. Everyone has been exceedingly kind since my arrival."

"If there is anything you need, you have only to ask," he said gallantly.

Meade laughed. "Watch yourself, Major. You don't know

what you're letting yourself in for. My sister's list of demands might stagger you.''

"Meade! How unkind,'' Libby chided, though her eyes were twinkling merrily. "Just because I asked you to build shelves for our books and a cabinet for Mother's china doesn't mean I'm unreasonable.''

"Certainly not, Captain,'' Forsythe agreed. "Fort Apache needs more of the amenities of civilization. Speaking of which, I assume you will be attending the party that Colonel and Mrs. Dunlevy are hosting in honor of you and your brother tomorrow night.''

"Certainly. Meade and I are looking forward to it.'' She lowered her voice and leaned forward. "Though, confidentially, I suspect that my brother and I are only the excuse for the party rather than the reason for it.''

The major laughed. "You're quite right. We use any excuse at all to relieve the boredom of post routine. But I assure you, a new surgeon and his fair sister are the best we've had in quite some time. And now I really should be going,'' he said, rising. Without calling undue attention to the gesture, he placed two of his calling cards on the mantel and stepped toward the door. Libby and Meade joined him there. "I shall look forward to seeing you tomorrow night, Miss Ashford.''

"Thank you, Major.''

"Captain.'' The two officers performed their parting ritual, and Libby's smile stayed in place until the major was gone. Then she rounded on her brother like a miniature virago. "Meade Ashford, you should be horsewhipped, and following that, you should be drawn, quartered, and hanged from the nearest yardarm.''

Meade laughed and dropped a kiss on his sister's brow. "Libby dear, you're mixing your military metaphors.''

She shook her head. "Clever alliteration will not get you back into my good graces. What do you mean, telling the major that I'm demanding? What must he think of me?''

"He thinks you're perfectly charming,'' he answered, still chuckling. "Libby, when are you ever going to realize the effect you have on the men of our species? One smile and a glance from those gorgeous dark eyes are enough to turn even the stoutest heart into a puddle of mush.''

"Oh, Meade, stop it," she said dismissively, heading toward the kitchen to find Sergeant Brogan. "I've had enough teasing for one day."

"I am not teasing you, Libby," Meade said, suddenly growing serious.

"I'm going to start supper," she said with a wave of her hand that reminded her she was still holding the buttonhook Meade had stuck her with. She turned and slapped it into his hand. "Why don't you make yourself useful and bring in the carpets?"

She breezed out. Meade started to follow her, then realized it was pointless. His sister's concept of herself had been formed years ago by a vain, neglectful mother and an uncaring father.

Meade suspected that he, too, should shoulder some of the blame for Libby's low opinion of her own beauty, but he was damned if he knew how to rectify the problem. She refused to believe him, no matter how often he tried to tell her she had blossomed into a lovely young lady, and these last few years there had been precious few others around to verify his claims.

He and Libby had been taking care of each other for nearly as long as either of them could remember. When he thought of their mother, Meade envisioned a bitter woman who had taken no joy in anything, particularly her children. Their father was an officer of the Seventh Cavalry who had never been anything but a disappointment to his wife. She had passed away when Libby was eight, and their father had been too preoccupied with his military career to take much notice of two affection-starved children.

Meade and Libby had been shuffled from one relative to another, treated like poor relations, and made to feel that they were subsisting on charity. Then their father had died shortly after the war, leaving a modest estate that allowed Meade and Libby to open their own home while Meade completed his education at Harvard.

Libby had attended a modest girls' school as a day pupil,

but spent most of her time taking care of their house and helping Meade with his studies. Throughout her late teen years, her only social contacts had been a few of Meade's friends from medical school and a distant cousin her own age with whom she corresponded.

As a result of her unusual upbringing, Libby was well educated and had been schooled in the social graces, but she was also headstrong and independent to a fault. She was a fighter and a survivor, but she had never learned the fine art of being a woman. Her soft heart kept her from being abrasive, but the few men with whom she had come in contact and who had expressed any romantic interest generally found her too outspoken and stubborn for their masculine sensibilities.

When Meade decided to put his medical training to use in the army, Libby went to live with their cousin, but she wasn't happy. The cousin's life consisted of a seemingly endless round of parties, social calls, and soirees. Libby was out of her depth and utterly miserable. To make herself useful, she took a position as a governess, but her cousin's family was appalled that one of their relatives had joined the ranks of the working class.

Though she did her best to keep him from seeing how unhappy she was, Meade knew Libby too well to be fooled. He was posted in Washington when he finally sent for her. He had missed Libby as much as she had missed him, and it had seemed right that they be together no matter what the circumstances.

Libby barely had a chance to become accustomed to life in the military when Meade was assigned the position of post surgeon at Fort Apache. The journey had been anything but easy, but Libby made the best of every situation they encountered. After living such a cloistered existence, she seemed to look upon the experience as a great adventure. Meade worried incessantly about bringing her to such a dangerous place, but she laughed at the notion that her life might be in peril.

And she was also determined to scoff at the idea that men found her attractive. But surely, Meade thought, in this isolated outpost where women were such a rarity, his sister would finally come to realize her own value. She had so much to give, and Meade couldn't bear the thought of her wasting her life taking care of him. For her sake, he wanted her to fall in love and marry a man who would treasure her intellect and her spirit as much as or more than her beauty.

Whenever he teased Libby about finding just such a husband, she usually turned the tables and promised to get married as soon as he took a wife. For some reason, though, Meade found the idea of marriage for himself unpalatable. He enjoyed the company of women immensely, but he had yet to see a marriage that was worth the inevitable complications it would bring to his life. Meade believed he was fated to live as a bachelor, but while he had no regrets about his own unmarried state, he couldn't bear the thought of Libby living a similar life. As long as they were together, they would never be truly lonely, but Libby deserved far more than a brother could give her.

So he worried about her constantly, and kept a keen eye out for a suitable match. Major Forsythe was certainly a likely prospect, and Captain Edgemont of Company C had been quite taken with the lovely Miss Ashford. Both were from fine families and had promising careers ahead of them. And there were others as well. One thing was certain—there was no shortage of eligible bachelors at Fort Apache.

If he could just get Libby to keep an open mind, curb her tongue, and behave like a lady, he might find a husband for her before the year was out.

ELEVEN

By THE FOLLOWING EVENING Libby was satisfied that she and
Sergeant Brogan had done as much as was humanly possible
to make the new post surgeon's quarters comfortable. With
the walls painted, the furniture arranged, and all their trunks
finally unpacked, Libby gave herself over to preparing for the
party that was being held in honor of her and Meade.

Dressing was more of a chore than she would have liked.
Two days out on the trail from Santa Fe to Fort Apache,
Libby had decided bustles and corsets had no place in the
desert regions of the Southwest. Fortunately her wardrobe
contained very few fashionable gowns that demanded such
accoutrements. Her shirtwaists, aproned skirts, and simple
day frocks had suited the journey admirably, and nothing she
had encountered thus far at Fort Apache had required she
dress more formally.

Tonight was different, though. It was important to Meade's
career that he make a good impression, and his superiors'
judgments would be affected by their opinion of the surgeon's
sister. For Meade's sake, then, she spent nearly an hour
combing, crimping, and styling her long chestnut hair into a
fashionable arrangement of thick braids and curls with a
fringe of baby-fine swirls that feathered onto her forehead.
Then, with considerable reluctance, she donned a crinoline
bustle and chose one of her best gowns, a full-skirted concoction of pale blue foulard with a form-fitting basque
trimmed in navy gros grain. After weeks of enjoying relative

freedom and comfort, Libby felt as though she were wearing a straightjacket.

Meade's lavish praise made her efforts worth the nuisance, though. He looked impossibly handsome in his dress blues, and when Libby took his arm to be escorted down the quadrangle to the home of the post commander, she actually felt almost as lovely as he claimed she was. Not even his hushed admonition as they knocked on the door—"Now, behave yourself, Libby"—daunted her.

She and Meade were greeted like visiting royalty, and Libby found it remarkably easy to relax in the comfortable, attractive quarters of Colonel Grisholm Dunlevy and his wife, Elaine. A veteran of numerous campaigns at her husband's side, Elaine Dunlevy had long ago learned that surrounding herself with heirlooms and a few of the niceties of civilization was the only way to make life on the frontier bearable.

Thanks to the officers' courtesy calls, which she had yet to begin repaying, Libby had already met everyone in attendance, including the famed Indian fighter, General George Crook, who was making his headquarters at Fort Apache. The general fascinated Libby, mostly because he looked so little like her image of him. He was not a tall man, nor did he cut a commanding figure, and he seemed shy almost to the point of reticence in the presence of ladies. Yet he was the only man in the last few centuries of recorded conflict—Mexican and American—who had managed to bring the Apache Indians under even partial control.

Libby had done a considerable amount of reading on the problem of dealing with America's aborigines, and she was eager to hear Crook's thoughts on the subject. But throughout Mrs. Dunlevy's excellent dinner Libby's time was so monopolized by the other ladies that speaking to the general was out of the question. The hostess was anxious to hear the latest gossip from Washington, and Mrs. Crenshaw, a woman of astonishing beauty whose husband was currently out on scout, eagerly questioned Libby about the latest fashions.

Both women covered their disappointment admirably when they learned that Libby could provide them with very little information of the type they were seeking. Libby found she had far more in common with Susannah Robertson, who was much closer to her own age and was more concerned with the realities of daily living on the frontier than with frivolous topics such as fashion. Susannah was in the final stages of her first pregnancy, and Libby felt a great deal of sympathy for her discomfort—both physical and emotional. Her husband was the captain of Cavalry Company B and, as such, might be called upon at any moment to place himself and his troops in grave danger.

As she patiently listened to Susannah's stories of her husband's harrowing experiences against the Indians, Libby said a prayer of thanks that Meade was not attached to any of the regiments. As post surgeon, his duties would be confined primarily to the hospital, so there would be little dangerous campaigning of the sort Captain Robertson faced.

Major Forsythe, seated across the table from Libby, disengaged himself from a conversation with Susannah's husband and directed his attention to Libby. "Tell me, Miss Ashford, what did you think of the journey from Santa Fe?"

For some reason all other conversations ground to a halt and all eyes focused on Libby, as though her answer was of great import. She suddenly found herself feeling quite self-conscious. "It was unlike anything I'd ever experienced—or even imagined, Major. We live in a truly remarkable country."

"I understand you had quite a scare in the area of Apache Pass," Captain Edgemont commented, giving Libby what she interpreted as a rather condescending smile.

"Unnerving reports of Apaches on the warpath followed us throughout the journey," she replied politely. "To my knowledge, though, the only 'scare' we had came in the form of a few smoke signals that were spotted from time to time. I believe there was some concern that they might be massing for an attack, but none materialized, thank heavens."

"You traveled with the Eighth Infantry, didn't you?" Major Forsythe asked, tactfully changing the subject so as not to alarm the ladies with talk of Indians on the warpath.

Libby recognized his ploy and was somewhat irritated by it. Did he really think that the women assembled wanted to remain blissfully ignorant of any danger to themselves and their families? Rather than make an issue of it, though, she allowed the topic to drop. "Yes. They provided us with excellent escort. I don't think we could have been in better hands," she replied, then realized to whom she was speaking. "Unless, of course, we'd been traveling with the Fifth Cavalry," she added quickly.

At the other end of the table, General Crook laughed, startling everyone. "Bravo, Miss Ashford. You have the makings of a true diplomat."

The others joined in his laughter, and Libby's cheeks flamed. "Thank you, sir. I am trying my best to learn military protocol."

"It appears you're doing a fine job," Crook complimented her.

"It's kind of you to say so, sir." Libby glanced at Meade and found him beaming at her. Having impressed the general, she supposed she should leave well enough alone, but there were too many questions she wanted to ask. "General, I noticed this afternoon that a number of Indians have begun congregating several hundred yards from the fort."

Crook nodded. "Quite right. Tomorrow is rations day. The Apaches come to the fort twice a week to be counted and to receive provisions from the commissary officer."

This wasn't news to Libby, but it provided her with the opening she'd been looking for. "Isn't that demoralizing to them? Being forced at gunpoint to accept charity, having their autonomy completely usurped, and being treated like recalcitrant children—"

Mrs. Dunlevy gasped. "Recalcitrant children? My dear Libby, you are speaking of the most bloodthirsty race of Indians in the Americas! Left to their own devices, those savages would kill us all without a second thought!"

"Is it any wonder? This is their country, after all," Libby replied equitably.

Colonel Dunlevy frowned at her. "Miss Ashford, we are sitting on the soil of the United States of America. This area was ceded to us by the Mexican government in the Treaty of Guadalupe-Hidalgo twenty-six years ago."

There was nothing Libby loved more than a lively debate, and her eyes sparkled as she leaned forward. "Yes, but who ever said it was theirs to cede? The Apaches were here long before even the Spanish conquistadores. What gave Spain the right to say, 'This land is ours'?"

"The right of conquest," the colonel replied.

"Ah, but the Apaches were never conquered. If they had been, there'd be no need for military intervention now."

Meade cleared his throat and tried to nudge his sister's shins under the table, but he succeeded only in rustling her skirts and petticoats. Before he could take a more definitive action, Captain Edgemont had stepped into the fray.

"Surely, Miss Ashford, you're not suggesting we abandon this territory altogether and leave its settlers to the mercy of the Apaches."

His condescending tone was beginning to irritate Libby. "Not necessarily. But this is a vast country—millions of square miles, so I'm told. Surely there is some better way of dealing with the natives than stripping them of their pride and independence. They are human beings, after all."

"They most certainly are not!" Edgemont responded hotly. "If you'd ever seen the depredations these savages are capable of, you'd know what I mean."

"I understand your point, Captain," Libby said in a placating tone, realizing she'd opened a can of worms that were about to wiggle out of control. She still wasn't ready to give up, though. This was the most fun she'd had since Meade's college days when his friends had descended on their home and Libby had inserted herself into their lively conversations.

Keeping her smile friendly, she spread her hands in a gesture that included everyone at the table. "But I ask you, is there any gentleman here who would not resort to savagery if he had no other recourse in defending his home and family from an invasion of the sort we have perpetrated on the native Americans?"

"Indians are not Americans, Miss Ashford," the colonel said sternly.

Libby shrugged. "This is America, sir, and whether we

like it or not, the Indians *are* here. What else should we call them?''

Mrs. Dunlevy started to reply and steer the conversation into a more appropriate direction, but when Crook cleared his throat, the colonel's wife sat back and allowed the commander to have his say. Secretly she hoped the general would put Miss Ashford in her place, but the general seemed more amused than irked by the Dunlevys' outspoken quest.

''Your sentiment is noble, Miss Ashford, and admirably humanitarian. But it might interest you to know that the Apaches and other Indians I've encountered would be quite offended to hear you call them Americans. All the tribes— Sioux, Pawnee, Apache—consider themselves independent nations.''

Libby smiled at the general graciously. At last someone was addressing her as though she had a mind capable of comprehending complex issues. ''Which makes negotiating with them virtually impossible, I suppose.''

Crook nodded. ''Exactly. They've been fighting among themselves for centuries. Why, the Apaches alone are divided into at least a dozen tribes that have rarely lived in peace with one another. Our culture is so vastly different from theirs that it would be sheer folly to believe we will be able to live in harmony with them until we prove our superiority.''

''But, General, is there really no alternative to destroying their way of life so completely?''

''None that I have found, Miss Ashford,'' he said with genuine regret. ''In bringing the Apaches under control on this and several other reservations, I have done my best to institute programs that would allow them to support themselves.'' He frowned, but his displeasure was not directed at Libby. ''Unfortunately there are circumstances that are simply beyond my control.''

''You're referring to the government's failure to arrive at a uniform Indian policy,'' she guessed, earning a look of amazement from Crook and some of the others.

''You're surprisingly well informed, Miss Ashford,'' the general replied.

''I read, sir,'' she said simply. ''And I must confess that

I find the workings of our government fascinating. Though I fear it will not happen in my lifetime, I look forward to the day when women are allowed to have a say in their own destiny.''

Meade and Colonel Dunlevy both cleared their throats loudly. Everyone shifted uncomfortably, and Libby realized she had gone too far—*much* too far, if the expressions on the faces around her were any indication. She was not at all surprised when the hostess painted on a strained smile and edged her chair away from the table. ''Gentlemen, the colonel has some excellent port, and I know how you all love your cigars. . . . If you'll excuse us, your ladies shall adjourn to the parlor and leave you to your diversions.''

The officers rose as one, and as Meade helped Libby with her chair she couldn't help noting that no one was looking in her direction. She gave her brother an apologetic half smile, and Meade replied with a resigned sigh and a little shake of his head. She moved obediently toward the parlor door and in so doing passed by General Crook. She avoided looking at him and was astonished when he addressed her.

''Miss Ashford . . .'' Libby stopped and somewhat reluctantly turned to face him. ''Thank you for a most lively debate. I hope we'll have a chance to continue our conversation in the near future. One of the few liabilities of being a general is that it's difficult to scare up a good argument.''

Despite the strain in the room, everyone chuckled, and Libby made a small curtsy to the general and gave him a smile that contained equal amounts of respect and gratitude. She knew better than anyone that the general had just saved her from being a social pariah. ''That would be both a pleasure and an honor, sir.''

She turned and resumed her trek to the parlor, but before she and the other ladies were completely out of earshot they heard the general say quite clearly, ''Captain Ashford, your sister is a remarkable young lady. I hope you appreciate her candor and intellect.''

Meade's answer was lost as Mrs. Dunlevy closed the door, and Libby breathed a sigh of relief. As she took a seat on the divan beside her hostess, though, she realized her relief was premature. Crook had let her off the hook with the officers, but their wives were another matter altogether. They seated themselves while Mrs. Dunlevy served coffee, but there wasn't a hint of merriment in the room. Libby realized that nothing but an apology was going to put her back in the good graces of the officers' wives.

"Mrs. Dunlevy," she said, leaning forward earnestly when her hostess handed her a cup and saucer, "if I misspoke myself earlier, I do apologize. It's only that I was eager to hear General Crook and the other officers expound on the controversies I've been reading so much about in the eastern newspapers."

"Think nothing of it, my dear," Mrs. Dunlevy replied graciously but without warmth. "Obviously General Crook was not offended."

"But I certainly never meant to offend you"—she looked at the others—"or any of you. Meade is forever telling me I'm much too outspoken for my own good, and obviously he's right."

"You'll learn, Libby dear. You'll learn," the hostess predicted.

"Indeed you will," Mrs. Crenshaw said frostily. "The first time you watch your brother go off on a campaign, knowing you might never see him alive again, you'll learn. When you see a slain soldier for the first time and start imagining the hideous tortures that might lie in store for someone you love, you'll learn, I guarantee it. And I'll be anxious to hear you sympathize with those heathens then!"

"Caroline, please," Susannah Robertson said gently, leaning over to pat her hand. "Libby is new to the life we've chosen."

Caroline Crenshaw drew herself up, and Libby realized that she was about to cry. "Speak for yourself, Susannah. I never chose this life; my husband did." She stood abruptly. "Excuse me, Elaine, I'd like a moment to freshen up."

Mrs. Dunlevy rose as well. "Of course, dear. Let me show you to my room."

Cursing her foolish tongue, Libby watched them go, wondering if she could have made matters worse had she been trying.

"Don't look so forlorn, Libby," Susannah said with a wry, sympathetic smile. "Caroline is a bit too high strung for cavalry life, and she has a few concerns right now that you probably aren't aware of."

"Concerns?" Libby asked, grateful that she hadn't alienated everyone.

Susannah nodded and kept her voice low. "Major Crenshaw is currently in the field with Company C in search of some hostiles who fled the reservation last month. We've had no word from them for several days now, and Caroline is understandably worried."

Libby shook her head at her own folly. "Why is it that I always speak without thinking?" she said to no one in particular.

Susannah grinned conspiratorially. "Frankly, I found your conversation most refreshing. I'm sick to death of parlor talk."

Libby managed a smile. "You're only saying that to make me feel better, but I do appreciate it. Truly I do."

"Don't be silly. It was a real delight to finally hear General Crook speak out. I've rarely heard him utter more than a word or two at a time. And when you mentioned women in government!" Her eyes grew bright with laughter. "I thought Colonel Dunlevy was going to have a fit of apoplexy."

Libby thought back to the moment and couldn't repress a giggle. "He did turn an uncommon shade of red, didn't he?"

Susannah nodded and covered her mouth to control her mirth as the colonel's wife returned. Libby sobered more quickly. "Is Mrs. Crenshaw all right?" she asked with genuine concern.

"She'll be fine," Mrs. Dunlevy replied.

"I can't tell you how sorry I am for the upset I've caused. As you said, I have a great deal to learn about the realities of life here."

Her sincerity touched the army wife. "There's been no real harm done, Libby."

She shook her head. "I hope not. It's just that until this

past month, the Indian question has been nothing more than a fascinating abstraction to me, while to you ladies it's quite literally a matter of life and death. I should have known better than to spout off as I did.''

Mrs. Dunlevy reassured her once again, and the discussion was dropped when the officers joined them. Mrs. Crenshaw returned looking much more composed, and the conversation was kept to the superficial. Only once did it threaten to turn controversial, when Major Forsythe offered to take Libby on a turn around the parade grounds the next day so that she could get a closer look at the Apaches who would come into the encampment to collect their rations. Libby was delighted to accept his invitation, and Meade, who was standing casually to one side of his sister's chair, was plainly stunned that the major didn't seem put off by Libby's earlier antics. Taking that as an excellent omen, he was only too happy to give his consent when Forsythe looked to him for permission to escort his sister.

No further mention was made of the Apaches, and it seemed that the party was about to come to a conclusion when there was a knock at the door. Colonel Dunlevy gestured to his adjutant, Lieutenant Wexler, and the young officer sprang to answer it.

Mrs. Dunlevy attempted to keep the conversation going through the interruption, but Libby's concentration fled the moment the door opened and a tall, rugged-looking Apache stepped onto the threshold. Indeed the visitor's unexpected arrival captured everyone's attention, and the room grew deathly silent.

Behind the Apache in the doorway, the porch lamps illuminated two more Indians, one carrying a bag of some sort, but Libby found her gaze riveted on the apparent leader. He was at least six feet tall, with a lean build and broad shoulders that bespoke considerable strength. His coal black hair had been bluntly cut on a level with his wide, square jaw, and was held in place by a red bandanna. His eyes were deep set, and even from a distance Libby could see that they burned with an inner fire. Though he made no threatening gestures, there was a fierceness about him that Libby found both terrifying and thrilling.

He was dressed in a conglomeration of clothing that was, to say the least, confusing; knee-high moccasins and fringed buckskin trousers, over which he wore an odd sort of apron that draped in front and back, contrasted sharply with the army-issue blue shirt.

It took only a moment for her to realize that this had to be one of General Crook's Apache scouts she'd heard about on the trip from Santa Fe.

The scout said a few quiet words to Lieutenant Wexler, but before the adjutant could relay the message, Crook was already on his feet, headed for the door with the post commander and Major Forsythe right behind him. Libby watched, fascinated by the drama unfolding before her and, even more, by the scout. He reached for the bag being held by one of the others and handed it to the general. Colonel Dunlevy looked nervously over his shoulder at the ladies, and Crook made a gesture that Libby took to mean they should all step outside.

Crook turned to his hostess and begged to be excused for a moment, and then the officers filed out. The general preceded the colonel, who preceded the major, until finally only the Apache was left at the door.

"Please forgive the interruption, Mrs. Dunlevy," he said with a slight inclination of his head in her direction. His voice was so deep and his English so precise that Libby was startled.

"I understand completely," Mrs. Dunlevy replied.

"Ladies . . ." He included them all in his apology with a cursory glance that swept the room, but when his eyes fell on Libby, he seemed to freeze. His black eyes captured hers with an intensity that stilled Libby's breathing, and she had the oddest feeling that the scout wasn't seeing her for the first time. For an instant she felt an immutable connection with the Apache, something as tangible as a touch . . . and then the connection was broken. He seemed to remember where he was and, without another word, slipped out of the room.

It took Libby a moment to collect her scattered senses.

She barely heard Mrs. Dunlevy remark on the scout's odd behavior.

"Who was that?" Libby asked, trying to sound casual.

"Case Longstreet," Captain Robertson answered. "He's one of General Crook's chief Apache scouts."

Libby mulled over the information. It didn't surprise her that he was a leader; he looked like a man who would find it difficult to bow to any authority. "Case Longstreet." She frowned. "Is that an Apache name?"

"Not from what I've been able to gather," Mrs. Dunlevy replied. "He seems to have some nebulous connection with Jedidiah Longstreet, a rancher in these parts who sometimes supplies cattle to the quartermaster."

"He's a—what's the term?—a half-breed?"

"Oh, no, he's a full-blooded Apache. Make no mistake of that. He's had the training of an Apache warrior. I know very little more about him than that, actually. He's something of an enigma."

"How so?" Libby asked.

Mrs. Dunlevy shrugged vaguely. "Well, for one thing he speaks impeccable English, as I'm sure you noticed. Grisholm says he also speaks Spanish and a number of different Apache dialects, and I've heard rumors that he reads English as well as he speaks it. That alone makes him uncommon."

For some foolish reason, Libby's heart was racing. "This is fascinating. Tell me more."

"Please don't," Caroline said disdainfully. "I've had about as much Indian discussion as I can handle tonight. I'd rather not spend the remainder of the evening talking about that pretentious heathen. No matter how many languages he speaks, he's still a filthy savage."

Libby was shocked by the woman's narrow-minded attitude, but before she even had the opportunity to curb her tongue, Meade placed his hand on her shoulder to silence her. It was everything Libby could do to keep from telling him she wasn't about to make another scene, no matter what the provocation.

A moment later the officers returned, making no attempt to explain the incident that had precipitated their absence.

Libby was bursting to ask about the contents of the mysterious sack the scout had delivered, but she knew better than to inquire. She sat passively for the remainder of the evening, barely taking notice of the conversations around her. She nodded politely when it seemed appropriate and laughed delicately when everyone else laughed at something that had been said. Her mind, though, was completely preoccupied with the enigmatic Case Longstreet. She found it impossible to erase the image of his dark, captivating eyes and the way he'd studied her so intently. She contemplated the meager bits of information she'd gleaned about him, and speculated on how it would be possible to obtain more. Not once did she stop to question her motives.

Longstreet was a fascinating paradox, and next to a lively debate, there was nothing Libby Ashford loved more than solving a good puzzle.

TWELVE

NAKED EXPECT FOR a breechclout, Case crouched by the fire, waiting for the stones at its perimeter to heat. Behind him stood his sweat lodge; to his left, his wickiup; in front of him, barely visible in the darkness, was Fort Apache, a hundred yards from his camp at the base of the hill. The distance between Case and the inhabitants of the fort was so wide, though, that it might as well have been a hundred miles.

With a stick he poked at the rocks, edging them closer to the fire. Time had taught him patience, but tonight he was eager to finish the preparations for the sweat lodge. The assignment he had just completed for Crook had left him feeling unclean. He needed purification. He needed to soak the stench of death from his body. Only sweat and prayers would accomplish that.

He carried the rocks into the lodge using a forked stick, lowered the blanket flap, dropped twigs of sage on the stones, and sprinkled them with water. Steam filled the tiny enclosure, and Case sang the prayer to prevent the ghost sickness. When he had finished and sweat was pouring off his body, he sang another song, this one to his spirit, the Thunder Eagle.

As he sang, he clutched the medallion that hung around his neck from a rawhide thong. This necklace had no silver beads or nuggets of turquoise; no eagle feathers were suspended from its base. It was only a disk made of bone, carved with the image of the Thunder Eagle. The day when he would replace it with the necklace that had been stolen from his mother would soon be at hand. Gato was close; Case's quest was almost at an end. Eleven years ago the eagle had taken him on a spirit journey, laying scenes from his life before him, and one by one those visions had become reality. The unknown faces in his dream were of people he now knew. The places he had visited with the eagle, he had later seen with his own eyes. Over the years Jedidiah had shown him many wonders of the white man's world, even taking him to cities in the East, but everything Case had seen there had earlier been revealed to him in his spirit journey.

And now one more vision had become a reality. Before he left on his last assignment, Case had heard that a new post surgeon was en route to Fort Apache and that he was bringing his sister with him. Their name was Ashford. If Case had been informed correctly, the woman he had seen tonight was the sister of the new doctor.

She was also the gentle-eyed creature in his dream who had tried so hard to erase his torment. The vision of her face had stayed with him through all these years, hovering on the edge of his consciousness. He held the image of her above all the others, because throughout the torturous spirit journey, she had been the only ray of hope, the only vestige of peace and contentment in an otherwise horrifying nightmare. In quite moments of despair and confusion, Case had sometimes called to her, and she had comforted him.

Even now, in the sweat lodge, she seemed to be calling to him. Case tried to ignore her voice, but she had been a part of him for so many years that it was impossible to turn away from her. He told himself that she was only one more omen that had been fulfilled, bringing him one step closer to Gato . . . to revenge.

Over the years he had been close to Gato many times. For months after the massacre, Case and Jedidiah had searched Mexico for some clue to the fate that had befallen their beloved Morning Star. They had found no trace. The little girl seemed to have vanished off the face of the earth. In his heart Case believed she was alive, but with every year that passed his hope of finding her grew weaker. She was a young maiden now. The memories of her former life had surely dimmed. Wherever she was, Case prayed that her life was happy, but he knew that was unlikely.

The thought of the physical and emotional tortures Morning Star must have suffered was one of the things that kept his hatred for Gato burning so intensely. Like Case, Jedidiah had been bent on killing the renegade, but the frontiersman had become frustrated at not being able to find him, at chasing him but always being one step behind.

Case had felt no such disappointment; he had known it was not time. Only when all of his visions had come true would he have his revenge on Gato. In the meantime he had been content with letting the Chiricahua renegade know that he was being pursued, that someone was waiting for him patiently, biding his time, gathering power until the moment of retribution was at hand.

In the world of the Apache, everything had a power all its own, and with the help of his grandfather, Case had learned how to use those powers. But the white man had powers as well—many kinds that went far beyond the capabilities of their rifles, cannons, and seemingly endless supply of ammunition. There was a kind of power that could be gained from association with a man of influence who controlled the fate of many.

General Crook was just such a man. When he had announced his desire to enlist Apache scouts in his effort to bring all the southwestern tribes under control, he had met with the White Mountain Apaches under a flag of truce and persuaded many of them to help him. When Crook learned about Case Longstreet, he had sought him out personally and in so doing had turned another of Case's visions into a reality. Case had found much to respect in the general and had agreed to help him bring peace to Apacheria. His knowledge of languages, his country, and his people had made him invaluable to the general. With the help of the Apache scouts Case led, Crook had come closer to achieving peace than any military man before him.

Case knew that a few men at Fort Apache would never look at him as anything other than a savage, but in the field,

when their lives were in peril, they respected Case Longstreet. More important, General Crook respected him, and
that gave Case tremendous power.

In the end, when it came time to meet Gato, Case knew
that this power above all others would help him meet his
destiny and prevail. He had lived for no other reason. He had
studied long and hard to master the white man's difficult language. He had learned their manners and customs. He had
learned to read their stories. He had visited their cities and
had suffered insults and even an occasional whipping, all in
the name of revenge. Gato would be his, and soon.

The knowledge of this should have made Case stronger,
for the hatred in his heart still burned as brightly as it had on
the day of his parents' death. Yet the strength he sought in
the sweat lodge would not seem to come. The vision of the
woman danced before him, replacing resolve with confusion.

For eleven years he had known he would meet her someday. When he thought of her, it was as *his* woman. It had
seemed a harmless enough illusion then. But Case was no
fool. *His* woman was white, and nowhere in his travels had
he found a place where an Apache could claim a white woman
as his own.

This white woman, with her wide, soft eyes and cream-
colored skin, had some place in the grand design of his revenge against Gato; of that Case was certain. But she had
never been meant to be his woman. He had no choice but to
accept that now and let go of his foolish fantasy.

He stayed in the sweat bath for an hour or more, praying
for the purification of his body and mind. He prayed for the
completion of his quest. He prayed for the eagle to take back
the vision of the woman named Ashford . . .

If not for his sake, then for hers.

Shortly before ten the next morning, Libby stepped out of
her quarters and surveyed the spectacle on the parade
ground. At the east end of the quadrangle near the stables,
four stakes had been driven into the ground, and hundreds of
Indians were lined up behind them. Some were sitting, some
standing, and the lines stretched almost the complete length

of the enormous parade ground. There had to be a thousand, at least, she decided, and possibly even more than that. One thing was certain—there were more than twice as many Apaches as soldiers in the fort today.

Common logic told Libby that being in such close proximity to so many "wild" Indians should imbue her with at least a modicum of fear, and yet she could muster none at all. She felt instead an overwhelming fascination laced with sadness. These were a conquered people; yet in every face she studied, she saw a flicker of pride or, just as often, a trace of humiliation.

Libby was eager to walk among them, but more than that, she wanted to talk to them, ask them about their lives, so that she could better understand what they were thinking and feeling. Conversation would be unlikely, though, if Mrs. Dunlevy's remarks last night were any indication; apparently Case Longstreet was one of the few English-speaking Apaches in the area.

Libby's thoughts drifted back to her strange encounter with the scout. Her desire to know more about him had not abated, but her only source of information since the dinner party had been Sergeant Brogan. As he assisted her in preparing breakfast, Libby had questioned the striker about the scout, but Brogan had muttered something about "that damned uppity Injun," and Libby had let the subject drop.

She hoped to have better luck questioning Major Forsythe if she could find a casual way of broaching the subject when he called for her. The major was to have met her at ten, though, and as Libby surveyed the parade ground she saw no sign of him. She glanced at command headquarters on the northwest end of the quadrangle, then at post HQ opposite it on the southwest end. She saw a number of officers coming and going, and even caught a glimpse of the insufferable Captain Edgemont as he entered Crook's command station, but no Major Forsythe.

She was about to return her attention to the Apaches when something new caught her eye. At the entrance to the fort, which was situated between the headquarters buildings, two tall posts topped with odd-looking ornaments had been

erected, flanking the entrance. She was certain they hadn't
been there the day before, and Libby's curiosity got the better
of her. Since there were no restrictions against her wandering
around the post unescorted, she slipped on her wide-brimmed
shepherdess hat, affixed it with pins, and took off past the
row of officers' quarters that stood between the hospital and
post headquarters.

Soldiers touched the brims of their hats in an informal salute to her, and Libby was aware that she had attracted the
attention of some of the Apaches across the compound, but
no one accosted her as she made her way toward the nearer
post. When she finally drew close enough to have a better
view of the "ornament," though, her steps faltered. A hideous, sinking feeling overcame her. It was . . .

No. Common sense—nay, common decency—told her she
couldn't be seeing what she was seeing. It simply wasn't
possible. . . . And yet every step closer seemed to confirm
her suspicion, until she was less than a dozen feet away and
there was no denying that the bauble adorning the post was
a human head.

A ragged mane of black hair, encrusted with blood,
streamed down the wooden pylon. The features were hideously contorted, and unmistakably Apache.

Sickened, Libby brought one hand to her mouth as she
whirled away. The world tilted crazily, and she closed her
eyes, fighting back a wave of nausea. When she opened her
eyes again, a man was standing in front of her, his broad
chest obscuring her view. The unexpected presence of someone so close startled her, but the moment of fear passed and
her shock mingled with anger when she realized that the man
was the Apache scout, Case Longstreet.

She stepped back, her breath still coming in short pants.
With a flash of appalling insight, she remembered the mysterious coffee sack the Apache had delivered to the colonel's
house last night. Now she knew what it had contained.

"Are you all right?" Case asked, concerned by her pallor.
He'd been leaving Colonel Dunlevy's office when he noticed
her passing by. He had hesitated a moment, fighting the impulse to call out to her, resisting the need to hear her voice.

There was no reason for an Apache scout to speak to any of the ladies on the post, though. He had started to turn away, until he realized where she was headed. He jumped off the porch to intercept her, telling himself that he would have tried to spare any of the ladies the shock Miss Ashford had coming, but he was too late.

She saw the bloody dismembered head of Alchinay. She whirled on unsteady legs, and Case fought the urge to steady her. When she opened her eyes and looked at him, his heart sank. The wide-eyed look of curiosity she'd worn last night was gone. The moment she recognized him, cold contempt seized her features.

Libby stared up at him, her image of him blurring with the image of the disembodied head. Her curiosity about the scout and all her humanitarian sentiments about the noble red man vanished in an instant.

"What is that doing there?" she demanded harshly as soon as she could find her voice.

Case took a step back, trying to separate himself from her contempt. His face became an unreadable mask. "I believe it's meant to be a warning, Miss Ashford." He gestured to the docile Indians behind him. "A reminder of what can happen to those who choose to reject the white man's . . . generosity."

The bitterness behind his words barely registered on Libby, nor did she stop to wonder how he had learned her name. "It's barbaric!"

"I quite agree."

"Then take it down at once."

"I didn't put it there, and if I had the authority to remove it, I would. My people don't believe in displaying the dead."

"But obviously you have no trouble dismembering them!"

Case finally realized that she believed he had beheaded the chief. She was like all the others, condemning him as a savage without knowing who he was or what he believed. His eyes grew cold. "You couldn't be more wrong."

"Then why did you do it?" she retorted. "That head was in the sack you brought to General Crook last night, wasn't it?"

Case had never justified himself to any white man; he wouldn't start with this woman, no matter how much her censure wounded him. "Yes."

Libby had never been so confused in her life. Last night she had felt something for this handsome, enigmatic Apache. She hadn't dared label it as physical attraction, but it had been a soft emotion enhanced by her innate curiosity. Now she felt nothing but disgust. "How could you do something so vile?"

"I did what General Crook ordered me to do."

Libby's eyes widened. "I don't believe you."

"Then I suggest you ask him yourself."

"I will," she said curtly. She whirled toward command headquarters and found herself looking once again at the head on the stake. A wave of nausea overcame her, and the ground began spinning beneath her feet. Her knees buckled, but before she could fall, Case's arms were supporting her.

"Longstreet! Unhand Miss Ashford at once!" Andrew Forsythe bellowed from the porch of post headquarters.

The order captured the attention of everyone on the parade ground, and in an instant a dozen officers and soldiers were bearing down on Case, with Major Forsythe leading the pack.

When she realized she had suddenly become a spectacle, humiliation compounded Libby's light-headedness, but she made every effort to stand on her own. She had never fainted before, and she wasn't about to start a trend at this stage of her life. "I'm fine," she said to the scout, but with less conviction than she would have liked. "Please let me go."

Case complied and stepped back as Forsythe reached Libby's side. Though she seemed steady enough, the major took her hand and placed his other arm at her waist. "Are you all right, Miss Libby?" he asked solicitously.

"I'm fine, Major," she assured him. "There's no need for all this fuss."

Forsythe pinned Case with a contemptuous glare. "You will wait for me in my office, Longstreet."

Though the major's proprietary air galled Case, he didn't let the officer see it. He'd spent years making sure that no white man could read the thoughts and feelings behind his eyes. He nodded curtly and glanced at Libby, but she refused to acknowledge his presence. Only when he had moved off toward command headquarters did she raise her eyes to follow his retreat. But he had no way of knowing that.

When the other soldiers who'd gathered saw that the situation was under control, they drifted off, leaving the major to see to the lady's welfare.

"I can't tell you how sorry I am, Miss Libby," he said in a tone that was meant to soothe. "I take full responsibility for this unfortunate incident. If I had been on time for our appointment, this could have been avoided."

Libby was having difficulty focusing on his words. Her thoughts were still preoccupied with Case and the horrible brutality he had committed. "I'm sure you had an excellent reason for being tardy, Major. I know what a demanding position you hold." His arm was still at her waist, and Libby was finding the closeness discomforting. Gently she eased away from him.

"Nonetheless, this never should have happened. I promise you, Longstreet will be severely punished for the liberties he took with you."

Libby frowned. "What liberties?"

Forsythe looked surprised by the question. "He placed his arms around you."

She sighed impatiently. "He prevented me from falling in the dirt when he thought I was going to faint." She pointed toward the dismembered head, but didn't make the mistake of looking at it again. "If you're going to punish him for something, *there's* all the excuse you need."

Forsythe glanced at the post, and the full picture of what had happened finally slipped into place. "I'm terribly sorry you were subjected to such a shock, Miss Libby. The heads of Alchinay and Klo-sen were placed out here as a deterrent to other chiefs who might be tempted to take their people on the warpath. I should have seen to it that you were warned."

"This is barbaric," she said again, but with considerably less force now that she had calmed down somewhat.

"But it is necessary," he insisted gently. "These two chiefs were responsible for the death of twenty-two soldiers and civilians in the past six months. Our troops have been dogging them so ruthlessly that their followers wanted to return to the reservation, but General Crook felt they couldn't be trusted. He refused to allow them to return and receive rations until they sent him the heads of their chiefs. Which they have done.''

Libby absorbed this new information. ''Then what you're telling me, Major Forsythe, is that Case Longstreet didn't actually behead these men.''

''Of course he didn't. He was merely acting as go-between on General Crook's orders.''

''I see.'' The savageness of the act still troubled Libby, but she was amazed at the relief she suddenly felt. No wonder Longstreet's handsome face had turned to stone when she accused him of committing this barbarous act. He'd only been following orders, and the war-weary Apaches had simply been ensuring their survival in the only manner open to them.

Libby was suddenly ashamed of having jumped to the wrong conclusion so easily. She had accused Case and judged him guilty without allowing him the opportunity to defend himself.

Forsythe read the expression of relief that played over her delicate face, and wondered why her mistaken belief that the Apache scout had committed the depredations had disturbed her so much. He remembered the sympathetic attitude toward the Indians she had voiced last night, and surmised that she was merely relieved because her beliefs had not been undermined.

''You're very pale, Miss Libby,'' he said solicitously, and gestured toward the hospital. ''Please allow me to escort you back to your quarters. We can postpone our tour of the post until another time.''

Libby hated being perceived as weak, but her legs were still wobbly and her curiosity about the Apaches had been dampened, at least temporarily. ''Thank you, Major. I believe I would like to return home.'' She accepted his arm, and they started down the quadrangle. ''I'm sure you have duties to perform.''

"You're quite right. And I assure you that the first of those will be to see to the punishment of Case Longstreet."

Libby was confused. "Punishment for what?"

"The liberties he took with you," Forsythe said as though speaking to a child. "That cannot be allowed to pass."

Libby stopped and withdrew her hand from the crook of his arm. "Major, I told you before, Mr. Longstreet did not take liberties with me. He was merely coming to my aid."

"Nonetheless, he should not have touched you."

Her shoulders straightened in indignation. "*You* touched me, Major Forsythe," she reminded him. "Are you going to see to your own punishment as well?"

She had a point that gave the officer a moment's pause as he tried to figure out a way to explain the difference to her.

"Well?" she demanded.

"It's not the same thing, Miss Ashford. However, if you feel that I took liberties, I will by all means apologize."

Libby's hands went to her hips and she sighed with exasperation. Was the major dense, or had the Arizona sun addled her own brain? "My point, Major Forsythe, is that *no one* took liberties with me. You acted out of concern, as did Mr. Longstreet."

"But *he* never should have presumed to touch you."

"Because he's an Indian?"

Forsythe smiled thinly. Now he was getting somewhere. "Precisely."

"Are you suggesting that he should have allowed me to fall on my face in the dirt?"

The major was becoming irritated. "He should never have approached you in the first place."

Libby thought back to the moment she'd encountered the scout this morning. "I believe he saw my distress and was—"

"Then he should have called an officer for assistance," Forsythe asserted forcefully.

Libby shook her head. "Obviously we're never going to agree on this. But let me make myself clear, Major Forsythe—I do not want Case Longstreet punished."

"Begging your pardon, miss, but that's not up to you. I

cannot allow any of the ladies of this fort to be manhandled by an Apache, no matter who he is or how much faith General Crook puts in him.''

Libby looked to the heavens. ''Now we're up to manhandling! My God, Major, at this rate you'll be charging Mr. Longstreet with attempted rape before the day is over!''

''Miss Ashford!''

She lowered her voice, but the intensity of her speech made the officer take notice. ''Major Forsythe, I do not want Case Longstreet punished for performing an act of common courtesy. Now, if you do not give me your word as an officer and a gentleman that you will drop this matter immediately, I will march into General Crook's office and explain the situation to him personally.''

The determined set of her jaw told the major that she wasn't bluffing. Because Crook placed so much reliance on Longstreet, Forsythe knew there was an element of doubt regarding whose side the general would take in such a situation. Though he was convinced of the rightness of his decision, it really wasn't worth the risk. ''All right, Miss Ashford. If you feel that you suffered no insult in being''—he started to say ''accosted'' and quickly switched—''assisted by an Apache, then I will allow the matter to pass.''

Libby remembered the incident and was surprised to realize that she'd felt far more comfortable with Case Longstreet's arms around her than she had in a similar position with Major Forsythe. It didn't seem prudent to tell him that, though. ''Thank you.''

''And now . . .'' He gestured toward her quarters, indicating that they should resume their stroll, but Libby stepped away from him.

''Please, Major, don't trouble yourself. I've been too much of a bother to you already. I'm sure I can find my way home without further incident.''

He bowed lightly and touched the brim of his hat. ''In that case, I'll leave you here.'' He started to turn away, but Libby suddenly had a pang of conscience for the way she'd spoken to him. She held out her hand to stop him.

''Major . . . One more thing.''

He looked at her expectantly.

Libby was uncomfortable. She wasn't good at apologizing, but she seemed to be doing a lot of it since arriving at Fort Apache. "I merely wanted to tell you how much I appreciate your concern for me. I realize that despite our difference of opinion, you were acting in what you felt were my best interests. If I reacted too harshly, I apologize."

Andrew Forsythe regarded her with open puzzlement. One minute Miss Liberty Ashford was salt and vinegar, the next she was honeyed wine. She had a sharp tongue, but her smile was sweet enough to take the sting out of anything she said. Her intelligence was obvious, but her unorthodox ideas only proved that educating women was a dangerous thing.

He's never met a woman so full of contradictions.

"Think nothing of it, Miss Libby. You're new here, and—if you'll forgive my saying so—you have a lot to learn. You'll soon come to understand the realities of life in Arizona."

An image of Alchinay's head flashed through her mind. "I believe I had my first lesson today," she said sadly.

With a nod of understanding, Forsythe touched his hat again and left. Libby returned to her quarters and, once she was inside, sank into her grandmother's rocking chair. A renewed bout of trembling seized her, and for the first time since she and Meade had left Washington, she truly regretted having followed her brother to this godforsaken wilderness.

THIRTEEN

"ARE N'T YOU TIRED of acting so brave, Susannah?" Libby asked, handing her new friend a cup of tepid water. The weather had turned miserably hot, and the pregnant cavalry wife was suffering terribly. Meade had taken a look at her, announced that her baby could arrive at any time, and advised complete bed rest. Since Susannah's husband and their striker were preoccupied with their post duties most of the time, Libby had started visiting several times a day to see to the poor woman's needs. "If I were about to have the first baby ever born at Fort Apache, I'd be absolutely terrified."

Susannah gave Libby one of her sweet, benevolent smiles. "I must confess that until you and your brother arrived last week I was worried, but having a bona fide physician on post rather than a rummy bone-cutter has eased my mind considerably." She reached for Libby's hand, and tears formed in her eyes. "And you, my dear friend . . . I can't imagine how I would have survived this week without you."

Libby patted her hand fondly, touched by her emotion. "I've enjoyed every moment. In case you haven't noticed, there's very little to do out here. One can see the guard mount only so many days in a row before it begins to lose some of its charm."

Susannah laughed. "You've been here ten days, Libby. You can't be bored out of your mind, yet. It's against army regulations."

"Well, for heaven's sake, don't tell anyone," Libby said,

her voice lowered conspiratorially. "I'm in enough trouble around here as it is."

"Things have been lively since your arrival," Susannah said wryly. She studied her new friend speculatively. "Have you seen that scout, Longstreet, since your encounter last week?"

Libby's smile faded. "Not even a glimpse, and I do want so much to apologize to him for the misunderstanding." She didn't add that she'd been spending far too much time thinking about him. She rationalized her curiosity by telling herself she was interested in learning more about *all* the Indians in the area of Fort Apache, but that was lame logic.

"And Major Forsythe?" Susannah asked.

"I've already apologized to him."

"No, I meant have you seen him again?"

"Only in passing. He manages to be polite." She sighed wistfully. "Meade is furious with me for alienating him. Confidentially, I think my brother is trying to marry me off."

"Men!" Susannah shook her head in disbelief. "Did you tell him you're perfectly capable of handling that yourself?"

"Hardly, since the facts would seem to suggest otherwise. So far I haven't done an exceptional job of attracting even the slightest prospect."

The comment was meant to be humorous, but Susannah chose to take it seriously. "Does that bother you, Libby?"

"Not particularly," she answered truthfully. "It is strange, though. Most women my age are at least *contemplating* marriage."

"And you never have?"

"Only in vague terms," she confessed. "Does that mean there's something wrong with me?"

"Not at all," Susannah assured her.

"I don't know . . ." Libby mused thoughtfully. "I guess I've always felt that there was something . . . special in store for me."

"All girls feel that way."

"No, not like this," Libby replied. "When I think of the future, trying to imagine myself in it, I don't see myself in ordinary settings."

"What do you mean by 'ordinary'?"

Libby shrugged. "Oh, social calls and lawn parties, fussy parlors and servants to bring in tea at four, playing lawn tennis . . . raising daughters whose deepest concern is what to wear to the next cotillion." She hesitated. She'd never told this to anyone, not even Meade, and she was amazed that she was doing so now. Libby had never formed a friendship as quickly as this new one with Susannah Robertson, but it seemed right to confess her darkest fear.

She leaned forward intently. "Sometimes I wonder if my inability to imagine myself in the future is a"—she struggled to find the words—"well, a sign of some sort."

Susannah frowned. "A sign of what?"

Libby shrugged helplessly. "That I'm not meant to have a future."

"You mean that you'll die young?" her friend asked, clearly astonished. "Libby, what a horrible thing to suggest. You're going to live a long and happy life, I guarantee it."

"You're probably right," Libby said with a chuckle. "I'll grow old taking care of my brother, or if he eventually marries, I'll play spinster auntie to his cotillion-clad daughters."

"Libby, you're impossible," Susannah told her. "I predict that before the year is out, you'll be married to some gallant officer of the Fifth Cavalry, and that special life you mentioned will be an exciting jounce from one military outpost to another."

"You're an optimist, Susannah," Libby accused. "But even you must admit that I'm not the sort of woman most men are looking for when they go to choose a wife."

"You make it sound as though men choose wives in the same manner they select their tailor or a fine bottle of wine." She shook her head. "It doesn't work that way, Libby. Any man worth his salt marries because he's found a woman he can't live without."

Libby sighed. "Well, thus far in my life I've met a number of men who are more than happy to live without me."

"But you're too beautiful for that to last long."

"That's what Meade keeps telling me. Perhaps if I could learn to curb my tongue I'd discover he's right."

Susannah laughed. "You go right on being yourself, Liberty Ashford. Somewhere in this world is a man who will appreciate all the wonderful things you have to offer."

With that pronouncement they changed the subject, and Libby prepared a light dinner for them. Afterward she helped Susannah move from the sofa to her bed, then left her alone for an afternoon nap.

But as Libby returned to her own quarters, the conversation stayed with her. Her unmarried state didn't really bother Libby; she hadn't seen enough examples of truly happy marriages to make her want the institution for herself. What was beginning to trouble her, though, was Meade's apparent determination to find her a husband. It made Libby feel she was becoming a burden to her brother, and that was one thing she had always sworn she would never be.

Unfortunately, the idea of marrying just to please Meade was totally unacceptable. And even if it hadn't been, there was a marked scarcity of suitable prospects. In the short time she'd been there, she'd met a score of unmarried officers, but not one appealed to Libby. That in itself wasn't bothersome; what was beginning to irritate her was her—and Meade's—preoccupation with the subject.

Determined not to give it another thought, Libby stepped onto the porch that ran in front of her quarters and the hospital. What she found there made her gloomy thoughts vanish. Sergeant Brogan had finally found the time to build her a flower box. It was long and crudely constructed, but it would certainly serve Libby's needs. She'd brought seed packets in the hope of having at least a modest garden, but the moment she'd seen the barren landscape around the fort, she'd known a garden was impossible.

A flower box was not out of the question, though. Sergeant Brogan had been skeptical about the venture and had cautioned her not to get her hopes up. Libby felt sure he had simply been too kindhearted to tell her that her plants hadn't a prayer of surviving an Arizona summer. But no matter what it took, she was determined to have flowers.

Elated by the challenge ahead of her, she set to work immediately. The first step had to be moving the box from the edge of the porch where Brogan had placed it, but her excursion into horticulture came to a grinding halt when she discovered that the box was too heavy for her to move. Undaunted, she dashed inside and called for the sergeant, but he was nowhere to be found.

"Splendid," she muttered, returning to the porch. Shading her eyes, she glanced over the parade ground, hoping to catch a glimpse of someone she knew, but luck was not with her.

And then she saw Case Longstreet standing in front of the sutler's store next to the hospital. Here, at last, was the chance to apologize she'd been looking for, and since she was in need of assistance, no one could possibly criticize her for speaking to the scout.

"Mr. Longstreet!" she called, hurrying down the boardwalk past the hospital. "May I have a moment, please?"

Case turned and was astonished to see Libby hurrying toward him. He'd noticed her, of course, the moment he stepped out of the sutler's store. She was the reason he'd paused instead of going on about his business. Though it was foolish—probably even insane—he'd been trying to think of an excuse to speak to her. There wasn't one, though. To approach her would have been inappropriate. He hadn't needed the degrading lecture of Major Forsythe last week to convince him of that. He knew better than anyone that the social chasm between himself and Libby Ashford was wider than the continent of America—and infinitely more difficult to cross.

He'd been prepared to slip away quietly; now there was no question of leaving. He stepped toward her as she approached, meeting her just as she reached the end of the porch. She was so beautiful that she nearly took his breath away, but he betrayed that emotion by not so much as a flicker of an eyelash. "Good afternoon, Miss Ashford," he said, his tone and his expression guarded.

Being on the porch afforded Libby the opportunity to look at the scout almost eye to eye. It was a unique sensation. On the parade ground last week, she'd been much too distraught to analyze her startling physical reaction to him, but now she was experiencing the same incomprehensible stirrings she'd felt at their first meeting. He was an incredibly handsome man, but the things that moved Libby were the intensity of his eyes and the aura of barely controlled power he exuded.

"Good afternoon, Mr. Longstreet. I . . ." Her heart was racing, her mouth was dry, and for a moment she completely forgot why she'd called to him.

Case found her sudden bout of shyness amusing. She didn't strike him as the sort of woman who would often be at a loss for words. "Yes?" he prompted, barely maintaining control of the smile that played around his lips.

When Libby realized he was trying not to laugh at her, she felt like a complete fool. But rather than turning red with embarrassment, she smiled. "I wanted to ask a favor of you, but I'm not doing a very good job of it."

"Not yet," he agreed, making Libby laugh. How anyone could call this man a savage was beyond her.

She turned and gestured toward the empty flower box at the other end of the porch. "I need that contraption moved, and I'm afraid it's too heavy for me to handle alone. Would you mind?"

Case knew he should call to one of the soldiers down by the stables to assist her, but he couldn't resist the opportunity to speak with the woman who'd haunted so many of his dreams. "Not at all."

He stepped onto the porch, and she strolled along beside him, adjusting her stride to his. "I also wanted an opportunity to apologize, Mr. Longstreet. Last week I made some very unkind assumptions, which I deeply regret."

Case looked down at her, surprised. "Considering the shock you'd had, I'd say that your conclusions were natural ones."

Libby noticed for the first time that he had a faint foreign accent that was quite pleasing. "Still, I'm not very proud of myself. It certainly put us off on the wrong foot, as they say."

Case wondered why it should matter that she make a good impression on him. "Does that make a difference to you?" he couldn't keep from asking. "We're not likely to run into each other often—formally or otherwise."

Was that bitterness or regret she heard in his voice? Or

perhaps a hint of both? Considering his intelligence, his command of the language, and his obvious knowledge of American customs and manners, bitterness would certainly be justified . . . but regret? Why would he have reason to regret their vastly different social standing? Instead of pondering those questions, she forced herself to concentrate on the one he had asked. "It disturbed me a great deal."

"Why?"

They had reached their destination, but neither of them gave a thought to the wooden box at their feet. Libby was looking up at him, astounded by how natural it seemed to talk to him so freely. "When I saw you at Colonel Dunlevy's, I was intrigued by the possibility that there might be someone here who could tell me about the Apaches—not just the wartime activities we read so much about back east, but about who they are in times of peace."

"That interests you?"

Libby could tell that he was surprised—and a little pleased as well. "Very much. But then, at our first real meeting, I jumped to all the wrong conclusions and spoke quite disgracefully to you. You see, when I discovered that my brother and I were coming to the Arizona Territory, I swore that I would take a broad view of the Indian question. I wanted to examine it carefully from both sides before forming too many opinions about what the army is doing out here."

Case found himself frowning. "You say that as though there's some question in your mind about the rightness of your government's expansion policies."

"Oh, I have plenty of questions, but I'm afraid they're all moot." She gave him a self-effacing smile. "President Grant and the members of Congress couldn't care less about the opinions of Miss Liberty Ashford."

Liberty. Her name was Liberty. Case clung to the piece of information. "They couldn't care less about the plight of the Apache either."

"I know."

Her voice was sad, and Case recognized her sincerity. "Why should that bother you, Miss Ashford?" he asked earnestly, without rancor. "You've never lived among my people, have you?"

"No." Libby thought back to the dismal years after her mother's death. "But I know what it's like to be torn from my home, to live on charity, and to be made to feel that I'm less than what I am. Your people have had their freedom taken away from them. I . . ." She hesitated, wondering if he thought she sounded terribly condescending. "I guess I feel a sort of empathy with them."

Case could hardly believe what he was hearing. "Your attitude is an uncommon one."

"And unpopular," she said ruefully.

"If you expect to make a home here, you should keep it to yourself," he advised.

She chuckled. "I'm afraid it's too late for that. I've already scandalized the entire post."

Case frowned. "Is that how I escaped punishment last week?" After the way Major Forsythe had bellowed at him and ordered him to wait in his office, Case had expected more than a reprimand. He had assumed the major was "generous" because of Case's long-standing relationship with General Crook, but now he realized he might have been mistaken.

Libby waved his question away airily. "The major and I disagreed on the interpretation of the events that transpired that morning, but I assured him that you were not at all to blame." She glanced away from him. "In fact, I told him that, considering the horrible accusations I'd hurled at you, you would have been justified in letting me fall on my face."

What she *didn't* say told Case more than her actual words. Forsythe had indeed wanted to punish him, and Liberty Ashford had damaged her own status by defending the actions of an Apache. Life here was hard under the best of circumstances, but because of him, her life had become much more difficult. The thought didn't please Case. "Don't ever defend me again, Miss Ashford."

She looked up at him, startled by the harshness of his tone. "I was only doing what was right."

"There is no 'right' when it comes to the Apache. You'll learn that soon enough."

Libby gasped with indignation. "I am sick to death of having everyone tell me I'll learn! What is so wrong with having beliefs and standing up for them? Aren't women allowed to possess a sense of honor, or is that just the purview of men?"

This time Case couldn't repress his smile. In his reading and study of the white culture, he'd learned the word "spitfire," but Liberty Ashford was the first person he'd ever been able to apply it to. He discovered that he liked her spirit very much. There was a word she'd used, though, that was not in his vocabulary, and when she scowled at him, demanding to know what was so funny, he felt no embarrassment about asking, "What does it mean—'purview'?"

Libby's irritation dissolved, and she smiled. "It means the limits of someone's authority or responsibility."

Case nodded, considering the definition, then gave her a gentlemanly bow. "Well, Miss Ashford, I'm not sure that this is a good time to discuss the boundaries of honor, but it is within my . . . purview to help you move this." He gestured to Sergeant Brogan's creation. "I would appreciate it if you'd answer one question for me, though."

Libby was only too happy to let their argument drop. There were too many things she wanted to learn about Case Longstreet to waste these few precious minutes quarreling. Already several soldiers in the quadrangle had noticed her speaking to the scout, and if past experience was any indication, she guessed they were probably debating whether or not to come to her rescue. "Ask anything you like."

He squatted beside the long wooden box. "How did a watering trough get onto your porch?"

Libby laughed. "That, sir, is a flower box."

Case looked up at her. "You're going to grow cactus on your front porch?"

She straightened her shoulders proudly. "No, I am going to grow zinnias, asters, and perhaps even a few daisies. By autumn the post hospital will be awash with color."

She looked so determined and proud that Case hated to burst her bubble. "By autumn your flowers will be withered and brown—if you can get them to come up at all."

"They will come up, Mr. Longstreet, and they will survive. A little . . . ordure from the stables mixed with the earth will make a quite acceptable potting soil."

Case had never heard the word "ordure," but he didn't need to ask the definition. "I'm afraid all the stable mix in Fort Apache won't be enough to make this soil fertile, Miss Ashford." He lifted one end of the flower box experimentally, and finding it too unwieldy to lift, he gave it a push in the direction of the wall. With Libby helping him guide it, they managed to get it into position under the parlor window while they argued.

"I'm going to have flowers," she insisted.

"Not with this dirt," he countered. "My people learned hundreds of years ago that nothing will grow on this particular piece of land but scrub and cactus."

Libby considered that. "Then I'll just have to find some more suitable earth. There, that's fine." She straightened as Case stood. "This is your country. Where would you suggest I look? General Crook has been encouraging farming on the reservation, so there must be some place where things will grow."

Case thought a moment. "There is a valley below a place called Cottonwoods Joining. Flowers grow wild there in the spring, covering two hillsides for as far as the eye can see." He smiled faintly, as though remembering something. "It is a favorite spot to place the courting stones."

"Courting stones?"

He explained the tradition, and Libby smiled, imagining the valley he'd described and a proud Apache brave in hiding, waiting for the girl he loved to walk the flower-strewn path. The image of Case Longstreet replaced the face of the imaginary Indian she'd conjured, and her smile faded a little. "That's a lovely custom."

"And practical," he replied. "It's kept many a young brave from being shamed. There's very little that's worse to an Inday than suffering humiliation."

"Inday?"

"It's what my people call themselves," he explained. "Apache is a name that was given to us by our enemies."

"I see." She paused for a moment, trying to curb her tongue, but she couldn't keep from asking, "Have you ever placed the courting stones out for a maiden?"

The warm lights in Case's eyes dimmed. "No."

"I'm sorry," she said quickly.

He looked down at her, his expression cold and unreadable. "Why should you apologize?"

"I spoke out of turn. That was impolite." She shrugged helplessly. "It's just that you looked as though you were remembering something pleasant when you talked about the stones. I thought perhaps it was where you courted your wife."

"I have no wife," Case said, more harshly than he intended. When his family teased him about not being married, he explained that he could not choose a wife until he had fulfilled his quest for revenge. That was only partly true, but Case could not explain to anyone—least of all Miss Liberty Ashford—that the image of a soft-eyed white woman had filled his mind so completely that there had never been room for any other maiden.

He softened his tone and explained, "The place I mentioned is where my father placed the courting stones for my mother. Their families had been enemies for generations, but their marriage brought many years of peace—the last my people ever knew. Or may ever know," he added quietly.

Libby felt his sadness as keenly as if it were her own. "I'd like to know more about your parents," she said, hoping it would encourage him to keep talking. "Perhaps I could even meet them someday."

His expression of sorrow did not change, but a shudder rippled down Libby's spine a moment before he replied, "That is not possible. They are dead."

Libby's parents were also deceased, but she knew instinctively that the grief she felt over the passing of her neglectful parents wasn't comparable to what Case Longstreet felt. When he spoke of his parents, it was with love. All Libby had of her own parents was regret for the things that should have been but never were. "I am truly sorry" was all she could manage to say.

Case looked down at her and was touched by her sincerity in ways he had only imagined possible. The look she wore was one he had seen in his visions a hundred times. It was soft and warm. It offered comfort and asked for nothing in return. He wanted to thrust the vision out of his mind, but he couldn't because this was real. "You must not apologize for things that are not your fault or for things you cannot control," he said gently.

He wasn't scolding her. Libby knew that. He was . . . making a connection between them, mesmerizing her with the power of his personality. She had never known such a fascinating man. And she had certainly never met one who made her feel quite the way she did at that moment, as though no one else in the world existed but Libby Ashford and Case Longstreet.

She struggled to find something to say, but the opportunity was denied her when a voice called out, breaking the spell Case had somehow woven around her.

"Libby? Are you all right?" Elaine Dunlevy asked as she and Caroline Crenshaw hurried toward the porch. Both women cast suspicious glances at Case, and he stepped back to make room for them.

"I'm fine, Mrs. Dunlevy," Libby assured her, then murmured a pleasant hello to Caroline, who, despite the afternoon heat, looked as though she'd just stepped from a page of *Harper's Bazar*. She realized that the ladies were curious about Case's presence and probably more than a little disapproving. "Mr. Longstreet was kind enough to help me move my flower box," she said sweetly, stepping aside so that they could get a good look and hating herself and the situation that demanded she have an excuse just to speak to the scout.

Elaine nodded, but admonished her mildly. "Surely your striker could handle such a menial task."

"I'm afraid Sergeant Brogan was nowhere to be found. He made the box for me and deposited it on the edge of the porch while I was visiting Susannah. I assume his post duties called him away."

Caroline was looking at the wooden trough with her delicately arched brows raised in disdain. "What on earth could you possibly want with a flower box out here?"

"Why, it's for growing flowers, what else?" She turned to Case. "But Mr. Longstreet had just informed me that the soil my gardening venture needs is some distance away from the fort." Remembering something Susannah had told her about the colonel's wife, Libby gave Elaine her most enthusiastic smile. "Perhaps you could put together one of the fabulous picnics I've heard so much about, Elaine. The spot Mr. Longstreet was describing sounds absolutely perfect—wildflowers in profusion near a cold spring. The weather is—"

"That sounds lovely, Libby dear," Elaine interrupted. "But my excursions have been somewhat limited of late, due to some unrest on the reservation. My husband feels that it's unwise to venture too far from the fort until such time as all of the Apaches have been brought under control."

"Mrs. Dunlevy is right, Miss Ashford," Case said respectfully. "A party such as the one you propose would require an armed escort, and a military force of any consequence might be misunderstood by my people."

Her eyes sparkled as she looked up at Case. "Oh, my. It would seem I have a lot to learn, wouldn't it?"

It was everything Case could do to keep from laughing out loud, particularly when it became clear that Libby was daring him to do just that. Straight-faced, they stared each other down for a moment, their private joke passing completely over the heads of their companions.

"Well, you'd be wasting your time, anyway," Caroline announced. "No matter what kind of earth you use for potting, you'll never get plants to grow in this miserable wasteland."

Meade had told Libby the same thing, as had Sergeant Brogan and Case Longstreet. But having Caroline decree it as though she were the voice of the Almighty made Libby fighting mad. If for no other reason than to confound the snooty Mrs. Crenshaw, Libby was going to grow the most beautiful bouquet of flowers in Arizona!

Libby glanced at Case and had the strangest sensation that

he could read her thoughts or that, at the very least, he shared her sentiments.

"I'm sure you have things to do, Mr. Longstreet," Elaine said, growing increasingly uncomfortable with the situation. She'd hurried up here only to save Libby from yet another social disgrace, but if the scout didn't depart soon, the disgrace would be Elaine's and Caroline's, too. "Please don't let us keep you from your duties."

"That's very considerate of you, Mrs. Dunlevy," Case said politely, though he knew only too well that he'd just been summarily dismissed.

And Libby knew it, too. She had to struggle to keep her irritation hidden. This was her home, after all; Elaine Dunlevy had no right to dictate when her visitors should arrive and depart. Still, she managed a smile. "I can't thank you enough for your assistance, Mrs. Longstreet. It was very kind of you to come to a lady's aid."

"It was my pleasure, Miss Ashford. Good luck with your garden." He nodded to Mrs. Dunlevy and to Mrs. Crenshaw, who had yet to look at him. "Ladies, good afternoon."

He stepped off the porch, and it was everything Libby could do to keep from watching him go. Instead, she turned her attention to her unexpected visitors. "Won't you please join me for tea?" she invited, only because it was the proper thing to do.

"No, thank you," Elaine said, trying to appear pleasant. "We only stopped by because we saw you with Longstreet and were concerned that he might be trying to force himself on you again."

Not again, Libby thought irritably. "If you're referring to the incident on the parade ground last week, let me assure you that Mr. Longstreet has *never* forced himself on me," she said tightly. "We've had two brief conversations, and he's been nothing but a perfect gentleman."

Caroline shook her head, making the tiny ringlets at the back of her neck bounce. "Don't let his manners fool you, Libby. He's still an Apache."

She said "Apache" as though it were a vile contagious disease, and Libby wanted to shake some sense into the sharp-tongued, narrow-minded little twit. Her missing husband had returned from his mission unscathed several days ago, but Libby had yet to see any difference in her vinegary personality.

"Caroline is right," Elaine said. "Case Longstreet has proven himself invaluable in General Crook's conquest of the Apaches, but—"

Libby didn't care to hear another criticism of the scout. "So I understand," she said quickly. "His knowledge of the country, the languages, and the various Apache tribes has saved countless American lives. Why, do you know that just the other day I heard one of the officers say that if it weren't for Longstreet and the other Apache scouts, there probably wouldn't be a single Indian on any reservation in the territory?"

"Well, that's true," Elaine admitted somewhat reluctantly.

"I've also heard that on most military campaigns it's the scouts who do most of the actual fighting."

Elaine's lips thinned into a tight line. "That has been true in some instances."

Libby gave her an innocent smile. "Then I'd say that Mr. Longstreet and his fellow Apache scouts deserve our utmost respect, wouldn't you?"

"I respect those Apaches who choose to be our allies, but that does not mean that I must grant them social equality."

"Have you ever had a conversation with Case Longstreet?"

Elaine looked shocked. "Certainly not. We have exchanged pleasantries when the occasion demanded it, but I have no reason to associate with an Apache, any more than I would embark on a friendship with one of the enlisted men under my husband's command. There is a proper way to do things in the army, Libby."

"That's right," Caroline interjected. "The social order must be maintained, or chaos will be the result. Why, my husband would never dream of fraternizing with any of the soldiers under his command—"

"So therefore you can't socialize with any of the wives of the enlisted men," Libby said, calling up one of the many inequities she'd noticed since her arrival. There weren't many wives of the enlisted, but the few who did live at Fort Apache worked as laundresses. That put them well out of the social class of the officers' wives.

"Exactly," Caroline declared.

"And the same applies to civilian scouts," Libby replied. "Even more so."

Libby knew that there was logic in the segregation of officers and the men who served under them. Officers had to command the respect of their subordinates, and they couldn't do that by becoming their genial companions. But Libby seriously doubted that these two ladies would be quite so up in arms if they discovered her conversing on the porch with Private Sloane from D Company. And she knew for a fact that Al Seiber, the civilian *Caucasian* chief of Crook's scouts, had been entertained by Colonel and Mrs. Dunlevy only three nights ago.

In Libby's mind, the distinction being made between the white scout and the Apache scout constituted bigotry.

For Meade's sake, Libby bit back that accusation. Though it nearly choked her, she thanked the ladies for their wise counsel and sent them on their way.

Once she had taken refuge indoors, however, it was everything she could do to keep herself from breaking a few pieces of the family china.

FOURTEEN

VENTING HER FRUSTRATION, Libby paced back and forth in front of her brother, her skirts swishing furiously. "Those silly old cats! Don't they understand that their intolerance is the very thing that's going to make peaceful coexistence with the Apache impossible? I swear, Meade, when they started preaching at me, I just wanted to scream!"

"Libby, calm down. And sit down, too," he added. "All that pacing is making me dizzy."

She stopped abruptly, arms akimbo, and glared at him. "Meade Ashford, the least you could do is summon a touch of moral indignation—if not for Case Longstreet's sake, then for mine!"

"I'm sorry, Libby, but I have to agree with Mrs. Dunlevy. You should never have engaged in conversation with that scout."

His attitude stunned Libby, but before she could open her mouth to protest, Meade stood and placed his hands on her shoulders. "I understand that the incident on the parade ground last week wasn't your fault, Lib."

"Well, thank you for that," she intoned sarcastically.

Meade ignored the gibe. "And I agree completely that Longstreet shouldn't have been punished. But this is different. You went out of your way to get him to help you when you know as well as I that you could have called to any soldier on this post to give you a hand with that planter."

"He was the only man in sight with whom I was acquainted," she said stiffly.

Shaking his head, Meade resumed his seat. He knew his sister too well to be fooled by her excuse. "He's a fascinating contradiction, and you wanted to know more about him."

Libby folded her hands and rested them in the pleats of her skirt. "What's wrong with that?"

"He's an Apache Indian."

Libby cast her eyes toward the heavens. "Why is it that whenever I ask that question, the only answer anyone can give me is"—she lowered her voice to a mimicking masculine pitch—" 'He's an Indian.' "

Meade chuckled despite himself. "My darling sister, you are truly unique and I love you beyond words, but you have to face certain realities. No matter how much you deplore it, prejudice exists."

"Does that mean that you and I have to propagate it?" she demanded.

"No, but we do have to live within the confines of a society that does."

Normally, Libby enjoyed philosophical discussions with Meade, but she was too embroiled in the practical applications of this one to garner any pleasure from their exchange. She joined him on the sofa, leaning toward him with her arm draped across the backrest. "Meade, we are now living among the Indians. You can't look beyond the confines of this fort in any direction without seeing their little huts. They outnumber us a hundred to one!" she pointed out emphatically. "No matter how much anyone might seek to deny it, the level of fear in this place is so potent that it's an actual presence."

"That's right," he agreed. "And it's perfectly understandable. Even as well fortified as this encampment is, no one can be sure that the Apaches aren't going to rise against us and slaughter us in our beds."

"Then what is wrong with trying to understand them?" she wanted to know. "Ignorance breeds contempt—and fear. If I'm not mistaken, it was you who taught me that."

Meade studied his headstrong little sister. There were times when he wanted to paddle her backside, and there were other times—like now—when the pride he felt in her nearly overpowered him. But for all the noble sentiments she expressed, he had an instinctive feeling that she wasn't being completely honest. "Tell me something, Libby. Does your desire for knowledge encompass the entire Apache race, or is it just one Apache in particular who fascinates you?"

Libby flushed guiltily. "I want to learn about them all," she said a little too forcefully to fool her brother.

Meade frowned. "That's what I thought." He rose and glared down at her. "If the opportunity to study the Indians from a safe distance presents itself, then by all means learn whatever you can, Libby." He pointed a finger at her sternly. "But you stay away from Case Longstreet. Is that clear?"

Libby bristled at his high-handed manner. "I am not a child, Meade," she said, coming to her feet. "Don't try to order me around like one."

"You are my responsibility. That gives me the right." He glared down at her with the sinking feeling that he was dominating her in height only. "In the future I don't ever want to hear your name linked to Case Longstreet's in any context. Is that clear?"

"Perfectly," she replied, completely uncowed.

"Good." He turned and headed toward his room. "I'm going to retire for the night, and I suggest you do the same."

"Yes, sir, Captain Ashford!" she barked, giving his back her best military salute.

Meade whirled and caught her, but she looked not the least bit penitent. Discipline had never been his forte, possibly because there was only a nine-year difference in their ages—or, more likely, because they were so close and thought so much alike.

Clearly a dictatorial attitude wasn't going to do the trick, so he softened his tone. "I'm only thinking of what's best for you, Libby. Surely you can't doubt that."

Of course she didn't. And it was impossible for her to be angry with him when he was looking at her with so much affection. He was, after all, the only person in the world who had ever loved her for what she was—thorns and all. "I know that, Meade."

He shook his head ruefully and gave her a smile that was filled with remorse. "You can't change the world, little sister."

She grinned impishly. "Can I try?"

He fought back a laugh. "No."

Libby crossed the room and gave him a good-night kiss on the cheek. "Spoilsport."

Over the next few days the tension Libby had commented on grew alarmingly as reports of a major campaign began to circulate. Factions of the Chiricahua, who had always been a thorn in Crook's side, were regularly slipping away from their mountain reservation and raiding rancheros in the south. Thanks to a private treaty between the formidable Chiricahua leader, Cochise, and a representative of the United States government, Crook had no control over the Chiricahua so long as they stayed in their mountains.

But rumors had it that a group of braves—variously reported as numbering between one hundred and one thousand—had been preparing to go on the warpath. While Crook tried to determine the validity of this rumor, he began readying his own troops for battle. The scuttlebutt around Fort Apache suggested that cavalry companies B and E would soon march against the Chiricahua in a massive campaign.

This news was particularly distressing to Susannah, whose baby was due at any time and whose husband was the commander of Company B. Her difficult pregnancy was already sapping her strength, and worry for David's safety was taking what little she had left. Libby admired the brave front Susannah maintained, but that wasn't going to do her much good when she went into labor. Only strength and endurance were going to matter, and Susannah had very little of either in reserve.

With every day that passed, Libby found herself spending more time with the frail cavalry wife. It felt good to have a purpose beyond caring for her brother's home. And, as Meade put it, it kept her out of trouble. It also gave Libby something to think about besides Case Longstreet.

The scout intruded on her thoughts at the most inopportune times. And she was reasonably certain he hadn't dismissed her from his mind completely, because the morning after their conversation, she'd discovered that sometime during the night her flower box had been filled with a rich, dark soil. She'd known immediately that it was a gift from Case Longstreet, but just to be sure, she'd questioned Sergeant Brogan, who'd sworn he hadn't the vaguest idea where the dirt had come from.

To most women, a few bags of soil would have seemed a totally inappropriate gift, but Libby wasn't most women. Longstreet had gone out of his way, no doubt traveling a considerable distance, just for her. It was a touching gesture, one Libby appreciated more than she could have said. Unfortunately there had been no opportunity to thank him for the gift. She'd seen him only once since then, as he was leaving Crook's command post, and if he'd seen her, he had given no indication of it.

As the days passed, Libby found herself haunted by Meade's insinuation that her fascination with the Apaches began and ended with Case. In her heart she knew her interest was broader than that, but she couldn't deny that the scout held a special fascination for her. She found herself dwelling on every look they'd shared, every word they'd spoken. Every time she worked in her improvised garden, she thought of him, sometimes with growing fondness, and sometimes with anger for the unjust manner in which he was being treated.

Questions danced in her mind with dizzying regularity. Where had he learned to speak such perfect English? What had prompted him to make the effort? What was his relationship to the rancher, Jedidiah Longstreet? What had happened to his parents? Had they been victims of the government's war of conquest? Considering what was happening to his people, it was obvious that he had suffered great personal tragedy; so why had he chosen to ally himself with the white soldiers?

Without Case to talk to, there could be no answers to her

questions, of course. In general terms, she had learned that the Indians he fought against were not technically *his* people. After some judicious questioning, Sergeant Brogan had informed her that Longstreet was a White Mountain Apache. For the most part, the bands of that tribe were living peacefully on the White Mountain Reservation that surrounded Fort Apache. In some ways, they were more fortunate than other tribes, since they were being confined to a place that had been their homeland for centuries.

But they were still a people in bondage, their survival almost totally dependent on the army's largess. And what was worse, the government of the United States didn't even officially recognize them as human beings. They were entities without rights, without status, and without any recourse for obtaining reparations for the land that was being systematically stolen from them.

Libby often thought about the bitterness she'd heard in Longstreet's voice and was amazed that it was not stronger.

Much too often she lay awake at night thinking about the scout, mulling over all the questions she wanted to ask him. She also thought about the wonderful, breathless way she had felt every time his black eyes looked into hers. In the dead of the night those same feelings would wash over her, and her nights became restless reminders that she was a twenty-two-year-old woman with no prospects for a home, children, or a husband who could take her breath away with a single look.

She was in the midst of one of those fitful nights of tossing and turning when banging at the door roused her and Meade from their beds. Meade was still groggy with sleep as he trudged to the door in hastily donned trousers, but Libby was wide awake, her heart beating with anticipation as she dashed into the parlor. She knew even before her brother opened the door that Susannah's time had come.

And she was right. In the faint glow of the lamp Meade lifted, Libby could see a disheveled David Robertson.

"Captain Ashford, please forgive the intrusion at this late—"

"Oh, for crying out loud," Libby snapped. She'd had about

all she could stand of military manners. "Susannah's gone into labor, hasn't she?"

"Yes." He looked at Meade. "She's in terrible pain, Captain. Can you—"

"I'm on my way," Meade assured him. "You hurry on back and hold her hand. I'll be there as soon as I collect my bag."

"Thank you, Captain." Robertson disappeared into the night, and Meade hurried toward the door to the hallway that connected the doctor's quarters with the hospital.

"I'm going with you," Libby told him as she headed back to her room for a pair of slippers.

Meade stopped at the front door and turned, frowning. "Libby, you have no idea what's involved in delivering a baby."

"You forget, brother dear, that if it hadn't been for me you wouldn't have passed a single exam in medical school." She grinned at him. "And besides, what could be so hard about it? Susannah's going to do all the work."

When Meade didn't respond to her teasing, Libby's heart skipped a beat. She recognized the real reason he didn't want her there and had to fight back tears. "You don't think she's going to survive the birth, do you?" she asked, her voice barely audible.

"That's a possibility," he admitted reluctantly. "I don't want to put you through an ordeal like this."

Libby squared her shoulders. There would be no tears tonight. "Susannah is going to need a woman with her, and you may need an extra pair of hands. I'm going with you," she said with finality.

Meade relented. "All right. Put on some clothes and be quick about it."

A few minutes later they were both dressed, after a fashion, and hurrying down the quadrangle to the Robertsons' quarters. Susannah was already exhausted and drenched with perspiration by the time they arrived, but her face lit up at the sight of Libby, and Meade was glad he'd allowed his sister to come along. If Susannah Robertson was going to survive the night, she would need all the help she could get.

Meade's first act was to shoo her husband out of the bedroom. While Libby held Susannah's hand and bathed her forehead with a damp cloth, Meade examined his patient and discovered, as he'd feared, that they were in for a long night. As the labor progressed, with Susannah growing weaker after every contraction, he was forced to give her a mild sedative to reduce the pain.

Libby proved to be an extremely competent nurse, but more than that, she did a remarkable job of keeping Susannah's spirits from plummeting. By dawn, though, his patient's shallow pulse told him that if the ordeal didn't end soon, he was going to lose both mother and child. Since nature didn't seem to be working on his side, he relieved Susannah of her misery with a heavy dose of morphine and, as soon as she was unconscious, used forceps to take the baby.

The wrinkled, squalling infant came into the world with an unsightly cone-shaped head, thanks to the forceps, but when Libby presented Captain David Robertson with a son, Meade assured him that in a few days his son would look normal. In all other ways, he was as healthy as could be.

Meade's real concern was Susannah. Though he tried to keep his apprehension hidden from Libby, he didn't expect the cavalry wife to live out the day. Morning sick call forced him to resume his regular post duties, but he checked on his patient often. Each time he visited, he found Libby there, tending the baby and the mother with unflagging determination and good cheer, as though she could keep the specter of death away with nothing more than the sheer force of her personality.

Her innate gentleness and devotion made Meade prouder of her than he had ever been before. He wished the ladies of Fort Apache could see Libby like this, exhausted but still smiling, pouring her heart and soul into caring for a friend. For all of his sister's strange notions, which she verbalized much too frequently, this was what Liberty Ashford was all about—doing what had to be done no matter what the cost to herself.

Unfortunately, Meade was fairly sure that if Mrs. Dunlevy and her shadow, Caroline Crenshaw, did walk into the Roberstons' quarters, they would see only a bedraggled young woman whose hair needed taming. They might smile pleasantly, but when they left, they'd be gossiping because Miss Ashford's behavior was unbecoming to a lady of breeding. Of one thing Meade was certain: Neither of those estimable army wives would have deigned to soil her hands as Libby had last night.

Libby maintained her bedside vigil for several days. She napped on the Robertsons' sofa whenever she could, but most of her time was divided between the baby, David Michael, and Susannah. Meade expected every day to be the mother's last, but with Libby's unwavering care and Susannah's determination to live, the doctor finally decided that his prognosis had been wrong. Both mother and son were going to survive. Libby stayed with them another day, but at sunset of the fourth day Meade put his foot down and demanded she come home to rest. Libby was too tired to argue. She gave David copious instructions on how to care for his wife and son during the night, and then Meade dragged her home and put her to bed.

It was just before noon the next day when she awoke. How she had slept through reveille, turnout for fatigue duty, sick call, and all the other noisy routines that kept Fort Apache humming was a mystery to her, but she had. Every muscle in her body ached, but once she was bathed and dressed she felt ready to jump back into the fray again. Sergeant Brogan came in just as she was starting dinner, and she was only too happy to allow him to take over the preparation of the noon meal. Meade came in from the hospital and assured Libby that Susannah was doing fine.

"But you can't keep this up, Libby, or you're going to make yourself ill," he told her as they sat down to eat. "Susannah and little Michael need more help than you can give them."

"There is no one else, Meade," she countered. "Susannah's so weak she can't even take care of herself, let alone the baby. David and Mumford, their striker, should be able to start helping out, though. Surely they can take care of her at night."

"Libby . . ."

Meade's somber expression told her there was something wrong. "What is it?" she asked.

"The rumors we've been hearing are true," he said reluctantly. "General Crook is preparing for a massive campaign against the Chiricahuas."

"Oh, no." Libby bowed her head. "When?"

"Sometime next week. He's sent to Fort Verde for infantry reinforcements. As soon as they arrive, cavalry companies B and E will head for Fort Thomas, below the Gila River."

"Is this an official transfer? Will Susannah be expected to move as well?" she asked, not daring to breathe until she had an answer. A journey out of the mountains and across the desert would certainly kill the new mother; surely the army wouldn't be so heartless as to force her to go until she was stronger.

"No, Lib. This is a campaign, not a transfer. I don't imagine the troops will stay at Fort Thomas for more than a day or two."

Libby was immensely relieved that she wasn't going to lose the only friend she had at Fort Apache. "Does Susannah know?"

He nodded. "David told her this morning. She didn't take it very well." Meade looked down at his plate, toying with a slice of beef as he tried to figure out a way to tell his sister the rest of the unhappy news.

Libby was too concerned about Susannah to notice that her brother had suddenly grown pensive. She folded her napkin beside her plate and stood. "I'd better get to her. Just the thought of David going into battle again will make her frantic. That's the last thing she needs right now." She hurried out of the dining room, but Meade's voice stopped her at the door.

"Libby?"

She turned expectantly. "Yes?"

Meade opened his mouth, but nothing came out. He wasn't sure he had the heart to tell her.

Libby's heart began to race. Something was wrong. She stepped toward him. "Meade, what is it?"

"Libby . . . Crook received word from Fort Thomas that the Fifth Cavalry's regimental surgeon has died."

"How horrible," she replied. "What happened to him?"

"I don't really know," he said evasively. It wasn't going to do Libby any good to know that the surgeon had succumbed to wounds he received in a skirmish with the Apaches. "The point is, though, that the general doesn't want the Fifth to embark on this campaign without a surgeon."

Libby's world turned upside down. "Oh, my God," she whispered. Somehow she made it to the table and into a chair before her knees buckled. "This wasn't suppose to happen, Meade."

He covered one of her hands with his own. "But we knew it could. I'm truly sorry—for your sake, Libby. But for my part, I'm rather looking forward to a little campaigning. We've been here nearly a month already, and so far I've done nothing but treat a case of the gout, sober up a few drunken soldiers, and deliver a baby." He shrugged and gave her his most boyish grin. "Not exactly a challenging medical practice. I could use a little excitement in my life."

"Congratulations," she said sarcastically, irritated that he could actually be enjoying the thought of what was ahead of him. Their father would have been proud of his son's attitude, but Libby had a different point of view. "You could be the first military man in history to die of boredom."

"I'm not going to die, Lib. I promise."

Libby tried to find a bright side, but there wasn't one. The best she could do to ease her fear was to run through a list of her brother's assets. "Well, you're a crack shot and an excellent rider. We can thank Father for that much, at least. And you do have the sense to know when to duck, don't you?"

Meade chuckled. No one he'd ever known could turn tragedy into humor quicker than his sister. "I think so."

She sighed lightly. "Then I suppose I have no choice but to allow you to go."

"Thank you. I'm sure General Crook will be delighted to learn that I have your permission."

A shudder of apprehension ran down Libby's spine, but

she squelched it. The last thing Meade needed was to be burdened by her fear for his safety. She rose from the table again. "I'd better check on Susannah now."

Meade stood and drew his sister into a firm embrace. "Don't worry about me, Lib."

She clung to him for just a second, then drew back and smiled. "Me, worry about you? What a silly idea."

She turned and hurried out on her mission of mercy, but not before Meade saw the unshed tears glistening in her eyes.

Susannah was in better spirits than Libby had expected, but now that she knew Meade was going away, she had a better understanding of the brave front her friend tried to maintain. Libby wasn't accustomed to keeping her emotions bottled up, but she was learning that some situations demanded it.

With her sunniest smile in place, she helped Susannah with a bed bath, changed her nightgown, and maneuvered her into a rocking chair where she could feed the baby while Libby changed the bed linens. Once all the necessities had been attended to and Michael was sleeping peacefully in his mother's arms, Libby and Susannah turned their attention to the very real problem of how they were going to manage once David and Sergeant Mumford left.

"I don't see any other solution," Libby said firmly, trying to override Susannah's objections to her suggestion. "I'll simply move in here with you until you're strong enough to do for yourself."

"I forbid it, Libby, and that's that. You've already done too much." Her voice was surprisingly strong for someone who couldn't have won a fight with a newborn kitten. "I can't allow you to turn over your whole life to taking care of me."

"What life?" Libby asked, drawing a wan smile from her friend. "I think I can manage to curtail my whirlwind social schedule for a few weeks. And besides, once Meade is gone, I won't have any responsibilities in our quarters. It will certainly be less lonely for both of us if I'm living here."

"But you can't do it all—cooking, cleaning, taking care of the baby *and* me. It's just not right."

"Then suggest an alternative," Libby challenged.

Susannah let her head fall back into the pillows as she thought. "What about one of the laundresses?" she said finally. "Surely one of them might like to earn a few dollars extra."

Libby gave her a doubtful look. "Susannah, those poor women already have more work than they can handle. Besides, I doubt that any of them could spare more than an hour or two a day."

"Well, at least that would be *some* relief for you."

The rocking chair creaked as Libby pondered the problem. She truly didn't mind taking on the extra work that caring for her friend would entail, but even she had to admit that having an extra pair of hands would be helpful. Michael's difficult birth was going to add weeks to Susannah's lying-in period. She was still feverish from the infection that had set in after the delivery, and there was simply no telling how long it would be before she could take care of herself, let alone her son.

Unfortunately Libby didn't see any alternative to doing everything herself. She promised Susannah she'd investigate the possibility of getting a laundress to help out a few hours a day, but she held out very little hope.

Susannah napped on and off the rest of the day, and when Captain Robertson completed his duties, Libby left the family in the capable hands of Sergeant Mumford, who arrived just in time to start supper. Libby and Meade spent a quiet but somewhat strained evening trying not to talk about anything important. They turned in early, and by the time the bugle called fatigue duty at seven-thirty the next morning, Libby was on her way to Susannah's once again.

The weather was abominably hot, but the water-filled clay ollas hanging from the ceiling gave them a surprising amount of relief from the heat. Susannah sat in the rocking chair for nearly an hour, then returned to bed exhausted. She managed to sit up again to eat the light dinner Libby prepared, then retired to her bed once more.

She had just finished Michael's afternoon feeding and had coaxed Libby into sitting down to rest for a while when they heard Captain Robertson's voice coming from the parlor.

Susannah frowned. "What on earth is David doing here at this hour? Isn't it nearly time for the cavalry drill?"

"I believe so." Libby stepped toward the door just as Robertson slipped inside and closed it behind him. She moved aside as the captain approached the bed hesitantly.

"What's wrong, David?" Susannah asked.

He gave her a perfunctory kiss on the cheek. "Are you up to seeing visitors, Sukie?"

The question surprised her. Several people had dropped in during the last two days, and Libby had been forced to send most of them away with thanks for their concern and their assurance that they would visit again when the new mother was stronger. As far as Susannah knew, though, David had never personally escorted a visitor into their quarters. "I suppose so," she said. Then an uncomfortable thought hit her. "It isn't General Crook, is it?"

David smiled tightly and cast a nervous glance toward the door. "No, my dear. I was just in his office, though, and he does send his regards."

"Then who's here, David, and why are you so jittery?"

He cleared his throat. "Well, it seems that the news of our son's birth has spread among the Indians, and some of the squaws took it upon themselves to make you a present."

Susannah gasped. "A present from the Apaches? How remarkable!"

"Yes, well, that's what General Crook thought, too," David told her. "It's a very encouraging gesture of goodwill, and he was hoping you might feel up to receiving the gift personally."

Susannah glanced across the room at her friend. "Isn't that wonderful, Libby?"

"It certainly is," she replied, moving to the bureau. "Shall we get you into a dressing gown for this momentous occasion?"

"Oh, by all means," Susannah replied.

David started for the door. "I'll just step outside and keep our guests company." He stopped and turned to his wife. "By the way, Longstreet came along to act as an interpreter, but if you'd rather not have him in our bedchamber—"

"Don't be silly," she chided lightly. "How else are we going to communicate?"

"All right, but I don't want you to tire yourself." He stepped out, closing the door behind him.

"Well, Libby, here's your chance to learn a little more about Mr. Longstreet," Susannah said slyly as Libby helped her to the edge of the bed so that she could slip on the rust-colored dressing gown.

Libby looked at her drolly. "I've been forbidden that pastime, remember?"

"Has that ever stopped you before?"

She chuckled. "I must do something to correct that image you have of me as an insolent hoyden."

Susannah fell back weakly into the pillows. "It's too late. The whole camp knows your secret."

"How true," Libby muttered as she moved across the room and took Michael from his cradle, then placed the baby by his mother's side. When Susannah was satisfied that she looked as respectable as possible under the circumstances, Libby went to the door and admitted their guests.

With David leading them, three Apache women entered the room. The eldest was wearing a lovely buckskin dress with elaborate beadwork down the front and sleeves. The other two, both much younger, wore short skirts made of stripped bark, and low-necked *camisas* of unbleached muslin. This was the costume Libby had seen most often on ration days, which she always watched with great interest. Two of the women wore their hair long and unbraided, but the third—a lovely young maiden with bright, inquisitive eyes—had pulled her hair back and fastened it with an exquisitely beaded bow of sorts.

All three looked curiously around the room as they entered, and Libby wondered if this was the first time any of them had been in a white man's home. The two younger women carried beautifully woven baskets, but Libby found her attention immediately drawn to the object the woman in buckskin carried. It was a baby carrier of the sort they used for their own infants. Libby had seen them before, but had never had the opportunity to study one up close.

As everyone crowded into the room, David took up a position at his wife's bedside. "Sukie, this is the wife of one of the White Mountain chiefs," he said, indicating the eldest woman. "And this is her daughter-in-law and her granddaughter." He looked to Case, who was standing just inside the door. "Is that right?"

"That's right." Case's eyes darted to Libby, then away before she could acknowledge him.

Susannah glanced across the room to Case. "Mr. Longstreet, please tell them I am honored by their visit."

"*Cìtc'ì-né* . . ." The old woman turned to him, and Case intoned a string of guttural, unintelligible sounds. The chief's wife replied, making a speech of some length.

When she had finished, Case looked at Susannah. "She says her heart is glad that you are honored. She knows you have been ill, and she has brought gifts to return you to health and to keep your baby strong. It will make her heart glad if you accept these gifts."

David gestured toward the object the old women held. "That's a papoose basket, isn't it?"

"A cradleboard," Case corrected. If he objected to the term "papoose," he gave no indication of it. "She made it herself and blessed each piece with the ritual prayers."

"May I see it?" Susannah asked, holding out her arms. The gesture spoke for itself, and the other woman handed her the cradle. "Why, it's the softest thing I've ever touched. And it's so light. See, David?"

She held it out for her husband, and he inspected the extraordinary craftsmanship. Susannah wanted to know how the cradleboard worked, and after a few words from Case, the older woman stepped forward and picked up little Michael. David started to protest, but Susannah shushed him and watched with delight as her son was strapped into the snug baby carrier. The other women gathered around as well, smiling and laughing in the gentlest manner imaginable as they admired the little boy.

Libby watched the proceedings with a kind of amazement. She glanced at Case to see his reaction to the cultural exchange, and found him looking at her. No, not looking, she decided. Studying.

Smiling happily, she moved toward him. "I was beginning to fear that you were going to ignore me completely, Mr. Longstreet," she said sotto voce.

Case tried to resist the urge to return her smile, but found he couldn't. He'd thought of little else but her smile in the weeks since he'd seen her. "I wasn't sure that speaking to you was appropriate," he replied softly.

"If you don't speak to me, how can I thank you for the wonderful present you left on my doorstep? I know how much trouble you must have gone to to obtain that potting soil. I was very touched."

"No thanks are necessary."

Susannah asked a question, and while Case translated, Libby watched him, trying to ignore the rapid beating of her heart. In her month at the fort, she had heard the Apache language spoken a number of times, but it was a shock to hear Case speak it so fluidly—much more of a shock, in fact, than she'd experienced weeks ago when she'd heard him speak English for the first time at Colonel Dunlevy's. It made her all the more curious to know everything there was to know about him.

When he finished translating and the women were once again cooing over the baby, Libby recaptured his attention. "You've called the older one Sit-say-i-nay several times. Is that her name?"

She said the word perfectly, and Case smiled down at her. "No. In your language her name is She Goes to War. *Cìtc'ì-né* is my paternal grandmother."

"You're the grandson of a chief?" she asked with surprise.

"Does that impress you?"

"Everything about you impresses me," she admitted honestly.

Her candor astounded him. More than anything, he wanted to tell her that the feeling was mutual, but he couldn't. She was a remarkable woman, but Case knew he was nothing but a curiosity to Miss Liberty Ashford. He couldn't allow himself to read more into her words than was there. "Then you should be truly impressed, Miss Ashford," he said lightly. "Since I am the grandson of not one chief, but two."

"Will you be a chief someday as well?"

Case's expression grew pensive, and he glanced away from her. "I don't know. I have not seen that far into the future."

She laughed lightly. "You say it as though you have seen at least some distance into the future."

He looked at Libby, and suddenly she found it difficult to breathe. "Some of my life has been laid before me," he said quietly. "But I do not know what it all means."

Libby was confused, not only by his words but the intensity of his gaze. It was almost as though he was seeing through her.

Before she could think of a comment, David announced that it was time for Susannah to get some rest, and Case began ushering his relatives out of the room. The Robertsons thanked the women profusely, and Case translated. Just as the youngest one reached the door, though, she turned back and spoke for herself.

"Baby pretty," she said in broken, halting English. "He make good warrior, like he father."

That said, she ducked her head shyly and darted out.

David moved toward the bedroom door. "I'll see them out," he said, but Libby wasn't paying him the least bit of attention. Her eyes were locked on Susannah's.

"Did you hear that?" she asked with a grin. "The young one spoke English."

Susannah nodded. "I know. She said a few words while you and Mr. Longstreet were conversing." She paused, trying to read her friend's mischievous expression and finally picked up her train of thought. "Libby . . . are you thinking what I think you're thinking?"

Libby nodded. "Why not?"

Susannah was too exhausted to come up with an argument. "You're right. Go ask her."

Grinning broadly, Libby dashed for the door and nearly collided with David. "Libby, what on earth is wrong?"

"Not a thing," she replied merrily, hurrying past him. "In

fact, I may have just solved the servant problem at Fort Apache!''

''What is she talking about?'' David asked his wife as Libby disappeared.

''A part-time nursemaid for your son,'' Susannah replied.

He made the connection immediately and frowned. ''Now just a minute, Sukie—''

''My darling husband, it's out of your hands,'' she said matter-of-factly.

FIFTEEN

⊏⊐⊏⊐⊏⊐⊏⊐⊏⊐

"Mr. Longstreet!" Libby dashed out of the house and looked frantically around, blinking against the blinding sun. At the far end of the parade ground, the cavalry units were preparing for mounted drill, and several hundred Apaches were still in their ration lines. With so much activity going on, it took Libby a moment to spot Case and his family, but she finally saw them headed toward the headquarters buildings.

"Mr. Longstreet!" she called, hurrying down the quadrangle.

Case stopped and turned to her. "Yes, Miss Ashford?"

"Could I have a word with you, please?"

Case hesitated a moment, then spoke a few words to his grandmother. The old woman fixed her dark eyes on Libby, studying her intently before she shepherded her young relatives away. Case turned back to Libby. "What is it?"

"I'd like to talk to you about your cousin," she answered, raising one hand to shield her eyes from the sun.

Case took note of her discomfort and gestured toward the ramada—the thatch-covered porch that ran along the front of the officers' quarters. "Why don't you step out of the sun?" he suggested, leading her into the shade. "You shouldn't come outside without a bonnet."

Libby gave him a grateful smile. "I know. My skin has already turned at least two shades darker. In another few months, I'll be able to pass for an Apache."

Case didn't return her smile. "That's doubtful, Miss Ashford."

She sobered. "I'm sorry. I suppose that wasn't a very funny jest, was it?"

"There's more to being an Apache than having dark skin."

"So I've been told. Someday I hope to have the opportunity to learn what that entails."

Case frowned. "Why should you want to?"

"Because I like understanding things. What's so wrong with that?" she asked defiantly, puzzled by his obvious displeasure.

"You could study and observe for a lifetime and never understand the Inday mind, Miss Ashford."

For some reason, prejudice was about the last thing Libby had expected from the handsome scout. "Because I'm a woman, you mean," she said with a touch of belligerence.

"Because you're white," he said, softening his tone.

Libby's heart responded to the gentleness of his deep voice, but her keen mind was primed, as always, for a good debate. "You're an Inday, but you've learned to think like a white man," she pointed out. "Why can't that understanding be reciprocal?"

Case shook his head. "I understand the white man's language. I've read some of your books, seen some of your cities. I have learned to imitate your manners . . . but that doesn't mean I think and feel as you do."

Libby had trouble seeing the distinction he was making. Before she could think of a suitable rejoinder, though, Case reminded her of the reason she had detained him. "What was it you wanted to say about my cousin?"

Though she was disappointed, she let go of their discussion. "I'm sure you've heard that several cavalry companies will be leaving next week."

"Yes."

She gestured vaguely toward the officers' quarters. "Well, you see, when Captain Robertson leaves, his wife is going to need someone to help her with the baby. She'd like to hire someone, and I thought—that is . . ." As she spoke, Case's face became such an unreadable mask that Libby suddenly found herself growing tongue-tied. Perhaps this wasn't such a good idea after all. "I've offered to help out, you understand. I'll be staying with her at night, but Susannah—that is, Mrs. Robertson—doesn't like being so reliant on me. So I thought . . . well, when I heard your cousin speaking English . . . She seems like such a sweet girl . . ."

"You wish to hire her as a servant," Case said flatly, putting Libby out of her misery.

Her heart sank at his tone. "Is that an offensive offer?"

"It is—" Case couldn't find the words for it. He was too astonished. "Your friend would trust an Apache to care for her son?"

Libby looked at him blankly. "Why shouldn't she?"

He raised one dark eyebrow. "Haven't you heard? Apaches torture women and children."

"Oh, stop playing the devil's advocate. There's no way you could convince me that that sweet-faced young girl would deliberately harm the Robertsons' baby," she said irritably, then remembered what Case had said about understanding the Apache mind. Her conviction slipped a little. "Would she?"

"No," Case assured her. "Tessa would not hurt anyone unless it was in defense of her loved ones."

Libby frowned. "Tessa? Is that an Apache name?"

"It's the name that was given to her by the missionaries who taught her to speak English. I use it because it is disrespectful to speak an Apache's true name."

Libby was fascinated. "Why?"

Case shrugged. "It is their property. Would you go into the home of a friend and use an article of her clothing without asking permission?"

"I see what you mean." She would have loved to question him further about Apache customs, but this time she remembered that she had a mission. "How do you think Tessa would feel about helping Mrs. Robertson? Would she like the opportunity to earn a little money, or would she find the offer insulting?"

Case thought it over a moment. The money would help her family buy goods at the sutler's store, but for Tessa that would not be the prime consideration. Case's young cousin had a keen interest in learning about the white man. The missionaries who'd spent two years trying to convert the White Mountain Apache to Christianity had left quite an impression on the girl.

At Tall One's request, Case had been teaching English to several of the braves in his grandfather's clan, and Tessa often found an excuse to be nearby when Case was giving lessons. Most Inday girls would never have considered toiling in the home of a white man, but Tessa just might. And one thing Case knew for certain: He would not have to worry about his cousin being mistreated as long as Libby Ashford was around.

"I will ask her father's permission," he said finally.

"Her father? Why don't you ask Tessa?"

"Because she would not agree if her father did not wish it." He grinned. "Is that not the way in the homes of white men? Mustn't the woman ask the permission of the man of the family?"

He was teasing her and Libby knew it. "Well, that's how it's *supposed* to be anyway."

"But your house is different?" he asked slyly.

Libby flushed guiltily, but she was thoroughly enjoying his needling. "My brother and I have an understanding. He gives orders, and then I do as I please."

"Isn't that called anarchy?"

Libby laughed. "I've been called many things, Case, but never an anarchist." Her laughter faded when she realized she had broken the bonds of formality between them. "I'm sorry. I meant, Mr. Longstreet."

"It's all right, Miss Ashford," he reassured her. "There is no disrespect in using the name that was given to me by a white man."

"Jedidiah Longstreet?" she guessed, and when Case's expression turned questioning, she explained, "I heard that you are somehow related to a rancher by that name."

"He is my very distant cousin by marriage," he replied. "And he has also been what you would call my mentor."

"Will you tell me someday how that came to be?" she asked hopefully.

Case frowned, thinking of the spirit journey that had set him on an impossibly twisted course. He still could not imagine what part this fragile, spirited woman would play in that journey. "Perhaps," he replied cautiously.

Since the subject clearly didn't please him, Libby changed it. "Do you also have an Apache name?"

He nodded and spoke a string of difficult sounds. "It means He Chases the Thunder."

Libby smiled. "That's lovely."

"It describes my life," he told her, his voice quiet and reflective.

For the first time Libby caught just a glimpse of the enormous sadness that engulfed Case Longstreet. "How so?" she asked gently.

"Miss Ashford!"

Libby turned at the sound of her name being called and saw Major Forsythe galloping across the parade ground on a huge gray stallion. "Damnation!" she swore under her breath, turning back to Case. "One of these days, you and I are going to have a conversation that isn't interrupted by some narrow-minded Samaritan who thinks he's doing me a favor!"

It was a struggle for Case not to laugh, but he managed to keep his face somber as Forsythe charged up.

"I'll handle this," Libby whispered, then turned a bright smile on the man towering over her.

"Is something the matter, Major Forsythe?"

The officer's horse danced a bit, forcing Libby to step farther into the shelter of the ramada. "I was about to ask you the same question." He pinned Case with a ferocious glare. "Longstreet and I had an agreement that he was never to disturb you again."

"I'm afraid *I* am the one doing the disturbing," Libby said with forced affability. "Mr. Longstreet has a young cousin who speaks passable English, and we were discussing the possibility of having her come work for Mrs. Robertson during the day once you and the general drag her husband off to war."

Forsythe scowled. "An Apache working as a domestic? That's unthinkable."

Libby's eyes widened with false innocence. "Why? Is there some rule forbidding such a thing?"

"Well . . . no," the major admitted reluctantly. "I suppose the possibility never occurred to anyone."

"Good," Libby muttered, then smiled. "As you know, Major, Mrs. Robertson has been desperately ill. Having someone to help me care for her and little Michael would be invaluable."

"I'm sure that's true, but an Apache—"

"Is my only hope for relief," she said smoothly. "I've grown quite exhausted caring for the little tyke, and once the captain leaves, there's going to be even more work to do." She batted her eyelashes at him as she'd seen her cousin do countless times when she wanted to get her way. "Please say you'll pave the way for me if I should need to obtain the permission of Colonel Dunlevy."

Forsythe knew he was being manipulated—and rather clumsily at that—but he couldn't think of a way out of this dilemma. He knew the girl Libby was referring to. She was clean and well mannered, and she did speak English remarkably well for an Apache. No doubt General Crook would think this was another excellent cultural exchange. "Very well, Miss Ashford. If the girl and her family agree, I'll see to it that daily passes are arranged for her."

"And I will see to it that she has a suitable escort to and from the fort," Case added.

Libby beamed and reached out impulsively, placing her hand on Case's arm. "Thank you." Her eyes met his, and the connection made by the glance and the touch took Libby's breath away. She withdrew her hand quickly and managed a smile that encompassed Case and the major. "My thanks to both of you." She took two steps backward. "And now I should be getting back to Susannah. Please let me know when you have Tessa's answer, Mr. Longstreet."

"I will."

Libby hurried away, and Case sensed Forsythe's eyes on

him. He looked up, unintimidated by the officer glowering down at him.

"You're treading into dangerous territory, Indian," the major warned him, his voice harsh and low. "You stay away from that white woman, or else."

"Or else what, Major?" Case asked evenly.

"We're going into battle with the Chiricahua." Forsythe leaned forward. "And all sorts of things can happen in battle. Remember that."

Forsythe straightened and jerked on the reins, forcing his horse to dance dangerously close to Case. The scout stepped back to keep from being trampled, but his expression betrayed no fear because he felt none—of the horse or of the warning.

If the dreams Case had had about the arrogant officer were true, Major Forsythe wasn't going to live long enough to make his threat a reality.

Libby's plan worked like a charm. The next day Case brought Tessa by to speak with the Robertsons, and Major Forsythe obtained all the necessary authorizations. The girl's English was halting at best, but thanks to the missionary wife who had so fascinated her, she had a rudimentary knowledge of the workings of a Caucasian household. She was bright and inquisitive, and best of all, little Michael seemed quite at home with her.

Although Libby's plan had been for Tessa to begin work as soon as David left on the campaign, the captain insisted she start immediately. He claimed it was only to give Libby a little freedom, but privately, Libby and Susannah speculated that he wanted to see for himself that the arrangement was going to work out.

And it did, splendidly. By the first of the following week, Libby felt completely comfortable leaving Tessa and Susannah alone for protracted periods. Her life returned to a more normal routine of taking care of Meade's home and seeing to the needs of their own little family. The time she spent at the Robertsons', though, became very special to her, because Tessa was so eager to learn whatever Libby cared to teach her. In return, the girl did her best to answer some of Libby's questions. The language barrier made lengthy conversations and explanations impossible, but Libby treasured every crumb of information she could get.

The bits and pieces of knowledge she put together convinced her that the Apache were an extraordinarily superstitious people. Tessa refused to kill spiders because she feared their relatives would miss them and take revenge against her. A brief thunderstorm blew up one afternoon just as Libby served dinner, and the girl refused to eat until it had passed for fear the lightning would make her teeth fall out.

Since leaving Washington, Libby had been keeping a journal, and as her knowledge of the Apache grew, so did the volume of her writing. Only facts and impressions about people and places went into her diary. Her feelings she kept to herself. She wrote little of her growing dread of her brother's imminent departure; she wrote even less of her growing attraction to Case Longstreet.

Every afternoon just before sunset he came to the Robertsons' to collect his cousin, and Libby always managed to find an excuse to be there. They rarely exchanged anything more than simple pleasantries, but the thought of seeing him at the end of the day became the highlight of her existence. The mask of stoicism he wore always seemed to dissolve when he looked at her, and Libby began to anticipate the change. When he appeared at the Robertsons' door, his eyes would be cold and lifeless, as though he had steeled himself against something unpleasant. Then he would see Libby and the coldness would begin to fade. His gaze would grow as warm as a caress.

Feminine instinct told Libby he was fighting that warmth—but losing the battle. He looked at Susannah with respect and a touch of admiration for her gentle ways and the patience she had shown toward Tessa. The emotions he transmitted when he looked at Libby were more intimate.

On Wednesday the moment Libby and Susannah had been dreading finally arrived. Companies E and H of the Forty-seventh Infantry completed their harrowing journey from Fort Verde. While the officers in charge reported to General

Crook, the men set up camp just outside Fort Apache. Before the end of the day, most of the ranking officers had been summoned to Crook's headquarters, and word had been passed around that the campaign against the Chiricahua renegades would begin on Friday.

When Case didn't come for Tessa that evening, Libby surmised that he, too, was meeting with Crook. Tessa's brother, a stern-faced young brave with the most hostile eyes Libby had ever seen, came to escort her home. Meade and David were meeting with the general, which left Libby and Susannah alone in the Robertsons' quarters, trying to pretend that everything was normal.

Sergeant Mumford prepared supper, but neither of them could eat. Together they passed the time as all proper ladies were supposed to—by engaging in ladylike pursuits.

"Thunder and tarnation!" Libby cursed as she stabbed her finger with her embroidery needle for the third time in an hour.

With her feet up on the parlor sofa and little Michael sleeping peacefully in his Apache cradleboard nearby, Susannah lowered her needlework into her lap and gave her friend a mildly reproving look. "Why don't you give it up, Libby? Those pansies you're embroidering aren't worth the loss of so much blood."

"No," she said obstinately. "I refuse to be defeated by a sofa pillow."

"I think it's your brother's impending departure that's defeating you," Susannah replied.

Libby lowered her embroidery hoop. "How can you be so calm?"

"You forget, I've been through this before. I accept it because I have no choice, and you're going to have to learn to do the same thing." She smiled and gestured toward Libby's needlework. "All the bloodletting in the world isn't going to help Meade."

"Is the first time the worst?" she asked hopefully.

Susannah would have liked to give her the answer she wanted, but she couldn't lie. "No, Libby. It doesn't get any easier."

"I was afraid of that."

"Look on the bright side. As post surgeon, Meade won't have to do this very often."

"I'll try to bear that in mind," she said, but in truth it was cold comfort. Her brother had never been in combat before. He'd been only fifteen at the outbreak of the Civil War. It had been surprising to both Libby and Meade that when he reached an age when most boys were signing up, their father had discouraged him from doing so. He insisted that Meade carry on with his medical studies as planned.

At first Libby had thought he was finally showing some concern for his son's welfare, but she had eventually come to realize that Martin Ashford's only concern was the war effort. Doctors were desperately needed, and Colonel Ashford wanted his son to be more than a hastily trained bone-cutter. Meade had to be the best so as not to disgrace his ambitious father.

But now Meade was going into battle in a war that Congress had never officially declared to be a war. Unfortunately the casualties were all too real.

When Libby fell silent, absorbed by thoughts she didn't want to think, Susannah let the conversation drop until the silence became too oppressive to bear. Without really intending to, she asked a question that had been nagging at her for days.

"You're worried about *him*, too, aren't you, Libby?"

"Him?" she questioned innocently, though she knew very well what her friend was getting at.

"Case Longstreet."

Libby focused her attention on her embroidery. "I'm concerned for the welfare of everyone who's going on this campaign."

"Libby, don't be evasive. I've come to know you too well. I see how your eyes light up whenever he calls for Tessa, and I know how disappointed you were this afternoon when her brother came for her instead. You're infatuated with the man."

She didn't bother to deny it. "Well, at least you called him a man instead of 'that Indian.' "

"He is an Indian, Libby." Her gentle voice also held a note of warning. "A relationship between the two of you is quite impossible."

"I know that," she snapped irritably.

"Then stop—"

"Stop what?" Libby demanded, tossing her embroidery hoop onto the table beside her. "Stop thinking about him? I've tried. Stop remembering what I feel like when he looks at me with those beautiful dark eyes?" She stood. "Believe me, I've tried that, too."

Susannah knew Libby's anger wasn't directed at her. "You could try not questioning Tessa about him."

"Yes, I could do that," she replied ruefully as she began pacing the room. "Particularly since she refuses to answer the questions I ask."

"Perhaps that's because she knows you're in love with her cousin and that such a relationship is hopeless."

"I am not in love with Case Longstreet," she insisted. "You said it yourself—I'm infatuated. There's a difference."

"But infatuation can lead to love."

"Don't be silly." She returned to her chair. "I was once infatuated with a young man Meade was tutoring in anatomy at Harvard. He came to our house twice a week, and I served him rum cakes and tea. When I put the plate in front of him, he always found a way to brush his hand against mine as he took a piece of cake or the cup. . . ." She sighed at the sweet memory. "He would look at me with the most adoring eyes imaginable, and I hung on his every word."

"What happened to him?"

"The day after he passed the anatomy course he came to our little house, hat in hand, to ask me what he called 'a most delicate question.' "

Susannah clapped with delight. "He proposed to you?"

"No, he asked if I'd send my recipe for rum cake to his fiancée in Boston." Susannah burst into laughter, and Libby assumed an injured air. "Don't make light of it! I was utterly devastated!"

Susannah covered her mouth to muffle her giggles. "I'm sure you were."

"My point is that women recover from these harmless lit-tle infatuations," Libby said, trying to remain serious. "They don't mean a thing."

Susannah's laughter finally dissipated. "To you, perhaps," she said seriously. "But what about Case Longstreet? What is he supposed to make of your flirtation?"

Libby gasped. "I'm not flirting!"

"Aren't you? When he's in the room, your eyes look no-where else. Your face positively glows, and you hang on his every word. What kind of an impression are you giving him?"

"That I find him . . . interesting," she answered, finding that their conversation was growing quite uncomfortable.

"But what if he begins to believe it's more than that? Libby, you can't toy with this man," Susannah warned.

"I'm not toying with him! I'm . . . I'm . . ."

"Just infatuated?"

"That's right."

Susannah shook her head. "No, Libby, I think it's more. You're obsessed with him. He's handsome, enigmatic, and, even more tantalizing, he's forbidden fruit. By word or deed everyone at Fort Apache has told you to stay away from him, but you're just stubborn enough to defy them all for spite."

The words were gently spoken, but their impact hit Libby like a slap in the face. Too hurt to be angry, she froze in the chair. "Is that really what you think of me, Susannah? You believe I'm that shallow?"

"No, of course not," she exclaimed quickly, realizing she'd expressed herself badly. "I'm just trying to impress on you the dangers of an infatuation with Longstreet. We're in a pre-carious situation here, Libby. You may feel sorry for the Apaches on this reservation, but you can't lose sight of the fact that they are a warlike race of people who could rise against us at any moment with only the slightest provoca-tion."

"Case would never harm me—or anyone else at Fort Apache!"

"Perhaps not," Susannah said evenly. "But you can't deny that a very real prejudice exists against him. What if Major Forsythe or some of the other soldiers took it upon them-

selves to punish Longstreet for the interest he's shown in you?
Longstreet's people respect him. Can you imagine what they'd
do if he was killed because of a white woman?''

''That's preposterous,'' she snapped, refusing even to en-
tertain the idea. ''Nothing like that is going to happen. Now
could we please change the subject before you decide to tell
me again how shallow I am.''

''I didn't mean to offend you, Libby.''

''I know,'' she replied, but it was difficult to accept the
notion that her only friend at Fort Apache thought of her as
a petulant child. Her attraction to Case Longstreet was not
an act of rebellion. Yes, she cared more for him than she was
willing to admit to Susannah, or even herself, but her obsession had nothing to do with his being ''forbidden fruit.''

They changed the subject to something harmless, but Libby
was suddenly too restless to stay still. Alert to every sound
on the parade ground, she rose frequently and went to the
window, but there was nothing to see except the lights in the
enlisted men's barracks across the quadrangle.

Finally, when she realized she was being anything but a
comfort to Susannah, she left, knowing that Mumford would
look after the mother and child until the captain returned.
The idea of going back to her empty quarters was unappeal-
ing, but there were precious few options open to her. The
evening was cool, with no moon to provide even a glimmer
of illumination. The stars were so vivid they looked close
enough to touch, though, and Libby stepped out from under
the ramada, leaned back against the support post, and began
looking for constellations.

Orion and the Pleiades were simple. The nearby Hyades
were more difficult. Pegasus proved so elusive that before she
could find it she grew dizzy from looking up.

''Have you lost something, Miss Ashford?''

The voice in the dark was so soothing that Libby wasn't at
all startled, but she did wonder how Case Longstreet had
managed to come so close to her without alerting her to his
presence. Then she remembered he was an Apache, and dismissed the question as foolish. Susannah's dire prediction
also passed through her mind, but she dismissed it as well.

Being with Case felt so right that she couldn't bring herself to believe it was wrong.

"Indeed I have, Mr. Longstreet," she replied wistfully, glancing up again. "Pegasus is missing."

Case looked up at the stars. "Perhaps if you told me what this Pegasus is, I could help you find it."

"He's a beautiful white winged horse from Greek mythology."

"Ah." That explained why he'd never heard the word before. He'd had trouble enough comprehending the white man's ways without delving into the fables of ancient cultures. He did know that men had once assigned mystical meanings to the stars, though. "I'm afraid I see no horse, winged or otherwise. Perhaps if you looked over the stable . . ."

Libby laughed and abandoned her search. "You're teasing me."

"A little," Case conceded, stepping closer as though drawn to her like a magnet.

"Don't your people ascribe meanings to the stars?"

"Not as specifically as some. A falling star is said to point in the direction of an approaching enemy. And that band of light there"—he used his thumb to point to the Milky Way—"is made by the pitching of a flour-laden burro."

"I suppose that makes as much sense as seeing a winged horse in a collection of random lights," she said with an airy laugh. "Tell me, is there a reason why you pointed with your thumb?"

He looked down, and for the first time in their brief acquaintance, Libby thought that he was actually embarrassed. "Pointing to any heavenly body with a finger gives you warts," he finally answered.

Libby stifled a laugh. "I see." There was a moment of silence as they looked at each other. The lights from the officers' quarters were the only illumination, and it was difficult to see clearly. For some reason, though, the darkness enhanced the strange connection Libby always felt to this man when she was with him—and sometimes when she wasn't. "Do you believe that?" she asked after a moment.

"I respect the beliefs of my people," he replied.

"But you've experienced so much more of the world than most of your people. Surely that's eliminated some of your superstitions."

Case knew she wasn't criticizing him or his people. She was simply trying to understand him. He took another step toward her, and Libby shifted so that her shoulder was leaning against the post. Case couldn't resist mirroring her position on the other side of it. "I once visited the home of my friend, Jedidiah, in Philadelphia. His family was quite suspicious of me, but they took me in and treated me as they would have any other guest," he told her, smiling fondly at the memory.

Libby was certain he hadn't changed the subject and was working toward an answer to her question, so she remained silent, enjoying the hypnotic quality of his voice.

"The first night we sat down to supper, his aunt spilled a little bowl of salt, and when she cried out in alarm, I jumped from my chair and began searching for a spider or snake on the tablecloth. Everyone assumed I was preparing to attack them, but dear Aunt Millie was oblivious to their fear because she was too busy throwing pinches of salt over her shoulder, muttering 'bad luck, bad luck.' "

Libby laughed merrily. "I retract my question."

Case chuckled, too. "No, it's a valid one," he said gently. "What you really want to know is whether I ever find myself confused by the differences between my beliefs and yours."

"Do you?"

"Sometimes," he admitted. "But I have learned to accept what is without asking too many questions."

"Whereas I question everything," Libby observed.

"It seems that way to me." He looked down at her, and it was everything he could do to keep from touching her face. "And if you don't like the answers you get to your questions, you fight to change them."

Libby could hardly breathe. "Is that bad?"

"It is wonderful."

Without thinking about what she was doing, Libby moistened her lips and realized that she had never wanted to be kissed so desperately in her life. The desire was so potent that she moved a little distance away from the pillar, trying to break the spell she had fallen under. It didn't work. She tried changing the subject, but feared that wouldn't do the trick, either.

"Obviously you've finished your meeting with General Crook," she observed somewhat belatedly.

Case took a step back as well. His thoughts were too dangerous. "Yes. The general is laying out his strategies."

"Is the meeting over?" she asked, wondering why she hadn't noticed any officers passing.

"No. I expect it will go on for several hours, but my presence was no longer required. I was headed for the Robertsons' to make certain that Tessa had left for her home."

Libby assured him that she had, then made a vague gesture toward the hospital. She murmured something about needing to return to her quarters, and Case bade her good night. As he started to walk away, though, Libby found that she couldn't let him go. "You'll be leaving with the cavalry, won't you?"

Case turned to her. "Yes."

"Will you be careful?"

He smiled. "An Apache is always careful."

A pause turned into a protracted silence, but neither of them moved. Finally it was Libby who broke it. "Would it be presumptuous of me to ask you to walk me home, Mr. Longstreet?"

"It would be foolish of you to ask and foolish of me to do you that courtesy," he answered quietly.

Libby took a step back. "You're right, of course. Forgive me."

"Anything."

His voice was as soft as the breeze against her face, and for reasons that made absolutely no sense, Libby suddenly felt like crying. "Good night, Mr. Longstreet." She turned and had taken only a few steps when Case fell in beside her.

Her melancholy vanished, and she couldn't bring herself to comment on their folly. They were simply two fools. Two fools in love, she thought, then quickly swept the ridiculous notion away. She was passing a few innocent minutes with an intriguing stranger on a dark, silent night. There was no reason to read more into it than that.

Case inquired after Susannah's health, and their discussion eventually turned to Tessa's thirst for knowledge. They strolled along at a leisurely pace, speaking of trivialities that didn't seem trivial to them, and when they reached the hospital, it was the most natural thing in the world for them to sit in the chairs Libby and Meade kept on the porch for those times when they needed to escape the heat of their quarters.

Case asked about her "garden," which was surviving despite the heat. He asked where she had come from and why she had chosen to follow her brother to Fort Apache. She told him the truth about her life—the loneliness that had been alleviated only by her brother, the restrictions and conventions that had always chafed her, the inadequacies she felt because she was so different from other women.

Case commented little, but he cherished the things she told him because they gave him a better understanding of her. In some ways, her past had been no less tragic than his, but she had a spirit that refused to be broken.

She also had a curiosity that was insatiable, and soon she was the one asking the questions. She asked simple ones at first, but it was impossible for her to resist becoming more personal. "Last week you told me that your Apache name, He Chases the Thunder, describes your life. What did you mean by that?"

"It is the name that was given to me when I became a man," he said evasively.

"But how is it descriptive of your life?"

He tried to find her eyes in the darkness, but she was only a vague shadow. He felt her, though, as he had felt her every day of the last eleven years. "You would not understand," he replied, but something inside him told him that was a lie. She would understand.

"Is it something you're forbidden to speak of?" she asked, remembering the few times that Tessa had refused to answer her questions because she feared that some harm might come to her.

"It is . . . complicated."

"Then I won't press you to talk about it." Libby was disappointed, but she tried not to let it show. Case heard it in her voice, though.

"I did not say that to hurt you, Libby."

He used her name for the first time, and she had never heard it sound so sweet. "I'm not hurt. It's just that I have so many questions about you. I'd like to understand how you became the man you are."

He was silent for a moment. "Would you be so eager to understand me if you knew that my life has only one purpose, that of revenge?"

"Revenge?"

"It is all I am, Libby," he told her, his voice growing hard. "I exist for no other reason, and until I have that revenge, I have no other life."

She leaned toward him. "Revenge against what? Or whom?"

"His name is Gato."

Libby didn't have to see his face to imagine the hatred she would see in his eyes. The depth of his loathing was in his voice. "What did he do to you?"

"He murdered my parents and all the women and old men of my mother's family. He took my sister, Morning Star, to be sold as a slave in Mexico, and he stole a necklace that has great meaning to my people . . . and to me."

Libby couldn't begin to imagine the horror of what he described, and her heart went out to him. "Where were you when it happened?"

"In the eye of an eagle. Watching," he answered quietly. He half expected her to get up then and leave without a backward glance. Had she known what was good for her, she would have; but she stayed.

"Do you mean that literally?" she asked.

"Yes."

Libby wasn't sure what to say. It was impossible for her to believe him, of course, but it never occurred to her to doubt that he believed it. In the final analysis, that was all that really mattered. "When did it happen?"

"Eleven years ago."

"And you've been searching for Gato all this time?"

"No," he replied, amazed at her acceptance. "I have spent these years preparing for my revenge."

"When will that happen?"

In the simplest terms he could find, he explained the spirit journey the eagle had taken him on and the many sights that had been revealed to him. "When all of the visions have come to pass, then I will take my revenge."

The memory of their first meeting was nagging at Libby. "Did you meet people on your journey?"

"Yes. General Crook I met. And Major Forsythe . . . and many others who have already come and gone from my life."

Libby hardly dared ask her next question. "The night you first saw me, at Colonel Dunlevy's, you looked at me as though you had seen me before." She held her breath. "Was I in your dream?"

The silence grew long and heavy before he replied. "Yes."

"What is to become of me?"

"I don't know," he replied honestly. "My journey was filled with signposts that have pointed me in the direction of Gato, in the same way that I would follow a shooting star to find my enemy. In meeting you I have passed another milestone that has brought me one step closer."

"How many . . . milestones are left?"

"Not many. A great battle is coming. Gato will be there, but I will not know it until later. I will find his arrow."

"How will you know it's his?"

"Each brave makes his own arrows, and on each one he carves a symbol to make it fly straight and sure. I have seen Gato's arrows before," he said coldly, remembering the shaft that Jedidiah had removed from his shoulder. "I will know it when I see it again. Soon after that we will come face to face. We will fight, and one of us will die."

"Do you mean your dream doesn't show you prevailing over Gato?" Libby asked, trying to quell her fear. What Case was telling her was beyond her comprehension, and it undoubtedly had about as much validity as the salt dear Aunt Millie had thrown over her shoulder to ward off bad luck; but for some reason Libby believed him. She felt like a child being frightened by a ghost story on a stormy night, but there was nothing childlike about her fear. It was painfully real.

Case heard the fear in her voice and was touched by it. He wanted to reach out to her, but didn't dare. Instead, he stood and moved restlessly to the edge of the porch. "The eagle promised me only that I would meet Gato," he told her. "I have spent my life preparing. I am ready."

Libby frowned at him through the darkness. A light from the barracks across the quadrangle cast him in silhouette, highlighting the perfection of his lean form. It was the hatred in his heart that induced her to go to him, though. "But you might die."

Case shrugged, refusing to look at her. "Then I will die."

"How do you know this Gato isn't already dead?" she challenged. There was more light at the edge of the porch than there had been in the shadows, and she could see the fixed, determined set of his jaw.

"I have followed him for years. He knows I am waiting, and he knows why."

"Where is he now?"

"At this second? I'm not sure," he confessed. "Last year he was hiding in Mexico, but he will return soon."

Libby placed her hand on his arm. The simple touch moved them both. "Case, your parents are dead. Wreaking revenge on Gato won't bring them back."

He looked at the soft pale hand on his arm, then at her delicate heart-shaped face. He couldn't allow the imploring look in her eyes to sway him. "It will bring the Thunderbird necklace back to me. Until I have that, my mother and father cannot be at peace. That is reason enough."

He believed every word of it. Libby realized that nothing she could say would sway him from the dangerous course he had set. Perhaps his visions were irrational, but his hatred was as much a part of him as his piercing eyes and the dignity with which he carried himself in the white man's world.

"Do I play a part in your revenge?" she whispered, unable to look away from him.

"I don't know."

Will I ever play a part in your life? she wanted to ask, but didn't dare.

They studied each other for a moment, bound together by a web of emotion neither of them understood or wished to explain. It was Case who finally broke the fragile strands by stepping off the porch. He bade her a good evening, then disappeared into the night. Libby stood on the porch watching the darkness long after he had gone.

She didn't notice the two soldiers across the quadrangle who'd been hidden in the shadows between the barracks buildings, passing a bottle of whiskey back and forth.

But they had noticed her. And Case.

SIXTEEN

THE NEXT MORNING General Crook tapped his foot thought-fully as he studied the map on his office wall. Between the Black River and Cochise's stronghold in the Dragoon Mountains, tiny red flags marked a score of locations that had been hit by renegades during the past month. Thanks to a treaty that had made the Dragoons a reservation—and an unsupervised one, at that—there was no way Crook could mount an assault against the wily old Chiricahua chief. However, with troops from Fort Thomas and Fort Bowie he was going to do his damnedest to make an impression on the bands of renegades who were leaving the reservation, attacking rancheros, and then hightailing it back to Cochise.

A knock at his door broke Crook's concentration, but he didn't turn away from the map as he called, "Come."

His adjutant stepped into the room and announced, "Case Longstreet reporting as ordered, sir."

"Good! Come in, Case." He turned as the scout entered, and his welcoming smile turned into a scowl of barely controlled outrage when he saw the bruises and cuts on the Apache's face. "That will be all, Lieutenant," he barked, and the adjutant left, closing the door behind him. "What happened?" he demanded once they were alone.

Case's battered face remained impassive. "It's nothing, sir."

Crook retreated to his desk. "That cut over your eye is not nothing, Longstreet." He sat. "Since I've never known an

Apache to engage in fisticuffs, I presume this was done by one or more of my men. Correct?''

"I'd rather not say."

"Is this person, or persons, still alive?"

"To my knowledge, none of your soldiers are missing, sir."

"But you're not going to tell me who did this to you?"

"No."

"Blast it, Case, I cannot have this sort of thing going on. I've got a hundred White Mountain Apache scouts on the army payroll. They trust me, and by virtue of that, they trust the army. If I allow whoever did this to go unpunished, I could lose that trust. I'd be in a devil of a fix then, and you know it."

Case shook his head. "The incident is already in the past, General. Believe me when I tell you that it will be much better for all concerned if you leave it alone."

Crook drummed his fingers on the desk. Longstreet clearly wasn't going to explain what had happened, why, or who had been involved. Unfortunately, the general had a pretty good idea about the why. And the who wouldn't be too difficult to determine, either. "I daresay it won't be too hard to find out who else was involved. I'll just search for the man or men who look worse than you do."

Case almost smiled. "As I said, sir, the matter would be best left alone."

"Because there's a lady involved?" Crook asked shrewdly. Case's silence was all the answer he needed. He shook his head, wondering how to handle what could become an explosive situation. At the Dunlevys' party, he'd found Miss Liberty Ashford's forthrightness refreshing. What he'd heard about her since had convinced him she was a lady of great conviction and spirit. Her association with the scout was probably quite innocent, but it could lead to problems that Crook shuddered even to think about.

"Longstreet, you're a civilian scout. I can't punish you, because to my knowledge, you haven't done anything wrong. And since you're not a soldier, I can't order you to stay away from . . . this lady. The most I could do would be to release you from your contract with the army and ban you from Fort Apache.'' He sighed heavily. ''Of course, if I did that, I'd probably lose about half of my scouts.''

''You're probably right.''

Crook had to smile at that. One of the things he'd liked most about this scout from the very beginning was his candor. He could always count on getting nothing but the unvarnished truth from Case Longstreet. ''Then I don't have any choice but to leave this matter up to your good judgment, do I?''

Case's glance didn't waver from the general's. ''Not that I can see, sir.''

''Well, if you don't wish to press charges against the men who did this to you, then officially I'll have to pretend that it didn't happen. I just hope there are no . . . repercussions.''

''So do I.''

Crook got down to business, questioning Case about the readiness of his scouts, who would be setting out in advance of the cavalry the next morning. Case assured him that the braves were ready. ''But they want to hold a ceremony tonight, General.''

Crook frowned. ''You mean a war dance, don't you?''

For the first time since he'd entered the room, Case smiled. The very mention of an Apache doing a war dance was enough to make even the most stalwart army man nervous, because there was always an element of doubt in the soldier's mind about whom the Apaches were preparing to make war on. Those who had actually seen a war dance got even more nervous. ''If they're not allowed to perform the ceremony, some of them will refuse to go,'' Case reminded him.

''I know.'' Crook sighed. ''Permission granted.''

''Thank you, General.''

They completed their business, but as Case started to leave, Crook stopped him at the door. ''One more thing, Longstreet. I want you to head over to the infirmary and see Dr. Ashford about that cut over your eye.''

Case immediately thought of the doctor's lovely sister and what had happened last night as a result of the time he had spent with her. For Case, a few cuts and bruises were a small price to pay for those precious moments, but when word of his fight and the reason for it began to spread, as it surely would, Libby Ashford might feel very differently. "That's not necessary, sir," he replied.

"I disagree, and since I'm in charge, what I think is the only thing that matters. I can't afford to risk that cut festering and putting you out of commission. You're too valuable to me. Report to the infirmary immediately."

Case had no choice but to acquiesce. "Yes, sir."

Crook looked at him archly. "And just in case Captain Ashford has heard about your little altercation, I trust you will bear in mind that he is to accompany us tomorrow. I wouldn't want him out of commission, either."

Case nodded curtly. "Understood."

He left Crook's office and headed for the hospital, mustering all the Apache stoicism at his command. The glares that followed him eliminated any hope that Libby's brother was ignorant of the fight—and the reason for it.

"They did what?" Meade demanded, glaring at Sergeant Brogan. The striker had apparently felt it was his duty to bring Captain Ashford the news as soon as he'd heard it. He'd found Meade in the infirmary and drawn him aside for a word in private.

"They ambushed him, sir," Brogan replied, looking a little embarrassed at having to recount the gossip. "They slipped away from the fort and hid themselves near Longstreet's wickiup. As soon as he got back to his camp, they gave him a good thrashin'. Or at least, they *tried*. From the looks of 'em this morning, it was the Injun who did most of the thrashin'."

"And you say they did it because they saw Libby with Longstreet?" Meade asked, scowling.

"Now, they're not sayin' that Miss Liberty did anything wrong, Captain. It was the scout."

Meade had never been so angry. "What did he do to her?"

Brogan shrugged. "No one knows for sure. Naturally, Reynolds and Cooper aren't talkin' much 'cause they're afraid of bein' punished. The facts have sorta been pieced together.

All anyone knows for sure is that Longstreet and Miss Liberty were seen on the porch, sorta . . . close, like.''

"Libby!'' Meade bellowed, storming through the ward. His only two patients watched him go, wondering what all the excitement was about. "Libby!''

In their quarters next door, Libby was preparing to visit Susannah when she heard her brother shouting to her. The behavior was so out of character that she was convinced something was seriously wrong. Her heart beating in her throat, she dashed into the connecting hallway and collided with Meade in the hospital anteroom.

"Meade! What's wrong?'' she asked urgently, then winced as he grabbed her arm and propelled her through the door of his office. "Meade, stop that. You're hurting me.''

He released her. "What the devil did you think you were doing?''

"What are you talking about?'' she asked, rubbing her arm.

"Last night you were seen with Longstreet!''

That was what the fuss was about? Libby was astonished. "What of it?'' she asked defiantly.

"What did he do to you?'' Meade demanded.

"Nothing! We just talked. What's wrong with that?'' she asked, beginning to get a little angry herself.

Meade could hardly believe she was treating this so lightly. "Someone saw you!''

"What difference does that make?''

"My God, Libby. You're a smart woman. Don't you see the damage you've done?''

Libby was getting frightened. She'd seen her brother angry before, but she'd never seen him act like this. "All we did was sit on the porch and talk. It was perfectly innocent,'' she insisted, though she knew very well the feelings she'd experienced last night were anything but.

"Well, because of your innocent little talk, two privates from Company D took it upon themselves to defend your honor.''

"Oh, God,'' Libby whispered, reaching for the back of a

chair for support. Susannah's warning flashed through her mind, and guilt and fear nearly overpowered her.

"They ambushed Longstreet in his camp last night."

"Where is he?" she asked frantically. "How badly was he hurt?" Assuming he was in the hospital, Libby dashed for the door, but Meade grabbed her arm again.

"Libby, stop worrying about Longstreet and think of your reputation!"

"The devil take my reputation! *Is Case all right!*"

Meade couldn't believe what he was seeing and hearing. "My God, Libby, you're in love with the man."

Tears pooled in her eyes. "Meade, please. Is Case hurt?" She held her breath. "Is he dead?"

"No, Libby, I'm fine."

Libby whirled at the sound of Case's voice and found him standing in the door Meade had left ajar. Relief flooded through her, and she ran toward him, stopping just short of throwing herself into his arms. She studied his battered face, knowing that what had happened was her fault. Biting her lower lip to force back tears, she gingerly touched the bruise on his cheek.

"It's all right," he said softly, wanting more than anything to draw her into his arms.

"I'm so sorry," she whispered.

"It's not your fault."

A tear escaped her control. "Yes, it is. I shouldn't have asked you to walk me home."

Unable to stop himself, Case reached out and brushed the tear away. "And I should have had the strength to say no," he answered softly.

The look on Longstreet's face told Meade much more than he wanted to know. "Libby, go to our quarters at once."

Fighting anger at his dictatorial tone, Libby lowered her head. "Don't order me around, Meade. I'm a grown woman."

"Then for God's sake start acting like one!"

She whirled toward him. "Don't yell at me."

Case placed a calming hand on her shoulder, and she glanced back at him. "Do as he says, Libby, please. I won't be the cause of trouble between you and your brother. Go home and calm down.''

She opened her mouth to argue, but there was nothing to say. Terrified of what her brother might do after she left, she hesitated for a moment, then went to Meade. "Have I ever lied to you?" she asked softly.

Meade felt his anger draining away, but the concern that replaced it was just as potent. "No, Libby. We've always been perfectly honest with each other.''

"Then you have to believe me when I tell you that Case and I didn't do anything wrong last night.''

Meade shook his head helplessly. Couldn't she see the damage she was doing, not just to herself, but to Longstreet, too? "I do believe you, sweeting.'' Gently he took her by the shoulders and placed a kiss on her brow. "Let me talk to Longstreet.''

Libby nodded and pulled away from him. "You'll take care of his cuts, won't you?''

"Of course.''

She stepped toward the door, stopping when she reached Case. She looked up at him, wanting more than anything to touch him, to feel the comfort of his arms around her, but that was impossible. There didn't seem to be anything to say, either. Though it was difficult, she hurried out of the office, through the anteroom, and into the hallway. She pushed the door to, leaving it ajar, and leaned against the wall, straining to hear what was being said, but there was nothing to hear because Meade had closed the door to his office.

Now that Meade's anger had cooled, he wasn't quite certain what to say to Longstreet. The Apache was standing by the desk, his face a mask of stoicism. Gone was the tenderness Meade had seen in his eyes when he'd looked at Libby, but there was no hostility there, either. They stared at each other for a moment; then Meade went to his desk and removed a bottle of whiskey from the drawer where his predecessor had left it. He wasn't a drinking man by nature, but the situation seemed to call for it.

"Would you care for a drink?" he asked, pouring a shot into the cup that had held his morning coffee.

"Haven't you heard? It's illegal to give an Indian liquor," Case said placidly.

Meade studied him for a moment. "You meant that as sarcasm, Mr. Longstreet, but actually you've hit upon the crux of this little mess we've landed in." He took a sip of whiskey. "See, you don't seem like an Indian, not to my sister, at least. You're as civilized and mannerly as any officer on this post, and apparently Libby can't see past the veneer."

Case didn't like what Ashford was saying, but he respected his directness. "Perhaps she sees me with better eyes than you do. She looks with her heart and sees me for what I am."

"And what are you?" Meade challenged.

For Libby's sake, because this man was someone she loved, Case knew he had to be equally honest. "A man standing between two worlds, belonging to neither, but a *man* just the same."

"A man who's in love with my sister."

Case found it difficult to hold Meade's penetrating gaze, but he did. "I respect your sister. I have great admiration for her openness."

"You're not going to admit you're in love with her, are you?"

"No," he replied.

"But you're perfectly willing to contribute to the ruination of her reputation."

This time Case had to look away. "That was never my intention."

Meade slammed the cup onto his desk. "Damn it all, Longstreet, just what were your intentions? Did you really expect to carry on an open flirtation with my sister and not have anyone object?"

Case frowned. This was becoming frustrating. "This was never a flirtation, Captain Ashford."

"Then what would you call it?"

"A friendship."

Meade looked at him in disbelief. "Can you honestly stand there and tell me that your feelings for my sister are strictly platonic?"

Case was beginning to feel like a child being reprimanded

by a parent, and he didn't like it. He'd been prepared to take whatever abuse Ashford wanted to fling at him for the damage done to Libby's reputation, but he hadn't expected to be asked to dissect his emotions. At the moment they were so tangled he couldn't even identify them himself, let alone explain them. Or justify them.

"You would not understand what I feel for your sister, Captain."

Meade was having a hard time, too, because he was finding it impossible to dislike Case Longstreet. He knew the man's reputation—both the good and the bad—and he had to respect him for the things he had accomplished. In the territory of Arizona, where hatred of the Apache ran at a fever pitch, Case Longstreet had earned the trust and respect of George Crook, one of the most important military men in the country. That hadn't happened without a reason.

And Meade also knew his sister. It was impossible for him to imagine Libby caring so intensely about someone who had no redeeming qualities. But Case Longstreet was an Apache. All the good diction and proper manners in the world weren't going to change that fact.

"You do realize that a relationship with my sister is impossible, don't you?" he asked finally.

Case's expression didn't change, but an intense pain seized his heart. "I know."

"Then for God's sake stay away from her. I don't want Libby to be hurt!"

"Her interest in me will soon pass," he predicted.

Meade shook his head. "You don't understand my sister, Longstreet. She gives with her whole heart, holding nothing back. That's what makes her so special, but in your case, it could destroy her. I won't let that happen."

"Neither will I."

"Then stay away from her."

Case looked down at the floor as he tried to sort through his emotions. It was a long moment before he spoke again. "Do you believe that some things in this world are beyond the control of one man—or many?"

The question took Meade by surprise. He hadn't been a

doctor long, but during his hospital apprenticeship, he'd seen patients die who should have lived, and some live who should have died. The lesson it had taught him was that all too often man was as powerless as any of God's other creatures. "Yes. I do."

"Good." Case nodded. "I will stay away from your sister, Captain," he promised, then took a step toward Meade. "But if this should turn out to be beyond your control and mine and Libby's you will have to accept it."

"Never," Meade swore.

Case shook his head sadly. "Then it is you who will destroy your sister."

Meade didn't want to admit it, but he knew Longstreet was right. He would just have to do everything in his power to convince Libby that she had chosen to care for the wrong man. There didn't seem to be anything more to say to the scout, though. Meade believed his promise to stay away from Libby, but in his heart he knew that wasn't going to be enough.

"Come into the infirmary and I'll dress that cut," he said shortly, heading for the door.

But Case didn't follow him. "Ashford." Meade turned. "You know that I must see Libby before I leave tomorrow."

Meade thought it over and nodded reluctantly. If Longstreet left tomorrow without speaking to Libby, she would magnify this incident in her mind. She might even romanticize it beyond recognition—or control. "You'll tell her that a relationship is impossible and you don't want to see her again?"

Case was silent for a moment. "I will say what needs to be said."

That wasn't a very satisfactory answer, but Meade knew he wasn't going to get a better one. "All right. You can see her after I've had a look at that cut."

Case met his gaze evenly. "I wasn't asking your permission."

Meade's anger flared again, but he controlled it when he realized that Longstreet wasn't being insolent, just honest.

He opened the office door, and Case followed him through the anteroom into the infirmary.

Waiting in the shadowed hallway, Libby heard them go, but that was all she had heard. She opened the door a few inches more. Case would pass by on his way out of the hospital, and Libby intended to talk to him, no matter what anyone said or thought. She had to make sense of what she was feeling. She had to know what Case was feeling. Most of all, she just had to see him again because he was leaving tomorrow and there might never be another chance.

She waited for what seemed like hours. When she heard the squeak of the infirmary door at last, she peeked into the anteroom. As Case passed her hiding place, she opened the door wide.

He stopped and looked at her. He could see that she had been crying, and traces of fear laced with confusion showed plainly in her eyes. For the first time Case realized that his woman had no defenses to protect her from the kind of pain she was feeling now. He wanted to provide that protection, but how could he when he was the cause?

"We have to talk. Please," Libby implored.

"I know."

She stepped back to make room for him in the hallway and closed the door behind him. She started to lead him into the parlor at the other end of the hall, then remembered the open windows. Anyone passing might see or hear them, and this nightmare could start all over again.

"We'll have more privacy here," she said quietly. The room on the other side of the wall was a supply room, so it was unlikely they would be heard. Sunlight coming in from the parlor made it possible for them to see each other clearly, but the knowledge that they had to hide in a hallway only added to Libby's confusion and pain. They stood a few feet apart, close enough for their hands to touch had they reached out, but neither did.

"What did my brother say to you?"

"What we already know. That you and I cannot be together, even as friends."

Libby started to protest, then looked at the bruises on his

face and remembered why they were there. "I don't have any choice but to accept that, do I?"

Case shook his head. "No."

She found it impossible to look at him. "When Meade told me what had happened, I'd never been so frightened. They might have killed you."

He smiled ruefully. "Fortunately for me, that was not what they had in mind."

Libby heard the humor in his voice and looked up. "They just wanted to teach you a lesson?" He nodded. "What did you do?"

"I fought them off without doing too much damage. They'd been drinking, so it wasn't difficult."

"But you'd have been within your rights to kill them."

"I'm not as much of a savage as everyone thinks I am."

Libby took one step toward him. "I don't think that."

"I know," Case said softly.

She wanted desperately for him to reach for her, but when he didn't, she turned and faced the wall, embarrassed by her overwhelming emotions. "I'm falling in love with you," she whispered. "You know that, don't you?"

Case wanted to tell her that he had been in love with her long before they'd met. It would have made her woman's heart open to him like a flower to the sun. But her brother was right. If she gave him all her heart, her trust, her loyalty, it would destroy her. But he wasn't going to lie to her and allow her to believe that she meant nothing to him. She wouldn't have believed it anyway. "You are the most priceless woman I have ever met, Libby. Your honor and honesty, your sweetness and compassion, are all any man could want in the woman he loves."

Libby clung to the words, gathered them into her heart, and stored them in a safe place. "What do Apache women do when they care for a man they can't have?"

"The same as white women. They carry on with their lives until a man comes along whom they can have."

"And what does a man do?"

Case remembered the story of how his father had fought the opposition of two tribes for the woman he loved. It made him want to claim Libby as his woman then and there and tell the white man's world to go to the hell they believed in. But there was his revenge against Gato to think of and the uncertain future he faced. Even when he came to the end of his quest, there would still be the world to deal with, to live in. Perhaps by the time his bones had turned to dust, an Apache would be able to love a white woman and the world would smile, but Case didn't really believe that would happen.

"If he cares for her enough, he lets her go," he replied sadly. "What does a white man do?"

Libby looked up at him, her heart shining in her eyes. "If he loves her enough, he fights for her."

She was disappointed in him. He saw it in her eyes, and it hurt him as much as not being able to tell her he loved her. "I must go, Libby."

"No." Her hand flew to his arm to detain him. "Not yet."

He looked down at her and placed his hand on hers, but did not pry it away. "There is nothing more to say."

"I have many things to say!"

He shook his head. "Nothing that will change what is."

"Case, please . . ." she pleaded softly, raising her hand to caress his cheek. "You're leaving tomorrow, and there may not be another chance. . . ." Stretching up, she pressed her lips to his.

The kiss was light and innocent, but it was the sweetest thing Case had ever experienced. His people did not kiss; it was considered unclean. But there was nothing repulsive about Libby's lips touching his. He had never felt anything like it.

His breath hissed between his lips. His eyes closed, shutting out the world that would not have approved, forgetting about the quest for revenge that had forced him to go places an Apache should never have gone. He pulled Libby into his arms, lifting her off her feet as he pressed her body to his. She wrapped her arms around his neck and tangled her fingers in his hair as their lips explored and tasted. The kiss and their embrace went beyond passion. It was the communion of one lonely soul reaching for another and finding it was no longer alone.

When Case finally released her, lowering her feet to the floor, they looked at each other. Both were breathless, aching, and more confused than ever.

"You should feel soiled," Case said in a deep, hoarse voice that made Libby tremble with need.

A sob welled in her throat, and tears coursed down her face. She brushed at the wetness on her cheek and looked down at the glistening teardrops on her fingertips. "I feel as though my heart is going to break in half," she whispered. She studied his face, memorizing every line, every angle, and especially the bruises that symbolized the reason she couldn't fight for this man's love. She touched a swollen spot on his cheek, then placed her fingertips against his mouth. "I can't bear the thought of causing you any more pain."

Case's breath hitched as his tongue tasted the residue of her salty tears. "The pain would be yours."

"I don't care."

He embraced her gently, pulling her close, resting his cheek against her hair. "You would, *cida'ké*. Someday you would."

Libby made no effort to control her silent tears, nor did she try to correct him, though she knew he was wrong. "What does that mean—*cida'ké*?"

Case hesitated. "It means 'beloved.' "

She clutched him tightly, then let go and stepped back. "Do your people have a god?" she asked, her voice broken with emotion.

The question surprised him. "We have many deities, but the spirit who leads me is the Thunder Eagle."

"Then I will ask your god and mine to keep you safe." She took another step back. "Good-bye . . . *cida'ké*."

She turned and walked slowly toward her quarters. The sunlight coming from the parlor cast her in a golden halo until she quietly closed the door.

For a long time Case stood in the darkness. When his parents died, he had never shed a tear. Was it wrong, he wondered, that his face was wet now?

SEVENTEEN

▱▱▱▱▱▱▱

SHE WAS SITTING in the rocking chair, staring blankly through the window when Meade finally found her late in the afternoon. It was the third time he'd checked their quarters, but there had been no sign of her. At first he'd feared she might have run off with Longstreet, but he had quickly discounted that notion. Libby had never taken the coward's way out of anything in her life, and it was unlikely that Longstreet had, either.

Meade stood in the door, watching her for a moment. She had to know he was there, but she refused to look in his direction.

"Where have you been, Libby?" he asked quietly.

It was a moment before she answered. "I had to prepare dinner for Susannah."

The terrible flatness of her voice frightened Meade. "Are you all right?"

"I will be."

Meade moved a cane-backed chair close to the rocker and sat, leaning forward with his elbows on his knees. "Libby, talk to me."

She looked at him finally, but there wasn't a flicker of life in her dark brown eyes. "It's over." She laughed bitterly. "And the truly funny thing is, I don't even know what 'it' was."

He touched her hands. They were as cold as death despite

218

the afternoon heat. "You fell in love, Libby. It had to happen sometime."

Tears pooled in her eyes. "It hurts."

"I know." Meade wasn't sure he could bear seeing her like this. "But, my sweet, darling Libby, you can't fight the world."

"Yes, I can," she replied with the conviction of a true idealist. "I would fight anyone or anything if it meant that Case and I could be together. But I won't," she assured him. "Yesterday Susannah warned me about what could happen, and she was right. It could be worse next time, and I can't let Case take that risk."

"You never cease to amaze me, little sister."

"Your little sister is growing up in a hurry, Meade." She patted his hand. "It's about time, wouldn't you say?"

"I love you exactly as you are, Libby. I don't want this experience to change you."

She managed a tired smile. "Maybe it will be a change for the better."

He raised her hand to his lips and kissed it. "I don't think so."

"I'll be all right, Meade," she assured him earnestly. "I don't want you worrying about me. In fact, I don't want you thinking about anything but getting yourself back here in one piece."

"I'll do my best," he promised, releasing her hand as he straightened. "Are you angry with me, Libby?"

"No," she replied.

"But you are disappointed in me, aren't you?"

Libby never would have told him that on the eve of his departure with Crook's army, but since he'd asked, she couldn't lie to him. "A little," she admitted. "You're not like Forsythe and the others who judge Case simply because he's an Apache, but I would have expected a little more tolerance from you. Or at least a little more outrage over the unfairness of it all."

"I'm only thinking of you, Libby. Obviously Case Longstreet is an honorable man. There's a great deal to admire about him."

"So long as he stays away from your sister," she said without rancor.

Meade couldn't deny it. "Yes."

"Because he's an Apache?"

He shook his head. "Because we live in a world that would never accept a relationship between a white woman and an Indian. In the long run, Libby, it would cause you enormous pain. Think of your children—"

Libby frowned. "Children? Meade, we didn't elope last night. We just talked."

"But the more you're with this man, the more you come to care for him. Can you honestly tell me you haven't thought about spending your life with this man?"

She looked away. "I haven't thought about the future at all."

"If that's true, it's because in your heart you know it's impossible for you to have a future with Case Longstreet. Libby darling, I know you're hurt, but in the final analysis, this is for the best."

"I'm sure you're right," she replied, but the part of her that was numb with pain and an overwhelming sense of loss didn't believe it.

She gave him a smile that was meant to reassure, then went off to start supper. For Meade's sake she did her best to appear normal. They both knew it was an act, but it was the only way either of them knew to get through the long night ahead. All through the meal Meade wrestled with a decision, and finally, as he helped her clear away the dishes, he made it.

"Libby, Captain Edgemont dropped by the hospital to see me today."

"That must have been pleasant," she said with a touch of sarcasm as she immersed their plates in the small tub of water on the counter. "Did he advise you to give me a sound thrashing?"

"Of course not," he scoffed, though her supposition wasn't too far from the truth. Edgemont liked Case Longstreet a great deal more than some of the other officers did—Forsythe, for example—but he still disapproved of the Apache's interest in Libby. When he made that known, it had been everything Meade could do to remain polite. Though he'd been expressing some of the same sentiments Meade felt, the cavalry captain's prejudice rankled him. Edgemont had made a suggestion, though, that had merit. "Actually, he wanted to inform me that the Apache scouts are holding a ceremony tonight, and since you've expressed such an interest in their culture, he thought you might like to attend."

Libby was surprised by the suggestion and amazed that Meade would countenance it. "Have the Apaches invited us?"

"Well, not specifically, but I checked around, and there's no prohibition against our attending. Edgemont's going, and he promised to drop by to see if we'd like to walk down with him."

"Walk?"

Meade nodded. "It's being held in a ravine near the river."

Libby mulled the idea over. Of course she was intrigued by the idea of witnessing an actual Apache ceremony, and anything at all would be better than spending a tense night alone with Meade in their quarters. But Case would surely be there. Part of her wanted to see him again, but another part warned her that the meeting might mean more pain.

The part that wanted to see him was the stronger of the two. "I'd love to go," she told him, then smiled wryly. "The idea of attending with Captain Edgemont casts a pall over the occasion, but I expect I can manage to ignore his condescension for one evening."

"Excellent. Why don't you get ready while I finish off these dishes?" he suggested.

"All right." She dried her hands and moved to the door, then paused a moment to study her brother's back, wondering why he'd told her about the ceremony. He, too, had to know that Case would be there. Why would he willingly throw her in the scout's path, unless, of course, he was convinced that his presence and Edgemont's could prevent her from spending any time with Case? That seemed the only explanation, and Libby finally slipped off to her room to don a pair of sturdier shoes and to collect her shawl.

Edgemont called as promised, and Libby was surprised to learn that the Crenshaws were accompanying them as well. Apparently the boredom of post routine had overwhelmed Caroline's aversion to the Apaches. They strolled out of the quadrangle through the egress between the hospital and the sutler's store, then picked their way across the rough plateau that led toward the river.

No one had thought to bring along a lantern, or perhaps, Libby thought, her more experienced companions knew better than to call attention to themselves.

Long before they reached the ravine, Libby could hear the insistent, steady beating of drums. The near horizon glowed a golden hue, and eventually they began to see tiny golden sparks as smoke from massive bonfires threw burning embers into the air. The drums grew louder, and when they came to the edge of the ravine the scene below sent shivers down Libby's spine. The fires sent dancing shadows up and down the sides of the vast arroyo. Hundreds of Apache men and women were seated on logs or on the ground, but the bright golden circles around the bonfires were eerily empty. The persistent drumbeats and the hissing crackle of the bonfires were the only sounds.

Meade held Libby's hand to steady her as they picked their way down the hill. No one seemed to pay them any heed as their vastly outnumbered party found a log and sat near the outer edge of the great circle.

Sandwiched between Edgemont and her brother, Libby sat spellbound as the drums picked up speed and intensity. Four braves, naked save for calf-high moccasins, breechclouts, and headbands, entered the circle of light from the east. They approached the fire side by side, then began dancing in single file around the great bonfire. They circled it four times, then separated and danced in a square pattern around the blaze.

When the drums stopped abruptly, the dancers left as they had come, and one brave stepped into the edge of the dance circle. Libby's heart skipped a beat when she realized it was Case. He was dressed like the others, and the light turned his bronze flesh to gold, highlighting every muscled contour of his naked torso and thighs. With his face raised to the ember-strewn sky, he brought his arms up and sent up a war chant that turned Libby's blood to ice. The drums began again, and the spectators began chanting and whooping as one by one the warriors entered the circle and began a furious dance.

Some carried bows; others carried spears and shields, or wicked-looking knives. They brandished the weapons, and the shouting from outside the circle rose to a fever pitch that completely drowned out Case's voice.

"He's calling the warriors by name, demanding that they dance to show how bravely they'll fight the enemy," Edgemont said, leaning close to Libby's ear. She registered the information, but was too entranced by the spectacle to acknowledge him. The whoops and yells were obviously meant as encouragment, but Libby noted that none of the dancers joined in. It was probably just as well. Their contortions were terrifying enough. They drew back their bows, they stabbed the air with their spears, they slashed with their knives. As the drumbeat quickened, so did their movements.

Libby couldn't begin to count the number of braves, nor did she try. She absorbed the primitive display like a sponge and tried to convince herself that she was not frightened. It was impossible to quell her instinctive fear, though. She was a civilized woman from a society that had long ago rejected the abandonment of inhibitions. Yet there were no constraints here. The dance was savage. The men who danced were savages. That was the image they meant to convey, and they did it with astonishing skill.

She watched them, mesmerized and horrified. This was the society in which the man she loved had been raised. She looked across the sea of warriors, searching for Case. He was not where he had been before, and she craned her neck, searching for him among the spectators. Then, without warning, a figure bathed in light and shadow suddenly leaped into the circle brandishing a rifle. He joined the frenzied dance, and Libby drew back with a start when she realized that dancer was Case.

Gripping the rifle in one hand, he held it above his head as he performed a series of dizzying twists and turns. He crouched and sprang, whirling in midair. Sweat glistened on his arms and torso as he bludgeoned imaginary enemies with the butt of the rifle. His dance was savage and horrifying, and yet it had an elemental power and grace that Libby found strangely seductive. His movements called up primal, erotic emotions Libby hadn't known she possessed. Shame merged with her fear, and her heart pounded ferociously as the cries of the spectators urged Case on until he raised the rifle and fired into the air, startling everyone.

The three army officers jumped to their feet, and Libby rose as well. Edgemont and Crenshaw reached instinctively for their revolvers, but Libby grabbed Edgemont's arm before he had the opportunity to remove it from the holster. Her fingers dug into his forearm, but what prevented him from drawing was the realization that it would be suicide to display a weapon while the Apaches were whipping themselves into a senseless frenzy.

Caroline demanded that her husband take her away immediately, and the major motioned to Edgemont and Meade. They stepped over the log, but Libby didn't move. Her eyes were riveted to Case's dancing silhouette.

"Libby? Libby . . ." Meade's voice barely reached her, but she finally glanced at him. "We have to go now. It may not be safe here. Come." His arm was at her waist, urging her to move, and she had no choice but to slip quietly away with the others. The chants and war whoops chased them out of the ravine, but when they reached the top, they all stopped and looked back. Even from that distance, Libby could pick Case out among the ferocious dancers.

She was utterly oblivious to Caroline standing beside her, until she spoke, pulling Libby out of her hypnotic haze. "Well, Libby dear," she said, her voice tinged with sarcasm, "do you still doubt that your precious Case Longstreet is a savage?"

Libby glared at her, her fear mingling with outrage and the sickening feeling that the malicious witch was right. She glanced at the others and found them all staring at her expectantly. In a flash of blinding insight, she suddenly realized why Meade had brought her here, and why Caroline and

Edgemont had come along. They all wanted to be on hand to see the moment of Libby Ashford's awakening.

"Damn you," she muttered, stiffening her jaw against a rush of tears that she refused to allow to fall. "Damn you all."

She whirled and began running toward the fort, away from her treacherous brother, away from the pulsating drums, away from the proud Apache she'd thought she knew . . . but didn't really know at all.

EIGHTEEN

LIBBY SPENT the next month in hell. After the war dance, Meade admitted that he'd known what kind of ceremony it was, and that Case would be dancing. He'd taken her because he wanted her to see the other side of the man she'd fallen in love with. He claimed to have done it for her sake.

Libby could see his actions only as a cruel deception. He had broken the bonds of trust and honesty that had always been the keystone of their relationship. Meade had always been the only person Libby could depend on, but now his dishonesty made her feel as though she'd lost the most important thing in her life. On the eve of his departure into a harrowing and uncertain future, his betrayal of her trust had cast Libby adrift in an emotional wasteland.

She watched him leave the next morning, torn between anger and the fear that she might never see him again. The scouts had set off on foot an hour before the cavalry, so Libby had no opportunity to see Case and reconcile the two hideously different images she had of him.

But in the month that followed, with word of the fate of the troops nearly nonexistent, Libby had more than enough time to think. For two weeks she devoted herself to taking care of Susannah and Michael, but every day her friend grew stronger and needed less help. Tessa continued to come, and there was little for Libby to do.

Everyone at Fort Apache knew about the cruel joke that had been played on her, and they watched her like buzzards circling their prey. "Well," their looks seemed to say, "has the high and mighty Miss Ashford learned her lesson?" Pride was about the only thing that kept Libby going. She kept her head up, her demeanor pleasant, and she refused to allow anyone to see her anguish and confusion.

Susannah was the only exception. They spent hours talking, trying to sort through Libby's tangled emotions and bring everything into perspective. It was the hours Libby spent alone, though, that did her the most good. She finally forgave Meade. He was only human, after all. He didn't want her to spend the weeks or months of Case's absence romanticizing him into something he wasn't. Meade had done what he thought was right, not out of spite or malice, but because he loved her. The breach in their relationship would mend, and Libby refused to consider the possibility that she would be denied that healing time.

Her feelings about Case were much more difficult to sort through. One minute she would laugh at herself for fancying that she'd been in love with him; the next, she would remember the desperate longing in the kiss they'd shared and the tender lights in his eyes when he looked at her. His deep, mellifluous voice spoke to her in her dreams, weaving a spell around her, drawing her to a place of warmth and safety that was very much like coming home after a long, harrowing journey.

But that was the Case Longstreet who'd sat on her porch and spoke to her in the darkness, revealing to her the demons that haunted him. That was the man she loved, and no matter how often or how resolutely she told herself that she couldn't love him, the emotion wouldn't go away. It clung to her, wrapping itself around her heart with unshakable tenacity.

There was another Case Longstreet, though—the one his people called He Chases the Thunder. Libby made no effort to block out the image of that warrior dancing in a fierce, unbridled frenzy around a ghostly fire. She forced herself to hear the war cries of his people and remember the way he'd responded. Meade had hoped the image of Case as a savage would destroy the love she felt for him. Libby hoped it would, too.

But it didn't. It was a part of him she didn't understand, one she might never understand; but after the shock wore off, she realized that Case was still the same gentle, haunted man who'd held her in his arms and called her his beloved.

Case Longstreet and He Chases the Thunder were two sides of the same coin. Just because one side was strange and savage didn't make the coin any less valuable. In some ways, in fact, it made it more so.

Unfortunately, that realization did nothing to assuage Libby's feelings of hopelessness. Meade claimed the relationship was impossible. For all her sympathetic understanding, Susannah said the same thing. Even Case believed there could be no future for them. Libby tried to accept that, but only because she feared a repeat of the incident between Case and the soldiers who had taken it upon themselves to punish him.

No matter how often she told herself it was impossible, though, she couldn't make herself believe it. She told herself she was being foolish and unrealistic. She tried imagining the isolation from society she would have to endure if she tied her life to Case's. She thought about the bleak future of the Apache nation and tried to convince herself it would be suicide to offer to share in it.

Nothing worked.

Her love for Case wouldn't go away.

Case stood at the back of Crook's command tent, listening to the officers congratulate themselves on the great victory they had won that morning. Three days earlier, the Apache scouts had located an encampment of Chiricahua braves and their families on the western slopes of the Santa Elena Mountains. The information was reported to Crook, and Case had argued in favor of going in with his scouts immediately before the Chiricahua realized they were in danger and slipped away. Major Forsythe had argued that, burdened as they were by their women and children, the renegades would be unable to escape. Crook had agreed and ordered his two cavalry companies into position.

Case and the other scouts had waited, shaking their heads at the folly of the Blue Coats. It seemed impossible that the advancing army had gone unnoticed by the Chiricahua, and yet miraculously, the renegades stayed where they were. Even more miraculously, when Major Forsythe led his troops in an attack against the encampment, the Chiricahua had put up only token resistance. Though there were a few injuries, not a single death had been recorded on either side. The Indians—thirty-three Chiricahua, half of them women, children, and old ones—had been rounded up and escorted back to Crook's field headquarters as docilely as lambs being led to slaughter.

The officers thought it was a great victory. Case thought the entire affair smelled like a rotted barrel of salt pork. When Case expressed that sentiment, though, Forsythe had laughed and accused him of being resentful because his scouts had been robbed of the credit for another capture.

"It was too easy," Case argued. "They had to know you were preparing for an attack. The cavalry does not travel quietly."

"Obviously they were just tired of running," Forsythe said dismissively. "We've been dogging them for a month now, and when we finally tracked them to their lair, they knew it was time to give up."

"Then why didn't they send someone to sue for peace?" Case countered. "Why put up even token resistance?"

"*Token* resistance!" Edgemont exclaimed. "We've got four wounded men out there." He gestured to the dried blood on Case's arm. "Even you took a shot."

"It was a ricochet, that's all. And I still say the Chiricahuas stayed too long and gave up too easily."

Clearly the other officers didn't agree with him, but Crook knew better than to discount his opinion completely. "If it wasn't because they were tired of being on the warpath, why do you think they did it?" he asked.

"I'm not sure," he admitted. "Perhaps they wanted to trick us into believing that we had found their main camp while the rest of them stay in hiding until we're out of the area."

"No, this is the main body," Forsythe argued. "I'm certain of it. Your scouts tracked them here and swore there were no signs of any others. This has got to be the group that's been causing all the trouble."

Edgemont agreed with the major. "My guess would be that these Chiricahua intend to allow themselves to be taken to the reservation so they can collect rations for a week or so; then they'll try to slip quietly away one night and go back to their raiding."

Crook nodded thoughtfully. "That's certainly happened before."

"Well, they're not going to do anything as long as we have their leader in irons," Forsythe pointed out.

Crook looked at the scout. "You've talked to them, Case. Do you get the feeling that they're going to give us any trouble before we can get them back to the reservation?"

"I wish I could say, sir." Case shook his head. "I just know something isn't right. I've got some of the scouts mixing with the prisoners to see if they'll say anything that would give us a clue, but so far nothing."

"What about the four missing scouts?" Crook asked.

That was troubling Case most of all. He'd sent four men out to scout the area before the battle this morning, and none of them had returned. "I haven't heard anything yet, sir. There's a party out looking for them."

"Keep me posted."

"Yes, sir. And there is one other thing," he added before Crook's attention could be diverted. "Apparently an old woman was wounded this morning."

"That's right," Forsythe confirmed. "I believe she was trampled by one of their ponies that was spooked by the gunfire. Captain Ashford tried to get a look at her, but she wouldn't allow him to touch her. I don't know what more we can do."

"She wants their medicine man to hold a ceremony for her," Case informed him.

"What kind of a ceremony?" Crook asked.

"For curing horse sickness, sir."

"Do you see any danger in allowing it?"

"I don't think so, sir. It's a simple ceremony."

Forsythe was appalled. "Begging your pardon, sir," he

said to Crook, "but you can't be considering granting this request."

"You know my policy, Major. I believe that whenever possible, these captives should be allowed to hold their ceremonies. It cuts down on resentment and makes it less likely that they'll create trouble."

Forsythe knew the policy and thoroughly disagreed with it, but Crook was in charge. "Then I would suggest that we post a company around them while the ceremony is in progress, sir."

"Doubling the guard would be more sufficient, sir," Case declared.

Crook looked from one man to the other. "I'll leave those arrangements up to Major Forsythe," he decreed after a moment. "Take whatever precautions you deem necessary, Major."

Case kept his displeasure hidden. Knowing Forsythe, he'd have every soldier in camp guarding a simple curing ceremony.

Crook dismissed everyone but Captain Edgemont, whose company would begin escorting the Chiricahua back to a temporary reservation at Fort Verde first thing in the morning. Captain Robertson's company had left the area that afternoon headed for Fort Thomas where they would pick up a supply train and then rendezvous with the rest of the troops, most of which were already on their way to the Graham Mountains.

Case left the tent, still convinced that the Chiricahua were up to something. He strode purposefully across the tent-strewn headquarters camp toward the separate piece of ground that had been assigned as sleeping quarters for the scouts. He wanted to speak to his uncle, Angry Coyote, to see if he'd learned anything from the Chiricahua he'd been talking to, but when he passed by the hospital tent, Meade Ashford stepped out.

The two men stopped and looked at each other. Both were surprised by the unexpected encounter, but Meade was the only one who showed it. Case had spent very little time among the soldiers during the campaign; generally he stayed with the scouts unless Crook sent for him. And since the scouts always traveled well in advance of the cavalry, there'd been virtually no occasion for Case and the doctor to meet. They'd seen each other from a distance a number of times, but that was all.

Case couldn't think of any reason to linger. He nodded to Meade and started to step around him, but the doctor seemed to feel differently about the encounter.

"I understand you were wounded today," Meade said before Case could pass him. He gestured toward the arm. "I'd appreciate it if you'd let me take a look at it."

"It's only a scratch," Case assured him.

"Nonetheless, it should be disinfected and bandaged." He stepped back and waved into the tent. When Case hesitated, Meade added, "Please, Longstreet. If you allow me to treat you, the other scouts, and even some of the Chiricahua, might do the same when the need arises."

A ghost of a smile played around Case's lips. "You want to make an example of me."

Meade chuckled. "I wouldn't have put it quite that way, but you're right. That is what I want."

Case nodded and stepped into the tent. Except for an orderly who was rolling bandages, it was empty. "You've released your other patients?"

"Yes. Fortunately, their wounds weren't much more serious than yours." Case slipped off his cartridge bandolier and his shirt, and Meade began swabbing the wound with alcohol. Though it had to sting like the blazes, the Apache didn't betray the discomfort by so much as a flicker of an eyelash. Meade worked in silence for several minutes, bandaging the cut, and when he finished, Case slipped back into his faded blue shirt.

Before he could leave, though, Meade dismissed the orderly who'd been covertly watching them. The young corporal left, wondering what fireworks he was going to miss.

"I've been looking for an opportunity to talk to you," Meade told him. "Can you spare a moment now?"

Case looked at him, betraying none of his curiosity, then nodded slowly. "A moment."

Meade sighed and turned away, pacing a few steps as he tried to figure out how to begin. For that matter, he wasn't even sure what he wanted to say. Finally he just jumped in. "The night before we left Fort Apache, I took Libby to the war dance."

Case wondered why he looked embarrassed. "I know. Your arrival did not go unnoticed by my people. Neither did your departure."

"Captain Edgemont told me you'd be dancing and that it was quite a violent display." Meade looked down. "But I didn't warn Libby."

Case shrugged. "You did what you thought was best for her."

"Damn it, Longstreet, why don't you stop this stoic Apache malarkey and talk to me!"

"I am talking to you," Case replied calmly.

"But you're not saying anything!"

"What would you suggest I say? That I'm sorry Libby saw me as my people see me?" He shook his head. "I'm not. She needs to know that side of me. Either she will accept it or she will not. I cannot control what she feels in her heart, and neither can you."

There was a desolation in Meade's eyes that Case couldn't keep from responding to when he said, "She's never going to forgive me for taking her to that dance without warning her. She thinks I betrayed her trust."

"You did," Case replied. "But she has already forgiven you."

Meade frowned. "How can you know that?"

Case paused. This product of the white man's world would never believe him if he told the truth—that he was connected to Libby in a way that went beyond even Case's understanding. He felt her every minute of the day; when he slept, she was with him in his dreams. "She loves you, Captain. People who love each other forgive each other."

"I hope you're right, because my sister is a part of me." He laughed humorlessly. "Sometimes I think she's the best part."

Case held Meade's gaze. "She is the best part of us all," he said quietly, unable to hide the sadness in his voice.

"How did you come to know my sister so well?"

"You said it yourself: she holds nothing back. All her thoughts and feelings are there in her eyes for anyone who cares to look."

"And you care," Meade said softly.

"I love her."

Meade ached for his sister and for this man. "But you can't have her."

Case moved toward the gathering darkness outside, then stopped. "Tell me something I don't already know," he murmured, then disappeared into the twilight.

When he returned to the scouts' camp, Angry Coyote was looking for him to report that the Chiricahua captives had invited the White Mountain scouts to attend the curing ceremony.

"They have tiswin, they say," Case's uncle told him in Apache.

Case shook his head. "That is not possible."

Angry Coyote shrugged. "Your general let them bring some of their belongings. The soldiers didn't search them good, maybe."

Case supposed it was possible, but it seemed highly unlikely. Crook had allowed them to bring only food and blankets; they had little else anyway. He didn't see how they could have smuggled jugs of the mild corn beer into the camp. "Tell the scouts they should not attend or they will be punished," he instructed. "And tell them they should be alert tonight."

His uncle nodded. "You suspect a trick."

"I do."

While Angry Coyote went from brave to brave, issuing the warning, Case walked down to the prisoners' encampment. As he had predicted, Forsythe had overreacted to the situation and stationed nearly fifty men around the area. The men, too, seemed to realize that their presence was unnecessary, for most of them were lounging about, talking among themselves, and grumbling about being denied a well-deserved night's rest.

The medicine man had built a huge bonfire and had already begun to dance by the time Case arrived. He found Forsythe and repeated what he had learned from Angry Coyote, then headed back to his own camp. He talked to the braves, questioning them to find out if anyone had seen signs of the four missing scouts or the men who had been sent to look for them. Every negative response increased his conviction that something was terribly wrong.

His conviction turned to certainty an hour later when Metal Knife, one of the second party of scouts, finally returned to camp. The brave was hungry and tired, but he didn't waste even a moment in finding Case. "What did you learn?" Case asked urgently.

"Two are dead," Metal Knife told him. "The others . . . I don't know."

"What happened?"

The scout handed him several arrows and followed him as Case moved toward his campfire to study them in the light. "There were signs of many Chiricahua. They had tried to hide their tracks, but I followed them."

Case squatted by the fire near his uncle. "Where?"

"The tracks led me here."

Case's heartbeat began accelerating. "We have been tricked."

Angry Coyote nodded. "They will attack at dawn, maybe. The Chiricahua do not like to fight at night."

Most Chiricahua, Case thought, remembering reports he had heard of night attacks perpetrated by the band led by Gato. It was rumored he had a large following who believed that their leader's power was great enough to keep them safe from the evil spirits of the night.

The possibility of being so close to Gato made Case's blood roar in his ears. He leaned toward the fire, studying the arrows Metal Knife had brought. None bore Gato's markings, but that only meant that Gato had not done the killing himself. Case remembered his spirit journey and the vision that had warned of an attack by Gato. Major Forsythe would die in that attack. Case would remove an arrow from his body, and it would be Gato's.

Another memory assaulted him, this one much closer in time, of fifty soldiers clustered around their Chiricahua prisoners, alert only to what was happening inside the huge circular formation, their bodies silhouetted by an enormous bonfire, making them easy targets.

The Chiricahua weren't going to wait for dawn to attack. If what Case suspected was true, they were surrounding the camp right now in the darkness.

Instantly Case doused his campfire and made a cooing sound like the call of the white-winged dove. In seconds a dozen scouts were gathered around him and more were coming. "Prepare for an attack," he instructed urgently. "Disappear into the night, and make a wide circle around the camp. We will surprise them from behind. See that it is done, Metal Knife." He looked at Angry Coyote, who spoke enough English to make himself understood to the Blue Coats. "Uncle, go to Forsythe. Tell him what we believe. I must warn Crook."

Snatching up his rifle, Case ran toward the headquarters camp, keeping low to the ground so that he cast no shadow. As soon as he reached the soldiers' camp, he made a hasty report to the officer of the guard, then hurried on to Crook's tent. As he neared the hospital he saw Meade sitting by the entrance at a makeshift desk. The lamp beside him made him an easy target. "Ashford, get your rifle and come with me!" he ordered as he ducked his head into the tent.

Startled, Meade frowned up at him. "What—"

"Just do it!" Case commanded, then disappeared.

Puzzled and more than a little alarmed, Meade did as he was told.

There was no question that the scout's warning saved Meade's life—and nearly cost Case his.

NINETEEN

THE ROUTINE of life at Fort Apache had become second nature to Libby. She knew the purpose of every bugle call and the significance of every sound that came from the parade ground. Experience had taught her which to ignore and which to heed. She had become so accustomed to them that she barely noticed them anymore, unless something out of the ordinary happened—which it seldom did.

But six weeks to the day after Meade and Case left, Libby and Susannah were sitting in the Robertsons' parlor with their needlework when a commotion in the quadrangle captured her complete attention. The bugle call that summoned a fatigue detail to fall into formation was completely out of place, as was the brief accompanying chaos.

"What is it?" Libby asked, but before she could put down her embroidery and go to the window, Susannah was on her feet.

"They're back," she said, but there was no joy in the way she announced it. "And they have wounded," she added as she snatched Michael from his cradle and rushed out the door.

Libby hurried after her, and they stopped in the shade of the ramada, waiting. Though it was only a matter of minutes before the first mule-drawn ambulance rolled in, it seemed like hours. Four mounted cavalrymen flanked the vehicle, and another four accompanied the second ambulance and the supply wagon. Two officers rode at the head of the sad procession.

"Meade!" With her skirts tangling around her legs, Libby ran onto the parade ground. Meade spurred his horse, urging him out of the path of the ambulances, then dismounted just as Libby reached him. She threw herself into his arms, and his embrace lifted her off the ground.

"You're all right . . . you're safe," she whispered.

"I'm fine, Libby." He kissed her brow and set her back on her feet. Tears of relief were streaming down her cheeks, and Meade brushed at them, but succeeded only in smearing her face with dirt. "Don't cry."

"I'm just so happy to see you." She tried to get control of her weeping, but when she finally looked at her brother—*really* looked at him—the tears only flowed more freely. He was hot, sweaty, and exhausted, but those things could be easily rectified. His eyes, though, were those of a man who had seen things no man was meant to see. Libby feared it would be a long time before that look went away. "What happened, Meade?"

"We were tricked by the Chiricahua . . . ambushed."

"Oh, God . . ." The ambulances rolled past them, and Libby realized the rest of the cavalry was not bringing up the rear. The lieutenant who'd been riding beside Meade was hurrying into command headquarters to report to Colonel Dunlevy, but there was no sign of David Robertson, Major Forsythe, Crook . . . or Case Longstreet. "Where are the others?"

"They're continuing with the campaign, searching for the renegade who masterminded the attack." Meade looked toward the hospital where the ambulances were stopping. "I have to get to the hospital and take care of the men, Libby."

"How many wounded?" she asked, walking with him.

A soldier from the fatigue detail assigned to assist with the wounded approached Meade and took his horse. "Eight have made it this far." His jaw stiffened before he continued. "Five died on the way, and twelve more didn't live through the night after the attack."

Libby was staggered. No wonder her brother looked as

though he'd been to hell and barely made it back. "My God, Meade," she said hoarsely. "How many deaths were there?"

"Twenty-six."

She swallowed hard. "Was Case—" She couldn't bring herself to ask if he was dead. "Is Case still with Crook?" she amended.

Meade was torn between his duty to care for his patients and his need to soften the blow that was in store for his sister. He stopped and looked down at her.

Libby shook her head, unwilling to believe the worst. "No. He's not dead," she said, grabbing his arm. "Tell me he's not dead, Meade," she said harshly.

"He's not dead, Libby." Meade closed his eyes. "But he is badly wounded." *And it's all my fault*, he wanted to add, but there would be time enough later to tell her how Longstreet had nearly lost his life saving Meade's.

She looked at the stretchers being unloaded from the ambulances. "I have to see him," she said, hurrying toward the hospital.

With two long strides, Meade caught up with her. "Let me get the men settled first, Libby."

"No, I have to see Case now!"

He grabbed her arm and pulled her to a stop. "Libby, most of these men are in agony. They've been jouncing in a wagon over nonexistent roads for nearly three days now. Let me do my job, and then you can come in."

"But Case—"

"Is going to be all right," he assured her. "That crazy bastard is too damned stubborn to die, believe me. Now go to our quarters, and I'll send someone for you as soon as I can."

Libby knew when it was useless to fight her brother. When he disappeared into the hospital, she stayed on the porch, out of the way of soldiers being carried inside. As each stretcher passed, she looked for Case, but she saw only bloodstained bandages and faces contorted in pain. The last man in the procession was staring up, his eyes glazed with agony. When Libby saw the bloody stump where his leg had once been, she whirled away, unable to bear seeing any more. She thought of her brother being forced to remove that leg, and tears flooded onto her cheeks again.

Was Case in that condition? she wondered. Or worse? How much could one man suffer and still survive?

"Libby?" Susannah hurried onto the porch, and Libby looked at her through a blur of tears. Mortified, she realized she hadn't asked about her friend's husband.

"I'm sorry, Susannah. I don't know what happened to David," she managed to choke out.

"He's all right," Susannah assured her. "I spoke to one of the men from the escort. David was on his way to meet a supply train when the Chiricahua attacked. But, Libby . . . Major Forsythe was killed."

Libby pressed her hand to her forehead. "This is a nightmare," she murmured.

Cradling Michael in one arm, Susannah reached out to her friend. "I heard that Longstreet was wounded. Is he going to be all right?"

"Meade says he is." She glanced at the hospital doors, then away. "He won't allow me to see him yet, though."

A frown creased Susannah's brow. "Libby, should you?"

"Of course!" Libby was appalled that she would even ask. "I have to see him."

"But you've said it yourself a dozen times—you have to stop thinking about him."

"This is different! I have to see for myself that he's all right. Can't you understand that?"

The dark-haired cavalry wife sighed wearily. "I'm beginning to understand that you're not going to let go, no matter what."

Libby looked at her beseechingly. "Susannah, please. Don't scold me. I need support right now, not trepidation."

Susannah squeezed her hand. "And you've got it. Just be careful with your heart."

Libby nodded and tried to smile, but the effort was wasted when she glanced down the quadrangle and saw Tessa standing under the ramada in front of the Robertsons' quarters. Since Susannah's recovery, the girl came only a few hours a day, and Libby had completely forgotten about her when the ambulances rolled in. "Case's family should be told," she said, glancing at the hospital doors again. She didn't want to abandon her vigil, but she couldn't leave the girl standing there wondering what was happening.

"I'll tell Tessa," Susannah volunteered, but Libby shook her head.

"No, I'll do it." Together they moved down the row of buildings. Tessa looked at them expectantly, and Libby did her best to make the girl comprehend what had happened. Her English was improving, but there were still huge gaps in their ability to communicate.

"He die?" Tessa said forlornly.

Libby shook her head. "No, Tessa. We won't *let* him die." Somehow she managed an encouraging smile. "Would you like to wait with me? Maybe we'll be able to see him soon."

The Apache maiden looked at the hospital. She had seen the bodies being carried in, and the infirmary now represented a place of death to her. She wanted to see her cousin, but she didn't want to go into that building. After a moment she shook her head vigorously. "I go now. Grandfather must know."

She hurried off, and Susannah looked at Libby. "Would you like me to wait with you?"

Libby was grateful for the support, but despite Susannah's sympathy, she knew that her friend didn't really approve. It would be better to wait alone. Libby thanked her and returned to her quarters.

One hour passed, then two, before Meade finally came for her. He escorted her into the hospital, where rows of once-empty cots were now occupied. Morphine had allowed most of the men to escape their misery, but one or two were beyond the reach of that painkiller. Libby's footsteps echoed off the plank flooring as she moved past the cots to the back of the room. A line of empty beds separated Case from the other men, and Libby frowned at her brother, deeply disappointed in him.

"You separated him from the others because he's an Apache?"

It hurt Meade to know that Libby believed him capable of

that kind of prejudice, but considering everything that had been said between them before he left, he'd probably earned her disillusionment. "No, Libby," he replied wearily. "I put him down here so that when he wakes up, you can speak to him without worrying that the others are eavesdropping."

Libby realized how deeply she'd wounded him. The chasm between them was wider than she'd ever imagined it could be. "I'm sorry, Meade. I should have known."

"It's all right."

They stopped at the foot of Case's bed. He seemed to be sleeping peacefully, but he was so pale that Libby knew it had to be a drug-induced sleep. A light sheet covered him to the waist, and a fresh bandage encircled the area below his rib cage.

Forcing back tears through willpower alone, she stepped to the side of the bed. "What happened to him?" she whispered.

"He took two bullets, one in the thigh and one in the upper abdomen," Meade replied quietly, moving to Libby's side. "I wasn't sure he'd make it through surgery. Field conditions are not the best," he added bitterly.

Libby couldn't help but respond to his pain. She placed a comforting hand on his arm. "You did the best you could, Meade."

Her eyes were filled with understanding, and Meade wanted to pull her into his arms and pour out the horror of it all. But that was a burden he was going to have to bear alone. Just knowing that she could feel his torment without having to be told helped a great deal.

He nodded to her, and Libby turned back to Case. She knelt by the bedside and gently reached out to touch his face. "I'm here, Case," she whispered. "For whatever it means to you, I'm here." She stroked his brow and wasn't surprised to find him feverish. Her fingers drifted over his lips as she remembered the bittersweet passion of their kiss, and then her hand moved lower. Gingerly, she touched the scar on his shoulder.

"One of the men said it looks like an arrow wound," Meade told her. "I don't know how old it is."

"Eleven years," Libby replied without looking up. "He was shot with a poisoned arrow on the day his family was massacred."

Meade was surprised by the extent of her knowledge. "You know a lot about him."

"Not nearly enough," she replied, reaching for Case's hand and enfolding it in both of hers. He knew she was there with him. She wasn't sure how she knew it, but she did. And he was glad she was there, too. "Do you know who ambushed you?" she asked Meade, thinking of what Case had told her about his quest for revenge. According to Susannah, Major Forsythe was dead. Was that another milestone? she wondered.

"No one knows for sure. Some of the scouts claimed they found arrows belonging to a Chiricahua renegade named Gato, and Case has cried out that name several times."

The prophecy was coming true, Libby realized. "You're getting close, *cida'ké*," she whispered, raising his hand to her lips. "Too close."

Meade frowned. He could barely hear her, but he could have sworn she spoke an Apache word. "What did you say?"

"Nothing." Libby stood and looked at her brother. "Is there anything I can do for him?"

"No."

She took Meade's arm. "Then let's get you home. You need a bath and a good night's rest." She led him down the aisle that separated the two rows of beds, and Meade didn't have the strength or the will to resist. "Once you've been taken care of, I'll come back and sit with Case."

He frowned again. "Libby, the orderlies can handle this. A hospital is no place for you."

"According to whose rules?" she asked defiantly.

"Mine," he said firmly.

"Then change your rules, Meade. I am coming back."

This time it was Meade who knew better than to argue.

There was no such thing as cold water at Fort Apache at that time of the year, but Libby did her best to keep cool compresses on Case's forehead. When she was nursing Susannah, she'd learned to dip a rag in warm water, then fan the air with it to cool it down, and that was what she did for Case throughout the night. The two orderlies on duty gave her strange looks, but she ignored them, certain they were less puzzled by her methods than by her gentle ministrations to a heathen Apache.

A single lamp at the opposite end of the room cast dim, ghostly shadows, but Libby ignored those apparitions, too. Case was restless, and all her attention was focused on him. She spoke to him softly, soothingly, and was convinced he was comforted by her presence.

It was nearing midnight when he finally awoke. Libby was running the wet cloth across the muscled contours of his chest and down his arms, but the second his eyelids fluttered open, she sensed his alertness. His eyes were bright with fever, but they focused on her instantly and he smiled.

"That is how you touched me in my dream," he said hoarsely.

Libby returned his gentle smile and reached for a glass of water. "In your spirit journey?"

"Yes."

"I didn't even know you existed then," she said, lifting his head so that he could drink. "I was only a young girl."

She lowered his head to the pillow, but Case's eyes never left her. "The eagle knew."

"Knew what?"

"That you were meant to be my woman."

Libby's heart skipped a beat, and she reminded herself that Case's mind was addled by fever. He reached out his hand toward hers, and when he winced, Libby started to rise. "I'll get something for the pain."

"No." Case managed to get hold of her hand. "It's not so bad if I don't move. I need to clear the fog from my mind."

"But I don't want you suffering."

"I will not suffer so long as you are here, *cida'ké.*"

"I'm not going anywhere," she whispered, smiling through a mist of tears. She wet the compress again.

"Do you know what happened?"

"Only that you were ambushed." She suddenly found it impossible to meet his eyes. "Your scouts said that Gato was responsible."

"I know. They brought me an arrow they had taken from Forsythe."

Libby stopped what she was doing. "You saw his death in your vision, didn't you?"

He nodded weakly.

"How many more are going to die, Case?"

"I don't know."

She wanted to ask him to give up his quest for revenge, but there was no reason to believe that his quest was in any way responsible for the ambush. She said nothing, but in her heart she knew that Case understood how she felt—not just about his revenge, but about everything.

She gave him another drink and continued bathing him until he drifted off to sleep again. Some time later, barely able to hold her eyes open, she stretched out on the empty cot beside his and fell asleep almost at once.

The first note of reveille brought her awake the next morning, and it took her a moment to recognize where she was. Slipping off the cot, she checked on Case and found him still asleep, and still feverish. A basin of fresh water was sitting on the floor between the beds, thanks to one of the orderlies, and Libby immediately began applying compresses again. Thirty minutes later the quiet that had pervaded the night finally ended when Meade and the relief orderlies reported for duty.

Meade checked his patients methodically, ordering their dressings to be changed and morphine administered when needed. He worked his way down the rows, and when he finally reached Case's bed, he addressed his sister with his sternest expression in place. "Libby . . ."

"Go home," she said for him. "I know. I was just waiting for you, lazybones. Did you sleep well?"

"Like a baby," he assured her, though in truth, he had tossed and turned, plagued by visions of the limbs he'd amputated and the men he'd buried.

Libby knew he was lying, but let it pass. "Case slept soundly most of the night."

"Good." Meade stepped to the bedside and was pleased to discover that there was no blood on either of the Apache's bandages. "You go wash up and get some rest. I'll take over."

"That's an offer you won't have to make twice." She stretched up on tiptoe and kissed her brother's cheek. "I'll come back later."

"Is that a good idea?" Meade asked with a troubled frown.

She sighed deeply. "Are you worried about what everyone on the post is going to think?"

"I'm worried about you."

"Well, don't. As long as Case needs me, I'm going to be here for him."

Meade knew it was pointless to argue. Obviously the lesson she'd learned about Case Longstreet at the war dance hadn't sunk in, or she had decided it didn't make any difference. Either way, six weeks hadn't done anything to change her feelings for the scout. Meade was beginning to fear that he could do nothing to save his sister from tragedy.

Libby waited to see if he was going to press the point, but before either of them could say anything, a commotion at the infirmary door captured their attention.

"What the—" Meade stared as three Apaches—two old men and a young girl—stepped into the cavernous room. "Isn't that Tessa?" he asked Libby, and found that her face was beaming.

"And those are Case's grandfathers, Blue Bear and Tall One," she informed him. One of the orderlies stepped in front of the old chiefs, and Libby hurried down the aisle. "It's all right, Corporal. They've come to visit their grandson."

"At ease, Corporal," Meade added when the orderly looked uncertain about whether to accept an order from the doctor's sister. Meade followed Libby down the aisle.

"Tessa, tell the *nant'an*s they are welcome here," Libby instructed. As the maiden translated, Meade noted that neither of the old men looked surprised that Libby had used an

Apache word, but Meade certainly was. Now she was even starting to speak their language!

In her halting English, Tessa told Libby that the chiefs wished to see Case. Meade nodded his approval, and Libby led the three visitors down the aisle. Meade explained the nature of Case's wounds, and Tessa did her best to translate. The two old men remained stoically silent, and Libby suspected that they were somewhat intimidated by the Blue Coats' hospital.

The chiefs stopped at the foot of the bed, and Libby went to the far side and knelt, gently running her hand over Case's brow, talking to him quietly until he awakened. "Your grandfathers are here," she told him. "They want to see for themselves that you're still alive." She motioned to the chiefs, and the old men crowded closer. When Case began speaking to them, Libby joined Meade at the foot of the bed.

"Am I mistaken," Meade whispered, "or do those two old men know you?"

"Tessa introduced us on ration day not long after you left, and I've talked to both of them a number of times since then."

He digested the information. "And Tessa has been teaching you as much Apache as you've taught her English."

Libby shook her head and smiled. "Hardly. She's a much better student than I am." Her smile faded. "Meade, there's something you should know, and you might as well hear it from me."

He sighed and prepared himself for a shock. "What is it?"

"I've been teaching while you've been away."

"Teaching?" He was relieved for a moment—until he realized what she was telling him. There were only a few children at the fort, and their parents took care of their education. "You mean you've been teaching Apaches."

"That's right. You see, before he left, Case had been teaching English to some of the young boys in his clan. When Tessa told me that, I decided to see if they would allow me to resume their lessons."

"What did Colonel Dunlevy have to say about that?"

"Actually, he didn't put up any opposition at all." She

smiled triumphantly at the memory. "Even he realizes that English-speaking Apaches would be a boon to his administration of the reservation. So, on ration days, I hold class on our porch."

She never ceased to amaze him. "How many pupils do you have?"

"I started with just one—Tessa—but I'm up to six now."

"And they don't object to being instructed by a woman?"

Libby shook her head. "No. You see, women are afforded a great deal of respect in Apache society," she said pointedly.

Meade chuckled. "I stand corrected." He sighed. "Well, since the colonel doesn't object, I certainly don't see any reason to. Not that that would stop you," he added quickly.

"Leebee?"

She turned to the bed. "Yes, Tessa?"

"Grandfather say the white man's medicine is strong. Make my cousin strong soon, too, maybe."

Libby smiled at the old chiefs. "Yes, he will be strong again soon. My brother studied many years to be a good medicine man. He has great powers."

"Thank you for the endorsement," Meade whispered in Libby's ear as Tessa translated.

Blue Bear spoke, and the girl turned to Libby again. "*Nant'an* say he think your medicine is more strong." The words were barely out before the chiefs turned to leave. They moved down the aisle, and Tessa followed.

"I'd say you just received quite an endorsement, too," Meade murmured, but there was no humor in his voice. "Obviously you have the old man's blessing."

Libby looked up at him, her expression guarded. "But I'll never have yours. Is that what you're saying?"

Meade ran a hand through his dark hair impatiently. "How can I approve of something that's going to destroy you?"

"I don't know what's going to happen, Meade," she said flatly. "But please don't make me choose between you and Case."

"Libby, if you stay on this path, you may not be able to avoid that choice." Meade looked down at his patient and discovered that Case was watching them. "I'll be back in a minute to change your bandages, Longstreet." He stalked away, and Libby moved to the bedside again.

"You mustn't argue with him, Libby," Case said with all the strength he could muster. "He loves you very much."

"I know. That's why he'll come around."

"Around to what?"

She looked surprised. "To us."

Case shook his head. "There is no *us*, Libby."

She leaned close and gently stroked his cheek. "Last night you called me your woman. You said it was meant to be."

Case looked away. "Last night I had a fever."

"You still do," she said equitably, reaching for another compress.

Wincing against the pain in his side, Case grabbed Libby's arm. "I cannot let you be hurt by me."

"And I don't want you to be hurt because of me," she said, cradling his hand in both of hers, stroking his palm gently. "But I'm willing to fight for you, Case. I came to that decision while you were away. I'll fight the army and my brother—I'll take on the whole damned territory if necessary. And if I have to, I'll even fight you."

Her determination and the love shining in her eyes filled Case's heart until he thought it might burst. "I could not fight a lizard and win today," he said with the faintest, most beautiful smile Libby had ever seen.

TWENTY

TWO DAYS LATER Libby finally met Jedidiah Longstreet. He was nothing like the tall, brawny frontiersman she had envisioned from what little Case and Tessa had told her about him. But when the gray-haired middle-aged man dressed in buckskins appeared on her porch, she knew instantly who he was. His bright blue eyes studied her with disquieting intensity as she ushered him inside, and she wondered what he'd heard that brought him to see her.

"Have you seen Case?" she asked as they sat.

"I just came from the hospital," he told her, his manner neither friendly nor cold. "Your brother says he's doing much better."

Libby nodded and clasped her hands nervously in her lap. "Yes. His fever is gone, and he was much stronger when I saw him earlier this morning."

"I understand you've been taking care of him."

Longstreet's penetrating gaze was beginning to unnerve her. She looked down at her hands. "I know my brother would never neglect Case because he's an Apache, but I'm not so sure of some of the orderlies. As you must know, there's a great deal of prejudice against him here."

"You've been feeling the brunt of some of that, haven't you?"

She gathered her wits and looked at him. "What, exactly, have you heard about me, Mr. Longstreet?"

His weathered face cracked into a network of deeply etched lines as he smiled. "Depends on who I'm talking to."

Libby had to smile, too. "Have you heard that I'm outspoken and willful to a fault?"

He nodded. "And I've also heard that you're loyal, intelligent, and caring." His smile faded. "But I have to wonder if you're very practical, Miss Ashford. Case is an extraordinary man, and I understand that you might be drawn to him out of curiosity. He's known a great deal of suffering in his life, and I'd hate to see him hurt once your curiosity is satisfied."

Libby's shoulders stiffened. "What I feel for Case went far beyond curiosity a long time ago."

"What is it you feel for him?"

"I mean you no offense, Mr. Longstreet, but that's between Case and me. It's something we're going to have to work out for ourselves."

Apparently she'd given him the right answer, because he chuckled ruefully. "That's just about the same thing Case told me not ten minutes ago. I'd like to give you a warning, though, Miss Ashford."

Her expression became guarded. "What?"

"Don't mistake Case's strength for sophistication."

She understood what he was trying to tell her, and it rankled. "I'm not exactly a jezebel, Mr. Longstreet. This is"— her voice faltered—"an unusual situation for me, as well."

Jedidiah nodded thoughtfully. "I guess maybe it is, at that." He stood. "I won't take up any more of your time, miss."

Libby walked with him toward the door. "Will you be staying at Fort Apache long?"

"I'll be in the area for a week or two, probably. I want to make sure Case in on the mend. Then I'll see if he'd like to come home with me to recuperate."

"Like old times?" she asked with a hint of a mischievous smile.

Jedidiah looked surprised. "Case told you about that?"

"He's told me many things, Mr. Longstreet. I know how

much you mean to him and what an important part you've played in his life.''

"Do you know about Gato?" he asked soberly.

Libby nodded. ":Yes."

"And his visions?" When she nodded again, Jedidiah looked openly amazed. "Do you believe in them?"

"I know that Case believes in them," she replied matter-of-factly. "That's really all that matters."

"He's not going to give up until he's killed Gato, or Gato has killed him," Jedidiah told her frankly. "Hatred is a very powerful force, Miss Ashford. It doesn't leave much room in a man's heart for softer emotions, like love."

Libby squared her shoulders. "I'll take my chances."

"You're not going to change him," he warned her.

"I wouldn't say that's something Case needs me for, Mr. Longstreet. He's spent most of his life learning to change himself."

Jedidiah shook his head and smiled ruefully. "Well, they were certainly right."

"Who's 'they'?" Libby asked suspiciously.

"All the people who told me about you—Blue Bear, Colonel Dunlevy, your brother . . ."

"And what did they say?"

"That you're a lot tougher than you look."

She smiled. "They were right."

Jedidiah nodded to her respectfully as he stepped onto the porch. "Thank you for your time, Miss Ashford. I expect I'll be running into you again."

"Sooner than you might think," she replied. "Do you have plans for supper tonight?"

A slow smile spread across his craggy face. "No, miss."

"In that case, would you care to join my brother and me?"

"I'd be honored."

"Six o'clock," she told him.

"I'll be here."

In the week that followed, Jedidiah became something of a fixture in the Ashfords' home. Meade and the frontiersman hit it off famously, but Libby suspected that had more to do with their mutual disapproval of her relationship with Case than with any commonality of interests between them. Neither of them said anything about the amount of time Libby spent with the Apache, though.

She went to the hospital several times a day, and as soon as she knew Case was out of danger she began expanding the scope of her ministrations to the other patients. She left the more delicate matters, like bed baths, to the orderlies, but it was not unusual for Meade to enter the infirmary and find his sister spooning broth or writing letters for those men who had family back east. She finally persuaded one of the orderlies to show her how to change bandages, and before long she was doing that as well.

Her smiles and soft words were the best medicine for the men, though, and Meade couldn't bring himself to deny them that. Nor could he deny it to Libby, for the new respect and gratitude displayed toward her were enormous. And the change wasn't confined to just the wounded men, either. The soldiers who visited their comrades were treated to a healthy dose of Libby's special charm, and word began to spread.

Libby noticed the change almost immediately. When she and Susannah took their daily constitutional around the quadrangle, pushing Michael in his perambulator, the friendly greetings they received included Libby as well. At the slightest encouragement, the soldiers would stop and visit a moment, always ready with a friendly word and a welcoming smile. For the first time, Libby began to feel that she was being accepted at Fort Apache.

Caroline and Elaine maintained a polite distance, of course, but Libby wasn't troubled by their aloofness. They weren't the sort of women with whom she would have enjoyed an association back east, so she had no reason to bemoan the loss of their friendship in Arizona. Caroline was particularly disapproving of Libby's teaching efforts, but since Colonel Dunlevy supported the project, Caroline confined her censure to reproving looks.

Both Caroline and Elaine made it a point to visit the hospital at least once a day to bolster the spirits of the men, and though they were greeted politely, the reception they received was a far cry from the warm smiles that lit up the room when Libby walked in. Libby knew it was petty, but she took a great deal of pleasure from the distinction the men made between the aloof officers' wives and the doctor's sister.

By the end of the first week, Case was ambulatory; by the end of the second, Meade was ready to release him from the hospital with the admonition that it would be several weeks before he was fit to return to duty. Jedidiah had little trouble persuading Case to complete his recuperation at his ranch on the western boundary of the White Mountain Reservation. On Saturday morning Libby and Meade stood on their porch watching as Jedidiah's supply wagon rumbled across the parade ground and disappeared from view.

Meade noticed that Case, on the wagon seat beside Jedidiah, didn't turn back once to look at the woman who'd devoted herself to nursing him back to health. He knew Libby must have noticed it, too.

"Are you all right?" he asked, looking down at her.

Libby pushed away from the post she'd been leaning on and glanced up at him curiously. Her eyes were dry, and she looked not the least bit distressed. "Why wouldn't I be?"

"I thought you might have trouble letting him go."

Libby smiled patiently. "Jedidiah will take good care of him, and Case certainly isn't going to do anything foolish to delay his recovery. Besides, he was getting restless from being confined indoors for so long."

Meade shook his head, a little amazed. How simple she made it sound; since leaving was what was best for Case, that was what Libby wanted for him. If there was another woman in the world who was this supportive and understanding, Meade had yet to find her. If he ever did, he hoped he'd have the good sense to marry her on the spot. For Libby's sake, though, he hoped Case Longstreet didn't harbor similar sentiments.

Now that the scout was gone, at least temporarily, Meade knew there were things he had to tell Libby—things he'd been putting off out of dread, things she had a right to know.

Libby was watching the emotions play across his face as

he wrestled with the subject he'd been avoiding ever since his return. "Are you ready to talk about it now?" she asked.

Meade was surprised, but he knew he shouldn't be. "I'll have to, eventually. It might as well be now," he replied wearily.

It was too hot to go indoors, so Libby sat in her chair on the porch stirring the air with the small, sturdy fan that Tessa had taught her to weave out of grama grass. It was a minute or more before Meade sat next to her.

"How much have you heard about how Case was wounded?" he asked, not looking at her.

"I heard that he saved your life."

Meade frowned. "Did he tell you that?"

"No. Case said very little about the ambush," she replied. "Lieutenant Watson told me about it one night while I was sitting up with him. He didn't go into details, but I know about the trap that was set up and sprung."

"Then you know that Case saved a lot of lives, not just mine."

"You don't seem very pleased about it," she commented mildly, trying to keep any trace of sarcasm from her voice.

"What do you expect?" her brother snapped. "He was a bona fide hero that night, and I almost got him killed." He rubbed his hands over his face and leaned forward, resting his elbows on his knees. "God, so much of it is just a blur."

Libby placed a comforting hand on his arm. "You don't have to talk about it if you don't want to, Meade."

"But you deserve to know. God knows I don't want you to idealize Longstreet any more than you already have, but you have a right to know how he risked his life to save your brother." He laughed humorlessly. "That's what he was doing, you know—saving *your* brother. I'm here today only because Case is in love with you."

"Is that what's eating you alive?"

He shook his head. "I don't know."

"Yes, you do. You don't want to feel beholden to him because you're afraid he'll mistake your gratitude for friendship—or worse, for consent."

Meade stood and walked to the edge of the porch. "Maybe so."

"Tell me what happened," she said after a moment.

He started talking, staring out at the parade ground, but Libby knew he wasn't seeing any of the activity there. He described the trap the Chiricahua had set up, and the chaos that resulted when the first shots were fired.

"By the time the shooting started, Crook and the soldiers in camp were ready, thanks to Case's warning, but the men guarding the phony curing ceremony were completely unprepared," he told her bleakly. "Case's uncle tried to warn Forsythe, but it didn't do any good. The major either couldn't understand the scout or just didn't believe him. There were fifty soldiers standing around like ducks on a pond. They were the easiest targets imaginable.

"Fortunately Case had ordered his scouts to circle the area, and we managed to catch the renegades in a cross fire that sent them running for their lives." He shook his head. "I don't even want to think about how bad it might have been if those scouts hadn't outflanked the Chiricahua."

"How did Case get wounded?" she asked.

Meade turned to her, stuffing his hands into his pockets as he leaned against the post. "I thought the fighting was over. Case and I were with Crook and a small contingent of cavalrymen who had worked their way toward the prisoners' encampment. We returned the renegade's fire, and then all of a sudden the shooting stopped. Case ordered me to stay down while he went off to reconnoiter, but I could hear several wounded men screaming for help, so like an idiot, I stood up and started toward them. I heard a couple of shots, but I didn't realize I was the target until an arrow went whizzing past my head."

Meade wanted more than anything not to have to look at Libby just then, but somewhere he found the courage to hold her gaze steadily. "I froze. I was just standing there, out in the open. I didn't even have the good sense to drop to the ground."

A short, bitter laugh bubbled up in his throat. "I guess the Chiricahua thought anyone that stupid deserved to die, because they opened fire full bore. Then all of a sudden Case was there, knocking me to the ground. We rolled through the dirt and managed to crawl into cover behind a cluster of rocks. It wasn't until the firing stopped again that I realized he'd been shot twice because of my stupidity.''

Libby was glad to know the details, but it was nearly impossible for her to imagine what might have happened to her brother if Case hadn't intervened. Biting back tears, she stood and wrapped her arms around Meade. ''Remind me to thank him for keeping you safe.''

''I should do that myself one of these days,'' he said hoarsely, returning her comforting hug. ''Oh, I told him he was a fool to risk his life that way. And when I administered the ether so I could operate on him I muttered something about doing my best to return the favor . . . but I never really thanked him.''

She looked up at him. ''That's between you and your conscience, Meade. The longer you wait, the harder it'll be.''

''I know. But I just feel like such a fool, Libby. He suffered so much pain because of me, and you know the worst part? He doesn't look at me with resentment, or even pity. He just watches me with those damned unreadable Apache eyes.''

Libby smiled. ''They're unreadable only because you don't know what to look for. I've seen him watch you with the other patients, and what I see in his eyes is respect.''

Meade shook his head. ''You're seeing what you want to see, Libby. He couldn't possibly have an ounce of respect for me.''

''You're judging yourself too harshly, Meade. You're a doctor, not a soldier, for crying out loud. And that was your first battle,'' she reminded him. ''When Case looks at you, he isn't seeing the man who froze; he's seeing the man who left his defensive position because there was someone in pain who needed him. He's seeing the man who stood in a field tent all night, up to his elbows in blood, giving everything he had to save as many lives as he could.''

Meade needed very much to see the love and respect that were shining in her eyes. ''Did Lieutenant Watson tell you that, too?''

"He didn't have to," Libby replied. "I know my brother."

"Thanks, little sister." He pulled her into his arms again. "You know, I once told Case you are the best part of me." He dropped a kiss on her silky hair. "I didn't know then how right I was."

Libby had no trouble keeping busy while Case was away. Most of Meade's other patients were returning to duty or being sent home in the convoys that routinely brought supplies to Fort Apache. But Libby still had English lessons to occupy her two days a week, and she had fallen woefully behind in her housework. She doted on little Michael, and her daily walks with Susannah became the highlight of her existence because of the warm, friendly greetings she received from the soldiers.

One man in particular, the adorable little Lieutenant Watson, whom Libby had helped nurse back to health, made it his personal mission in life to see that Miss Libby had anything she wanted or needed. In a casual conversation one day he learned that Libby had never ridden a horse; naturally he offered to teach her, and she didn't hesitate to take him up on it.

Susannah, an accomplished horsewoman, was only too happy to lend Libby her sidesaddle, a riding habit, and a few pieces of advice that proved quite helpful. Lieutenant Watson knew all there was to know about horses, but the special problems created by a sidesaddle were beyond the realm of his expertise. After several lessons, Libby decided that she'd rather use the McClellan saddle the cavalrymen used, but she'd already scandalized Fort Apache enough as it was. And besides, Watson was quick to inform her that the McClellan had been designed for the comfort of the horse, not the rider, so she wasn't missing anything.

Though she was not an instinctive horsewoman, she gamely persevered, and the audience of soldiers who gathered to offer their encouragement grew daily. Libby enjoyed the challenge and the exercise, but her greatest pleasure was the camaraderie her efforts engendered. It was wonderful to feel that she belonged somewhere.

Meade suspected that sense of belonging was responsible for the little changes he saw in his sister. For as long as he could remember, Libby had possessed all the subtlety of a battering ram. He knew it was only a defense against her feelings of inadequacy, but that was beginning to change. She was as direct and outspoken as ever, but she displayed a new confidence in herself that was unmistakable—at least to Meade.

He knew, of course, that her feelings for Case Longstreet could have been responsible for the change, but he preferred to ascribe it to her sense of belonging. Thinking that made it easier for him to sleep at night. He respected Case, and sometimes he even wished he could get to know him better, because he suspected that they could probably become good friends. He was obviously a man of great strength, honor, and courage. But nothing was going to change the fact that he was an Apache or diminish the hardships Libby would suffer if she pursued a relationship with Case.

One thing Meade had realized, though, was that fighting with her or ordering her to forget about Case Longstreet would do about as much good as wearing a piece of cheesecloth in a sandstorm. All he could do at the moment was wait around and be ready to pick up the pieces when Libby was shattered by the emotions she couldn't seem—or didn't want—to control.

That became much more difficult when Case returned after two weeks on Jedidiah's ranch. He seemed as healthy as ever and ready to return to duty. A few days earlier, though, Colonel Dunlevy had received word that Crook and the cavalry were on their way back to Fort Apache, so there was nothing for Case to do but wait. He spoke to Libby only briefly when Meade checked him over at the hospital; then he disappeared for several days.

When Meade asked Libby if she knew where he had gone, she informed him that Case was spending some time with his grandfather. She seemed not at all resentful of the fact that he hadn't hurried to her side the moment he returned to the fort. The quiet nature of their relationship was completely beyond Meade's comprehension. Unfortunately, he understood only too well the look of love that sparkled in her eyes every time she saw him.

That look was very much in evidence on ration day when Case returned. Meade had been standing in the doorway of the hospital watching Libby and her Apache students. Tessa hadn't shown up for the lesson for some reason, and Libby had found the going rough without her. Rather than allow herself to become frustrated and curt, she dismissed the boys earlier than usual, then turned a surly look on her brother.

"If you laugh, so help me, I'll lace your supper with cayenne pepper tonight."

"What are we having?"

"Leg of mutton and lemon tarts."

He held up his right hand solemnly. "I won't laugh, I swear. Although I must say I was particularly impressed by your valiant effort to explain the difference between 'look' and 'see.' " With his forefingers and thumbs, he formed two circles and brought them to his eyes as he'd seen Libby do during the lesson. "I'm sure this helped a lot."

Libby swatted his arm and laughed. "You'll regret that when you sit down to eat tonight."

Meade laughed, too, but when he looked over Libby's head and saw Case approaching, his laughter faded. "I believe we have a guest."

His expression told Libby all she had to know. Her face was glowing with anticipation even before she turned and saw him. Mustering all the restraint she possessed, she stepped to the edge of the porch. "If you've come to collect Tessa to escort her home from her lesson, I'm afraid you're out of luck. She didn't come today."

"I know. She's preparing for an important ceremony." Case managed to tear his gaze away from Libby to look at Meade. "Good afternoon, Captain."

"Case. How are you feeling?"

"I'm well."

"Good." Meade considered insisting that he come into the hospital to verify that, but since his only valid reason for doing so would have been to keep Case and Libby apart a while longer, he restrained himself. "Well, if you'll excuse me, I have some paperwork to do.'' He stepped toward the hospital, but Case stopped him.

''If you have a moment, Captain, there is something I'd like to ask you,'' he said, his features composed into that unreadable look Meade hated so much.

Libby looked back and forth between the two men she loved. Meade was hesitating, and she almost laughed when she realized that he was afraid Case was going to ask for his sister's hand in marriage. ''Of course he has a moment, Case,'' she said, grabbing Meade's arm and all but dragging him to the edge of the porch. ''Don't you, Meade?'' she asked pointedly.

''Of course,'' he answered reluctantly.

''Shall I step inside while you talk?'' she offered.

Case looked at her, and Libby could see from the bright twinkle in his eyes that he, too, had guessed Meade's thoughts. ''No, Libby. This concerns you as well.''

Libby felt Meade's arm tense beneath her fingers, but she said nothing.

''Tomorrow Tessa is going to become White-painted Woman,'' Case told them. ''A ceremony will mark her ascent into womanhood. There will be dancing and a great feast.'' He looked at Libby. ''She has requested that you attend.''

Libby was deeply touched. ''I would love to.''

Case looked at Meade. ''And naturally you're invited as well, Captain. I'm sure you'll want to be certain Libby is properly chaperoned.''

Meade cleared his throat. ''That's very considerate of you, Case. Has this been cleared with Colonel Dunlevy?''

''He knows of the ceremony and has made no objections.''

''Well, then . . .'' Meade looked down at Libby. There was no way he could have persuaded her not to go, so he didn't even try. ''Where is the ceremony being held, and what time should we be there?''

''I'll come for you at eight tomorrow morning.''

Libby couldn't have been happier. ''We'll be ready.''

''Good.'' With one last, lingering look, he turned and walked away.

"Thank you, Meade," Libby said sincerely.

He tried not to be moved by her happiness. "What choice did I have?"

"You could have let me go alone," she replied with wide-eyed innocence.

Meade disengaged his arm from hers and headed for the hospital. "As I said, what choice did I have?" he muttered irritably, and the delightful sound of Libby's laughter followed him all the way inside.

TWENTY-ONE

THE MAIDEN CEREMONY was as beautiful and reverent as the war dance had been savage and frightening. Tessa wore the most exquisite garment Libby had ever seen—a buckskin dress with delicate fringe, ornate beadwork, and tiny tin cones that jingled airily when she moved. Her black hair hung nearly to her waist, with two white eagle feathers braided into the back and an iridescent shell dangling on her forehead.

While a shaman sang blessing songs, Tessa performed the rituals that sealed her bond with White-painted Woman, one of the Apaches' most important deities; in so doing, she assured her people and herself of health and prosperity. It was a display of optimism that Libby found most poignant.

Under an open tipi-shaped arbor, Tessa danced on a buckskin carpet. With a beautifully decorated cane, she kept time with the drumbeat, the fringe on her skirt swirling around her feet.

"This song tells of the Creation and the part White-painted Woman played in it," Case told his two guests.

"How many songs are there?" Libby asked without looking away from the beautiful young dancer. Her two escorts flanked her like tall, solemn sentries, making her feel very small but well protected.

"Dozens," Case replied. "But the ceremony itself has only nine parts that continue throughout the day and into the night. For the next four days, though, my cousin will be revered as we would revere White-painted Woman, and she can be called by no other name.''

''Four days?'' Libby glanced up at him.

''Yes. During that time it is believed she has the power to cure.''

She grinned up at her brother. ''Pay attention, Meade. You may learn something.''

He laughed out of obligation, but it was clear he wasn't enjoying himself. As Case had expected, Libby was utterly captivated by the proceedings; Meade, on the other hand, was doing his best not to appear nervous at being surrounded by Case's people. The ceremony was being held a considerable distance from the fort, and no other officers had elected to attend. Case had done his best to put Meade at ease, but he knew that only time would convince the doctor that he had nothing to fear.

After each phase of the ceremony, the drums stopped, and during those resting periods Case introduced Libby to members of his family she hadn't met yet. Since the Nah-ih-es ceremony was a time for celebration among friends, both of Case's grandfathers were there along with relatives from all sides of Case's family. Some greeted her with varying degrees of suspicion, while others were openly friendly.

The things she had learned about Apache customs from Tessa kept Libby from making too many social blunders, and Meade took his cues from his sister's behavior. By late morning, he had relaxed a little and was actually beginning to enjoy himself.

The fourth ritual—''Cane set out, she runs around it''— commenced with Tessa's decorated cane being planted upright about twenty-five feet east of the arbor. The drums began a new rhythm, and Tessa ran toward the cane, circled it, and returned. Some of the women encouraged her with shrill whooping sounds, while other women ran behind her.

''She will do this four times, representing the four stages of life,'' Case informed his guests. ''Each time the cane will be placed farther away from the arbor. When she has finished, she will own her life, and it will be a long and happy one.''

"Why do the other women run, too?" Libby asked, her face wreathed in a glorious smile.

"So that they may share in her long life and good fortune."

"That's—" Whatever she'd intended to say flew out of her mind when she turned back to the ceremony and realized that Tessa's mother was standing directly in front of her looking very stern and solemn.

"Dee-dah nejeunee, itsa nuest-che shee," she said firmly.

Libby frowned up at Case. "What did she say? Does she want me to leave? Have I done something wrong?"

Case shook his head and smiled reassuringly. "No, you've done nothing wrong. In fact, you've just been accorded a great honor. She says that because you are her daughter's good friend, you must come, too."

Libby was surprised and delighted. "And do what?"

"Run with the other women." He nodded to Tessa's mother, and she grabbed Libby's hand.

"Nuest-che shee," she repeated. Come here.

Before Libby could say yea or nay, the woman was dragging her into the circle of attendants who surrounded the arbor. When the third cycle began, Tessa's mother gave Libby a push, and after a quick glance back at Case and Meade, Libby joined in. Laughing with delight, she ran with the other women who were chasing White-painted Woman. Then she waited for the fourth cycle and ran again.

"Does this disturb you?" Case asked Meade.

Meade glowered at him. "What do you think?"

"I think your sister is happy today," he replied quietly, not flinching from Meade's fierce gaze.

"For how long?"

Case shrugged. "Who can say? Sometimes one day of happiness is all we are given in this life."

Meade's hands clenched into tight fists, and he had to make a concerted effort to relax them. "I want more for Libby than that. So should you."

He turned back to the ceremony, and Case let the conversation drop. Meade was right; Libby deserved more than Case could give her. While he was staying at Jedidiah's ranch, he had told himself a hundred times that he should find a way to release Libby from the unspoken bond that seemed to be pulling them closer together with every passing day. He couldn't seem to do it, though. She was too much a part of him. For years, she had been the softer side of his tormented soul; he could no more tear her out of his heart now than he could have severed a limb from his own body.

From across the ceremonial ground, he watched her laughing with his people, at ease and comfortable despite the barriers of language and culture that separated them. She reminded him of a beautiful, delicate flower that had opened its blossoms to a soft shower of rain. She drank in every moment of the experience, and when it was over, he knew that she would have grown in some way.

She was remarkable, and she was *his* woman. No matter how hard he tried, he could think of her in no other way.

When the drums finally stopped, Libby returned to her escorts, her face flushed and glowing. Laughing, she adjusted her shepherdess hat, then laced one arm through Meade's and the other through Case's, binding the three of them together. "I will now have a long and happy life," she decreed.

Her head barely came to their shoulders, and she didn't see the dark look Meade gave Case as he said, "Of course you will. I'll accept nothing but the best for my darling Libby."

Case caught the look, but refused to acknowledge it. "It's time to eat now," he said, gesturing to the baskets of food that had been placed in a line from the east of the arbor.

Knowing there was to be feasting, Libby had dipped into her household savings and purchased a large quantity of dried peaches at the sutler's store. She had soaked them in honey and cinnamon overnight and contributed several jars of the concoction to the feast. Tessa had loved the sweet treat when Libby made it for her and Susannah, but since White-painted Woman was fed separately from the others, she wouldn't have a chance to sample it again. Libby was anxious to see what her family and friends thought of it, though.

"There is no formality in this part of the ceremony," Case told them as they strolled toward the food. "It's every man for himself.'' He smiled down at Libby. ''Should I jump in and get something for you, or would you prefer to fend for yourself?''

The crowd was a little intimidating, but Libby was willing to risk it. Before she had the opportunity, though, several men approached Case and spoke to him in tones that indicated concern. Case answered, and the men left.

''What is it?'' Meade asked.

''Two soldiers are coming from the direction of Fort Apache. They're riding hard.''

In the heat of early July a man pushed his horse to its limits only if there was an emergency or he wanted a dead horse. ''Something must be wrong,'' Meade said. Concerned, he took Libby's arm and the three of them hurried away from the ceremonial ground. A telltale cloud of dust was rising in the southeast, and they stopped, waiting for the riders to arrive.

It was only a matter of minutes before Lieutenant Wexler, Dunlevy's adjutant, reined in his horse, dismounted quickly, and offered Meade a crisp salute.

''What's wrong, Lieutenant?'' he asked, returning the salute.

''Forgive the intrusion, sir, but there's been an accident at the fort,'' he said, trying to pretend he wasn't winded by his breakneck ride. ''Some of the men were trying to saddle-break that new herd of horses we received Friday, and Private MacDermott was thrown. The horse trampled him pretty bad. He's unconscious, and he can hardly breathe, sir.''

Meade nodded and glanced up at the private who'd accompanied Wexler. ''You men rest your mounts. I'll be ready to go as soon as I saddle the horses. Come on, Libby.'' He took hold of her arm and ushered her toward the remuda where their horses were hobbled.

Rather than challenge Meade in front of the soldiers, she allowed him to drag her away, but as soon as they were out of earshot, she gently disengaged her arm from Meade's grip. ''Is there any reason why you'd need me at the hospital?'' she asked, hurrying along beside him. Case, on the other hand, had no trouble keeping up with Meade's long strides.

"No, but—" He realized where she was leading and stopped in midstride. "Libby, you can't stay here."

She turned to face him. "Why not? I'm in no danger here. Surely you realize that."

"It's not a question of danger," he snapped. He glanced at Case, hoping the scout would support his decision, but he had gone ahead to the remuda. Meade looked uncomfortable and lowered his voice. "It's a matter of propriety."

"Case will see that I get home safely."

"No." He stalked off toward the horses.

She darted after him. "I am not leaving this ceremony."

"And I'm not arguing about it."

"I'm a grown woman, Meade! This is my decision to make."

"Longstreet, will you talk some sense into her?" Meade said harshly as they came to the remuda. "She's determined to stay."

Case was already tightening the cinch on Meade's horse. He didn't want Libby to leave, but he didn't want Tessa's special day to be the cause of an argument between Libby and her brother. "Perhaps you should go," he told her quietly, handing the horse's reins to Meade.

She looked up at him, and the fire left her eyes. "I want to stay with you," she replied softly. "Please assure my pig-headed brother that you'll get me home safely."

Case wasn't sure what to do. Libby had placed him firmly between the devil and the deep blue sea, as Jedidiah used to say. "If the captain agrees that you may stay, I will be happy to escort you home."

That wasn't the answer Libby had been hoping for, but it made her realize how wrong she had been to pit the men against each other. "I'm sorry," she whispered to him, then turned to her brother and took his hands. "Meade, please. Let me have this time with Case and his people. General Crook is due back any day now, and for all we know, he might drag Case away on another campaign. I might not have this chance again. Please don't fight me on this."

Meade knew that, for Libby's sake, he ought to insist that she return with him, and he also knew that she would eventually forgive him if he dragged her back. But she was right about one thing. It was her decision to make. If there were consequences to be dealt with later, she would deal with them.

What was it Longstreet had said earlier? "Sometimes all we get is one day of happiness." If this was meant to be Libby's day, he couldn't bring himself to deny it to her.

Heaving a world-weary sigh, he looked at Case. "Will you have her home by nightfall?"

"But there is a dance toni—" Libby started to interject, but Case cut her off.

"Yes," he replied. "I'll have her home by the time the bugle sounds retreat."

Meade mounted his gray stallion and glared down at Case. "I'll hold you to that, Longstreet." He glanced at Libby, then rode off to join his escort party.

Standing side by side, with not even their hands touching, Case and Libby watched the soldiers disappear.

"Your friends at the fort will not understand this, Libby," he cautioned her quietly.

"My friends *will* understand. The others don't matter." She looked up at him and smiled. "Shall we go see if there's any food left?"

He smiled ruefully. "Your brother has had a difficult life, controlling you."

Her chin jutted out pugnaciously. "You think you could do any better?"

His gaze grew very tender. "I would not even try, *cida'ké.* The wind cannot be tamed. Come." He motioned toward the ceremonial ground. "We must eat before the next ritual begins."

The afternoon passed much too swiftly for Libby, and the daytime ceremonies ended much too soon. There were still several hours of daylight left when White-painted Woman shook out the buckskin carpet and threw it out of the arbor to the east. Then she threw a blanket toward each of the other three compass points to ensure that she would always have plenty of blankets and her camp would always be clean.

More feasting followed, but Tessa disappeared into the little wickiup where she had stayed between rituals, and Case hated having to tell Libby that nothing more was going to happen until dark. The men drifted off to challenge one another to games of hoops and poles, and the women began preparing more food.

"We should start back now," Case said reluctantly. At a slow but steady pace, it would take them an hour to reach the fort, which would get Libby home nearly three hours before the curfew at sunset.

Libby performed the same calculation, and decided that there was no reason to waste so much time. "I'd rather have you show me where you grew up, the places where you played and hunted."

His smile was patience personified. "Libby, you could go a hundred miles in every direction and still not see all the places I knew as a boy."

"Then show me a place near here that was special to you." She remembered something he'd once told her about his parents. "I know. You can show me the valley where your father placed the courting stones for your mother. Is it far from here?"

"No. It will take us only a little out of our way."

"Then you'll show me?" she asked hopefully.

"There will be no flowers in the valley at this time of the year," he warned her.

"I have an excellent imagination. Come." She took his hand and headed toward their horses.

He hesitated only a moment, wondering what her brother would think of this deviation from their agreement. But his woman was smiling at him expectantly, filling him with a joy he had no will to deny. Wearing a smile of happiness that matched Libby's, he saddled her horse, slid an Apache blanket-saddle onto his own, and guided her to Cottonwoods Joining.

"It's beautiful," Libby said, surveying the little valley as she leaned back against the trunk of a cottonwood. The tree provided delightful shade, and Libby had happily removed her shepherdess hat and tossed it to one side. On her left ran a stream that would soon be nothing but a dry creek bed; on her right Case was sitting Apache-style, watching her.

"You are seeing with your heart, not your eyes," he teased her. "Only in the season of Little Eagles is this valley beautiful."

"But I can imagine how it looks carpeted with flowers. . . . " She sighed wistfully. "Where did your father place the courting stones?"

He frowned. It was something he had never thought to ask, and now it was something he could never know. "I'm not sure. Near the top of that hill, I imagine, so that he could watch her from the underbrush."

She studied the hillside, trying to visualize an event that had taken place before she was born. "Did they have a long courtship?"

"No," he replied, realizing that Libby had never heard the legend of how his parents met and fell in love. "Their families had been at war with each other for many years. At my father's urging, they met near here to talk of peace, but the elders could reach no agreement." He went on to describe the first meeting of Willow and Gray Wolf, their long rides through the countryside, and the disapproval they had to face. As he talked, his face took on an expression of sweet sadness, as though the story was both cherished and painful.

Libby couldn't help but think of her own situation with Case. The disapproval they faced was no less formidable, and perhaps even more so. "But they married despite the opposition," she said, unable to hide the hope that was beginning to be the foundation on which her life was built.

Case nodded. "They married and lived happily for many years."

Libby smiled. "Is the Inday wedding ceremony as beautiful as the White-painted Woman ritual?"

"No. There is very little ceremony. A woman comes to the man she has chosen and spends the night in his wickiup. The family of the husband must pay for the bride with gifts, which are delivered to the girl's father. Sometimes this is done before the wedding night, sometimes after, but once gifts are exchanged, the marriage is made."

Libby was surprised. "It's as simple as that?"

Case looked into her eyes and wished he could allow himself to become lost in their warm depths. "Committing your life, your happiness, and your love to another person is never simple, *cida'ké*."

Libby held his tender gaze, wishing she could read his thoughts. He gave so much when he looked at her, but always there was something he held back. "You know, don't you, that if you asked it, I would make that commitment to you now . . . this minute."

"I cannot ask it, Libby."

She had known how he would answer, but it wasn't what she wanted to hear. "Today? Or ever?"

He shook his head. "I don't know."

Libby swallowed hard and looked away. "Gato?"

"Yes. *Cida'ké* . . . ?" He waited until her eyes met his again. "The necklace Gato took from my mother's throat was one my father gave her on the day their marriage was sealed. It had beads of silver, nuggets of turquoise, and a carved medallion like this one." He reached beneath the open collar of his shirt and showed her his simple Thunderbird emblem. "When he placed it around her throat, the spirit of the Thunder Eagle flew overhead and blessed them. That day two eagle feathers hung from the medallion, and through the years, one was added for every child my parents bore."

He replaced the medallion beneath his shirt. "I have been told by those who have seen Gato that he still wears the necklace. Only two feathers remain. One is mine, the other is that of my sister, Morning Star. As long as Gato wears the necklace, he possesses our souls." He reached out and touched Libby's face. "And as long as he possesses my soul, I have nothing to give you."

Tears filled Libby's eyes, and she turned her face into his hand and pressed her lips to his palm. "Nothing I can say will heal your hatred, will it?"

"I have told you before that I exist for no other reason." He cupped her face in his hand and forced her to look at him. "But you are the only gentle part of me, Libby," he whispered.

"That's not true," she said, grasping his hand fiercely. "There is a kindness in you, Case Longstreet—a gentleness that has nothing to do with hatred or revenge, or with me."

"Libby, what you saw the night of the war dance—that is me. To take revenge without a second thought, to show no mercy to an enemy, to kill with cunning and guile—that is what it means to be Apache. That is what I am, and not even your love for me can change that."

"Two sides of the same coin," she murmured, remembering the conclusions she'd come to during Case's absence.

"What does that mean?"

She regarded him sadly. "It means I must accept you for what you are, not what I would wish you to be."

He frowned in frustration. If he could have been different for this woman, he would have tried, but that was not possible. "Can you do that?"

Libby wanted to accept him as he was, and she thought that she had. But when he talked of killing and hatred in such a cold, flat voice, when he placed his need for revenge above his love for her . . .

He would do what he had to do. He believed in a destiny that was unchangeable. Libby knew she could accept that. She found it more difficult to embrace the knowledge that if he ever came to believe she had no place in his destiny, he would leave her in true Apache fashion. He would walk away without ever looking back.

TWENTY-TWO

"WE SHOULD GO NOW, or your brother will begin to worry," Case said, rising in one graceful motion.

Libby hated to leave the little valley, but Case was right. It would be wrong to worry Meade. And besides, there didn't seem to be anything else to say. She offered him her hands, and he pulled her to her feet. The movement brought them close together, and though they both knew they should back away, neither of them did.

She stared up at him with dark, expressive eyes, inviting Case to look into her heart and see everything she was feeling. Love, sadness, hope, and desire were all there, shimmering just beneath the surface.

Case recognized the emotions, for they matched his own, but he dared not act on them until he had more to offer her than the passionate fire that consumed him. He couldn't let her see the need that swelled in him when he thought of her; she mustn't be touched by the hunger that threatened to overwhelm him every time he looked at her. He ached to hold her, to make her truly his woman in the ultimate sense of belonging; but such an act would be a betrayal of everything he was as a man and everything he believed as an Apache.

He stepped back, just as Libby had known he would. And she knew why. She tried to resent his sense of honor, but she couldn't; it was one of the things she loved about him. She couldn't help fearing, though, that it was also what would keep her from having a life with him.

They resumed their journey to the fort, but had covered less than half the distance when Case noticed a rider coming from the northeast on a path that seemed likely to intersect theirs. The rider was Apache, but that was all Libby could tell.

"Do you know who it is?" she asked, wondering if there was a reason to be concerned.

Case studied the indistinct form for a moment. "It's my uncle, Angry Coyote," he replied finally, changing course to intercept the rider. "General Crook has returned. Come."

Libby followed him, trying not to think of the consequences of Crook's return. There was no telling what mission he'd send Case on next, but she knew she could count on it being dangerous.

When they met Angry Coyote on the trail, he paid little heed to Libby. The scouts spoke to each other in Apache while Libby sweltered in the sun, watching Case's face grow colder every time his uncle spoke. Crook's name was mentioned several times, and Gato's, as well. From Angry Coyote's manner, Libby surmised that Crook had sent Case's uncle looking for him.

That supposition was confirmed when Angry Coyote abruptly departed. "Crook has asked for me," Case told her. "When my uncle did not find me at the ceremonial camp, he followed our trail."

"What else did he tell you?" Libby asked, dreading the answer.

Case's face was like a mask of cold, sculpted bronze. "The scouts tracked Gato and his braves to the Dragoon Mountains. He has taken refuge on the Chiricahua reservation with Cochise."

Libby held her breath. "What will you do?"

Case looked toward the White Mountains on the eastern horizon. His quest had begun there, but would end in the mountains to the south. "I have no more visions to guide me, Libby. The death of Forsythe was the last one." He looked at her. "I must go after Gato now."

* * *

"I forbid it!" Crook said, slapping his desk as he jumped to his feet. Although Case was considerably taller, the general allowed no one to intimidate or dominate him. "You cannot resign, Longstreet. You have a contract with the army."

Case studied Crook impassively. The moment he and Libby returned to the fort, Case had been summoned to headquarters. It had saved him the trouble of making an appointment. "And we had an understanding, you and I," Case said. "When you came to me three years ago and asked for my help, I told you I was seeking only one man. I agreed to scout for you on the condition that when the time came for me to face Gato, you would not interfere."

Crook remembered that agreement. He'd never broken a promise to an Apache before, and he didn't want to have to do so now. "But things have changed since then, Case. With the exception of a few incorrigible renegades like Gato, all the Apaches in Arizona and New Mexico are settled onto reservations. We're as close as we've ever been to the end of this abominable war, and I can't risk having the delicate fabric of this peace ripped apart by one man's obsession with revenge."

"You credit me with too much power, General."

"Not at all. You've been with me in every battle. You've acted as a translator at every powwow and treaty negotiation I've undertaken. There's not a tribe of Apaches in this territory that doesn't know you or know of you. Like it or not, Case, you're as much a symbol of the authority of the Army of the United States as I am. If you set one foot on the Chiricahua reservation with the intent of committing mayhem on one of Cochise's people, you could very well be giving that old fox the excuse he needs to initiate a full-scale war."

Case wasn't certain Crook was right. Cochise was more dedicated to keeping the white man's peace than any other Apache leader Case knew, but there was no denying the possibility existed. The old chief had become a pacifist in his waning years, but he had forced the Blue Coats to accept peace on his terms, not theirs. And he was still an Apache. "May I point out to you, sir, that you've been complaining about your inability to touch Cochise for nearly two years now. Wouldn't a full-scale war be easier to suppress than these hit-or-miss skirmishes with raiding parties?''

Crook paced behind his desk, his hands clasped behind his back. It was several moments before he spoke. "Case, I'm not a political man. I don't like the intrigue and the posturing. I've gotten where I am simply because my methods get results." He stopped pacing and looked at the scout. "But I'm also smart enough not to commit political suicide. I haven't exactly been circumspect about voicing my objections to that treaty General Howard made with Cochise. If I let you go after Gato, my detractors are going to claim that this was my way of maneuvering Cochise into breaking the treaty.

"Now, I don't expect you to give two figs about the ups and downs of my career, but I don't have to tell you what could happen to your people on this reservation if I'm replaced or stripped of my influence."

Finally the general had made a point that Case had to respect. There were men, both military and civilian, who had become wealthy by misappropriating funds and supplies that were meant for the Apaches. Case knew for a fact that Crook had never been guilty of that kind of dishonesty. The Indians in his charge received not only his respect but also the full rations they had been promised when they agreed to settle on the reservations. Without Crook to protect them, the White Mountain Apache might soon be starving.

Case couldn't allow his revenge to bring harm to his people. Since Major Forsythe's death, Case had felt somewhat disoriented. His resolve was as strong as ever, but there were no more signposts to show him the way to his objective. The Thunder Eagle had brought him this far; the rest of the journey was his to make alone.

The time was his to choose as well, and he wanted it to be now. But Crook's arguments were persuasive. The chances were slim that the repercussions the general feared would come to pass, but Case couldn't take the chance.

"Very well, General," he said finally. "I withdraw my resignation."

Crook returned to his chair, greatly relieved. "I'm grateful, Case. And I'm not unmindful of the agreement you and

I had. In fact, I may be able to help you confront Gato.'' He gestured to a chair and waited until Case was seated. ''You see, I want that renegade as much as you do. I lost a lot of good men because of his treachery, but it's just barely possible that his retreat to Cochise's stronghold was the biggest mistake he could have made. I want to turn that mistake to my advantage.''

''What do you have in mind?''

The man the Chiricahuas called Gray Fox smiled. ''Tomorrow, I want you to start for the Dragoon Mountains to arrange a meeting between me and Cochise.''

Case wasn't sure he'd heard correctly. Crook had just talked him *out* of going to the Dragoons. ''To what end, sir?''

''I want you to show him the arrows we collected after the ambush. That's proof enough that Gato was responsible. If Cochise is as honorable as he pretends to be, he'll have no choice but to turn Gato over to the army.''

Case smiled. Crook's plan had merit. Cochise repeatedly denied accusations that the renegades terrorizing the area around his reservation were his braves. He claimed that his people were all living peacefully according to the treaty, and no one had been able to prove otherwise. However, if he was confronted with proof of Gato's treachery, he would have to turn the renegade over to the army or risk being accused of violating the treaty. Then he could be forced to leave his stronghold and resettle his people on less desirable reservation land.

''Very well. I'll meet with Cochise.''

Crook looked at him gravely. ''You realize, of course, that since you'll be traveling under my flag, you can't take any personal action against Gato.''

''I know that.''

''And you also know that Cochise might have you killed and your body disposed of in such a manner that we'd never know what happened to you.''

Case nodded. ''Yes.''

Crook wove his fingers together and looked down at his desk. ''If we're successful in getting our hands on Gato, I'll find a way to let you have him, Case. It will be just the two of you, man to man.'' He looked up. "But I'm not doing you any favors by sending you on this assignment.''

Case stood. "I know that, too, sir.''

He rode into the Dragoon Mountains wearing only his breechclout and moccasins, and carrying a standard bearing Crook's flag—two gold stars on a field of red. The strap of a courier pouch slashed a dark line across his chest, but far more noticeable were the two scars on his torso—one still angry and red, the other faded. Both were physical proof of Gato's treachery. Case wanted them plainly in view when he met with Cochise.

He followed the mountain trails, letting instinct guide him. He knew he was being watched. Eventually someone would confront him, ask his purpose, and either try to kill him or guide him to Cochise. His rifle was resting in its sheath on his blanket-saddle, and a bowie knife was strapped to his waist. He made an easy target, but he was counting on Cochise's sense of honor to keep him alive.

Though he was alert to every sound and sign, Case was having difficulty concentrating on the mission Crook had sent him to perform. He wanted to think about Cochise, plan what to say to persuade the chief to surrender Gato to the soldiers who were camped just beyond the boundaries of the reservation. Those thoughts wouldn't come, though. Libby kept intruding. The memory of their parting had been echoing through his mind for a week now. The scene played over and over, no matter how hard he tried to push it away.

He had gone to her that night after his meeting with Crook because he had known he couldn't leave without seeing her. He had marched onto the porch, not caring who saw him or what they thought. Meade had been there, but after a few uncomfortable moments, he had reluctantly gone next door, using the excuse that he needed to check on his patient. With Libby standing near the unlit hearth and Case standing near the door, he had explained Crook's plan.

"This is dangerous, isn't it?'' she asked quietly, her hands clasped in front of her, half hidden by the folds of her muslin tea gown. Her hair was down, flowing around her shoulders as

Case had never seen it before. The golden glow of lamplight made her seem more fragile than she was, and though she looked completely composed, Case wasn't fooled. Her hands were folded together so tightly that they had turned white.

He had never lied to her before, and he couldn't do so now. "It could be dangerous, yes."

"You won't be able to act against Gato, but what if he decides to kill you? He could arrange an ambush—"

Case shook his head, cutting her off. "I don't believe he'll do that. Setting a trap for the army was a great tactical victory that earned him the respect of his men. Ambushing one man who rides under a flag of truce would bring him dishonor. He would not risk having his men turn on him."

Libby's chin came up. "And if he decides to fight you face to face?"

"I would like nothing better than for him to give me no other choice."

She moved toward him. "I won't ask you not to go." She managed a small self-deprecating smile. "Because it wouldn't make any difference if I did."

"It would make it much harder for me to leave you, Libby."

"Well, that's something, anyway." She reached out and took his hands. "I guess the only thing that really matters is that you come back."

He raised her hands and pressed one, then the other, against his lips. "If I am meant to return, I will." It was as close to a promise as he could give her.

She looked up at him, her eyes sparkling with unshed tears. Her hands tightened on his, and she stretched up, placed a soft kiss on his lips, then retreated. Her love and concern moved Case beyond words, beyond thought. That afternoon she had wanted him to take her into his arms and show her that he loved her. He had wanted the same thing, but his reasons had been selfish. Now, though, Libby truly needed the reassurance of his embrace, and he could not deny her—or himself—that comfort.

"Do you know that the Apache do not kiss?" he asked softly.

"I'm sorry," she said, fighting a flush of embarrassment. "You kissed me once before and—"

He brushed her lips with his fingertips, silencing her. "Of all the white man's customs I have learned, it is the one I like the best." Slowly he lowered his mouth to hers, and Libby's lips parted breathlessly. The sweet simplicity of his kiss unleashed her tears and a wave of desperate longing. His arms went around her waist, and he pulled her close. One hand tangled in her hair, and Libby arched up as sweetness blossomed into passion. The kiss deepened, intensified by urgency. Her hands dug into his shoulders, and she clung to the precious moment, relishing the feel of her breasts crushed against his chest, savoring the strength of his arms and the gentle caress of his hands. An ache of physical need consumed her, bringing undreamed of sensations to life, and she glimpsed for the first time what belonging to someone in every sense of the word truly meant.

Case was no less moved by the kiss. All of the fire he had been suppressing surged to the surface, carrying him beyond the place where it was safe for him to go. He lost himself in the kiss, and in the touch and feel of Libby's body against his. The blossoming of her passion swept reason aside.

But he was who he was. In that moment he could have forgotten Gato. He could have severed himself from his vow of revenge. He could have made Libby his woman without remorse or regret for what loving her would cost him. But there was more at stake than his own needs. Libby deserved more than a moment of breathless passion; she deserved a man who could come to her whole. She deserved a man who had fulfilled his destiny and who had the strength to fight a world that would condemn them.

Leaving her that night was the hardest thing he'd ever done. But she had not left him. As always, she was with him everywhere he went, only now he had the memory of their shared desires to haunt him. For the first time in eleven years, he was impatient for his quest to come to an end.

It was late afternoon before a welcoming party of four Chiricahua braves on horseback finally confronted him. Case had been conscious of the fact that they had been tracking him for hours, so he was not surprised when they suddenly appeared in front of him, blocking his path. He recognized their leader as Little Face, one of Cochise's clansmen.

"I have words your chief must hear," Case said when Little Face demanded to know why he was trespassing on Chiricahua land.

The brave studied Crook's flag contemptuously. "You speak for Gray Fox?"

"I do."

"Then come." Little Face gave a signal to the other braves, and they surged forward, flanking Case's horse. Not another word was spoken as they led him to Cochise's encampment.

As he approached the *nant'an*'s wickiup, the old chief came slowly out of the dwelling. His shoulders were stooped with age, and he looked a hundred years older than he had when Case first saw him nearly ten years earlier. In one decade a fearsome warrior had become a tired, sick old man. Case noticed, though, that he still carried himself with the same nobility of spirit that had impressed every white man who'd ever met him and lived to tell the tale.

Case dismounted and planted the flag. There was only a slight breeze to stir it. "I come to you in peace." Though Cochise knew English, Case chose to address him in their own language.

The old chief studied his face. "I know you," he said after a long moment. "We met long ago, before the days of the Gray Fox, when you were little more than a boy. You are the White Mountain Apache who bears two names."

"Your memory is good," Case replied, flattered that the great man had remembered him. "My people call me He Chases the Thunder."

"And the white man calls you Longstreet." Cochise gestured to the flag. "Since you come in the name of Gray Fox, I will call you Longstreet, too." He turned to his wickiup and sat in front of the door. Case needed no other invitation to join him. He settled across from the chief, and two other braves—one old, one young—took their places by Cochise. "What has Gray Fox to say to me?"

"I bring a message from the soldier chief." He reached

into his pouch, extracted five broken arrows, and handed them to Cochise. "Do you recognize these?"

Cochise studied them thoroughly, passing them back and forth to the men flanking him. Finally, the men placed the arrows on the ground between Case and Cochise. "Maybe."

"On a night before the last full moon, a band of Chiricahuas attacked a camp of soldiers near the Santa Elena Mountains." He picked up the arrows. "These and many more like them were left in the bodies of the soldiers."

"That attack was not of my doing," Cochise said calmly. "My people live here peacefully. We no longer make war on the Blue Coats."

"These arrows prove otherwise. They belong to the brave known as Gato and to those who follow him. The Gray Fox followed Gato here, to your mountains, but because he respects the treaty you made with Howard, he could not follow Gato beyond the boundaries of your land."

The old chief's face gave away none of his thoughts. "The Gray Fox is as wise as he is powerful."

"And he is also angry," Case said. "The warriors he commands are like family to him. They count on him for protection, and when one of them dies, he is expected to avenge that death."

"My people did not kill his soldiers. He should not look to me for revenge."

"You have allowed Gato to live in your mountains. As long as he enjoys your protection, he is one of your people and you must bear the burden of the crimes he commits."

"I have not said that Gato is here," Cochise said shrewdly.

Obviously age had nothing to dull his wits, Case realized. "But Gray Fox knows that Gato *is* here. For you to deny it would bring shame to a life that has been filled with honor."

The chief was silent for several moments. Then he gave an almost imperceptible nod, and the young brave on his right stood and disappeared behind the wickiup. Gato was being summoned to the meeting. "What does Gray Fox want of me?" Cochise said finally.

"You must send him Gato and his followers, the ones who attacked the soldiers," Case replied. Though outwardly his demeanor didn't change, he became acutely aware of everything going on around him. If Gato was coming, Case had to be ready for anything. "Gray Fox is waiting by the river. If your braves bring him the renegades, he will go in peace. If not, he will know that your treaty with Howard has turned to dust."

This was the speech Case and Crook had agreed upon. It was meant to give only the implication of a threat. If Cochise didn't accede to the demands, Case was to press him for a meeting with Crook, who would make the threat more specific.

If Cochise was concerned by the implied threat, though, he gave no indication of it. "I cannot give him to you."

"Why not? Long ago Gato was rejected by your people because he practiced dark witchcraft. Why do you now protect him?"

"Once, in the days when I was making war on the Blue Coats, before I brought my people to these mountains, Gato saved me from a trap that had been set by the horse soldiers. For that, I owe him my life."

"Do you owe him the lives of all your people, too?" Case asked sternly. "If you continue to protect him, those who trust you will suffer for his treachery."

Cochise considered the words, but did not comment on them. Instead, he gestured toward the arrows. "How do I know the proof of guilt you bring me is not false?"

"What reason would Gray Fox have to lie?"

Cochise cocked his head to one side as he studied Case's face. Then he allowed his eyes to move purposefully to the old scar on his shoulder and the fresh one on his abdomen. "When I met you many years ago, you were with a white man. Together you searched for Gato, and you spoke openly of your terrible hatred for him. He is the reason you bear two names, is he not?"

"He is," Case said coldly.

"Maybe you come to me now to trick me into helping you wreak revenge."

"If that was my purpose, I would not hide behind the flag

of the Gray Fox as Gato is hiding behind you. I will have my revenge, but today is not the day.''

Case sensed Gato's approach even before the renegade and several of his braves appeared in the clearing. Obviously he had been waiting nearby, which meant that Cochise had guessed the reason for Case's visit long before he arrived in camp. It meant, too, that Cochise had known about Gato's attack on the soldiers. Case had suspected as much, and now he was certain of it.

Those jumps of logic barely registered on his consciousness, though. They were insignificant compared to the overwhelming surge of hatred that flooded Case the moment Gato actually appeared. He looked exactly the way Case remembered him. Time had not changed him in any detail. He was still tall and strong; his expression was still the personification of arrogance and evil. And at his throat . . .

Case saw the necklace and wondered desperately how he was going to control his rage. Like Gato, it had changed little with time, but what had once been a beautiful symbol of love on his mother's throat was now an obscene exhibition of contempt and conceit. Two feathers still remained, but they were not as Case remembered them. For so many years the power of the necklace and his mother's love for her family had kept them like new, but now they were worn and frayed. Like Case, they had lost the thing that should have kept them whole.

Case rose slowly to his feet and faced the man who had been the center of his existence for too many years.

Gato approached him, his expression arrogant. ''Longstreet, the Apache with two names who worked so hard to make sure Gato knew them both. At last you have found me,'' he said casually. ''I had begun to worry that your words were like the air—hot, but full of nothing.''

''Is that why you ran from me for so many years?'' Case replied, unable to keep his voice from betraying his hatred.

Gato laughed. ''If you had truly wanted to find me, you would not have failed so many times. You wanted only to frighten me, but Gato cannot be frightened, Longstreet.'' He grabbed the medallion and held it out contemptuously. ''Not as long as I have the thing you desire most in the world. Your hatred will betray you, and you will fail, as you failed the day I took this from your mother.''

Blind rage surged through Case's veins, and had it not been for the calming hand that took his arm, he might have killed Gato then and there—or died trying. Through a red haze of anger, he looked at the hand, then at Cochise. Case had no idea when the chief had risen and moved to his side.

''You told me revenge was not your purpose, or did you lie?'' he asked quietly.

Case stiffened his jaw, desperately trying to bring his hatred under control. ''I did not lie.''

''Then sit, and I will tell you what I have decided.'' Cochise returned to his place, then looked at Gato. ''Come and sit beside me.'' Gato started to move, confident of his position of superiority until Cochise said quietly, ''For the last time.''

For just a moment the renegade's eyes betrayed a degree of uncertainty that neared the proportions of panic, but he quickly controlled it. He sat, but Case noticed that some of the edge had been taken off his arrogance.

When Case was seated as well, Cochise picked up the arrows and showed them to Gato. ''Longstreet has brought these, and a message from the Gray Fox. I must give you to the soldiers or the treaty will be undone.''

''Surely the great Cochise does not fear the Gray Fox!'' Gato exclaimed, clearly hoping to shame the old chief.

''I fear what will happen to my people when I am gone,'' he said reflectively, as though looking toward a faraway place. ''I have been at war most of my life. I do not wish that fate for my grandchildren.''

''But you—''

Cochise raised his hand, and Gato fell silent. ''Hear me. The time of my death is coming soon. I have seen it, and I am ready. There is only one thing I can leave behind when I go from this world, and that is peace for my people.'' He looked at Gato. ''But there are many like you, and like Geronimo and Nolgee, who hoped that I would fail. When I am gone, there are others, like my son, Taza, who will try to hold the peace for which I have worked so hard. If I break faith with the treaty, I will make it impossible for Taza to hold our people together, for the Gray Fox will cut off our rations and chase us out of the mountains. I cannot allow that to happen," he said gravely, then looked at Case. "But I cannot renege on my debt to Gato."

"You are a great and wise chief," Case replied. "But you must do one or the other."

Cochise shook his head. "No. There is always a third choice. You, Longstreet, will stay here through two nights. You will eat my food and keep me company. I will tell you stories of the battles I have won"—he grinned sadly—"and I will tell you lies about the ones I lost."

His smile faded as he looked with regret at the man who had once saved his life. "And you, Gato, will take your people tonight and leave my mountains, never to return. By the time Longstreet tells the Gray Fox of my decision, you will have had time to vanish. He cannot pursue you if he does not know where you have gone, and he cannot punish my people if you are no longer here."

Gato was plainly astonished. He had never dreamed anything like this could happen. "You have lost your wits, old man! And your courage!" he shouted, jumping to his feet.

The *nant'an* stood and silenced the renegade with one piercing glance. "Cochise has spoken. If you are here at the rising of the second sun, I will take you to Gray Fox myself." He turned and watched as Case rose. "I offer you friendship, Longstreet, but if you try to leave before the appointed time, I will have my braves kill you."

"I understand," Case said, his eyes shining with respect. Crook wasn't going to be happy about the outcome, but Cochise had resolved a difficult situation without compromising his honor. "I will be happy to eat your food and honored to listen to your stories."

"Enju." Without looking at Gato, he slipped inside his wickiup.

Case turned to the renegade. "You have little time, my enemy. You should hurry."

Gato lifted his chin belligerently. "I am not afraid. Gray Fox will never find me."

"But I will," Case replied evenly. "The time has come for one of us to die."

"You are right, Longstreet," Gato sneered. "But you need not come looking for me. I will find you and make you pay for turning Cochise against me. Count your days, for they are few in number."

He whirled, and Case watched as Gato and his braves hurried out of camp. The moment they were gone, the cry of an eagle reached Case's ears. He looked up, but there was no bird, only a second cry, and a shadow that passed over Case's face, then disappeared.

The spirit of the eagle was with him once more.

TWENTY-THREE

~~~~~~~~~~~~~~

"COCHISE IS DEAD," Case told the general, his voice flat and colorless. His enforced holiday as the old chief's "guest" had ended that morning, and he'd ridden hard all day to reach the field headquarters.

Crook came to his feet behind the makeshift desk. "When? What happened?"

"Today, just after dawn," Case replied. "His family was with him. He passed from this world very quietly."

The general sat as he digested the news, his expression somber. "Is that why you were gone so long? Were you able to get an audience with him, or was he too sick?"

"We met," Case told him, then went on to explain what had happened. He described his meeting with Cochise and the old chieftain's final act as leader of the Chiricahua. He told him how Gato and his band of forty followers had left the mountains that first night.

Case didn't tell Crook about the hours he had spent with the sick old man, listening to stories while Cochise's voice grew weaker as his time to die grew nearer. He had been a fearless warrior and a great man; Case wasn't sure Crook or any white man could understand how honored he felt to have shared the chieftain's final days.

Crook listened to Case's narrative, then shook his head in amazement. "We always did underestimate that wily old fox," he said quietly. "With Cochise dead, will the Chiricahua allow Gato to return?"

"No," Case said with absolute conviction. "Taza is now the chief of the Chiricahua. He is not the brilliant leader his father was, and he may have trouble holding his people together, but he will honor Cochise's decision."

Crook sighed heavily. "Then we've lost Gato."

"No, sir, we have not," Case corrected him with a bloodless smile. "Gato blames me for what happened, and he has sworn revenge. He will come for me, and I will be ready."

The look on Case's face was chilling, and the general repressed a shudder. "He won't fight fair," he warned him.

"But he will fight. After all these years, nothing else matters to me." And it was true. Seeing Gato had changed Case. The soft emotions that had so recently seized control of his heart had now been devoured by hatred, leaving room for nothing else.

Not even Libby.

The chicanery Crook anticipated came sooner than he or Case expected. After a brief, fruitless search for Gato, Crook had decided to return to Fort Apache to formulate a new strategy. They had been on the trail only four days when a dozen ragged, exhausted Chiricahua approached under a flag of truce.

Case recognized the leader of the small band as one of the braves who'd been present on the day of his meeting with Cochise. The brave, Gusalá, readily admitted to having been a member of Gato's band, but he swore that he had broken faith with the renegade. His family was tired of being on the warpath. They had hoped to live out their days in peace with Cochise, but Gato's banishment had denied them that respite. Now they wanted to go with Crook to the White Mountain Reservation and live out their days as good Indians.

Crook had heard similar speeches so many times that he would have had trouble believing Gusalá even if he hadn't known about Gato's desire for revenge against Case. Under normal circumstances he would have offered these Chiricahua the same deal he'd offered the war-weary followers of Alchinay: Bring me the head of your leader, and I will allow you to stay.

But since he was certain this was another of Gato's tricks,

Crook knew that sending them away under those circumstances wouldn't have done any good. They would simply
return to Gato and report their failure to dupe the Blue Coats.
Gato would then be forced to formulate another plan. At least
now the opening gambit had been made; Crook and Case had
agreed that they should pretend to be fooled so that they
could see where the game was headed.

Crook's only overt concession to caution was to inform
Gusalá that he would be placed in the guardhouse the mo-
ment they reached Fort Apache, promising to release him
only if his people behaved themselves and made no trouble.
The others would be given a plot of land near the fort where
Crook could keep his eye on them.

Alert for any sign of Gato, Cavalry Company B resumed
its journey home. Their arrival was met with the usual fan-
fare; everyone turned out, hoping for the best but fearing the
worst as they scanned the returning troops for the faces of
friends and loved ones.

Libby was no different from the others. She heard the four
notes of the attention call being blown on the bugle and hurried outside. Down the quadrangle she saw Susannah standing under the ramada, her eyes glued to her husband; to
Libby's right, Meade was just stepping out of the hospital.
With guidons flying, the arriving cavalry company lined up
in a double column and came to attention until Captain Robertson dismissed them.

Libby looked for Case and finally saw him riding next to
a small group of Apache captives. Her heart sank when he
rode past the hospital toward the guardhouse without looking
at her. She waited expectantly while one Apache brave was
incarcerated.

"Is that Gato?" Meade asked, stepping to her side.

"I don't know." She looked up at him. "Can you find
out? Maybe this whole nightmare is over."

Meade wanted to tell her that as long as she was in love
with Case Longstreet, the nightmare couldn't possibly end,
but he held his tongue. "I'll go over to headquarters and see
what I can find out," he replied, stepping off the porch.

"Thank you." She returned her attention to the captives

and to Case, but he seemed totally oblivious to her. With the assistance of two cavalrymen, he took the Apaches to the quartermaster's, obtained rations for them, and then, after a brief conversation, began escorting them out of the quadrangle.

He passed Libby again, and this time he did stop, but only for a moment. His eyes met hers, but his face didn't soften with the expression of love that made her weak with longing. The man looking at her with cold, lifeless eyes was someone she didn't recognize.

The shock immobilized her, and before she could even think of crossing the parade ground to go to him, he had moved on with the Apaches in tow, like a shepherd tending his flock. Certain he would come back soon, she waited on the porch, watching for any sign of him.

Meade came back a half hour later to report what little he'd learned about Cochise's death and Gato's banishment. "Crook isn't saying much more than that, but he is warning everyone to use extreme caution where these Chiricahua are concerned. Apparently he thinks it's another one of Gato's tricks."

"Did Case see Gato?" Libby asked anxiously.

"I have no idea."

She looked out over the parade ground. "He'll come tell me about it as soon as he has a chance," she replied with strained optimism.

But one hour passed, then two, and Case didn't come. Libby waited all evening, alert to every sound in the quadrangle, but nothing out of the ordinary happened. She tried to read, but couldn't focus on the words. She tried sewing, but succeeded only in turning her fingers into pin cushions. She paced the floor, conscious of the way Meade watched her with concern when he thought she wasn't looking at him.

At ten o'clock she finally accepted the fact that Case wasn't coming and told Meade she was turning in for the night. She wasn't sleepy, but she would have done anything to escape her brother's scrutiny. Case's name wasn't mentioned, but as she stepped to the door of her room, she looked at Meade and said curtly, "Obviously Crook had some pressing duties for him."

"I'm sure you're right," he replied. He watched her go, puzzled by her agitation. Weeks ago, when Case returned from Jedidiah's, he had made no attempt to see her right away, and Libby had accepted it with an equanimity Meade found remarkable. What had happened to change her so much?

Of course, this situation was different. Case hadn't been returning from a hazardous assignment then. Was it only the thought of the danger he'd been in that was making Libby so desperate to see him, or had something about their relationship changed without Meade's knowledge? Libby certainly didn't confide in him these days. They existed peacefully only so long as he kept his disapproval of her relationship with Case to himself.

By the following afternoon, when the scout still had not put in an appearance, Libby was beside herself. At her insistence, Meade asked a few discreet questions of David Robertson and learned that, to the captain's knowledge, Case had been given no special assignments. He had come into the fort once to confer with Crook and visit Gusalá in the guardhouse, but as far as anyone knew, he was spending most of his time with his people or at his camp outside the fort.

Though personally Meade was delighted that Case was keeping his distance, it hurt him to see Libby so upset.

"Something has happened—I know it," she said when he related what David had told him. "I have to see him, Meade."

"If he wants to see you, Libby, he'll come. You two have certainly passed the point of needing to meet covertly."

Libby ignored the mild sarcasm in his voice. "You don't understand what getting revenge against Gato means to Case. It's an obsession. But something is different about him now— I can feel it. Something happened when he met with Cochise, and I have to know what it was. I have to know what he's thinking and feeling."

"Maybe it's better that you don't know, Libby."

"I don't believe that."

Meade shrugged. "Obviously Case does."

She swallowed hard, hating the idea of asking her brother for a favor that had anything to do with Case. She didn't see any other choice, though. "I need you to find him, Meade. I can't go—Crook has issued orders that no women are to set foot outside the fort without permission and a military escort. Please go talk to him for me and tell him I have to see him."

"Damn it, Libby—" He looked down at the floor and rubbed his forehead with one hand. "Don't you think he knows you want to see him?"

"Then at least find out why he hasn't come!" She grabbed his arm and forced him to look at her. "Please."

Meade had never denied Libby anything, and it hadn't been a hardship on him because her wants had always been so simple. She had never asked for fancy gowns because she knew their resources had been limited, and such things hadn't really mattered to her, anyway. She had never demanded he provide her with a houseful of servants, as a lady of quality deserved; instead, she had made do with one maid to help her with the demanding job of keeping their home. Her requests had been for small things, and Meade had been happy to give them to her because she gave him so much in return.

But this was something he simply could not do for her. He'd spent most of his life taking care of Libby, protecting her, trying to keep her safe and happy. He couldn't do something now that he believed with all his heart was wrong. Meade knew that even though she hadn't said it outright, the real reason she wanted him to go to the scout was that she was afraid Case had stopped loving her. He hoped to God it was true, and that Libby would eventually realize that her infatuation with the Apache had been a will-o'-the-wisp.

Though it tore at his heart, he had to deny her this for her own good. "I'm sorry, Libby. I can't. If Case wants to see you, he'll come." His refusal did more than surprise Libby. It filled her with intense disillusionment. Meade turned away and headed back to the hospital, unable to bear the look of pain in her eyes. He stopped at the door, though, with one piece of sad, parting advice. "And if he doesn't come, Libby . . . if he can cause you this much anguish without giving you a second thought, maybe you should face the possibility that he's really not the man you wanted to believe he was.''

Libby didn't like to admit that her brother had become heartless and intractable, but the proof was right in front of her. ''Maybe I should face the possibility that you're not, either,'' she said with wrenching sadness.

Meade turned without another word and went back to the hospital.

With only routine cases to attend to, Meade had too much time to think that afternoon. None of his thoughts were pleasant. He cursed himself for bringing Libby to Fort Apache. He cursed Libby for the streak of curiosity in her nature that had prompted her to pursue an acquaintance with the scout. He cursed Case Longstreet for the bizarre Apache beliefs combined with civilized behavior that had so entranced Libby.

Meade wanted to approve of the relationship. Truly he did. Like Libby, he believed there was too much intolerance in the world, too much hatred bred by ignorance and greed. There wasn't a doubt in his mind that Case was a decent man. He was possessed of enough courage for any ten men, and his intelligence was unquestionable. He wore honor like a badge. When he looked at Libby, the tenderness in his gaze was heartrending, even to a man like Meade, who didn't really believe in love.

If Case hadn't been an Apache, Meade would have blessed the relationship in an instant. Knowing that made Meade sick to his stomach. He had always prided himself on judging people by what they were and how they behaved, not by their station in life. But too many people in the world lacked a similar tolerance. If Libby followed her heart blindly and—God forbid—married Case Longstreet, her life would become a living hell. The hatred and alienation she would suffer because of Case would soon turn her love into bitterness and recrimination. The sweet, loving Libby he knew would eventually dry up and blow away.

No matter what it cost him, Meade couldn't allow that to happen. He'd taken on the responsibility of protecting Libby long before their father died. He couldn't shirk his duty now.

He'd been hoping she would come to her senses, but that clearly wasn't going to happen.

Meade tried to keep busy, but there was just too little to do. His operating room was spotless. His only patient—a snakebite victim—was sleeping peacefully. Finally he ended up in the storeroom checking supplies against an inventory sheet one of his orderlies had prepared.

When he heard the door to the infirmary creak as it was opened and closed, he sent up a hopeful prayer that an interesting case was coming his way. He hurried out of the storeroom and stopped dead in his tracks when he saw a very healthy looking Apache standing just inside the door. He recognized him as the scout known as Angry Coyote, Case Longstreet's uncle. As Meade recalled, the Apache spoke a little English.

"May I help you? Do you need a doctor?" he asked.

"You come," the Apache said sternly.

Through careful observation, Meade had learned that the more uncomfortable an Apache was with a situation, the more fierce he became. For that reason, he took no offense at Angry Coyote's brusque order. Clearly, he didn't like being in the white man's hospital. "Come where?"

"Longstreet want you. He say you come. Now. I take." With that, he turned and slipped out the door.

Meade hesitated, surprised by the summons. What on earth could Case want with him? The most obvious possibility was that he had been injured and needed a doctor. But if that was so, why hadn't his people brought him to the hospital?

It made no sense, but Meade knew he couldn't refuse to go. And in a way, he really wanted to see Longstreet. It was time he took a stand.

After a brief word with one of his orderlies, he collected a medical kit from his office and followed Angry Coyote outside. Two horses were waiting, Case's uncle was already mounted . . . and Libby was standing on the porch.

"What's happening, Meade? Has someone been hurt?" she questioned him anxiously. "I asked Angry Coyote, but he won't say anything to me."

"I don't know what's going on," he replied. "Apparently Case wants to talk to me."

"Why?"

Meade unhitched the horse and tucked his medical kit in the saddlebag. "I have no idea."

"Will you—" She stopped abruptly. Pride wouldn't allow her to beg Meade a second time to find out why Case hadn't come to her. "Never mind."

Meade knew what she'd been going to say, and why she'd stopped. "I'll ask him, Libby," he promised.

She managed a smile. "Thank you."

"Don't thank me," he told her bluntly. He mounted hastily and looked down at her. "What I want to hear Case say and what you want to hear are two very different things."

Case saw Meade and Angry Coyote coming moments after they rode out of the fort, but he made no move to prepare to greet him. His rifle—cleaned, loaded, and ready for use—was folded in a blanket beside him. With buckskin he had purchased from a cousin, he had sewn a new pair of moccasins; tonight he would pay a medicine man to bless them with pollen and prayers that would make them more durable. Gathered around him were the utensils he needed to repair his arrows, and he had already restrung his bow with sinew. He had reinforced the stitching of his rawhide-covered war-club and was sharpening his bowie knife with a whetstone.

All was in readiness for war. His battle with Gato was a game of wits now, but soon the renegade would make his move, and He Chases the Thunder would be prepared.

As Meade rode up, Angry Coyote veered off, allowing the doctor to complete the journey alone. Case did not vary his movements or acknowledge his presence by so much as a glance. Meade dismounted and strode toward him, medical kit in hand. Case continued honing the blade of his knife.

Puzzled by the Apache's failure to acknowledge him, Meade stood there uncertainly for a moment. The knife in Case's hand looked vicious; so did the man sharpening it. When Case finally looked up at him, Meade realized Libby had been right. This was not the Case Longstreet they knew.

"Sit," he ordered bluntly.

Curbing his temper, Meade did as he was told. Rudeness was easier to take from someone like Angry Coyote than from a man like Case, who knew better. "Your uncle said you wanted to see me?"

"There are things you need to know, for Libby's sake."

"About what?"

"About Gato. Crook has warned everyone that we suspect a trick, hasn't he?"

"Yes. But what's that got to do with Libby?"

"Maybe nothing, maybe a great deal if Gato should learn that she is important to me."

Meade's frown turned into a deep scowl. "Are you saying that Libby could be in danger?"

Case returned to sharpening the blade. "I don't know. All I can be sure of is that Gato will come for me. He blames me because Cochise banished him from the reservation."

Meade was incensed. "Damn it, Longstreet! I don't know much about this grudge between you and Gato, but I'll be damned if I'll let some ridiculous Apache mumbo jumbo bring harm to my sister!"

Case looked at him, his face chillingly impassive. "That is why you must tell her to stay away from me. The Chiricahua we brought back here are spies. They watch everything I do. If I go to Libby, they might suspect something."

"Does Crook agree with you that Libby might be in danger?"

"I don't think he's considered it. He doesn't know Gato as I do."

"Then we have to tell him. I want Libby protected."

Case shook his head. "She is safe as long she stays away from me and does not leave the fort. If we put a guard on her, it will only draw the Chiricahuas' attention to her. They might begin to wonder why."

"Let them wonder!" Meade exclaimed. "What difference does it make?"

Case controlled his irritation, reminding himself that Meade knew virtually nothing about the Apache mind. "The Chiricahua are already moving among my people, asking questions. They want to know if the rations are good and plentiful. Is Crook a man of his word? Will he deal fairly with them?''

Those sounded like harmless enough questions to Meade, but he kept silent, waiting for Case to make his point.

"Soon their questions will change, though. In a few days they will begin asking how many soldiers are stationed at the fort, how many Apache scouts are employed there. And the questions will then turn to me. They will subtly learn all they can about my life and my family, and they will report it to Gato.''

"You think Gato is somewhere on the reservation?''

Case nodded. "If not now, he soon will be. This land is riddled with canyons and caves. There are many places where he can hide with a small group of his braves.''

"Then Crook should increase his patrols,'' Meade declared hotly.

"No. That would be useless. Soldiers could look for months and never find a trace of Gato, even if he was right under their noses.''

Meade's jaw stiffened. "You have a very low opinion of the army that employs you.''

Case sighed deeply. "Soldiers cannot find what they have not been trained a lifetime to look for. Crook has assigned the Apache scouts to comb the area for Gato. We are the only ones who have a chance of spotting him without alerting him to the fact that we are looking.''

That was some consolation to Meade. "But what about Libby?''

"My people have been warned about Gato. They will not tell the Chiricahua anything about me,'' Case assured him. "If I stay away from Libby, they should never suspect a thing.'' He looked down, and for the first time Meade caught a brief glimpse of the man who was in love with his sister. "Tell her to be patient. When it is over, I will come to her.''

"What if she doesn't believe me?'' Meade asked. "She might think I'm lying just to keep you apart.''

The question surprised and saddened Case. He hadn't realized that the wedge he'd driven between Libby and her brother had gone that deep. "Libby would never believe you could lie to her."

Meade rocked back, unable to believe he'd even suggested such a thing. Case was right. The fact that he even considered the possibility was an indication of just how much his relationship with Libby had deteriorated. "I'll keep her away," he promised. "But there's something I want you to tell me."

That didn't sound like a question to Case, and he saw no reason to answer. The White Eyes had an absurd need for reassurance when they were speaking to someone. They expected one to nod and murmur approvingly so they could be certain that they were being listened to. The Apache had no such expectations. As long as a man was speaking and his companion did not leave, it was assumed the companion was listening.

Case had long ago adapted his behavior to make the White Eyes more comfortable, but he felt no need to offer such assurances now. In order to prepare for Gato, he had put aside every part of himself that had ever accepted the white man's ways.

When it became obvious Case wasn't going to ask what Meade wanted, the doctor leaned forward intently. "I want to know what you meant when you said you would come to Libby once all this is over."

"I meant exactly what I said."

"Come to her and do what?" Meade challenged. "Surely you've thought about the future—do you expect my sister to share it with you? Presuming you survive this business with Gato, of course."

It was a fair question. Case had given it no thought since his confrontation with Gato, but the deep feelings he had for Libby made his answer instinctive, as natural as breathing. "When this is ended, I will bring you the bride price and ask your permission to marry her."

"Bride price?" Meade was astonished. "You expect to *buy* my sister?"

"I want to spend my life with her."

"Where? On the reservation? Will you put her in buckskins and force her to carry water for miles? Cook over an open fire? Collect rations from the fort twice a week?''

"No," Case replied calmly. "Libby could no more live among my people than I can."

"Then what do you plan to do?"

"General Crook has paid me well for my services these last three years. I have saved money. It's always been my plan to buy a ranch someday. I will take Libby there."

"You can't own property, Longstreet. Or have you forgotten you're an Apache with no legal rights?" Meade said, hating the sarcasm he heard in his own voice.

Case's expression didn't change. "I have not forgotten. The property will be purchased by Jedidiah Longstreet."

"Have you talked this over with him? He doesn't approve of your relationship with Libby any more than I do, you know."

"He will do as I ask. There is government land around his property, but no one will buy it because it borders the reservation. Jedidiah and I will join our lands and raise cattle together. It's a dream we have spoken of many times," Case told him. "He will be happy to have Libby share in that dream."

Meade stood up, frustrated and disgusted. It sounded so reasonable, but it was all so wrong. "You're a fool, Longstreet."

Case looked up at him. "Your sister does not think so."

Well, that was certainly true. "What if I don't accept this . . . bride price you mentioned?"

Case had no choice but to consider the consequences if Meade refused to sanction their marriage. "If you force her to choose between us, you will lose her."

"I know that." It was the most painful admission he'd ever made in his life. "But no matter what it costs me, I can't stand by and watch you destroy her. You've got her so besotted that she doesn't know what's best for her anymore."

"But you do?"

"Do you really have to ask that question?" Meade asked bitterly. "Can you honestly say that marrying you, living as an outcast, is the best thing that could ever happen to my sister?''

No, Case realized. He couldn't say that. He wanted Libby. Until a few moments ago she had been the quiet center of the maelstrom raging inside him—set aside, but never forgotten. She was the light he wanted to walk into when his dark quest ended. Nothing could ever be better for Case than loving Libby and spending his life with her.

But that did not mean he was what was best for Libby. He would be asking her to live a harsh life, to be shunned by her society and to raise children who might never be accepted by her own people. In his heart he believed that his love for her could make up for all those things, but his reason told him Libby Ashford would be better off without him.

Case studied Meade carefully, feeling no malice toward him. He was only protecting someone he loved. But Case knew that if Libby was forced to make a choice, she would marry him with or without Meade's approval. The loss of her brother would destroy her, though. By marrying Case, she would be giving up so much; he wasn't sure he could ask her to give up the man who had been the center of her existence for so many years as well.

Case realized that his only hope for a life with Libby was to trust that somehow this man would come to realize they were meant to be together. And there was very little chance of that.

For the first time since he'd met Case Longstreet, Meade could read the thoughts behind the inscrutable Apache's eyes. Even before Case spoke, he knew he'd won. There was no joy in the victory, though.

''I love your sister,'' Case told him. ''Somewhere in this world there is a man who could give her more of the things you white men seem to think are so important, but nowhere is there anyone who would love her more than I. I love her enough, in fact, to do this for her.'' He stood and faced Meade squarely. ''If you do not agree to the marriage, I will not take Libby as my wife.''

''If I refuse to give my consent, Libby will never forgive me,'' Meade pointed out. ''We will both have lost her.''

Case shook his head. "She will never hear the reason from me," he promised.

Meade believed him. So why didn't he feel better? Why wasn't he happy? "I am truly sorry, Case."

"I know."

Meade returned to his horse, but turned back before he mounted. "I'll keep Libby away from you until this thing with Gato is over. If she doesn't see you for a while, maybe your parting will be easier."

"Now it is you who are being foolish, Doctor," Case said softly. "Nothing is going to make it easier."

TWENTY-FOUR

"APPARENTLY Gato holds Case responsible for his being banished from Cochise's reservation," Meade told Libby as soon as he returned. She'd been wearing a path on the boards of the porch with her pacing, and Meade ushered her inside, reassuring her that everything was all right. "Case thinks Gato's planning some sort of a showdown, and he doesn't want you caught in the middle."

He saw no reason to tell Libby that Case was actively worried about her safety. Meade would see that she was protected, so there was no reason to compound her worry about Case with a fear for her own life.

"He is all right, then?" she asked, only slightly relieved by Meade's explanation.

"He has changed, Libby. You were right about that," he told her. "There's a . . . deliberateness about him that's very disturbing."

"Meeting Gato must have brought back some terrible memories for him." Saddened by what Case must have gone through, and what he was still facing, Libby sat in her grandmother's rocker and leaned her head back. "I wish I could take the pain away."

"But you can't," Meade said firmly. "He asked that you stay away from him."

She looked at her brother, hesitating a moment before asking, "Was that his only message for me?"

Reluctantly he told her, "He did say he'd come to see you once this is over."

"That's all?"

"Yes." He didn't look away from her as he told the lie, but the only way he could control the guilt was by telling himself this was for her own good.

Libby accepted Meade's word at face value. She hadn't really expected anything more. Case would never have asked Meade to relay a message of an intimate nature, and she couldn't see Meade saying, "Oh, by the way, Libby, Case said to tell you how much he loves you."

She was disappointed, though. Memories of her last parting from Case were haunting her. She had experienced her first taste of passion, and she wanted to know that incomparable joy again. But there was more to loving someone than aching to feel the strength of his arms and to know the thrill of having his lips pressed to hers. There was a communion of spirit that went beyond the physical.

Libby and Case had that, and she clung to the knowledge. What made it hard, though, was the coldness she'd seen in his eyes. Just as Case had spent too many years living only for revenge, Libby had spent too much of her life feeling inadequate, as though she wasn't really worthy of being loved. As hard as she tried to fight them, doubts began creeping in.

As the next week passed, she grew more restless every day. Tessa was still coming to Susannah's several hours a day, but when Libby questioned her about Case, the girl couldn't tell her very much: Case had warned his people to be on the lookout for Gato, so now two of Tessa's brothers, instead of just one, escorted her to the fort and back. Several scouts, relatives of Case, had offered to make their camps alongside his, but he had declined their help. He wanted nothing to deter Gato from seeking him out.

He spent most of his days combing the hills and canyons near the fort, looking for any sign that Gato and his followers might have slipped onto the reservation, but if he had found such a sign, Libby knew nothing about it. She did learn that he had visited the post on two occasions, staying only long enough to meet briefly with Crook and spend a few moments with Gusalá.

The Chiricahua captive was also allowed visits from his family, and Libby had heard that the guards often found his wife outside the guardhouse, speaking to her husband through the barred window of his cell. Libby thought it ironic that a prisoner of war played host to more guests than she did.

It was a great relief to her when Jedidiah Longstreet arrived. She assumed that if anyone could talk Case into taking more precautions against the threat posed by Gato, it was his mentor. Her assumption was totally in error. Jedidiah's only contribution to making Case safer was to set up camp alongside him, overriding his objections by reminding him that he, too, had a stake in seeing that Gato paid for what he had done eleven years ago.

Jedidiah came to the fort no more frequently than Case, but Libby did get to speak to him briefly one afternoon as he came out of the sutler's store with supplies. Unfortunately, he wasn't able to assuage her growing apprehension. After only a few moments of conversation, she realized that his need for revenge was nearly as strong as Case's. She watched him go, feeling more discouraged than ever.

Meade had only routine cases in the hospital, so there was nothing to keep Libby busy there, and her English lessons consumed only two mornings a week. She tended her flower box diligently, but it did nothing to cheer her. As everyone had tried to warn her, the plants were not surviving. No matter how often she watered them or how much fertilizer she gave them, they withered before her eyes in the intense Arizona heat.

Her one and only comfort was her friendship with Susannah and the hours they spent playing with Michael, watching him grow more alert and active every day. He, at least, was proof that *some* things could thrive in this hostile environment.

"Libby, that's the fourth time you've gone to that window," Susannah said patiently without looking up from her needlework. "There's nothing to see but a few thunderheads in the sky and a river of mud on the parade ground."

"Well, you'd think Case would at least have enough sense to seek shelter from this storm," she snapped, shifting the baby from one arm to the other and stroking his back. He'd started to cry when the storm struck, and Libby had been successful in calming him. Unfortunately the process hadn't worked in reverse.

Susannah chuckled. "Liberty Ashford, of all the outrageous things I've heard you say, that is the most nonsensical. The Apaches have survived rainstorms for hundreds of years without benefit of our log cabins."

Libby managed to smile at her own folly. "I'm sorry. It's just that I can't bear the thought of him sitting out there like a clay pigeon in a trap shoot."

"Is that really what's bothering you?"

"Of course it is," she replied a little too quickly, turning to the window again.

Susannah glanced up at her, then looked back at her embroidery. "You're not upset that Case still hasn't made any effort to see you?"

"Of course it bothers me," she admitted reluctantly. "But I've accepted his need for revenge."

"Just as you've accepted his Apache heritage?"

Libby turned to her. "Yes."

"And nothing is going to keep you away from him, is it?"

There was a challenging note in her voice that irritated Libby. "You're beginning to sound more like my brother every day, Susannah. If I'd wanted to listen to criticism of Case, I could have stayed home."

"I'm sorry, Libby. I just find it all so difficult to understand. I know you're in love with Case, and you've almost convinced me that he's in love with you, but—"

"He *does* love me, Susannah. I know it."

"Then why hasn't he come to see you to set your mind at rest? Isn't that the least he could do for the woman he supposedly loves?"

Rocking Michael to and fro, Libby resumed her vigil at the same window. She didn't want to admit that she'd thought the same thing a hundred times or more. Had it not been for that one cold, lifeless look he had given her on the day he returned, she might never have suffered the doubts that were going through her head. But he had looked at her with the eyes of a stranger, and she couldn't wipe that memory from her mind, no matter how hard she tried.

"He's doing what he has to do," she said after a moment, ending the conversation.

Private Samuel Reynolds leaned negligently against the wall of the guardhouse, eyeing Case Longstreet with ill-concealed malignance as the scout spoke in hushed tones to Gusalá. Since the Chiricahua had been incarcerated at the fort, it galled Reynolds every time he pulled guard duty. When Longstreet showed up, it only made his irritation worse. The black eye and the cut lip Reynolds had received the night he had attacked the scout had long since healed, but he could still taste the blood every time he saw the Apache.

Why Longstreet had the run of the fort and the complete trust of General Crook was a mystery to him. If Reynolds had his way, every Indian in the territory would be hanged. But privates in the army seldom had their way about anything, so he kept his mouth shut and fumed while Longstreet talked to the renegade in that gibberish heathen language of theirs.

Fortunately it wasn't a long conversation. Longstreet finally turned away from the prisoner and started toward the door. The arrogant set of his shoulders and the unreadable look on his face nettled Reynolds.

"He tell you anything you want to know?" he asked snidely.

Case barely spared the private a second glance. He wasn't about to tell him that Gusalá was still denying any knowledge of Gato's plans or whereabouts. "Enough," he replied as he stepped out of the guardhouse.

"Goddam Apache bastard," Reynolds muttered under his breath. He followed Case to the door and watched him move down the quadrangle toward Crook's headquarters. One of these days, somebody was going to teach Longstreet a lesson about looking down his nose at his betters, and Reynolds wanted to be the one to do the teaching.

He was about to step back to his post in the anteroom, but

as he cast a quick glance over the parade ground, he saw
Libby Ashford standing on the porch outside her quarters.
Obviously she'd been tending her ridiculous flower bed; she
was wearing gloves and holding a tin watering can. Reynolds
could tell even from a distance that flowers were the last thing
on her mind, though. She was standing at the edge of the
porch watching Longstreet.

Now, there was a pair that really made his blood boil. But
he was happy to see that at least the Apache had come to his
senses. Longstreet seemed to be keeping his eyes straight
ahead, ignoring the woman who watched him with such obvious adoration.

"Something wrong, Private?"

Reynolds glanced at Lieutenant Watson, the officer of the
guard, who'd somehow managed to sneak up on him. Watson
was one of the most easygoing officers at Fort Apache, so the
private saw no reason to snap to attention. It wasn't required
on guard duty, but some officers demanded a lot more pomp
than others.

Reynolds spit a wad of chewing tobacco into the dirt.
"Nothin' wrong, sir. I was just wishin' the ground would
open up and swallow that high-and-mighty bastard, Longstreet. Be doin' us all a favor, I'd say."

"That's enough, Private," Watson said without much force
behind the order. He gestured toward the anteroom. "I believe your post is inside, isn't it?"

"Yes, sir." Reynolds stepped back to his post opposite
Gusalá's cell, and Watson followed him inside to make his
routine inspection. " 'Course, you know, sir, there is one
good thing?"

"What's that, Private?" the lieutenant said absently as he
looked over Gusalá's cell, trying to ignore the hard stare
the Apache fixed on him.

"Seems like the romance has cooled."

"Romance?"

"Between Miss Libby and Longstreet. I guess he got the
message that we ain't gonna put up with no filthy heathen soilin'
one of our women. Can you 'magine the nerve of that . . ."

Watson turned on his heel and glared at him with such intensity that Reynolds took an involuntary step back. "That is enough, Private! You will refer to the lady only as Miss Ashford, and you will get your mind out of the gutter!"

"Sorry, sir," he muttered, realizing his mistake. He'd forgotten that Watson was one of the men Libby had nursed back to health after the Chiricahua ambush. "I just meant— that is, the whole camp knows how she feels about Longstreet. And how he feels about her."

"Miss Ashford's private life is none of your business, and if I ever hear you speak another disparaging word about her, you'll be occupying that empty cell next to Gusalá."

"Yes, sir. Sorry, sir. I didn't mean no disrespect to the lady. It's all Longstreet's fault, of course. He's the one—"

"Don't push it, Reynolds," Watson barked, heading for the door.

"Yes, sir," Reynolds said meekly. He turned and saw that Gusalá's black Apache eyes were watching him. "What the hell are you looking at?" he growled, then cursed himself for having wasted his breath. Gusalá didn't understand a word of English.

At least that was what Gato wanted everyone to believe.

The rocky spires rose out of the valley floor, casting long shadows that reached the base of a great cliff. From a distance, the cliff looked smooth, like the unbroken surface of a quiet river. Up close, though, there were fissures in the rocks—some no wider than a man's hand, others as wide as a man's shoulders, and one broad enough for a horse to pass through. Like a tunnel to the sky, the widest fissure wound through the mesa until finally it opened into a red canyon riddled with caves. Unless the sun was directly overhead, the canyon was always shadowed and cool. The space was not large, and it was a dangerous place to be, for there was no escape route, but it suited Gato's purpose well. As long as he lit no fires, he and his braves could hide in the caves indefinitely.

This was the place he had chosen to meet the Apache with

two names. If the news Hacké'tisé had brought him tonight was good, the meeting might be very soon.

"The Blue Coats still speak freely in front of Gusalá. They have not yet realized he understands much of what they say," Hacké'tisé told his leader, proud of his own part in relaying messages between Gusalá's wife and Gato. On ration days, when the soldiers were busier and there were more Apaches for them to watch, Hacké'tisé took a place at the head of the rations line. The number on the neck tag he had been assigned was marked off by one of the soldiers, and as soon as he took his rations back to his camp, he slipped away. He kept to the rocks, and when that was not possible, he covered his tracks carefully so that he could not be followed to the red canyon.

In that fashion, everything Gusalá had heard in the two weeks of his confinement had reached Gato's ears.

Gato listened to Hacké'tisé's recitation of what had been learned in the last three days. His expression was dispassionate, but his mind was churning. He hatched plots and rejected them without betraying any of the frustration he was feeling.

"Is there more about the white woman?" he asked when the messenger went off on a tangent about Longstreet's cousin, a young girl who came to the fort daily. For a time Gato had thought he might be able to use the girl, but she had two brothers who stayed with her constantly. His braves would never be able to get close enough to kill them quietly, and any other way of disposing of them would sound an alarm among her people or the soldiers. Gato wanted his revenge to be private, so he had discarded thoughts of abducting the girl in order to lure Longstreet to the red canyon.

The white woman he had heard about, though, was more promising. On the day they had arrived at the fort, Gusalá's wife had seen a look pass between Longstreet and a beautiful white woman. The woman's face had been that of one in love, but the Apache with two names had looked at her with no emotion. It had been learned that she was the sister of the white medicine man, and on ration days she taught English to several young braves from Longstreet's clan. Once two old women had been overheard as they spoke of the white woman with great respect. Longstreet's name was mentioned, and they had clucked sadly about something that was "hopeless."

The thought that his enemy might have foolishly fallen in love with a white woman brought Gato great pleasure. Longstreet had given too much of himself to the white man; it would be delicious justice if he had condemned himself to the pain of wanting—but never having—a woman from the white man's world. But while Gato enjoyed thinking of that interpretation of the scant facts, he did not truly believe that even Longstreet could be so foolhardy.

Still, he was not ready to give up hope that the woman might be of use to him. He waited expectantly for the messenger to answer his question.

Hacké'tisé hid his disappointment at not being able to tell his narrative in his own way. "There is much about the white woman, Ahsh'ford," he assured him. "Two soldiers argued about her. Gusalá did not understand all their words, but he now believes that Longstreet has been close to her. One of the soldiers spoke against her, mentioning the name of the scout as well. The other became very angry. He spoke of Ahsh'ford with much respect, and the first man looked ashamed."

Gato could barely contain his excitement, but there was no outward display of it. "What do you know of her? Where does she live? Is she often alone?"

Hacké'tisé picked up a pointed rock and drew a large square in the dirt. Gato already knew the design of the fort—every building and its purpose as well as every nook and cranny where a man might slip in and out unseen. He knew how many guards patrolled the post at night and when their shifts changed.

Inside the big square the messenger drew a smaller one indicating the hospital. "Here is her home. The white medicine man lives with her."

"Where are the windows and doors?"

The messenger showed him.

"And only one man lives there?"

Hacké'tisé nodded. "Sometimes another soldier comes, but he leaves before it is night."

Gato thought a moment, and then a slow smile spread across his face. "So, Longstreet . . . perhaps I have found something that means more to you than this." With malicious glee, he fingered the medallion of the Thunder Eagle necklace. "Something to make you do foolish things," he whispered to himself, then laughed.

The ugly sound echoed off the walls of the red canyon and was lost in the darkness settling above.

TWENTY-FIVE

"YOU LOOK LOVELY," Meade told Libby as she stepped into the parlor. The party they were supposed to attend required that Meade wear his dress uniform, but it had taken a little persuasion to get Libby to change into something formal. In fact, it had taken quite a bit just to get her to agree to attend, and Meade could tell from her expression that she was having second thoughts.

His assumption was correct. Libby had put on the same gown she'd worn to the welcoming party the week she arrived at Fort Apache, but she was no longer the same woman. The time that had passed since then, measured in days, wasn't long, but Libby felt she had aged a lifetime in just a few short months; tonight in particular she felt a hundred years old. It had been three days since Case had walked past her on the parade ground without even looking in her direction. She was sure he'd had a good reason, but she couldn't begin to imagine what it was. The waiting and uncertainty were taking a toll, and the last thing she felt like doing was attending a party.

"I don't feel up to this, Meade," she told him wearily as she opened the fan that matched the blue foulard of her dress. "It's too hot for crinolines, and I don't think I can smile at Caroline all evening while she gloats over her husband's promotion."

Meade gave her an encouraging smile. "I thought you'd be delighted to attend your nemesis's going-away party."

"Hardly. I already have plenty of snide remarks to remember her by."

"Well, you can add a few more to your collection. It's only one night, after all."

Meade's forced good cheer was beginning to grate on Libby's jangled nerves. She'd agreed to attend the party for his sake, but considering the toll these last few weeks had taken on her, going to the party was probably the worst thing she could do for her brother. Her nerves were so taut that one ugly remark about Case would be all the provocation she needed to push someone into the punch bowl.

It just wasn't worth the strain. She never should have agreed to go. "I'm sorry, Meade. Truly I am," she said as she started back to her room. "I thought I could bluff my way through it, but I can't. You go on without me and convey my apologies and good wishes to Caroline."

"Now, wait a minute, Libby," Meade said, taking several steps toward her. "You have to go."

She stopped. "I don't *have* to do anything, Meade," she said with slow deliberation.

"You sound like a petulant child."

"Well, I'm not. I'm a grown woman who simply doesn't feel like being a hypocrite tonight. You know people will discuss Case and this business with Gato—and not in favorable terms. I don't want to have to smile and pretend their disparaging remarks don't bother me."

Meade didn't want to argue with her, but her comment was too revealing to pass up. "Are you finally admitting that you can't handle the controversy your relationship with Case has caused?"

Libby gritted her teeth and stared down at the floor. She'd managed to live in peace with her brother since Case's return only by walking on eggshells. She did her best to keep her anxieties hidden; he pretended not to notice that her nerves were frayed to the breaking point. "All I'm admitting is that I can't handle a party tonight. Case's life is in danger, and mine is in limbo. I don't feel like pretending otherwise."

"It's not going to get better, Libby."

"It will be better once Case is out of danger."

"You're being naive, Libby," Meade said with more rancor than he'd intended. "If you pursue this relationship with Case, disparaging remarks will be the least of your worries."

Libby put up her hands as though to ward him off. "I don't want to listen to this, Meade."

"Well, maybe it's time you did."

"Just stop it!" She turned and fled into her room, but Meade pursued her. He couldn't bear what this ill-fated relationship was doing to his sister, and he couldn't keep quiet about it any longer.

"I won't stop, Libby, until you face a few cold, hard facts."

"Meade, don't," she pleaded. "Don't force us both to say things we won't be able to forget or forgive."

"Since when is the truth unforgivable?"

"Since you began trying to impose your own interpretation of it on me. That's when." With a sweep of her skirts, she sat at her makeshift vanity table and began removing the ribbons from her upswept hair. "Do you really believe I haven't thought about how hard a life with Case would be? I'm not the little dunce you seem to think I've become. I know it won't be easy. My God, how could I *not* know it?" she said bitterly, her voice broken with emotion. "My own brother—the kindest, most generous and understanding person I've ever known—can't even accept the man I love. Do you think I expect anyone else to?"

Meade heard her description of him and gritted his teeth against the hot tears that suddenly pressed his eyes. He no longer possessed the traits she ascribed to him. This godforsaken place called Arizona had wrung them out of him. He had become narrow-minded and small. He had proved himself a coward in battle, and the things he had seen and done had forced him to close off his emotions so that the next time he was forced to amputate a man's limb or dig an arrow from a festering wound he would feel no more than his ethernumbed patient.

He'd arrived at Fort Apache feeling mightily superior to his predecessor, who had lived in squalor and left only empty liquor bottles as his legacy. He no longer felt superior. He understood the forces that had driven that doctor to drink, and Meade was terrified of walking down the same road. He hadn't resorted to the bottle yet, but he could fight his own guilt for just so long, and then . . . who could say?

The only thing in Meade's life that hadn't been tainted and twisted by grim reality was Libby. She was still the shining center of his existence. Her hope and idealism were still intact, and Meade didn't think he could survive watching them get ground out of her little by little until there was nothing left but pain and disillusionment.

He'd voluntarily joined the army and brought her along with him, and now he was terrified that this harsh land would eventually destroy him. He couldn't let it destroy Libby, too. That was why he'd forced Case into the deceitful bargain they'd made, and it was why he had to make Libby understand how wrong she was to believe she loved him.

He looked at her reflection in the little mirror over the vanity. The sun had turned her skin to a pale gold. She looked tired and drawn, but she was still incredibly beautiful. He had to see that she stayed that way.

Libby knew Meade was still behind her; she could see his reflection in the mirror. He looked so sad that it nearly broke her heart, but she knew he hadn't given up. He was collecting his thoughts, preparing his arguments. Fighting her anguish at his disapproval, she steeled herself against whatever he was planning to throw at her.

What he said, though, was something she couldn't possibly have anticipated.

"The Crenshaws are leaving for Santa Fe on Monday with a full infantry company as escort. It will probably be the best-protected caravan leaving Fort Apache in the next six months." He paused for a moment. "I want you to be on it, Libby."

Her eyes darted up to his in the reflection of the mirror, and a handful of hairpins clattered onto the vanity. "You can't be serious."

"I am."

"I won't go."

"Then I'll have Colonel Dunlevy revoke your permission to stay here. You'll be forced to leave."

Libby couldn't believe what she was hearing, but she didn't doubt for a moment that Meade would make good on his threat. "Don't do this to me, Meade. Don't do it to *us*," she begged, her voice tremulous.

"I'm sending you back east, Libby. That's final." He turned to leave.

Libby twisted around on the stool. "Case won't let this happen, Meade!"

He stopped at the door. "Longstreet doesn't have any say about it."

"You're wrong!" she insisted, too frightened to be angry. "I'll go to him—"

"You can't leave the fort," he reminded her.

"Then I'll find Jedidiah. He'll be at the party tonight. I'll tell him what you're planning, and he'll bring Case to me."

Meade shook his head. "Case can't stop me."

"He can if we're married!"

Meade took a deep breath and looked away from her. He knew Case wouldn't marry her without his approval, and Libby was never supposed to know the reason why. He'd hated making that bargain with the scout, but most of all he'd been sickened by his willingness to deceive Libby. If he was going to break her heart, the least he could do for her was give her the truth. "Longstreet won't marry you, Libby."

"Yes, he will. He loves me!"

He nodded. "Yes, he does. Very much. That's what makes this whole thing so damned tragic. He's a brave, honorable man who loves you so much that he's willing to give you up for your own sake."

That had always been Libby's worst fear, but she'd never expressed it to anyone—not Meade, Susannah, or even Case. "How do you know that?" she asked hoarsely.

"He told me," Meade admitted reluctantly.

Libby came to her feet. "When?"

"After he returned from the meeting with Cochise. That day he sent for me, I asked him what he envisioned for the future, and he told me he wanted to marry you. He wants to go into ranching with Jedidiah, and he wants you to be a part of that.''

Libby's heart expanded with joy, but it was short-lived. ''Then why did you say he was giving me up for my own good?'' she asked, hardly able to breathe.

Meade's face and voice were absolutely emotionless as he confessed, ''I told him that I'd never endorse the relationship. I made him realize that marriage to him is not in your best interest.'' He'd gone this far, and Libby was never going to forgive him, anyway. He knew he had to tell her the rest of it. ''I also manipulated him into promising that you'd never know I was responsible for his rejection of you.''

Libby's face drained of color. ''How could you do that to me?''

''It's for your own good, Libby. You can't see what this relationship is going to do to you, but I can.''

''You see nothing!'' she cried, moving to him. ''I love him, Meade. He's inside my heart and my head. I can't make him go away. And I don't want to! What I feel for him is too precious.'' She looked up at him imploringly, tears glistening in her eyes. ''Can't you understand that?''

''No, I can't, Libby,'' he replied sadly. ''The kind of love you *think* you feel is nothing but a mirage. It doesn't exist.''

She took a step back. ''That's it, isn't it, Meade? This isn't about Case and me. It's about you . . . and our parents. You're so disillusioned by their failure that you can't believe it's possible for two people to have something more than what they had.''

Meade didn't want to explore the possibility that she might be right. ''Take your head out of the clouds, Libby, and—''

''And you take your head out of the sand!'' she exclaimed. ''I'm not afraid of life, Meade. I'm not afraid of loving someone and risking the pain that can cause. Don't inflict your fear on me!''

''This isn't about fear, Libby! It's about reality!''

''No!'' she said harshly. ''It's about love, Meade. It's about what I feel for Case and what he feels for me. That's reality!''

''What about your children?'' he asked hotly. ''How can you condemn your half-breed children to live with that reality you think is so precious? What about the hate and ridicule they'll suffer because of you?''

Libby had thought about that often, but she had no clear-cut answer to give Meade. ''If Case and I have children, we'll give them all the love and security you and I were denied by our parents.'' Twin tears slipped down her cheeks. ''And I hope to God we can teach them that there can be a better world than this. Oh, please, Meade . . .'' She placed her hands on his chest. ''Help me. I want you to be a part of my life.''

He pulled her into his arms and held her tightly, pressing his cheek against her hair. ''I can't, Libby,'' he whispered, his voice broken with emotion. ''I just can't. I'm sorry.'' He set her away from him abruptly and hurried out the door.

Bereft, and more frightened than she'd ever been in her life, Libby collapsed on the bed. Her sobs were the wrenching, uncontrollable convulsions of a woman whose world had just been shattered into a thousand irretrievable pieces.

''I'm sending Libby back to live with relatives in the East,'' Meade told Jedidiah. A harvest moon bathed the Crenshaws' porch in silvery light, but Meade saw nothing romantic about the situation. He'd made a brief appearance at the party, staying only long enough to draw Jedidiah outside. ''I know Case doesn't want to see Libby right now, but I promised her that I'd arrange a meeting between them before she leaves. I'm hoping you'll help me make that happen. It's the only way I'm going to keep her from doing something stupid, like running off to find him herself.''

Jedidiah looked out over the quiet parade ground. Someone was playing a guitar in the enlisted men's quarters across the way, and every now and then a burst of raucous laughter split the night, but other than that, Fort Apache was silent and bleak. ''I find it hard to believe that Libby is giving up without a fight.''

Meade chuckled bitterly. ''Oh, she hasn't given up. She's holding on to the hope that Case will find a solution—maybe by forcing me to change my mind or by beating me into submission.''

"Libby wouldn't want that, and you know it." Jedidiah hadn't realized until just that minute how much self-loathing his new friend was carrying around.

"Don't be so sure. My Libby is a fighter. After I told her she was leaving she cried for a while. Then she pulled herself together and came at me with both barrels."

Jedidiah paused thoughtfully. "Have you considered giving her what she wants?"

"I tried that, remember? I stood back and kept my mouth shut during Case's recuperation, praying that she'd eventually come to her senses. Obviously it didn't work."

"That's not what I mean," he replied, turning to face his companion.

Meade digested the look on Jedidiah's face. "You mean let them get married? Watch Libby ruin her life?"

Jedidiah shrugged. "Who are we to say that's what would happen?"

Meade frowned. "I thought you were as opposed to this as I am."

"I was for a while, when I thought Libby was just a bored white woman whose fancy had been piqued by an exotic, forbidden Apache," he admitted. "But that's not the way it is. To tell you the truth, Meade, I was afraid Case would never be able to love anyone the way he loves Libby. He's been so consumed by hatred that I didn't think there was room for that kind of emotion. But he does love her"—he glanced up at the moon hanging low on the horizon—"and I know what that feels like."

And I don't, Meade thought bleakly, remembering Libby's indictment of him. He pushed the thought aside and concentrated on his purpose. "Will you help me arrange a meeting? I know Case is worried that Gato might learn about Libby, but maybe he could sneak into the fort one night . . . ?" He left the question hanging.

"I'm sure he'll take some action."

Jedidiah spoke cautiously, but Meade understood his meaning and shook his head. "He won't spirit her away and marry her," he said flatly. Then he explained the bargain he and Case had made.

Jedidiah shook his head sadly. "Isn't it amazing that one woman can be loved so much and still be made so unhappy? And all in the name of what someone else thinks is best for her."

Meade didn't want to hear the older man's philosophizing. "Just arrange the meeting, Jedidiah," he said shortly as he stepped off the porch and started down the quadrangle toward the hospital.

The lights in his quarters were out when he arrived.

Frowning, Meade hurried across the porch and opened the door. "Libby?" No answer. He'd been gone less than half an hour. Surely she wouldn't have gone to bed without hearing what Jedidiah had to say.

The horrible thought that she'd struck out on her own to find Case sent Meade flying to the lamp on the mantel. He lit it quickly, adjusting the flame as he rushed to the door of his sister's room.

"Libby? Lib—" His voice failed him when he saw the overturned vanity table. The scattered ribbons, bows, and pins hardly registered. He didn't notice the broken mirror or spilled pots of face cream. Blood roared in his ears when he realized in that moment that Case's worst fear had just come true.

"*Libby!*" He whirled and saw the Apache only a split second before the Chiricahua war club crashed onto his skull.

Patience had become Case's friend. Eleven years of following the eagle's signposts and preparing himself for Gato were now paying off. The calm he felt was forced, but real nonetheless. He was ready, and the waiting was insignificant.

Every day he and a handful of scouts scoured the canyons and valleys on foot, searching for some sign of Gato. They covered the area methodically, one section at a time, working in a clockwise circle around the reservation. So far they had seen nothing, but Case was not fooled. He knew his enemy was near and the time was almost at hand. The eagle had shown him no more visions, but Case's certainty came from within. It was as potent as any dream his guiding spirit had ever brought to him.

Exercising the caution that had been heightened by his awareness of Gato, Case stealthily made his way back to his camp, letting the shadows created by the full moon conceal his progress. He had separated himself from the other returning scouts a few minutes earlier, when only the steep hill at the rear of his wickiup stood between him and his camp.

At the top of the hill he surveyed the area and was surprised to realize Jedidiah was not in camp. Normally he spent his days among Case's family, keeping a watchful eye out for any sign that Gato might be planning something that involved them. He always returned by nightfall, though, and was usually waiting for Case with a pot of coffee and a hearty meal on the fire.

There was no fire tonight, though. Case was concerned for a moment, until he remembered that Jedidiah had been invited to a party at the fort. When he came back, he would have news about Libby, and that would be welcome indeed. Tonight Case would turn the tables and have dinner waiting for Jedidiah. He would ask his friend how she had looked, what she had worn. Jedidiah would tell him if her eyes still sparkled with love and tenderness when she spoke of him.

Letting the thought of Libby drift over him like a cool breeze, Case continued his careful descent, circling around to approach the camp from the front. He was still a dozen yards away when he spotted the footprints.

Every day before he left his camp, Case swept the area with a branch of sage to keep a fine layer of dirt loose on the hard soil and to obliterate his own prints. These new footprints had been made by someone who had arrived after Case left.

With his breathing controlled and steady, he squatted beside the impressions, which appeared to lead directly to his wickiup. The prints were not Jedidiah's, nor were they from the round-toed, hard-soled shoes worn by the soldiers. These had been made by moccasins, but not the kind sewn by the White Mountain Apaches. The stitching left a different kind of mark—like the impression Case had seen in the mud eleven years ago on the day of his parents' death. A Chiricahua moccasin had made that print.

Surely Gato would not be so foolhardy as to leave a trail this clear, he thought, but he knew better than to take foolish chances.

Keeping low, he doubled back, slipping up the hill a little way, then back down again, directly behind his wickiup. The blanket-flap door faced east, but at the back of his dwelling he had devised a cleverly disguised escape route—a trapdoor of woven yucca and buckskin that was indistinguishable from the other parts of the circular walls.

With his knife drawn, Case crept silently toward that secret door. As he crouched beside it, he heard no sound coming from inside, and when he threw the escape route open, he saw that the wickiup was empty.

He stepped back and moved through the camp, checking his sweat lodge and Jedidiah's lean-to, which protruded from the side of his wagon. His mule and horse were stabled at the fort for safekeeping, so there were no other structures that could hide an assassin.

Puzzled, he looked in the direction of the Chiricahua encampment. It was too far away to be seen, but he looked anyway, wondering if one of the "captives" had paid him a visit and found him not at home. The footprints did not come from that direction, though; they led directly from the fort.

With his eyes focused on the ground, he covered the area again and found the set of footprints leading away from the wickiup. The ground in front of the door was scuffed, and clear prints showed the direction the visitor left in. Someone wanted Case to know he had been here.

He returned to the front of the wickiup, prepared to search it more thoroughly, when the steady clip-clop of a horse alerted him to the approach of company. He looked toward the fort and recognized Jedidiah. Sheathing his knife, he jogged out to meet him.

As Jedidiah neared, he realized something was wrong. Case's movements were tense and deliberate, even for him. Jedidiah cursed himself for having stayed at the party after his disturbing conversation with Meade, but he'd known it would be an hour or more before Case returned, so he hadn't seen any reason to rush back to their camp.

"What's happened?" he asked as he slipped off his horse. "Is something wrong in camp?"

Case told him what he'd discovered as they walked slowly toward his wickiup.

"They made no effort to hide the prints?" Jedidiah asked, as puzzled as Case.

"No."

"You searched the wickiup?"

"Not thoroughly," Case replied. "I was about to do that when you rode up."

Jedidiah harrumphed. "You don't suppose someone left you a little surprise in there? Like a nest of rattlers?"

Case repressed a shudder. To an Apache, snakes were the most dangerous kind of evil. No Inday would willingly touch one, but Gato might believe that his witchcraft was strong enough to protect him. Case had no such beliefs.

"You want me to do it?" Jedidiah asked, reading his thoughts.

He shook his head. "If there is a trap inside, it is meant for me. I will look."

"Well, at least light a fire first," he advised. "You're going to need more light—and a good long stick with a flame at the end wouldn't hurt, either."

While Case kept watch, Jedidiah prepared a small campfire, then handed his surrogate son a lengthy torch. Case had only a minimal knowledge of the ritual prayer that was sung to give a man snake power. He had never paid a shaman to teach him, but as he approached the wickiup, he wished he had taken the time to learn. Expecting the worst, he threw back the blanket flap of the wickiup.

What he saw hanging in the opening, swinging wildly back and forth, made his dread of snakes pale by comparison.

TWENTY-SIX

WHEN CASE FROZE, Jedidiah looked over his shoulder and stared at the doorway in astonishment. Firelight glittered off the silver beads and made the cobweblike veins in the turquoise sparkle like gold. "The necklace?"

Case reached out and stilled the swinging pendant. His hand caressed the stones lightly, reverently, but there was no joy in him as fingers traveled down, brushing the medallion, then lower, to the tiny disk from which the eagle feathers had hung. The two feathers that represented Case and his sister were gone. In their place was a lock of long, dark, silky hair.

Gato cannot be frightened, Longstreet . . . as long as I have the thing you desire most in the world. The words flashed through Case's mind like uncontrollable stabs of lightning. He remembered too clearly the way Gato had held the medallion out to him, sneering contemptuously.

The thing you desire most . . .

Libby.

Blinded by fear and rage, Case untied the necklace.

"I don't understand," Jedidiah said. "Why would he leave you the necklace?"

With the medallion crushed into his palm, Case rose and held out his hand. The lock of hair tumbled down the back of his hand. "Gato has taken Libby. That's why the tracks are so clear. He wants me to follow."

Jedidiah couldn't believe it. "Now, wait a minute, Case.

There's no proof that that's Libby's hair. How the devil could Gato had known about her?''

"He knows," Case said with certainty as he headed for Jedidiah's horse.

"Where are you going?"

"To find her."

Jedidiah struggled to keep up with him. "At least go to the fort first! For all you know, she could be sound asleep. If Libby had been kidnapped, Meade would have raised an alarm that could have been heard for miles."

"Not if he's dead," Case replied.

"At least check it out," Jedidiah insisted.

Case paused. If Gato intended to harm Libby, Case was already too late, but that seemed unlikely. Gato would want Libby alive, to use as a pawn to manipulate Case into doing something foolish. If that was Gato's plan, a few minutes more weren't going to make any difference. It would be better to go into battle with all the facts.

Case tossed the horse's reins to Jedidiah. "Ride in calmly, sound no alarm. I'll enter the fort through the opening beside the hospital."

He turned and started running at the brisk, steady pace that enabled Apache warriors to travel miles without stopping. Jedidiah mounted quickly and set off for the fort, keeping his pace unhurried, as Case had instructed. He didn't need to be told that if Libby had indeed been abducted, sounding an alarm was the worst thing they could do for her. Sending a contingent of soldiers to follow the trail Gato had left would be signing Libby's death warrant.

He nodded politely to the sentries at the main entrance and tipped his hat to the guard walking his prescribed route. Crook had doubled the guard mount when he incarcerated Gusalá, but there was no way that all of the little outlets between the buildings could be protected at once. If Gato had been daring enough to make the attempt, it wouldn't have been too hard for him to sneak into the fort without being seen.

The proof of that came when Jedidiah sauntered onto the porch of the hospital just as a lamp was lit inside. He knocked, and seconds later the door opened. Case was already hurrying back across the room by the time Jedidiah stepped onto the threshold and saw Meade lying on the floor outside Libby's bedroom, bound, gagged, and apparently unconscious.

"Close the door and check the rest of the house," Case snapped as he knelt beside Libby's brother.

While Jedidiah did as he was told, Case removed the rags that had been stuffed into Meade's mouth, then carefully turned the doctor's head to inspect the dark, abraded circle on his temple. It was the wound made by a war club.

"There was a struggle in Libby's bedroom," Jedidiah told Case when he returned to the parlor. "But there's no blood. Obviously she was alive when she left here," he added.

Case didn't react to the news. "Get me some water. I have to wake him up." If Gato had left Meade alive, he must have a reason, and Case wanted to know what it was.

By the time Jedidiah returned with a basin of water from the barrel by the kitchen door, Case had Meade's hands and feet untied. "The back door is unbarred," Jedidiah said, kneeling beside Case. "Looks like they came in through the little window in the kitchen and went out through the door."

Case began bathing Meade's face, resisting the overwhelming temptation to dump the whole basin of water on him at one time. He had counted on the doctor to keep Libby safe, but Meade had failed. Case wanted to blame him for that; that would have made it so much easier for him to accept what had happened and deal with it rationally. But Meade was not at fault. Case knew the blame rested firmly on his own head. For that reason he kept his movements gentle as he brought Meade back to consciousness.

It was only a matter of moments before the doctor's eyes fluttered open. He looked up at Case, his expression blank and puzzled as he tried to figure out why the Apache scout was hovering over him, and then the memory of Libby's abduction flooded back to him. He sat up with a jerk, then grabbed his head, wincing against the pain.

"It would be better if you didn't move for a while," Case

told him, edging back. "Just tell me what happened to Libby. How long ago did they take her?"

"I don't know. An Apache stunned me with a club and tied me up. I must have lost consciousness right after they left," he said irritably as he tried to stand. The room swam, and he eased back to a sitting position. "They were waiting for me in the dark when I returned from speaking to Jedidiah."

Case looked at his friend. He knew nothing about a conversation between them and couldn't have cared less what was said. "How long ago was that?"

"About an hour and three-quarters," Jedidiah supplied.

Case looked at Meade again. "Why did they leave you alive?"

"Gato had a message for you," he replied venomously. "His English wasn't too good, but he managed to make himself clear. He said you're to come alone. If you bring any 'horse soldiers,' Libby will be killed."

The hard, cold expression on Case's face didn't change. "Did he say where?"

"He made a circle with his hands, like this"—he demonstrated—"then pointed to the northeast and said something that sounded like 'red canyon.' Do you know what he meant?"

There were a dozen red canyons in that section of the reservation, but only one that was completely enclosed as Meade had indicated. "Yes." Case stood and looked at Jedidiah. "Stay with the doctor. If I am not back with Libby by morning, tell Crook to send a company to Snake Canyon."

"Now, wait just a goddam minute," Meade ordered harshly, wincing against the throbbing in his temple as he stood. "You're not going after her alone. Gato will kill you on sight, and then God knows what he'll do to Libby—if she's not already dead!"

"If I take soldiers with me, he will kill her anyway. He would see us coming from miles away."

"Not a whole company of soldiers," Meade corrected. "Just me."

"No." Case shook his head adamantly. "You're in no condition to travel. You would slow me down."

Meade's concern for Libby tangled with the guilt he felt over having allowed her to be taken from his own house, and that, in turn, compounded the humiliation he still felt for having nearly gotten Case killed. All the emotions twisted together and became a blinding anger directed against Case. "That's not really what you're thinking," he accused. "You're thinking that I wouldn't be any good to you even if I did come along."

Case held his temper. He wanted to be off in search of Libby, not arguing with her brother. "You can't travel like an Apache."

"You mean I can't fight like a man," Meade growled.

Case neither confirmed nor denied the supposition. "I must do this alone."

He turned to leave, but Meade grabbed his arm and whirled him around. "This is all your fault, Longstreet. Do you hear me, *all of it!* My sister is going to die because of some ridiculous Apache vendetta! Well, you've got your showdown now, but you're crazy if you think I'm going to leave Libby's fate in the hands of a man who cares more about revenge than about my sister!"

The indictment cut Case to the bone. He'd spent most of his life savoring the thought of revenge without realizing the price he would be forced to pay for it. It was much too high. "You cannot stop me," he said defiantly.

"I can try," Meade said, his voice low and dangerous.

"Stop it, both of you!" Jedidiah commanded, stepping between them. "Stop arguing and think about what's important."

"Libby is the only thing that's important," Case replied, stepping back.

"Well, that's one thing we agree on, at least," Meade said.

"Then let me go after her."

Meade shook his head. "If you leave without me, I'll go to Crook and tell him what's happened. A cavalry company will be no more than twenty minutes behind you."

"You would be killing Libby," Case warned, not certain if Meade was bluffing.

"Then take me with you."

Case glared at him a moment. "We can travel only part of the way on horseback. If you go, you will cover the last miles on foot, Apache-fashion. Otherwise, Gato will see us coming."

Meade nodded, ignoring the pain in his head. "All right."

"If you fall behind, I will leave you," Case warned.

"Don't worry. I'll keep up."

"Then get your rifle and revolver." He turned to Jedidiah. "And you, old friend . . ."

Jedidiah knew better than to insist on going along. He was too old to run across the high desert at night. And besides, someone had to stay behind to pick up the pieces once this endless night was over. "Take my horse with you. The rifle is loaded, and there's ammunition in the saddlebags." He grabbed Case's shoulders and hugged him close for just a moment. "Take care, my son."

Case wrapped his arms around the older man. "I will come back, *Ci nah-kee tà*." My second father.

Jedidiah cleared his throat and stepped back just as Meade returned. Gone was the restrictive uniform coat he'd worn to the Crenshaws' party. In its place was an unadorned blue-black army blouse that would allow him to blend into the night.

"Enju," Case murmured. "Wait here while I go to the stable and get my own horse. No one will question me as they would you. Jedidiah will lead this horse around to the back door for you. Meet me there."

"How do I know you won't leave without me?" Meade asked.

Case shook his head in disgust. "When will you White Eyes ever learn that the word of an Apache means something?"

He brushed past Meade contemptuously as he headed for the back door.

Hidden by the black shadows of the rugged mesa, Case studied the wall of rock above him. At his side, Meade was leaning against the wall, struggling to control his breathing. Case knew the pain in his head and in his chest had to be enormous, yet the doctor had said nothing during the torturous journey to the mesa that hid Snake Canyon inside its belly.

They had ridden only a few miles before they began traveling on foot. Through open terrain where they might have been spotted by a lookout atop the mesa, they crawled. When there were hills and ridges to conceal them, they ran.

"Now . . . what?" Meade gasped hoarsely, irritated that he was the only one who appeared to be out of breath.

They were on the eastern side of the mesa, almost directly opposite the narrow, winding entrance that had earned the canyon its name. "Above us is an entrance to a cave," Case replied, never raising his voice above a whisper. "It winds through the rock until it reaches the canyon, maybe forty feet above the floor. From there you should be able to see everything that happens below."

"Me?" Meade questioned, looking up. All he saw were jutting rocks. "Where will you be?"

"I'll circle the mesa and enter through the passage. It's what Gato will expect of me."

"What makes you think this cave won't be guarded?"

"Gato was not raised in this part of the desert. He doesn't know it as I do."

Meade still wasn't convinced. "That may be true, but if he's been hiding in there for weeks, he's had plenty of time to explore."

"The opening is hard to see from the floor of the canyon, and the rock wall below it is as smooth as glass. My people say that many thousands of years ago, in the time when only the Mountain Spirits walked here, a river ran freely through the cave and tumbled down the wall inside."

"A waterfall?"

Case nodded. "Yes. There are many caves inside, but this is the only one that goes all the way through the rock. Even if Gato knows it is there, his men cannot climb up to it, and he would not suspect that it contains a passage leading outside."

"How long is it?"

"A quarter of a mile, maybe more," Case answered. "You will have to crawl part of the way, but there is only one tunnel, so you cannot become lost. Come. I'll take you to it; then I'll come back down and circle the mesa while you get into position." Slinging Jedidiah's rifle over his shoulder, he found a handhold and began to climb. When he had secure footing on a plateau above Meade, he crouched and extended his hand, but the doctor ignored it. With his rifle slung, he found his own handhold and followed Case up.

The long climb was made more difficult by their need for stealth, but finally they emerged onto a recessed plateau. Crouching, Meade followed Case as he ducked under a low overhang.

"Through there," Case told him, pointing into the darkness. "Crawl into the cave in a straight line. You should reach the back wall after only twenty feet. Follow the wall, moving to your right. You will know you're in the tunnel when you can extend your hands and touch both sides. You can stand then, but keep one hand up so that you will know when the ceiling begins to lower."

"Like playing blindman's buff," Meade muttered, peering into the pitch blackness.

Case didn't know that game, but the image was clear enough. "Even if you move slowly and carefully, you should reach the canyon long before I do."

Meade settled back on his haunches and looked at Case. The moonlight created strange shadows, but still provided enough light for him to see the harsh lines of the Apache's face. "Tell me what I can expect when you arrive," he instructed.

"I will shame Gato into fighting me."

"Then what?"

"After I have killed him, I will take Libby and leave."

He made it sound so simple. Meade knew it was anything but. "Assuming Gato doesn't shoot you down the moment he sees you, and assuming you win, what the devil makes you think his men are going to allow you to waltz out of there with Libby?"

Case ignored the sarcasm, reminding himself that this was a white man who understood nothing about the Apache mind. "This is a fight between Gato and me. His men will not interfere; by doing so they would lose all honor. If I defeat their leader fairly, they will have no choice but to let me go."

"And if Gato kills you?"

The question hung in darkness, and when Case finally answered, his reply chilled Meade far more than the eerie silence or the lifelessness of Case's voice. "If I die, you must kill Libby."

"What?" he exclaimed. "I can't kill my sister!"

Case fixed him with a hard glare. "Then you will watch her die a horrible, painful death."

Meade looked down at his hands and discovered they were trembling, but the emotion that made him quake was rage, not fear. "If we get out of this alive, Longstreet, you're going to answer to me for what you've made Libby suffer."

"A man answers only to himself, Doctor. Think about that before you judge me." Case placed his rifle on the ground between them and started to remove the cartridge bandolier from across his chest, but Meade grabbed his arm.

"What the hell does that mean?"

Case looked at him, his face expressionless. "It means that you must deal with your own guilt, just as I must deal with mine."

"My guilt?" Meade questioned, though he knew very well what the Apache meant.

"For your behavior in battle and for allowing Gato to take Libby," Case replied. "If you forgive yourself for these things, you will find it more difficult to hate me." He handed over the bandolier. "You will need these more than I."

He moved down the ledge, and Meade turned to watch him go, wondering if he was right about forgiving himself. Was he allowing his own guilt over his treatment of Case to color his decisions? The guilt was there, of course, but he didn't see how it could be responsible for his determination to keep Case and Libby apart. "Longstreet."

Case stopped and looked back at him, waiting.

"I'm sending Libby away when this is over," he said into the darkness.

Another moment of silence fell between them. "We all do what we must," Case replied quietly, then turned and disappeared down the cliff.

Juggling both rifles, Meade edged into the black cave and began crawling.

Hugging her knees to her chest, Libby huddled by the fire. The two Chiricahua braves flanking her seemed to know that she was too terrified to move, for they had paid little attention to her since removing her gag and the binding on her wrists shortly after entering the ghostly canyon. Gato had given a flurry of orders, and his men had rushed to obey. Some climbed the steep cliffs and hid among the rocks. Others were positioned on either side of the entrance. Libby had counted ten braves, including Gato.

The men had built a fire in the center of the huge canyon floor, and shoved Libby down beside it. She didn't believe it was a gesture of consideration because the canyon was so cold, though. From the way Gato had positioned her, she suspected he wanted Case to see her clearly the moment he arrived.

Libby dreaded that moment, but at the same time she was terrified it wouldn't happen. She didn't want to die, but she couldn't bear the thought of Case dying, either. She could only pray that when he came, he'd have some plan that would enable both of them to escape with their lives. But Gato appeared to be holding all the cards, and she had very little faith in that outcome. All she knew for certain was that Case *would* come.

The wait seemed endless. When they arrived, the moon had been barely visible over the eastern rim of the canyon; now it was almost directly overhead. It looked close enough to touch, and its iridescent glow bathed the entire circle in silver light. Libby thought about Case's quest and his belief in the guiding spirit of the Thunder Eagle. The setting could not have been more perfect if the eagle truly had chosen the time and place for the meeting of these bitter enemies.

Perhaps it was fated to be this way all along, Libby thought, then realized Case would be proud of her. She was finally starting to think like an Apache.

Out of the corner of her eye, she could see Gato sitting on a flat rock to her left. His legs were crossed, and he seemed to be deep in concentration. Occasionally Libby would hear the soft cry of some night creature, and Gato would raise his head and smile. Then he would return to his meditation. No one moved or made a sound, and the stillness reminded Libby of a tomb. That analogy brought her thoughts back full circle, and she wondered if she would go mad waiting, wondering, not knowing when or how she was meant to die.

When Case finally arrived, she cursed her impatience. His entrance was heralded by a cooing sound, like that of a dove, originating from somewhere far above them. Gato raised his head again, but this time he stood and turned his malicious smile on Libby.

"He come now." Gato gestured to the braves on either side of Libby, and they rose. He gestured for her to rise, and when she stubbornly refused to obey the order, the braves pulled her roughly to her feet. She struggled against them briefly, until one of the braves showed her his knife. She stopped struggling, and after Gato murmured something in Apache, the braves released her. The knife stayed in view.

With quiet deliberation, Gato walked a little distance away from the fire and waited. A moment later Case appeared in the mouth of the canyon. His eyes went first to Libby, then to Gato as he stopped a few yards beyond the portal.

"You have sent for me, and I am here," he said in Apache. His voice echoed off the canyon walls.

Gato laughed. "Have you come for me or for the woman?"

Moving his hand slowly, Case reached into the buckskin pouch that hung from the belt of his breechclout. He heard a noise to his left, but Gato raised one hand and the brave who had sprung forward stopped. Case withdrew the Thunder Eagle necklace and held it up.

For eleven years it had stood for revenge, but the moment he had seen it hanging in his wickiup, he remembered the true meaning of the necklace his mother had worn for so many years. It was a symbol of love, not hate. That was what Libby had tried to tell him in his dream so many years ago; it was everything she believed in and all she had represented since she came into his life a few months ago.

Knowing he should have learned the lesson sooner, he tossed the necklace onto the ground between himself and Gato. "If I can have only one, I will take my woman."

Gato laughed again. "You will have neither, Longstreet!" He gestured to the braves behind him, and suddenly Libby found herself being dragged away from the fire toward two wooden poles near the north wall of the canyon.

When she began struggling against them, Case cried out to her. "Don't, Libby! Don't fight them! Trust me, *cida'ké!*"

"Case, please!" she cried, but had no idea what she was begging him for. She stopped struggling as he instructed, and the braves tied her hands with rawhide thongs that hung from the tops of the poles. By the time they were finished, her arms were stretched above her head so far that only her toes touched the ground.

One of the braves stepped behind her, and Libby screamed when he grabbed her unbound hair, yanked her head back, and placed the blade of his knife at the edge of her scalp.

"Gato, no!" Case commanded. "You shame yourself! Your fight is with me, not the woman!"

"*Your* woman!"

"Yes!"

The renegade moved a few paces forward until he was standing almost on top of the Thunderbird necklace. "Then as my revenge I will make you watch her suffer and listen to her screams of agony before you die."

"You are no man." Case spat on the ground to show his contempt. "You have run from me like a coward for almost a dozen harvests, and now the only way you can have revenge is by torturing a woman." He raised his voice so that it rang into every corner of the canyon. "Your braves should turn on you so that they will not be tainted by your shame!"

"You cannot sway them," Gato scoffed. "They owe their lives to me."

"And a fine life it has been, yes, Gato? Even Cochise could not bear to look at you."

"That was your doing!" the renegade roared.

"Yes," Case agreed emphatically. "But do your men know why? Do they know that I seek revenge because you took gold from a white man to kill my parents?"

Two of Gato's braves looked at each other, surprised by Case's accusation, but the others did not react.

"What matters is that *you* pay," Gato replied, then looked to the braves on either side of the entrance. "Take him."

Four men sprang toward Case, and he tensed for their attack. To his left, though, he heard Libby cry out as her head was yanked back even harder. It was Gato's way of warning Case not to fight, and it worked. Case stood still as two of the men grabbed his arms and twisted them behind his back.

He allowed himself to be taken toward a pair of poles opposite Libby. They were going to bind him and make him watch while they tortured her, and Case wasn't sure there was anything he could do to stop them.

TWENTY-SEVEN

MEADE WAS LYING on his stomach watching the grisly drama unfolding below him. He'd heard the angry exchange between Case and Gato, but even if he'd understood Apache, he wouldn't have comprehended much of what was being said. The echoes in the canyon had distorted even the words Case spoke to Libby almost beyond recognition.

Meade understood the meaning of the actions all too well, though. Case had done his best to goad Gato into hand-to-hand combat, and he had failed. He was being marched toward the posts, and once he was tied up, he would be able to do nothing but watch helplessly as the braves tortured Libby to death.

Unless Case had an ace up his sleeve he'd neglected to tell Meade about, the scout had done all he could do. He'd marched fearlessly into a nest of vipers, but it was going to be up to Meade to get him and Libby out.

He'd made efficient use of his time while he waited for Case. His Colt .45 was loaded and lying within easy reach, and Jedidiah's seven-shot Spencer was right beside it. His own Springfield carbine was in his hands, and the barrel was trained on the brave who was holding a knife to Libby's head. It could discharge only one shot at a time, but the shells were easy to load; and at this distance, it was far more accurate than the Spencer.

The bright harvest moon was a blessing. He had counted ten Apaches—seven on the canyon floor, three on cave ledges similar to Meade's hiding place. The ones in the caves had rifles, and the ones on the floor either carried rifles or kept them within easy reach.

All in all, Meade was in an excellent position to pick them off one at a time—providing they didn't move, return fire, or use Case and Libby for target practice.

The only other asset Meade could count was Case. Because he'd put up no resistance to the braves who had taken hold of him, they had neglected to confiscate his knife and the wicked-looking war club that hung from his belt. Meade knew from personal experience how much damage a weapon like that could do.

And he also knew his time was running out. In a matter of seconds Case would be tied up. He was speaking to Gato again, but the renegade seemed oblivious to whatever insults were being hurled at him. He laughed once. The ugly sound echoed off the canyon walls, and Meade knew he could wait no longer. Praying for the accuracy he knew he was capable of, he took aim at the Apache holding Libby. If he was so much as a hairbreadth off, he would probably kill his sister— but if he didn't shoot, she'd be better off dead. He was convinced of that now.

He controlled his breathing and ignored the moisture on his palms and the thundering pulse of his heart. He prayed to God that he wouldn't freeze again. He steadied his aim . . . but just as he was prepared to squeeze the trigger the shrill cry of an eagle echoed through the canyon. The sound startled him, but more important, it startled the Chiricahua braves. The close quarters magnified the sound, making it seem twice as loud as any eagle had ever sounded—and twice as close. Alarmed, the Chiricahuas looked up, as did Meade, and saw the shadow of an enormous eagle soar across the harvest moon.

Chaos erupted below as the frightened, superstitious Chiricahuas called to their leader. The brave holding Libby's hair released her and moved toward Gato. The instant he did, Case took advantage of his captors' surprise and broke free of them. His knife was unsheathed in an instant, and one brave was dead before the other realized what had happened.

Gato was waving his arms, trying to calm the men, and Meade joined the fray. His first shot dropped the brave closest to Libby, then he grabbed the Spencer and fired one shot after another as the startled Chiricahuas dived for cover and tried to determine where the shots were coming from. Each report of the rifle echoed deafeningly, providing a confusion Meade hadn't counted as one of his assets.

He saw Case dash across the canyon toward Libby, and when Chiricahua rifles began firing at him, Meade concentrated his own fire on the braves who had taken cover. He kept them ducking until Case reached Libby and sliced through her bonds. She fell into his arms like a rag doll, and Meade's heart stopped beating.

She was dead. He knew it. He had gambled that the braves would be so intent on firing at him that they would forget about Libby. He had been wrong.

Blinded by rage, he emitted a hoarse cry of pain as Case carried Libby to a cluster of boulders and took cover there himself. A second later he saw Case crawling toward a rifle that one of the felled braves had dropped.

Meade grabbed his Colt and began firing. The part of his mind that could still reason tried to count the number of Chiricahua renegades who were still alive. Case had killed two; Meade knew he had taken out at least three. But there were still three in the caves, and Gato had taken cover with one of his men behind some boulders on the south side of the canyon. They had all spotted the muzzle fire from Meade's weapons and now knew his location, but as long as Meade kept his head low, he was in comparatively little danger.

But that didn't matter. Libby was dead and Meade's life had lost all meaning.

When the Colt was empty, he quickly reloaded, but moments after he stopped firing, so did the Chiricahua. The echo of gunfire began to subside, until finally all was quiet.

Meade began reloading the rifles, grateful for a respite from the deafening roar. The silence made it easier to think, but thinking wasn't Meade's problem. Feeling was the problem. A fist was squeezing every drop of life out of his heart. Libby . . . his Libby . . . Case's Libby . . .

They had both failed her.

Meade nearly jumped when a Chiricahua voice shouted something unintelligible, breaking the unearthly silence. Another voice joined the first. Gato answered, and from his tone, Meade judged that the renegade wasn't happy with whatever his men had said. There were more angry shouts, and then Meade heard Case's deep voice. He said something, and one of the men in the caves answered; then a second voice from another cave replied.

Case spoke for a long time, and it took Meade a moment to realize it when the scout started speaking in English.

"Meade! Can you hear me?" he called up into the darkness. "Ashford!"

"Yes!"

"Gato's braves want to give up. They think you are the spirit of the Thunder Eagle, and they don't want to fight you. They say this is Gato's fight, not theirs, and it is not worth dying for. If you will let them leave without firing another shot, they will go in peace."

Even though Case spoke slowly, the echo made him hard to understand. Meade got the gist of it, though. "What about Gato?" he asked. "I won't let him leave alive! He's got to pay for what he did to Libby!"

"Gato is mine," Case replied. "One of his own braves has disarmed him, and he's willing to exchange him for safe passage out of here."

Meade thought it over. He wanted Gato dead, and the only real way to ensure that was to let the others go. "All right. Tell them to come out in the open and throw their guns next to the fire. Then they can go."

Case repeated the message, and a few moments later a brave prodded an angry, defiant Gato toward the fire in the center of the canyon. Three figures silently emerged from their caves and quickly clambered down the rocky cliff. They deposited their rifles by the fire as instructed; two of them even added their bows and arrows.

Case met them in the center and picked up one of the rifles. A moment later the four braves were trotting out of the canyon, leaving Gato facing Case across the blazing campfire.

With the loaded carbine cradled in his hands, Meade stood. Gato and Case were staring at each other. If they were speaking, their voices were too low for Meade to hear. The fist squeezed his heart even tighter, and he raised the rifle, sighting it directly at Gato's head.

"Kill him, Case!" he shouted. "Kill the bastard now, or I will!"

"Meade?" Rubbing her chafed wrists, Libby stumbled out from behind the rocks where Case had ordered her to stay. The hatred in Meade's voice terrified her, and she'd already had enough terror to last a lifetime.

Meade looked away from Gato, not even conscious that he had lowered the rifle. "Libby? *Libby?*" The fist released his heart. "Oh, God," he whispered and began desperately searching for a way down the canyon wall. But there was none. "Libby, are you all right?"

"I'm fine now," she assured him. Then she moved slowly to Case. Her legs still felt wobbly, but they were better than they'd been when Case released her. A tremor of fear ran down her spine when she looked at Gato, but Case was her real concern. "What are you going to do now?" she asked quietly.

Case had been asking himself the same question. Eleven years ago he had sworn to his grandfather that he would slit the throat of this renegade. A year ago, even a day ago, he would have thrown away the rifle, unsheathed his knife, and demanded Gato do the same.

But that was before he realized there was something more important to him than revenge.

"Throw down your knife, Gato," he said in Apache.

For the first time, the renegade's arrogance turned to fear. "You would kill me unarmed?"

"I will not kill you at all. I will let the Gray Fox hang you for the soldiers you killed at Santa Elena."

"No!" Gato shouted. "That is not the way for an Apache to die!" He unsheathed his knife and feinted toward Case.

Case pushed Libby back and cautiously circled the fire. "Put down the knife, Gato. Killing me will not spare your life. If I die, my friend above will shoot you."

"That is a better way to die!" Gato exclaimed, lurching toward Case again. His panic made him careless, and Case feinted to one side, bringing the butt of the rifle level with his shoulders. He extended his right arm sharply and clubbed Gato on the head. The renegade dropped like a stone.

Libby released the breath she'd been holding and glanced up at Meade. He was lowering his rifle. She looked at Case, who was standing over Gato's inert body.

"Is it over?" she whispered.

Case took a deep, cleansing breath and nodded. "It's over."

A sob welled up in Libby's throat, and Case opened his arms to her. She flew into them, and he pressed her close. He felt the warmth of her tears on his chest, and something inside his breast expanded until it burst, releasing the last ounce of hatred from his heart, leaving nothing but his love for Libby.

He looked up and saw Meade on the cliff . . . watching them.

Dawn was just beginning to break as Fort Apache finally came into view. Libby was riding with Case, both of her legs draped over one of his, her cheek resting on his shoulder as he cradled her in his arms. She was so emotionally drained and physically exhausted that she had nearly fallen asleep twice, but the horse's movement over the uneven ground kept her awake. She didn't mind, though. The security of Case's arms was all she really needed. Meade had tried to get her to ride with him, but she refused. She could see in his eyes the hurt her rejection caused him, but he hadn't protested.

Gato had fought them every step of the way while they'd all been on foot, but when they reached the horses and tied the renegade on a long leash, he became too busy trying to keep pace with the horses to cause his captors much trouble. He was tethered to Meade's saddle, and Gato seemed to know that the white medicine man would like nothing better than to drag him over the rocky terrain.

They were still a half mile from the fort when two columns of cavalry rode out, their pace brisk.

"Looks like Jedidiah's done his job," Meade commented.

Libby raised her head and saw the soldiers coming. She squinted into the distance, and when she realized that General Crook was with David Robertson and Jedidiah at the head of the columns, she straightened. Her dress was torn and filthy. Her face was smudged with dirt and streaked with tears. Her hair was a frightful, uneven mess thanks to the brutal trimming Gato had given one side of it.

But she really didn't care. She was alive, she was in Case's arms, and the nightmare was over. The soldiers could think whatever they wanted to think.

Mustering her pride, she squared her shoulders and waited for the cavalry to arrive. It took them a while to spot the small party headed toward the fort, but when they did, they corrected their course and rode at a gallop to intercept them.

"Lieutenant Simmons! Take charge of the prisoner," David Robinson ordered as soon as both parties had faced off and stopped.

Crook looked them over and decided they were none the worse for wear. "Gato?" he questioned, eyeing the belligerent Chiricahua who was being led away.

"Yes, sir," Case replied. "I promised him you would hang him for the ambush at Santa Elena."

Crook looked Case over speculatively, wondering why he'd allowed the renegade to live. "Curious," he muttered, then edged his horse forward, fixing Case with a stern glare. "You I can do nothing about," he told the scout. "If you want to go off half-cocked, chasing renegades in the middle of the night, that's your business." He frowned at Meade. "You, on the other hand, I could have court-martialed for desertion. And you"—he looked at Libby, and his expression softened into a gentle smile—"are a very great lady who has suffered far too much."

Libby's eyes misted over. "Thank you, General."

His smile turned into an impish grin, and he leaned toward her conspiratorially. "So, tell me, Miss Ashford, has this little escapade changed your opinion of our noble Apache brethren?"

Libby knew he was referring to her encounter with Gato,

but it was Case she looked at when she replied softly, "Not a bit, sir."

Crook studied the tender look that passed between his scout and the doctor's sister. "Somehow I suspected as much," he muttered, then raised his voice to the troops. "Captain Robertson! Let's get Miss Ashford home, shall we? I expect the captain and Mr. Longstreet have quite a story to tell us."

David gave the orders, and the cavalry escorted them home. As they rode between the headquarters buildings, the bugler sounded attention, but it was a wasted gesture—everyone at Fort Apache was already out to meet them. David dismissed the troopers, and a crowd of anxious spectators surged toward Libby and Case.

Jedidiah, who hadn't waited for permission to dismount, was the first to reach them. With a smile that warmed Libby's heart, he raised his arms and plucked her off Case's lap, drawing her into a gruff embrace as soon as her feet touched the ground. She hugged him tightly. Then he released her as Susannah finally succeeded in fighting her way through the crowd.

"Oh, Libby," Susannah murmured tearfully as they embraced. "I was so frightened."

Libby drew back and smiled through her own tears. "So was I."

Susannah mumbled something about the whole camp being roused long before dawn, but Libby was too exhausted to care how everyone had learned of her kidnapping. "Come on," her friend urged. "Just let me get Michael out of his cradle, and we'll get you home and into a nice hot bath."

Like a mother hen, Susannah tried to usher her away, but Libby hung back, glancing up at Case as he slipped off his horse. His eyes caressed her tenderly, but when David Robertson approached him with orders that General Crook wanted to speak with him, Case was forced to turn away and Libby allowed herself to be led through the crowd.

Some of the soldiers who had been especially kind to her in the past were pressing around her, eager for reassurance that she was unharmed. Their concern touched Libby, but when she saw Elaine and Caroline fighting their way through the crowd, all her good feelings vanished.

"Libby dear, are you all right?" Elaine Dunlevy said with genuine concern.

"I'm fine, Elaine."

"I was just going to take her home," Susannah informed the women. "She's exhausted."

"I can see that," Elaine replied sympathetically as she reached out gingerly and touched Libby's partially shorn hair. "You poor dear. I can't even begin to imagine what you must have gone through."

Caroline was far less charitable. "Well, I hope this has finally brought you to your senses, Libby." Her shrill voice carried farther than she might have liked, and a dead silence fell over the group. Caroline flushed under the scrutiny of so many disapproving eyes. "What I meant was . . . well, surely you can see that your association with Longstreet—"

"Shut up, Caroline," Elaine said succinctly, then placed a comforting arm around Libby's shoulder. "Come, dear. I'll help you get settled."

Astonished, Meade watched the exchange, barely able to believe his eyes and ears. While Susannah dashed into her quarters to get Michael, Elaine ushered Libby down the quadrangle. The men began to disperse, leaving a speechless Caroline Crenshaw standing alone and ignored.

No, not ignored, Meade realized. Shunned. Temporarily, at least, Libby Ashford was far more popular with the residents of Fort Apache than Caroline Crenshaw had ever been.

"Sort of makes you wonder, doesn't it?"

The voice startled Meade, and he turned to look at Jedidiah, wondering how long he'd been standing beside him. "Wonder about what?" he asked.

"If maybe you were wrong about these people accepting Libby and Case." He looked pointedly at the matron who was shepherding Libby toward the hospital, then at Caroline Crenshaw, who had finally recovered her dignity and was flouncing off toward her own quarters. "Looks to me like the question has two sides. You're going to have to decide which one you want to be on."

The thought of aligning himself with a bigoted twit like Caroline infuriated Meade. "The only side I've ever been on is Libby's," he snapped.

"Then maybe you should start considering what she wants to do with her life, and not what everyone else is going to think about it."

Fuming, Meade wanted nothing more than to tell Jedidiah the same thing Elaine had told Caroline, but good manners and the bond of friendship he felt for the aging rancher stopped him.

"Meade, Case and the general are waiting for you," David Robertson called to him.

"Excuse me, Jedidiah," he said as he stalked off toward the command post.

Wearing a rueful half smile, Jedidiah followed the captain at a more leisurely pace. Meade was wearing down. Jedidiah was sure of it. He wasn't there yet, but he was getting there.

Libby allowed herself to be petted and pampered because she was too weary to protest. While Elaine issued orders to Sergeant Brogan, overseeing the preparation of a hot bath, Susannah straightened Libby's bedroom. Her friend laid out a fresh nightdress, and as soon as Libby had bathed and washed her hair, Susannah brushed it for her until it was nearly dry. Elaine applied a soothing ointment to her chafed wrists, and within an hour Libby was in bed, sound asleep.

When she awoke, she had no idea how long she'd slept, but the heat and the slant of light in the room told her it was probably late afternoon. What was more important to her, though, was that Meade was there, sitting on the edge of her bed, studying her with the most unreadable expression she'd ever seen.

"My poor Meade," she whispered drowsily, touching the bruise on his forehead with gentle fingertips. "Are you all right?"

He nodded. "I was going to ask you that."

"I'm fine," she assured him as tears welled in her eyes. "Thank you for saving me."

"I'm just glad you're safe." He took her hand and raised it to his lips. "I love you, little sister."

A tear slipped down her temple. "I know. Please don't ever stop."

"I won't." He kissed her hand again, then lowered it to the bed beside her. "Now, you get some more sleep. Doctor's orders."

"Don't worry. I plan to sleep until Tuesday."

He stood and smiled. "I'll see that her ladyship is not disturbed."

"But that means I'll miss the infantry escort on Monday," she reminded him.

His smile faded. "I know." He went to the door, but by the time he turned back to look at her, she was already asleep.

Meade moved through the parlor and founded Sergeant Brogan in the kitchen preparing supper. "Sergeant, would you be so kind as to see if you can locate Case Longstreet for me? I'll be waiting for him in my office."

"Yes, sir," Brogan answered with a touch of uncertainty, wondering what was in store for the Apache scout now. The striker had overheard enough arguments in the house to know which way the wind had been blowing these last few months.

Right now, though, the captain didn't look particularly happy, or particularly angry, either. It was amazing the way a few hours in hell could change a man. Given the recent chain of events, Brogan didn't feel inclined to guess what kind of changes the doctor had undergone.

After removing a kettle of beans from the stove, he went off in search of Longstreet.

Meade waited in his office with his feet propped on the desk and one eye on his predecessor's half-empty whiskey bottle. It seemed to be looking at him, too, daring him to pick it up, take a swallow, and erase the memory of the last few months he'd spent in purgatory.

Then he thought about the night he'd survived. He thought about the tears Libby had shed when she made him promise to always love her. He remembered the way he'd tried to get her to ride with him this morning and how she had regretfully turned her back on him and sought refuge in Case's arms.

With a weary sigh, he reached for the whiskey, dropped his feet to the floor with a thud, and shoved the bottle into the farthest recesses of the desk drawer.

"Sergeant Brogan said you wanted to see me."

Meade closed the drawer and looked up at the enigmatic Apache he both detested and admired. "Have a seat."

Dreading the inevitable, Case sat in the chair opposite Meade's. At one time he had been able to read every thought on the doctor's face, but those days had passed. Case didn't have to be told why he'd been summoned, though, and he didn't see any point in beating around the bush. "Have you told Libby you're sending her away?"

Meade rubbed his hand over his face, wishing he'd been able to sleep this afternoon when he'd finally gotten away from General Crook. Unfortunately, sleep hadn't come to him. His energy was depleted, but his mind had been racing too fast to allow him any peace. Finally he'd realized that he wasn't going to get any peace until he'd settled a few things with this man.

"Actually, last night, before the . . . kidnapping, I told Libby I was going to send her away," he answered after a moment. "And you should know that I also told her about the deal I forced you into."

Case almost smiled. Maybe there was hope for this white man, after all. "What did she say?"

Meade shook his head. "It doesn't matter. I've already agreed to let her stay."

"Why?"

He looked down, unable to hold the Apache's intent gaze. "Last night when you cut Libby down, I thought she was dead. It made me realize that losing her—whether to death, or to you—would be the worst thing that could ever happen to me."

Case's face grew hard again. "I've already told you I won't marry her without your approval. I won't deprive her of someone she loves more than her own life."

Meade looked at him. "Neither will I."

Case took a moment to digest what Meade was telling him. "You are withdrawing your objections to our marriage?"

"No," he said with an ironic laugh. "I still have plenty of objections. But I won't cut myself off from Libby just because I don't approve of the choice she's made—and it is her choice," he added quickly. "She loves you, and as hard as that's going to make her life, she deserves a chance to find out if there really is a kind of love that's strong enough to survive anything." He leaned back in his chair. "Personally, I don't think it exists, but I can't convince Libby of it."

Case did smile then. "If you keep trying, she'll spend the rest of her life attempting to prove you wrong."

Meade laughed, and this time there was weary but genuine humor in the sound. "How well you know her."

"I love her."

Meade stood and extended his hand. "Then don't ever give me a reason to regret this."

Case rose and took his hand. "After what you did last night, I wouldn't dare."

He smiled. "We did acquit ourselves rather nicely, didn't we?"

"You saved my life, and I thank you."

Meade tightened his grip on Case's hand. "Then I guess that makes us even."

TWENTY-EIGHT

"AND THE PARLOR will go here," Libby said, pacing off the space between the imaginary dining room and the spacious parlor Case had promised to build her on the piece of land they had just purchased. She spread her arms. "We'll have a big window here, looking out over the river." She turned to her brother, who was leaning negligently against one of the cottonwoods that had helped them choose the location of the house. "What do you think?"

"I think a big window is just going to let in a lot more dust," he replied grumpily.

Libby shook her head. "Case has promised me glass-paned windows."

"This I'll have to see," he muttered.

Laughing, Libby went to him and laced her arm through his. "Meade, if you think this is such a rotten idea, why did you put the ranch in your name and contribute half the money?"

He glanced away from her, unwilling to admit even to himself that he'd made the right decision in allowing Case to propose to Libby. He'd never seen her happier, and it irritated him almost as much as it pleased him. "It's an excellent investment," he responded.

"Oh, Meade." She sighed and placed her head on his shoulder. "You like Case, but you're just too stubborn to admit it. You'll come around one of these days, though."

He dropped a kiss on her forehead in the familiar way that

meant so much to both of them. "As long as you're happy, that's all that matters."

"I am," she assured him. Nothing had ever been truer. In the weeks since the ordeal with Gato, Libby's life had taken on a whole new meaning. Case had asked her to marry him, and Meade had given his blessing with the proviso that they be married by a minister. The Baptist minister in Bledsoe had refused when he learned that a white woman was marrying an Apache, but Jedidiah had found a clergyman at the Spanish mission in San Manuel who had been pleased to perform the rites.

Libby was now Mrs. Case Longstreet, and she could not imagine being happier.

Case had been amenable to the Christian ceremony because it was what Libby wanted, but he also wanted to follow the customs of his people. That was why Libby had dragged Meade out to the site of their proposed ranch house; with considerable reluctance, he had agreed to go through with whatever ceremony the Apaches demanded.

Libby had assured him it wasn't too complicated, and she hoped she wasn't lying. Case had briefly described it to her once, and as she understood it, the most important part of the occasion had already been taken care of. Jedidiah was staying with Meade at the fort, and every night Libby shared her husband's bed at Jedidiah's ranch. The joy and fulfillment she had found in his arms, and the delight she had taken in discovering her womanhood, had made Libby complete.

The only thing that could possibly make her happier was to know that she was completely accepted by Case's family. With luck, that would happen today.

"Libby?" Meade frowned as he looked into the distance. "What's that?"

She looked downriver and smiled. "It's Blue Bear and the rest of Case's clan. And there's Jedidiah, too."

Meade frowned. "Where's Case?"

"He's not expected to be here," she replied, watching the procession.

"Well, *I* expect him to be here," Meade snapped. "It's his wedding, for crying out loud."

"Actually, it's really the joining of my family to his," she explained a little sheepishly.

He looked down at her. "You didn't tell me I was going to be marrying the Apaches, too."

She grinned. "For better or worse?"

He sighed and straightened as the procession drew near. Blue Bear appeared to be leading a horse, and several braves herding a dozen head of cattle veered off to the east. The women walking behind Blue Bear were carrying baskets and blankets. Obviously this was what Case had meant when he mentioned the "bride price." Even Meade had to admit that it was an impressive display, considering the poverty in which these people were living.

Instinctively Meade stepped forward when Blue Bear and Jedidiah rode up and dismounted. The ancient Apache still moved with a dignified grace. He pointed from Jedidiah to Meade, grunted, and then fell silent.

"My friend, Meade," Jedidiah began. It was clear that he was trying to remain serious, but every so often the rancher's eyes darted to Libby, and a smile crept across his face. "My good friend Blue Bear has asked me to speak for him, and I am happy to be able to grant his request. You have a sister who has found favor in the heart of Blue Bear's grandson, and so he brings you presents.

"The Apaches are not so rich as they once were, but if you find these gifts worthy of the sister of a great white medicine man such as yourself, Blue Bear would wish to join your family to his own. His people will be as yours, and your people will be his. You will stand together and help one another, as all families must."

Meade was a little amazed to realize that he felt touched by the beauty of Jedidiah's speech. He glanced at Libby, and was not entirely surprised to see tears in her eyes. He looked at Jedidiah, not sure how he was supposed to respond. "I have already given my consent to this marriage, but . . . uh . . . I agree?"

Libby knew she wasn't supposed to have any part in the ceremony, but she couldn't resist leaning toward her brother and whispering, "Your eloquence is truly awe-inspiring."

He threw her a disgusted glance, then returned his attention to Jedidiah. "Please tell Blue Bear that the gifts he has brought are more than adequate to pay for my sister." He heard Libby gasp, but he ignored her. "And tell him, too, that I will be honored to accept his gifts . . . and even more honored to call his grandson my brother." He looked down at Libby and brushed a tear off her cheek. "Was that better?"

"It was wonderful," she whispered, rising on tiptoe to kiss his cheek.

Jedidiah translated the message, and at a signal from Blue Bear, the women came forward and deposited their baskets near Meade. The sound of a horse approaching drew everyone's attention, and the women began murmuring and smiling as they stepped back.

Wearing only his breechclout, moccasins, and the simple Thunderbird necklace he had worn for so many years, Case rode slowly past his family until he reached Blue Bear's side. He threw one leg over the neck of the horse, slipped to the ground, and approached Meade.

"My friend . . . the gifts my family has brought are for you to do with as you please," he said formally. "I wish to add a gift to the bride price, but it is only for your sister."

He looked down at Libby, stepped closer to her, and held up the Thunder Eagle necklace. Two beautiful, perfectly formed eagle feathers were suspended from it. "*Cida'ké*, many years ago my father came to my mother as I come to you now. He said these words, and I would say them to you, for no words were ever spoken that had more love or meaning in them." Raising the necklace, he placed it around her neck.

"Since the day I became a man, the Thunder Eagle has been my guiding spirit," he said, quoting from the legend that had been told about his parents. "He has protected me from harm and given me strength against my enemies." When the necklace was in place, he stepped back and lost himself in Libby's tear-filled eyes. "I give this necklace to you so that you will always know the protection of my spirit. So long as you wear it, my beloved, we can never be separated . . . even by death."

Smiling through her tears, Libby pressed the medallion to her breast. "I love you," she murmured.

"And I cherish you with all my heart."

She slipped her hand beneath the engraved disk and looked at it. The two frayed feathers that had once hung from the medallion had been found in her bedroom the morning after the kidnapping, but these were not the same ones. As Libby gently caressed the feathers that represented her life joined with Case's, her other hand reached out and stroked the single battered feather that now hung from the medallion on Case's chest.

"I would have been proud to wear your sister's feather next to my heart," she told him quietly.

Case covered her hand with his own so that she could feel the steady throb of his heart. "It is next to my own now. If the Thunder Eagle wills it, my sister and I will be reunited some day."

He closed the distance between them and gathered her into his arms. His head dipped toward hers, but Libby pulled back a little. "Apaches don't kiss, remember?" she reminded him with a teasing, tearful smile. "What will your family think?"

"They will think as I do," he said huskily, "that an Apache can learn a few good things from the White Eyes."

"And that the White Eyes should learn a few from the Apaches," she whispered as Case's lips sealed the bond of love that transported them to a place where only the eagle soared.

EPILOGUE

━━━━━━━━━━━━━━━━━

New Mexico Territory, August 1874

THE FIRE CRACKLED, and the stars overhead sparkled like diamonds on black velvet. Hugging her knees to her chest, Skylar Templeton looked at the stars and tried to visualize the things the old Mescalero storyteller, Consayka, was describing. He had recited the legend a hundred times, but Skylar never tired of hearing it, because it called up visions that seemed almost like memories.

"It was a necklace of great beauty, with stones of turquoise and a shell carved with the image of the Thunder Eagle," the ancient Apache said, relishing the delight on the faces gathered around him. Only a short distance away, the lights of the Rancho Verde spilled through the wrought-iron gates of the hacienda's walled gardens; but here by the fire, Consayka was re-creating a world very different from the one Anglos had built in this New Mexico valley.

Things changed so quickly that the old storyteller was afraid that before too many years, his people would forget the old ways, the old legends. That was why he was always happy when the young mistress of the hacienda slipped out of the house to listen to him. For her, he finished the story in his deepest voice, keeping his words so clear that they could not fail to touch the young girl's heart.

"The People were astonished that a brave would be so bold as to come to the ceremony, but when Gray Wolf placed the

357

necklace around Willow's throat, the Thunder Eagle cast his shadow over them, and the People smiled.''

Skylar looked across the fire at Consayka. ''Thank you for the story,'' she said.

He nodded. ''I know it is your favorite.''

''And mine!'' one of the younger children exclaimed, making them all laugh.

''Skylar!'' a voice called in the darkness, and Skylar turned just as her sister Rayna crouched down beside her, grabbing the sleeve of her robe. ''Skylar, what are you doing out here? If Mother finds out we're not in bed, there'll be hell to pay!''

''Rayna! Your language!'' Skylar rebuked mildly, knowing her sister wasn't really angry with her.

''Who cares about my language? It's my backside I'm worried about,'' Rayna replied, tugging Skylar to her feet. ''You know I'm the one who always gets punished.''

Skylar giggled. ''That's because you're the only one who misbehaves.''

''No, I'm just the only one who gets caught! Now come on. Mother will be up to wish us good night in a few minutes, and if we're not in our room, I'll get the blame.''

Like giggling thieves, the girls dashed to the garden. They were as different as night and day, these two sisters. They celebrated their birthday on the same day, but Skylar was quiet and shy; Rayna was bold and boisterous. Skylar was malleable; Rayna was stubborn. Skylar was timid; Rayna was absolutely fearless. Skylar had hair as black as jet; Rayna had inherited the corn-silk blond hair of both her parents.

They reached the gate and opened it carefully, wincing with each creak it made. They slipped through, hurried down the tiled path, and tiptoed across the veranda. Rayna glanced into the hall that led to the central courtyard, and when she was certain the coast was clear, she darted toward the stairs.

Behind her, Skylar paused a moment and looked back at the Apaches by the fire. She loved her sister, this house, and the devoted parents who had purchased a frightened little Apache girl from a trio of Mexican slavers and raised the child as their own.

Skylar could not imagine growing up with more love or

security than she'd been given here, and yet she was drawn back time and again to the Indians who worked at Rancho Verde. They were her only link to a world she could barely remember, and to which she no longer belonged.

"Skylar!" Rayna whispered.

Taking one last look at the fire, Skylar Templeton raised the hem of her nightdress and dashed into the hacienda.